A New War

ALEXANDER FARAH

For David, my strength and spirit when completing this work. I love you and I miss you.

THE KINGDOM OF NATAAROS

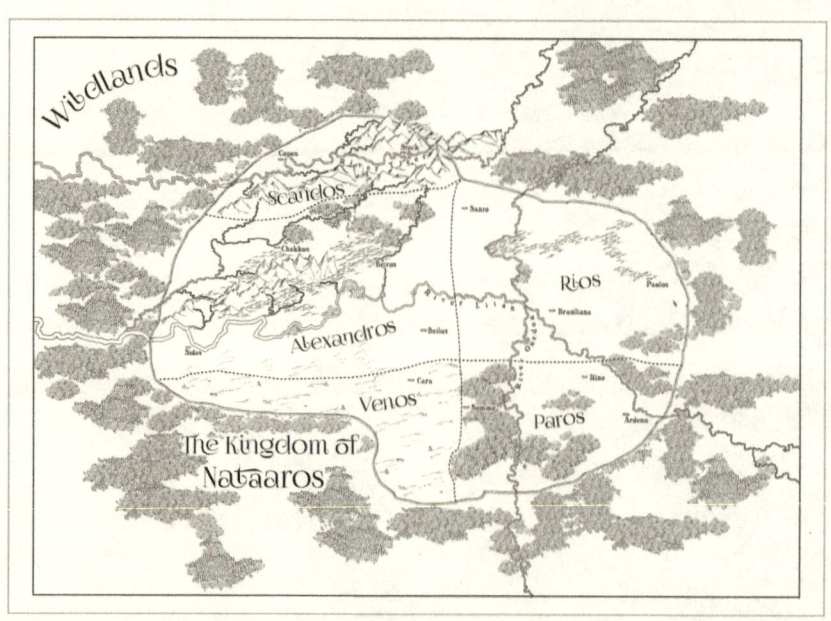

A NEW WAR

As we mourn the dead, we should also celebrate the living, and life itself, for life is a precious gift that should not be wasted.

— KING MICHEL AOUNIS

CHAPTER 1
A NEW THREAT ARISES

As the night blackened and the rain poured, the world slept. Many enjoyed warm beds, satisfied with a living made and another day survived. The soldiers of the king's army had no such luxury.

"This is ridiculous," complained Salal after a day's march through the harsh climate of western Alexandros, the largest province on the continent of Nataaros. "I didn't join the army for this. I joined to defend my king and my people."

Salal had only just reached adulthood, and now found himself thrust into service alongside the toughest warriors in the land, tasked with investigating a disturbance along the border wall that surrounded their country, separating the civilisation behind it from the unknown of the Wildlands without. Like other newcomers to the king's army, he had been assigned grunt work to test his mettle.

His friend Ahmid tried to be more optimistic, and to reassure Salal of the importance of their job. "This is fighting for the king. Who knows what lies ahead in the Wildlands, beyond Alhayit, the wall at the frontier? It's our duty to sniff it out." Patriotism and pride were strong in the people of Nataaros, particularly the Alexandrosians, who populated the largest and wealthiest province on the continent. While it was scary, and the risks high due to the lack of knowledge of what they faced, Ahmid considered the post as a blessing from his god, and a favour from his king.

Such optimism belonged to the young and naive. You wouldn't have seen it in an older soldier, had they been tasked with this investigation. And Salal wanted nothing to do with it. "You and I both know what lies beyond. The army of the dead." The anger in his voice before had been a mask for his fear. "We've both heard the stories that they will rise again one day. That's what this is. Their time has come."

Ahmid tended to steer away from spooky ghost stories and fairy tales. To him, the so-called army of the dead was a myth to scare misbehaving children. "Even if that were true, look on the brighter side. The army has tasked us with defending the people from them. That's got to be an honour." Ahmid wasn't interested in mirroring Salal's fear.

"Brighter side? Honour? Are you stupid? They've sent us here to die; we're nothing but fodder. No one's dared to cross the frontier into the Wildlands in who the hell knows how long? Centuries?" Salal's tone became more aggressive as his frustration that Ahmid just wouldn't see his side of things grew. "It's not an honour for us to go and face the army of the dead. It's a death sentence."

Ahmid was taken aback by Salal's insistence. Perhaps he was right. For the first time that night, Ahmid had no answer for Salal.

~

THEY CONTINUED their walk towards Alhayit.

In the west of Alexandros rose the Snowy Mountains, a range that stretched across nearly half the province, and through the northwest into neighbouring Scandos.

To avoid going through the largest stretch of mountains in Nataaros, they had met up in Sidos, where the province's famous gladiator fights took place. From Sidos, they had marched west towards the wall, with the Snowy Mountains in all their glory still an omnipresent sight.

Outside the thriving city, Salal and Ahmid entered the forest, whose tree trunks became thicker and the grass longer as they approached the wall.

Oddly for such an important structure, Alhayit had been unmanned for centuries. While it had been built to keep out the supposed threat of a dead army, the failure of that threat to appear in the years that followed had made the frontier an afterthought for the rulers of Nataaros. Though it still stood tall, it was now little more than a symbol of a time when the continent had still been forging its identity.

Yet anxiety was filling the air. These were uncertain times.

BEFORE THE TWO young men ventured from Sidos, they had to respond to the cry for help that had led them there. As they had travelled from Beiros, the capital, into Sidos, they were astounded by the difference in the architecture. Where Beiros was covered in landmark after landmark, Sidos was more modest, with the only building of real note being the arena where the gladiatorial games were held.

When the two men arrived, a guard gave them directions to a small house in the centre of the city. The family inside had made the distress call, to alert the army that there was something suspicious beyond the frontier.

They approached the door and knocked, but it took a while for anyone to answer.

"What a waste of time," Salal remarked. He had been sour even while they were still within the bounds of civilisation. "No one is even home."

But before he could grumble more, the door slowly creaked open. Behind it stood a little girl, eyes as wide as the horizon, with her face full of fear—mixed with curiosity—as she stared at Salal and Ahmid. She'd never seen a soldier before.

Before either man could get a word in, a woman rushed in and opened the door fully.

The girl's mother was rather embarrassed that it was her

daughter that answered the door. "My apologies," she said, ushering her daughter back inside. "You must be from the army."

She smiled as politely as she possibly could, but she too was struggling to hide her fear. Whatever it is they wanted to report must have shaken them both.

"Yes. My name is Salal and this is Ahmid. We've been told of a disturbance beyond Alhayit." Salal tried his best to sound inquisitive, but he didn't have the confidence or gusto. You could tell he was new at this.

The woman didn't seem to mind; she just wanted to tell them what had happened. "Something really bad," she said. "Please, come in."

They all made their way inside the house, but Salal shot Ahmid a worried look, clearly shaken by the woman's seriousness. Ahmid was stone-faced, not really buying into it, but Salal was panicky as usual.

"Take a seat." The woman tried her best to be a gracious host, but it couldn't amount to much in these circumstances. There was too much tension in the air for anyone to be comfortable. "May I get you both something to drink?" Manners were important to the people of Alexandros, after all, especially when hosting soldiers in your home.

Luckily for the woman, neither Salal nor Ahmid cared for the niceties. "No, thank you for offering." Then Salal insisted they get onto the topic.

But the young girl was still standing within earshot. Naturally, her mother wanted to protect her, and tried to get her to leave. "Not now, darling. Please, go to sleep."

The daughter went into her room but, unbeknownst to the three outside, knelt with her ear close to the door, trying her hardest to listen in.

The woman returned her attention to Salal and Ahmid, who had been patient enough to allow her to be a mother before anything else.

"Now, we were discussing what happened beyond the frontier," Salal said, gaining in composure and confidence. "First, we'll need your name."

4

The woman was surprised. "My name? It's Malia. "But why do you need my name?" She was guarded but ultimately willing. She still had to make sure she could trust the two strange men in her house.

"We need to know who's making the report, so we can come back to you should anything further arise," Ahmid responded reassuringly.

Malia gave a nod of approval as Salal took notes. Both men listened intently. It was imperative they did not miss one detail.

Salal kept leading the questioning. "Please, Malia, tell us everything. What happened on the night of the disturbance?"

Malia took a moment to breathe and collect her memories before laying out the events that had unfolded. "It was two nights ago. In fact, it was a night much like this one. I was outside, collecting the clothing that was out to dry, while my daughter was running around." Malia smiled briefly. Her daughter was all she had in the world. "You know how kids are."

Salal took notes of every detail while Ahmid listened.

"And as we were outside," the woman continued, "we looked towards the Snowy Mountains. Beautiful as they are, something seemed off about them. My daughter and I felt strange, as if forces outside of our control were at play."

Salal had to interject for a moment, "If you please, Malia, what's your daughter's name?"

Malia felt she could trust Salal with confidential information. "Her name's Lana. How sweet she is. Anyhow, we looked towards the mountains, with that uneasy feeling growing bigger inside of us. Suddenly, a light shot from the ground towards the sky…"

Malia's face changed. She was no longer smiling at the thought of her little girl, but showed dread as the memory of what she saw, heard, and felt that night crept back into her mind.

Salal and Ahmid's faces changed. Ahmid sceptical of ghost stories, was curious. But Salal, fearful of the myths surrounding Alhayit, started to show panic. "L-l-light?" he stuttered. "What sort of light?" Whatever composure he had begun to muster fled.

"A sharp beam of light. A white light, straight and thick like a tree, but it shot towards the sky, never ending." Malia's face now showed the horror of a memory she would rather repress. "And a scream! A scream that pierced through the air like a blade through flesh."

In Salal's vivid imagination, it was a scream of the highest pitch, confirming all his fears of the army of the dead.

"And then what?" He had to ask, though any answer Malia would give would be sure to frighten him.

"Then... Nothing. The light shot back down to the ground, and the screeching stopped. I've been fearful ever since." Malia began to tear up. "I'm just worried: what if it is the army of the dead? We've all heard the stories; we've all read what they will do to us if they come. I have a daughter. I have to protect her." Malia started to cry.

Ahmid went to calm and comfort her. "It's okay. We'll find out if it *is* the army of the dead. And no matter what, the king will do whatever he can to protect us." Ahmid's calmness came from his scepticism; he still didn't buy the idea of the army of the dead. But Malia did, and the thought of it frightened her. Ahmid had to make sure she was comforted, and to respect that whatever that beam of light and that screeching may have been, Malia was petrified for her life—and her daughter's.

Salal, meanwhile, was struggling to take down the rest of his notes. His hand was quivering so much with fear that his handwriting would be illegible to his superiors.

"Thank you, Malia. Your information was most helpful." His eyes were as wide as Lana's had been when she first saw the two soldiers at the door. Stoicism had never been his strength.

Lana had heard everything through her bedroom door, and was just as scared as her mother, but rather than breaking down and crying, she was expressionless, as if numb to the situation. Rather than making her presence known, she got up from the door and lay down in bed, staring at the ceiling.

Salal and Ahmid had to carry on. "We'd best leave you to rest." Ahmid got up and readied himself to head off. "Thank you very much for your time."

Salal got up too, still doing his best to hide his fear.

Malia saw the men out. "I hope, whatever it is, you can stop it."

She tried to stay hopeful, and felt she could at least trust Salal and Ahmid with the information she'd given them.

She closed the door as Salal and Ahmid made their way outside, both in quite different moods.

"The army of the dead? She cannot be serious, can she?" Salal exclaimed, praying that this was the end of their trip and they could head back to Beiros with their report.

Despite his empathy towards Malia for showing the same fear, Ahmid almost laughed at Salal. "Well, there's only one way to find out," he replied keenly, delighted at continuing to scare his friend.

Salal wasn't having it. "This is a suicide mission," he cried. "We're going to die."

Ahmid came closer to Salal as they started to make their way west. "We still have a job to do," Ahmid retorted. "Whether or not it's suicide is irrelevant. We were asked to investigate. Interviewing Malia is only half of it, and we have to see for ourselves whether or not this is actually real."

~

SALAL AND AHMID continued their journey ever closer to the frontier, Salal dreading whatever they would find, while Ahmid was unfazed. As the trees and the forest grew thicker and greener, they knew they were close, and they began to see the structure itself.

Standing tall and large, Alhayit was estimated to be precisely half a mile high, and stretched the entire length of the continent, not missing an inch. Its thickness was anyone's guess, so long had it been since anyone had scaled it to truly measure. Texts from centuries past claimed it was around a third of a mile thick, but no one had dared to verify it.

Daring, it seemed, was not in the nature of the people of Nataaros. To scale or pass the wall would take an order. Alas, Salal and Ahmid were there to see its true state, and not voluntarily, as Salal had spent the night reminding his friend.

"Guess there's no turning back now, is there?" Salal puffed out, in awe at just how big Alhayit actually was.

The stories they'd heard did not do it justice. It was bigger than any building in Beiros, Alexandros, or anywhere else in Nataaros. In fact, it dwarfed them.

Yet it was in ruin, a shell of the glory it had been associated with.

"Look at this thing: it's huge." Salal was awestruck as they approached its foot. "It really is as tall as they say."

Ahmid, too, was astounded by its size. "It could do with a bit of a clean, though." He smiled, proud of his quip, and for keeping his composure while Salal was still shaky.

Nonetheless, Salal spoke as if nothing were bothering him, "It's been unmanned for who knows how long. Why leave something so important unguarded? Are they not fearful of the army of the dead?" Salal dreaded the unknown. If it were up to him, half the army would've been up on the wall.

"There's no need for it. The dead haven't risen. It's a waste of resources to defend against what doesn't exist, or what doesn't pose a threat," Ahmid said, dismissing Salal's fears. "Well, we'll see for ourselves."

Salal's face shrunk. He'd silently hoped that Ahmid would empathise with him and they would turn back. But it's hard to empathise with someone you don't understand or agree with.

This was it: they were at one of the gates, unguarded as they had suspected it would be, and there was no turning back.

The gate was operated via a pulley system, which still worked after all these years.

Salal wasn't in any mood to be opening gates to his worst fears, so Ahmid did the honours, staying confident and without fear of whatever might lie ahead.

Salal chose not to retaliate. "I'm not going to dignify that with a response," he replied, trying his best to take the high road, even if it was difficult.

"That was a response, though." Ahmid never quit, but Salal stuck to his word, ignoring him as they went forward beyond the gates.

After a night of bickering, fear-mongering, and dark humour, Salal and Ahmid finally made it through the frontier.

It was no secret that they were the first men to have crossed over in hundreds of years, even since most of the population, including the royal family, had stopped believing in the myth of the army of the dead. They didn't feel the need to man or maintain Alhayit. It was a symbol of a simpler time, where the fear of the unknown was as common as the language spoken among the people.

Only a few shared Salal's opinion that the threat remained and was not to be taken lightly. But even then, it was a small group, almost cultish. The royal family dismissed the idea, and had only sent the two men now because of Malia's report.

The king's scepticism did still show, in that he had only sent two men to investigate a threat rumoured to be capable of wiping out all those that stood before it, rather than sending a group of elite soldiers.

As they crossed the gates of Alhayit and into the Wildlands, the scenery changed. Gone were the lush forests on the borders of Alexandros, along with the majesty of the nearby Snowy Mountains. It was dark, cold, and grey, unnerving to a point where the men felt haunted.

The trees had grown taller, as tall as any building found in Beiros, and were darker green, not the bright, vibrant green seen within Nataaros. They showed not the colour of nature, but of sickness, ill health, and death.

Salal realised they were no longer within the protection of their own country. "Wow, the first time either of us have left Nataaros. Can't say I was ever looking forward to travelling." Even the thought of leaving home bred anxiety within him.

Ahmid laughed at the notion that leaving Nataaros was such a terrible thing. "Think of it as an adventure. How many people can say they've left the country? Besides, every place is different. Do you honestly think Alexandros is the same as Rios, or Scandos, or, Lah forbid, Venos? Of course not, yet we've ventured out to these places. This is nothing." Ahmid always had a knack for putting things into perspective; it was a large part of why he felt no fear.

And for someone as well-travelled within Nataaros as he was, the other side of the frontier was just another destination among the many he'd seen and stayed at.

Salal still wouldn't buy it, "This is different, though. In Rios,

9

we're still inside our home country, under a king that protects us... Well, theoretically." Salal remembered it was the king who had ordered him to face his worst fears.

"What's that supposed to mean?" Ahmid was curious why Salal would be dismissive of their king, who they were supposed to fight for.

"You know why." Salal felt he didn't need to explain himself any further. "If he were truly a protector, he wouldn't send us to our graves like he has."

Ahmid only pondered the thought for a moment. "And if you were truly a soldier, you'd shut up, stand up, and accept any order from our generals, or better yet our king," he retorted.

They had bickered the whole trip, and by now both men were sick of it.

"Still, there's no reason we should be sent away from home like this," said Salal, still adamant this was a bad idea.

"I'll tell you why." Ahmid stopped and paused, certain he'd found a way to keep Salal quiet for the rest of their mission. "You're afraid. The king has every right to order this from us if he sees fit. You're a soldier. Be a man of your word and protect those you've sworn to protect. If this dead army is so bad, make sure no one ever feels their wrath. Besides, the only reason you feel homesick is because you were so attached to this idea of a wall that keeps the bad guys away. You've left home hundreds of times, and you've travelled to so many different places, but the moment you step outside of this irrelevant wall, you claim you are being sent away from home."

For the first time that night, Salal had no response. Ahmid patiently waited, but Salal had nothing.

Ahmid considered it a minor victory and flashed a smile as the two continued onwards.

～

AFTER ABOUT AN HOUR, Salal and Ahmid were approaching their destination. They had only a rough estimate of where the flash of light had come from for Malia to see, and the scream for her to hear.

The scary part about the Wildlands was that it all looked the same. There were no landmarks, roads, or tracks, and so no way of knowing which direction you were going in, save a compass, or the sun and stars. Otherwise there were only the tall, dark, grey trees. You could have gone further and further away from Nataaros, or moving in circles, and never know.

Salal began to grow weary. "How much longer?" he asked, his feet and lungs tired.

"Not long now, by my estimations. Just a bit further west." Ahmid took over as the navigator, as he, unlike Salal, was still in the right state of mind to lead them on. Salal was barely fit even to be there.

"Oh, great. 'Further west'," he complained. "You want to know what that means? Further away from Nataaros." It took Salal about a second to get through each word, between all his huffing and puffing. Fitness had never been his strong suit.

Ahmid was still trotting along. "You want to know what that also means? Closer to where we need to be. Now, come on, let's keep going!"

They both began to notice something strange about where they were.

The trees around them began to be more spread apart, not crowding or surrounding them as before. Even the thick, long grass on the ground began to thin out, with patches of dirt showing through. Nothing about this seemed natural.

"There's less trees, now," Salal observed. "What if this is the work of the dead army?"

"Well, there's only one way to find out," Ahmid was somewhat excited, knowing that they are about to make a big discovery.

They ventured further forward until there were no more trees or grass, only a circular patch of dirt about thirty metres round. This was definitely man-made.

Salal's dread deepened. "Look at this. Just a patch of dirt," he whispered, eager to keep his voice down.

"You're right. Just a plain old patch of dirt." Ahmid didn't try to stay quiet the way Salal did.

"Keep your voice down!" Salal whispered loudly, lambasting his companion. "The dead army could be here!"

Ahmid looked around. "All I see is a patch of dirt," he said, shining with confidence. He had been right all along. There wasn't a dead army to be worried about at all.

Salal wasn't convinced, though. "No. That scream and beam of light had to have come from somewhere. It wouldn't have been nothing."

Ahmid, after walking around the patch of dirt for a moment, went face to face with Salal. "Did you ever think that the lady was imagining things?" he said, curious to see Salal's response.

"What?" Salal didn't know what more to say.

"You know that it was all in her head. The scream, the flash of light—perhaps it was all fiction. Or, perhaps, she made it up on purpose?"

Salal refused to dignify the idea. "No. No way. That cannot be the truth. You saw her face; you saw the look in her eyes. Look at me and tell me that wasn't the look of fear." Salal was close to insulted that Ahmid would suggest a thing.

"The look of fear has been on your face this entire night," Ahmid retorted. "All I know is that this is the spot, and we're not being devoured."

Salal walked off. Even if he knew in his heart that there was more to this, it angered him that Ahmid might, for now, be proven right.

As he walked, Salal noticed something strange on the ground. Writing. As he got closer, he saw the characters were foreign to him.

"Ahmid, come look at this!" His comrade ran over.

"What? Is it another ghost story?" Ahmid almost laughed at Salal before he noticed the strange writing on the ground. "That could be anything," he said, trying to remain sceptical.

"No, it's the dead army," Salal said. "The stories say that through an ancient magic they will be awakened. This isn't in our language. What if this is the magic that was used to raise them?" Salal was now convinced he had been right all along.

"If it is the army of the dead, then they can *strike me down where I stand*!" He shouted the last.

Salal couldn't believe Ahmid's cheek, to dare risking his life like that.

But nothing came to strike him down. Both of them were still alive.

Ahmid smirked, happy to have been right.

"See, Salal? No dead army." He turned away, and as he did, a figure stood before him.

It looked human, but wasn't. It was lifeless, yet conscious. As tall as Ahmid, in the dark it appeared only as a silhouette, with a pair of bright eyes, red as blood.

They heard a shrill screech from the figure, and before Ahmid or Salal could react, Ahmid's head fell to the ground, followed by the rest of his body.

Salal now saw the silhouette. *He* had been in the right. The army of the dead was real, and it was there. More silhouettes were appearing from among the trees.

Salal was too scared to even draw his sword and fight. He stumbled backward, whimpering and cowering with the fear that had consumed him the entire night.

"*Run!*" The silhouette hissed loudly, as if death itself had a voice.

Without a moment's hesitation, Salal turned and ran as fast as he could. He didn't know exactly where he was going, but he tried to go back the way they had come, hoping to reach the frontier and Nataaros beyond it.

He could barely keep his balance as he hurtled forward, crying and panting, but soon he had a chance to rest—the army of the dead had let him go.

Back at the site of the attack, Ahmid's decapitated body lay on the ground, with the shadowy, red-eyed figures surrounding him.

After only a minute, a hooded figure approached Ahmid's corpse, picked it up and carried it away. Then it and the rest of the dead army moved quietly into the Wildlands.

CHAPTER 2

THE YOUNG BLACKSMITH

A way from the chaos at Alhayit, and away from the politics and violence of Beiros, lay Chekkos, the blacksmithing capital of all Nataaros. Despite its small size, its significance couldn't be understated, for when the king and his armies needed armour and weapons, that was where they got it. And so its people lived comfortably, though otherwise the place was unassuming.

In fact, many towns and cities across Nataaros survived this way, from the largesse of the monarchy, and through trade. Every province on the continent supplied goods or commodities to the king, and to the people of surrounding provinces.

Rios was the centre of agriculture. Paros was the centre of fashion and clothing. These two, along with Alexandros, made their income by providing for the continent. Only Scandos and Venos had fortunes less linked to Nataaros as a whole.

Scandos was wealthy on its own, second only to Alexandros, but its society spread the wealth out, with a middle class and a relatively even income distribution compared to its southern neighbour. It was largely autonomous and did its own thing.

On the other side of Alexandros, almost a world away from Scandos, the poorest province Venos, did its best to contribute to the king, but not through trade. Venos was home to all the prisons in Nataaros, and there the perpetrators of the most heinous crimes suffered the smouldering desert sun.

Giving the provinces distinct roles worked well but often left people boxed in a certain life. Those born in Paros, whether in the capital, Somme, or elsewhere, were likely to work as tailors. The only question for those in a trade, whatever their province's speciality, was how successful they would be. Would they stay a simple workshop hand, earning enough to live but never standing out, or make a fortune as a renowned master of their craft?

Young Melhel Barak, who lived in the Alexandrosian town of Chekkos with his uncle Fares, was taking the second route.

Together, they ran one of the highest-quality smithies in town, and Fares had managed to earn enough of a fortune from his work that he could afford a more than comfortable life for himself and his nephew. Among cottages and huts, they lived in a two-storey home a mere fifty yards from the smithy. It may have seemed rather average for a rich man's home, but in Chekkos it was a mansion.

Although the life of a Chekkos smith was humble, Melhel knew he wasn't bound to it, and had the talent and the time to go far in any profession. He was still only in his early twenties. His wise uncle knew it, too, but had seen and done enough in his time that he was more than happy to stay put in his business. And at that point they had a big job on their hands.

"How's it all coming along, Mel?" Fares said on walking into the workshop to check how his young nephew was managing.

"It's going well, uncle." Melhel was always confident, even when his energy had left him and his dark brown hair and tanned skin were grimed with soot.

Like any Alexandrosian, Melhel and Fares had dark features: a natural tan, brown hair and eyes. But they also had a rugged handsomeness that screamed mystery. Their eyes suggested there was more to them than looks alone revealed.

As Melhel carried on with his work, he noticed a letter in his uncle's hand.

"What do you have there, Uncle?" He wanted to know if the

letter was more work for him, which would mean less time practising his swordplay as he'd have preferred.

"Just a letter from the royal family," Fares replied.

"What could they want with us?" Melhel had lived his whole
life in Chekkos and its orbit, and had no idea what he or his uncle
could offer the king.

But it was rather common for the people of Nataaros to receive
letters from the king himself. Often, they were sent in bulk, for the
king to keep up his reputation as a man of the people.

Melhel had a strange sense that this letter was different.

Fares took the young man to one side of the smithy and they
opened the letter. It read:

Dear Fares Barak,

It has come to my attention that since your time in the army,
you have established yourself as one of the leading blacksmiths in
all of Chekkos. As you were one of my most trusted soldiers, it is
only fitting that I should pay you a visit and discuss you
becoming mine, and my army's, personal blacksmith. I have
already left Beiros en route to Chekkos, so I should expect to see
you within a week. I look forward to discussing the terms of our
arrangement.

King Michel Aounis of Nataaros

"Hm. Trust him to already be on his way before I can even
agree to anything," Fares grumbled.

The king knew how to get what he wanted.

Melhel wondered why his uncle would object to such an offer.
To be contacted by the king and asked to work for him personally
should have been an honour.

"Is that a bad thing, Uncle? This is a great opportunity for us,"
Melhel remarked. Though he was new to all this, it sparked his
ambition.

Fares made his way back to the forge, and Melhel followed suit
as they continued their discussion.

"I retired to Chekkos and started this life for a reason, Mel,"
Fares said. "I did my service to the king, to Nataaros. I wanted to

escape from it, not have that life come back to me. If I wanted it still, I wouldn't have come out here."

Fares smashed away at the metal with more aggression, letting out the anger and frustration that his old life looked like catching up with him.

Melhel still wasn't convinced.

"Is it still not a great honour to work for the king?" he asked. "To have him come to you directly for your work?" Melhel was determined to get every last bit of information out of his uncle.

"Some honour," Fares retorted sarcastically. "Working for the king and country is great to an extent. But, eventually, you get caught in a life you don't really want, and quarrels you'd be better staying out of. You're at the king's beck and call whether you like it or not. You answer to him, not anyone else—even yourself."

"Does King Michel not care for his people?" Melhel was certain the king's reputation was the reality.

"Sure, he does care," Fares said, "but he's still a king, and still the absolute authority in the land. There is no disputing it, so working for him means you do as he pleases. You'd hate it."

"Why is that?"

"You're too stubborn," Fares said. "When you don't listen to me, I get annoyed at you, but I can put up with it. I'm just your uncle; when you don't listen to the king, you end up in Venos. And believe me, you don't want that."

"I've heard the stories," Melhel hadn't been far outside Chekkos, so stories were all he had of the world. "It's supposed to be a nightmare."

Fares laughed at him. "*Supposed* to be! Say that after you've seen it for yourself."

There was a world-weariness about Fares, who had fought and killed for the king and for Nataaros. Because of it, his nephew still hung on every word he says, even as a grown man. Experience cannot be bought or taught. It is earned, and someone with it is worth more than one whom has read all the books in the world but never lived the contents.

Although Melhel was excited for the king's visit, Fares' words had given him second thoughts. Now he had the chance to see

17

things for himself, with the benefit of the perspective of one who really knew.

"The king coming to Chekkos!" Fares scoffed at the idea. "What a way to draw attention to yourself. Now, let's get back to work."

~

LATER THAT NIGHT, as the sun set on the Alexandrosian countryside, the orange sky contrasted beautifully with the green of a wide, close-shorn swathe of grass. Fares and Melhel were at a different kind of work.

Behind the shop and their home, they had a significant amount of land to themselves. Fares had made it a training field for he and his nephew. Though the older man claimed to have left the soldier's life behind, he still found it important to keep up his fighting discipline and instil some of it into Melhel.

This was not mere routine: the countryside was rife with bandits and other criminals, and their wealth and the arms they kept made them and their smithy a target. It was imperative that the two men were ready for anything. Nataaros was not lawless—that would diminish the good work the king and his men did in keeping order —but every society has villains, no matter how hard you try to keep them down. Towns like Chekkos and the countryside around them were well away from Beiros and the king's influence, and that was an advantage for lawless men, which was exactly why Fares felt reason for him and Melhel to be prepared.

Being blacksmiths, and excellent ones at that, gave them access to the best equipment in Nataaros, and Fares was battle-hardened, so their training was the best practice next to real combat.

Each man stood in the field with his weapon of choice. Melhel, being shorter, preferred a smaller, one-handed sword and a standard shield, to make use of his speed and ability to weave between enemies. Fares was much taller than his nephew. His size gave him an advantage, and there was nothing more suited to his build than a longsword. Their training swords were blunted so no one would get killed, but that's not to say they wouldn't get hurt.

As they began to spar, Melhel held his shield in front, in his left

18

hand, adopting a defensive stance. Fighting a larger opponent, he needed to be more cunning, and could not be the aggressor. Too many times he had tried to dominate in a match-up against his uncle, who had merely knocked him down, showing his advantage not only in size but in expertise. He had been a fine soldier in his youth, among the best.

Fares led with his sword as he approached Melhel, poking and prodding at his nephew, who had his shield raised, ready to parry and counter at any moment. Before long, Fares' attacking instincts kicked in, and he aimed a large swing at Melhel, who quickly blocked it with his shield and ducked out of the way, opening space between him and his uncle. Fares took advantage of this and extended his sword forward to keep Melhel at bay. The shorter fighter wanted to get in close and eliminate the taller fighter's reach advantage, but Fares didn't want to give Melhel an inch. He'd always been tough on the boy, to harden him up and prepare him for the worst.

From a distance, Fares took repeated swings at Melhel, who blocked each hit, then closed the space between them and knocked his uncle down with his shield. Fares couldn't believe it; this had never happened in all their time training together. Melhel was getting physically stronger, but Fares had never seen this coming.

He had no time to dwell on it, as Melhel was looking to finish him off, but Fares' quick reflexes let him roll out of the way of Melhel's attack, get back on his feet and recover.

Melhel's face showed a wry smile. He knew he'd rattled his uncle and that this might be the first time he could finally beat him.

His blood was up. Maybe it was his youthful energy or naivete, but for the first time in years, Melhel decided to turn on the aggression and come right at Fares. Screaming with every move, every swing of his sword, and every hit, he gave Fares everything, hoping his newfound strength and fitness would finally see him triumph over his uncle.

He forced Fares back, and the older man even showed signs of panic, but with a calm underneath it. It shocked him to find Melhel actually succeeding with an all-out attack, but he knew he still had some tricks up his sleeve. Nothing beats experience, and Melhel had never been in a real battle before. He had never fought someone with real skill, only measly bandits and would-be crooks.

No matter how fit and strong Melhel might have become, that was no substitute for the battle-hardened experience flowing through Fares' veins, along with the trademark Alexandrosian aggression and hot-headedness that was also in Melhel.

As Fares backed away, panting as the strength in his old legs seemed likely to desert him, he raised his sword to prepare for his nephew's continued assault.

Melhel was relentless, and charged at Fares to deliver the final blow. But out of nowhere, Fares swung up and faked a strike, before dropping his sword to the ground and ducking down as Melhel came near him, confusing Melhel as he ran past.

As Fares dropped down and threw his sword behind him, he quickly reached for a small dagger in his belt, grabbed it, and sliced across Melhel's Achilles tendon.

"That's your heel," he growled, dragging Melhel down and holding the dagger to his throat. "And if this were a real battle, your life."

Fares dropped Melhel on the ground, struggling to make sense of the move his uncle just pulled off.

"Sorry, nephew. Maybe next time." He helped Melhel up, proud of himself for showing that he was still the best fighter in the family, or what was left of it.

Melhel looked at his uncle, perplexed by what had just happened.

"What did you just do?" This was a chance to learn. "I've never seen such a move from you before."

Fares laughed at his nephew, purely for the joy of winning, such was their competitive spirit.

"Do you not think I'd have several moves up my sleeve?" He smirked. "Did you really think I wouldn't be prepared for the day you finally man up and take me head-on?"

At that moment, Melhel didn't even care that he had lost.

"Yeah, you're right. You bested me... again," Melhel said begrudgingly. "Whatever. I just want to know what that move was."

Smiling, Fares explained.

"I knew you were going to rush at me, so I feigned raising my sword, then dropped it at precisely the right moment to naturally draw your attention. That's when I planned to strike. I ducked down and pulled out my dagger, slicing your heel, which would've dropped you to the ground instantly if this were real. And as you fell, I'd have grabbed you and sliced your throat."

Fares' detailed explanation made sense, though Melhel struggled to see its practicality. "You never used it in a battle, did you?" Melhel asked.

"No," Fares' reply confirmed Melhel's suspicion. "But as you can see, it's a handy move in a duel if you feel overwhelmed."

"Reckon you can teach it to me now?" Melhel asked. Any time he came upon a new idea, he wanted to learn everything about it right away. He could handle being beaten, but being beaten by the same move twice, without knowing how to do it himself or how to stop it, would have irritated him.

Fares decided that their training must finish though, as it had gotten dark.

"Not right now," he said. "It's dinner time."

"Fine," Melhel grumbled. "Next training session, though, I'm winning."

Competitive spirit was what had driven the Alexandrosians to the top of the social order in Nataaros, a trait handed down to them by their ancestors. You wouldn't find more typical Alexandrosians than the Baraks, not just in looks, but in values, beliefs, and personality. But Melhel knew when it was best to quit and listen to his uncle. He knew he could save the sparring session for another day. In the meantime, he'd practice any time he wasn't working.

AS THE NIGHT WORE ON, Melhel and Fares sat in the living room behind their shop, winding down with a cup of tea to cleanse their bodies and calm their nerves before they went to sleep. It was a nightly tradition for them, with the fireplace burning in the cool evening, lighting the room with a husky orange glow.

They would converse on many topics during this ritual, and that night the letter from the king—and his uncle's frustration with it—had piqued Melhel's interest. Melhel knew Fares had fought wars under the king, but never asked him about it in detail. Whenever a reminder of those times popped up, Fares' face changed. The wars had never truly left him, and Melhel was usually afraid of prodding this soft spot in his uncle.

That night, though Melhel was determined to know why the wars had been so harsh, and why his uncle so resented the king, even though it had been his free choice to take up arms.

"Uncle..." Melhel had finally mustered the courage to ask these questions. "When we got the letter from the king, you were furious. Why?"

Fares looked at him and sighed, feeling he'd already explained himself enough. "You know why. That was my old life, serving the king. I've done my part. I don't want it coming back to me."

That was the typical answer. Melhel knew there was more to it than that, and wouldn't let Fares evade the question. "That doesn't make sense, though," he said. "You chose to risk your life for the king. Why be so spiteful towards him now, when he clearly trusts you for this job?"

Fares almost pitied Melhel for his youthful curiosity. These were more than a boy's innocent questions: he knew that Melhel wanted to pry as much out of him as possible, to know the full story at last. Fares had known this day would come.

He pulled himself up in his chair and took a big sip from his tea.

"What do you know about the Scandosian wars?" It was a rhetorical question.

"About as much as you've told me," Melhel retorted, confused why his uncle would ask a question with such an obvious answer. "They were fought because the Scandosians wanted greater power in the senate, as they were an economic power almost equal to Alexandros. Either they gained more power and representation, or they would declare a civil war."

Melhel recited this like a litany; it was practically the only information his uncle had given him on the topic, and that had been drummed into him.

The Scandosian wars had happened twenty-five years earlier, a few years before Melhel was born, so he had no memory of them. He and the rest of his generation could only go by what they were taught in schools and the stories their parents and grandparents told. Naturally, few of these stories told the whole picture. Melhel had read of the glory of the wars—how the king quashed the Scandosian forces, putting the rebel province in its place and restoring Nataarosian national pride. But from an early age he had known something was up, as he'd to seek that information himself. His uncle barely spoke about it beyond those few sentences Melhel had just repeated.

"Let me tell you what really happened." Fares said.

Melhel shifted in his chair, focusing his attention, excited to find out what had been hidden for so long.

Fares leaned forward.

"The basics of what you know did happen," Fares explained. "Scandos wanted more power, and fought for it. And the king didn't want it that way. He would rather it remain the same, with Scandos and the other provinces on an equal footing in government and in the senate, with ultimate authority going to the king."

Melhel was ready to ask questions. "Why did the Scandosians want more power?"

"Scandos has for a long time been wealthy and progressive," Fares said. "They believed that they did a lot of work for the country, but the king knew that giving them the power they wanted would disturb the balance in Nataaros. He couldn't allow our traditional system to be threatened, and he definitely couldn't allow that threat to his own power."

Fares relayed everything fluidly. The events had stayed with him as fresh as they had been twenty-five years ago, ready for the day when he would finally reveal the truth.

"Make no mistake about it," he said. "The Scandosians were hungry for more power, but diplomacy wasn't an option for anyone. That's the thing with war: everyone has an agenda; no one is inherently good or evil. We wanted to protect our ideals and interests, and the Scandosians were arrogant enough to think they could further theirs."

"Arrogant?" The accusation perplexed Melhel. He'd never met a Scandosian before. He didn't know what they were like.

"Very," Fares scoffed. "It's what makes them who they are. Must be an elven thing."

The native Scandosians were all elves. Tall, with long, flowing blonde hair, elongated ears, and an otherworldly beauty.

"So, they really are elves?" Melhel had only heard this, never confirmed it for himself.

"Yes, the natives are all elven," Fares confirmed. "It's probably why they're so arrogant to begin with. Hell, if I were that tall, beautiful, and naturally intelligent, I'd probably have a sense of entitlement myself." Fares spoke with an understandable disdain for Scandos and its people, given what he had gone through.

"But that still doesn't explain the war." Melhel was eager to get things back on topic.

"Right." Fares cleared his throat to continue his history lesson. "Where was I? Ah, yes," he remembered. "Throughout its history, Scandos was able to accumulate much wealth and prosperity. The elves were so intelligent and efficient, and Scandos is much more progressive than anywhere else in Nataaros: everyone has the chance to receive a high education and enter a profession of high class, such as law, government, or medicine. Alternatively, you could enter a trade or work at manual labour, such as we do with blacksmithing. Everyone has that freedom to do as they please. They have their own industries; they don't really rely on the provinces, like Alexandros does, to fuel their economy."

Fares took a breath.

"The system worked for decades," he went on. "Scandos was somewhat isolated from the rest of Nataaros and took care of itself. They were still allowed a place in the senate and had representation on laws and policies that affected Nataaros as a whole, and their autonomy was respected."

"So, what changed? Why did they start a war?" Melhel asked.

Fares pondered the best way to answer.

"For the reasons I gave," he said. "They felt that compared to wealthy Scandos, the other provinces weren't pulling their weight. When the king refused to give in to their demands, they declared war, and thus the Scandosian civil wars were fought. Five years of fighting people that were meant to be your own countrymen ... how about that?"

Fares gave a wry chuckle at the futility and pettiness of war.

To Melhel, it seemed as though Alexandros had legitimate reasons. After all, Scandos had declared the war for selfish motives. What choice did the king and the rest of the country have but to defend themselves?

"I don't get it. Why was it such a bad thing that you went to war, then?" Melhel asked. "Did Scandos not instigate it? Did they not threaten the ideals and foundations of this country?" Melhel was confused by his uncle's tone of regret and frustration, which Fares kept up as he explained why the war had been so bad for him.

"Remember when I said no one is inherently good or evil? That's why," Fares said sternly. He believed this with his whole heart. "We did horrible things. Any elf in Nataaros was captured and tortured or killed, even those simply working in the other provinces and not involved in the slightest with the war. Even if it happened on the battlefield, killing my countrymen is something I have to carry with me. Doesn't matter if they were elves; they were still from Nataaros. And like me, they were following orders, fighting on the whim of a bunch of politicians who wouldn't dare to fight themselves. They send young men out to die for them, and reap the rewards. What kind of leader won't lead his own soldiers into battle?"

The thought still angered Fares.

"We're not cattle, Melhel, we're men," he said. "I was told to kill any blond man with pointed ears, and in the moment, it's easy. In the heat of battle, you don't think of the beautiful faces under your enemies' helmets; you just slice the bastards open. It doesn't matter if they're twice your height and twice as advanced, you're expected to kill them ruthlessly, if you can. It's only after the fact that you realise what you have done.

"I couldn't fight for a king who wouldn't fight himself. I couldn't kill people who were in the same boat as me, simply doing their duty. That's why I left the king's service after the war. I retired out here with your parents and started a new life." Fares' voice was thick with emotion as he thought of how his life had gone, and how the past was finally catching up to him. "But it looks like the old ways simply won't completely leave me."

It was a lot for Melhel to take in. He sipped his tea, looked Fares in the eye, and could see his uncle's pain. The man's eyes showed the turmoil and suffering in his soul. It was a weight the size of the world, and just to speak about it showed how heavy a burden it was.

War is never easy for anyone involved. Not for the kings, generals, and officers who make the decisions, nor for the soldiers who carry out those orders at the cost of their lives. Those who kill their countrymen and survive carry a terrible burden, and none was so heavy as the one that Fares bore.

CHAPTER 3
THE KING ARRIVES

I n the week following Fares' revelations about the Scandosian Civil War, Melhel hadn't dared to mention it to his uncle again. He'd seen how painful it was for Fares to reveal it all, and tension filled the room after their discussion. They'd said nothing more; after Fares had finished, Melhel leaned back, running his hands through his dark brown hair. His brown eyes met Fares' only briefly, and he saw the suffering inside.

It does not do well to dwell on hurt. Sometimes, it is best to let time calm the situation and heal the wounds. So, Melhel and Fares went on with life as normally as they could, knowing that the king was on his way. It was incredibly rare for the king to visit anywhere outside of the three major cities in Alexandros: Beiros, Beilos, and Sidos. His willingness to come to Chekkos spoke volumes of his regard for Fares, even if Fares didn't necessarily reciprocate the feeling.

The men carried on with training, and paid extra attention to their work to make sure it was of the highest standard. Though Fares didn't particularly want to work for the king, there was still a custom of presenting one's best work when royalty visited—especially when it was the king of all Nataaros. The quality of the work reflected on his rule, and testified to what its maker contributed to the nation. Fares' duty to perform was only greater given that the king had praised his work and put faith and trust in him. Fares had to make sure it wasn't misplaced.

"The king is still the king," he would often say to Melhel, between resentful tirades. Even he treated the throne with respect and dignity. Only if a ruler directly harmed the country could that respect be withheld. And for all his flaws, and all the mistakes that had been made in Scandos, King Michel was just and fair, and spoke with a calm that drew people to his side. He'd forged a close relationship with Fares, and even though war tore them apart and left Fares bitter, the blacksmith knew the king was a good man.

"If he's as good as you're telling me, you're certainly not showing it," Melhel said to Fares in the week before King Michel's arrival.

"All good men have their imperfections," Fares assured his nephew. "The king will at least make good company. I know I don't sing his praises. But he is a good man, who cares deeply for his people. Even if he's a bit out of touch with the common man, like most kings are."

"Like *all* kings are!" Melhel laughed.

For all his ignorance and isolation from the king and the capital, he had still managed to get the impression, and not only from Fares, that kings didn't care about common people such as him. The king was in for quite the meeting with the young Alexandrosian.

IN A HORSE-DRAWN carriage whose opulence testified to the prestige of the royal family, the king, queen, and crown prince were now a mere mile from Chekkos.

The carriage was covered in royal red, trimmed with reefs of gold. You could spot it from a mile away, a boast that the king was here and commanded respect and honour. It was pulled by two of the finest horses in Nataaros, strong and fit and as heavily ornamented as they could be without weighing them down. The driver sat in front, a well-spoken man of Parosian descent who had gladly dedicated his life to the king's service.

Next to him were two of the king's bodyguards, the more senior of the two being the Sword of the King, Rafiq Harrira, general of the king's army and his representative and voice on the battlefield. Only the king had higher authority than he in combat, and his booming voice and six-and-a-half-foot frame made him an ideal candidate for his role. Rafiq was a natural leader, whom allies and friends naturally followed, and whose enemies feared and shook at the sight of him.

Inside the carriage, King Michel waited patiently to arrive in Chekkos, eager to see his old friend Fares after so many years. The carriage had been enlarged since his father's reign, to accommodate his height. Neither as large nor as stocky as his Sword, Rafiq, Michel had long legs that exemplified his lanky build. A toothy grin now stretched across his handsome face, showing his excitement. His grey hair gave him a silver fox type aesthetic, which could lead all the women in the land to have swooned over him during his speeches, while his calm demeanour allowed anyone else to follow him.

By his side was his beloved, Queen Rania, the most beautiful woman in the land. They were childhood sweethearts, having met when King Michel was but a teenage prince learning to rule and she was a scholar hoping to use her ambition and intellect to benefit the people of Nataaros. It was said that she was even more charismatic and a better conversationalist than her husband, attributes that she had showcased as queen. While her husband served the people, especially the downtrodden, in politics, Queen Rania was perhaps the greatest humanitarian in modern history, always visiting orphanages and hospitals, spending many of her days with the poor and the sick children of Nataaros, letting them know they were loved. She had raised millions of gold coins towards these causes, using her charm and wit to draw Nataaros's most prominent people to charity events and to donate to and join her causes. She was truly a queen of the people—beautiful, intelligent, and generous beyond measure —and her love for her husband was as strong as ever, as was his for her.

They sat in their carriage with hands locked together as always;

their love had stayed constant from the beginning until now, like in any beautiful marriage.

Across from them was their son, Prince Sirhan, continuing to read through a pile of scrolls. The spitting image of his father, though slightly shorter, the prince was a fearsome young man. A voracious reader with an encyclopaedic knowledge of his country's history, he had been learning from an early age how to be a king, and had accumulated much knowledge as a starting point. Unlike his parents, though, he was more shrewd and cunning than compassionate, and considered the poor a hindrance more than anything else. There was still hope his parents could instil some of their kindness in him, but that remained to be seen. They would also need to give him their charisma and command. Perhaps due to his upbringing, he was not a natural speaker or leader in the way his parents were: he had been spoiled, and sheltered to focus on his education, and lacked many of the social skills needed in a king. But he was the monarchs' only child, which put him beyond their criticism. He was the golden boy: the queen would have done anything to protect him, and the king believed he could do no wrong. And despite his flaws, his intellect would be an asset to him in power.

"Not long to go now," King Michel enthused aloud. "It'll be very interesting to see what Chekkos has to offer."

"I'm sure Fares will make himself a great host and guide," Queen Rania said, also full of warm feeling for the village.

Prince Sirhan did not share the sentiment.

"I can smell the shit from here," he sneered. "Tell me, mother and father, why must we waste our time visiting such an insignificant little hole? Do we not have more important matters to attend to?"

Slightly annoyed, King Michel quickly looked at his son to set him straight.

"Now, now, son, don't be so dismissive." His voice was full of calmness and authority. "That armour you're wearing, and the sword in Rafiq's sheath, can be credited to the hard work of Chekkos blacksmiths."

Prince Sirhan still wasn't buying it.

"And what does that have to do with us?" he asked. "Let these people send us their metal while we remain in Beiros taking care of the real issues."

King Michel sat up and almost managed to lean over his son despite them being confined in the carriage. The king's height intimidated the prince, who retreated slightly, knowing that once again his vanity and his tongue would earn him an earful from his father.

"Do watch your manners, Sirhan," King Michel warned his son. "The man we are going to visit was one of my best soldiers during the civil war. In fact, had it not been for the bravery and discipline of him and others, your beautiful mother and I would both be dead, and you wouldn't be even a speck of dust in this world."

Prince Sirhan shrank subtly. The king had humiliated him once again. The prince despised being made a fool, even by his own father.

Queen Rania sighed in disappointment and shook her head, but held onto the hope that Prince Sirhan's wicked tongue was purely a matter of youthful angst and rebellion, and not a reflection of his character and leadership traits.

"It's trust in loyal and faithful soldiers like Fares that has made this country thrive," King Michel reiterated. "You cannot find loyalty and effectiveness easily; you must make the best use of it when possible. I've heard great things of his work as a blacksmith, and I cannot think of a better candidate to serve me and my army."

The contrast between what King Michel thought of Fares, and what Fares thought of King Michel, was ironic. It was all a matter of perspective. Fares had helped win the king a war and consolidate his power. King Michel had ordered Fares into war to kill innocent people, leading to decades of inner pain and turmoil.

As a king, Michel's main concern was for his power and authority in the kingdom. Despite his compassion and care for his people, his first priority was to secure his rule, and anyone that could help, he treated as an asset, regardless of the long-term consequences to them. Fares and many others had to pay the price. Fighting and suffering for one's country bore a cost all the heavier when that country seemed not to acknowledge the sacrifice. The payments that Fares had been given on his retirement from the army wouldn't heal his wounds or anyone's, and for all the good in him, King Michel simply couldn't comprehend it.

~

ON THE DAY the royal family were to arrive, Fares and Melhel were preparing themselves for their esteemed guests.

Following Alexandrosian custom, chickens were being roasted over several hours while Fares prepared the bread and the vegetables. Gracious hosting and hospitality were essential in their culture, especially when the royal family were the guests. A feast was in order, as a proud Alexandrosian, Fares was sure to follow the customs.

Outside in Chekkos, the small town and houses were bustling as usual. The air was full of the rhythmic clank of hammers striking iron. Even if Fares and Melhel were occupied that day with hosting the king, theirs was not the only smithy in Chekkos. The sun was on full display, rare at this time of the year, as the clouds typically loomed large despite the heat of the sun. Perhaps the sky itself knew the king was arriving and wanted to present him with a glittering sun and a shimmering sky.

Light shone off the houses and buildings, making Chekkos glow like the sun itself. As men worked in the forges, the butcheries and taverns, and the fields and the offices, the women took care of the babies, and the children were tutored privately if they could afford it or otherwise played freely in the streets, without a care in the world or a thought of the wars that preceded their young lives, the political strife that was even then upon Nataaros, or the mythical threat of the army of the dead. Even the king's impending visit barely intruded on their world.

As Melhel helped Fares prepare, he wondered aloud, "How will the people here receive the king? Do they love him or hate him, uncle?"

Fares thought back on every situation in which he'd gone with the king on a visit outside of Beiros.

"He will be received warmly, or at least met with wonder," remarked Fares. "Whatever people think of him or his rule, when someone of that stature arrives, all eyes are on him. Especially in a small place like Chekkos. His carriage is twice the size of anything we have here, and ten times as extravagant. They will be awestruck."

"But we are meant to be simple people who care not for the glory of kings and queens," Melhel said.

"We are," Fares answered gently. "But make no mistake, we are still people. I've learnt that all coherent responses go out the window when you are dumbfounded. No one is going to remember their beliefs; they are going to look at the king and his family like a child looks at a new toy, with wonder and amazement like it's the greatest thing they've ever laid their eyes on."

Fares approached his nephew.

"Remember something, Mel," he said. "People may be more than happy to pick apart your achievements or your character behind your back, but once you're in their presence, the same person may be your best friend. Status breeds contempt, but also envy and wonder."

Melhel pondered this for a moment while he watched his uncle preparing the largest meal he had ever seen.

"Isn't that what you're doing?" Melhel pointed out. "You've criticised him and his actions for the past week, yet here we stand slaving in our kitchen for hours to greet him."

Fares' gaze focused on his nephew. "Following our customs and showing our respects as hosts and subjects doesn't make us hypocrites, if that's what you're getting at. I'm more than happy to criticise him if I have to, and to his face. I did so the last time we spoke. But that doesn't excuse me from being hospitable. You can show someone respect and grace without being two-faced, but by being honest and forthcoming."

That honesty ran thick in the blood of the Baraks. Fares was renowned for his bluntness, and Melhel, too, was more than happy to be straightforward, just as he did by questioning his uncle.

33

THE TIME HAD COME. As the middle of the day hit Chekkos and the sun gleamed as ever over the landscape, Melhel and Fares finished preparing their feast and waited in their home for the imminent arrival of the king.

Melhel was calm and stoic, eager to meet the revered king and make his own impression on him. But Fares was agitated; he bit his nails to the flesh and shifted his feet restlessly rather than standing in his place. Melhel smiled at his uncle's nerves, knowing Fares would never completely let go of the past. Forget the war, Fares couldn't even let go of protocol and convention. He had already assumed the deference of a knight in the presence of a king.

People had noticed the king's carriage making its way into Chekkos. As humble labourers, they'd never seen anything like its extravagance. They saw the red shining through the streets in stark contrast to the brown of their buildings and green of their pastures. The gold that adorned the carriage glistened like the sun in the sky. The people couldn't help but stop and look, drawn not only by the glamour of the carriage, but by the very idea of royalty.

"The king in Chekkos? Of all places?" one remarked. No one could conceive of it. Why would he have any business there? Most guessed it was to do with the smithing industry, not that many of them could have guessed exactly how. Like Melhel, they had never ventured far from town, nor gotten involved in or taken note of politics and governance.

Never one to pass up a public-relations opportunity, and noticing the awe with which the people in streets regarded the carriage, the king turned to his wife. "I think it'd be best if we pop our heads out," he said.

Queen Rania concurred. They opened the windows on the sides of the carriage and begun to wave at each citizen as they passed by. Most waved back excitedly; others simply couldn't, not only dumbfounded but paralysed with wonder.

Prince Sirhan, still of the mentality that they were beneath him, did not care even to acknowledge the people he would one day rule.

Inside, Melhel and Fares heard the clamour around the carriage passing through the streets, and Fares' nerves continued to show as they realised the royal family was close by now.

"Calm down, Uncle, it's only the king," Melhel said with barely suppressed laughter.

Fares wasn't having any of it, and determined to maintain authority over his young nephew. "Any comments out of you when the king is here, and so help me Lah, I will send you to him myself," Fares said through clenched teeth. But there was no time for back and forth, as they could hear the sound of horses' hooves and cartwheels growing nearer. King Michel was just around the corner.

"Mel, I'm serious; he's almost here. Please, just be on your best behaviour," Fares pleaded.

"Uncle, be grateful. I at least brushed my hair and trimmed my beard for the occasion." One last sarcastic jab wouldn't hurt.

"Melhel..."

Fares' dark eyes met Mel's brown, wide ones, and the young blacksmith realised his uncle was right. This was no time for silliness.

The moment had arrived; the king was there at the front of the Baraks' residence. The king and queen's Parosian escort made his way down from the carriage and pulled out a scroll to read to Melhel and Fares.

"On this most glorious day, I present to you Michel and Rania, king and queen of all of Nataaros!"

The neighbours watched as Melhel and Fares played host, and whispered among themselves about how it was that Fares was able to land an audience with the king and queen. Rafiq, the king's Sword, and the other bodyguards made their way down to open the carriage doors, and then out stepped the king and queen, regal as their reputation would suggest. Prince Sirhan followed them with a slight scowl, and momentarily met the eyes of Melhel, who realised he may have met his match.

Fares, on the other hand, on seeing the king and queen for the first time in a quarter-century, immediately bent his knee.

Melhel looked at his uncle and remained upright, forgetting the custom.

Rafiq began to anger at the insult.

The Parosian escort began to chuckle nervously, and Sirhan was about to unleash a barrage of insults at Melhel, but Fares quickly stepped in.

"Melhel, remember to kneel for the king," he said quietly, his eyes still downcast.

"But what of all you said about the king?" Melhel said. "You were criticising the life out of him, and now you want me to kneel?"

That trademark honesty was coming back to haunt the Baraks; it will hurt you in the world of politics if you're not careful about it.

King Michel and Queen Rania remained patient and forgiving, understanding of this was Melhel's first royal encounter. But they were also confused—what criticism could be referring to?

"Forget what I said." Fares' tone grew frustrated. "Just kneel, nephew."

Melhel remembered Fares' asking him, not even five minutes before, to not act stupid, and went down on one knee for his king and queen.

Rafiq and Prince Sirhan relaxed. The escort still chuckled anxiously: "Well, then, glad we have that sorted," he stammered.

"Quiet," King Michel hammered back at him, "It's clear this young man was unaware of our customs. No matter," he gestured to Melhel and Fares, "you both may rise."

The blacksmiths stood and took a deep breath, glad their little mix-up was over. Melhel got his first proper look at royalty as he rose, and was slightly intimidated by King Michel's height.

"Your majesty, it's been a while," Fares said, managing to smile at the king.

"Too long, Fares," King Michel reciprocated. "I'm sure you remember the queen."

Fares beamed at the sight of her. "Of course. My queen, I am humbled by your presence."

"And I am humbled by yours, Fares." The queen stayed graceful amid the commotion.

King Michel brought Prince Sirhan over.

"And this is my son, Prince Sirhan," King Michel exclaimed proudly. "Sirhan, this is Fares, one of my best warriors in the civil war. Had it not been for his services during the Battle of Beiros, neither of us would be here."

Fares was flattered. "You humble me, Your Majesty."

While everyone was being introduced, Melhel's gaze was fixed on the queen. Never in his life had he seen a woman so beautiful.

Fares remembered he still had to formally introduce the younger man. "This is my nephew, Melhel."

King Michel laughed, figuring Melhel had a similar personality to the younger Fares. "He has your honesty," the king said.

Prince Sirhan saw an opportunity to acquaint himself with Melhel, who was around his age but far less powerful. It was a chance to exert his dominance.

"Pleasure to meet you, Melhel, I'm the prince," Sirhan said with an air of pride.

"I know; I heard the king." Melhel couldn't shake his bluntness for long, and everyone was taken aback by it.

Fares had spotted Rafiq and quickly seized the chance to break the tension.

"Rafiq, old friend! So good to see you." Fares went and shared an embrace with his former brother in arms. "What has our king got you up to?"

Rafiq let go of his cold demeanour and smiled at the sight of a close friend.

"I am now his Sword, Fares," Rafiq held his chest out, proud of the honour bestowed upon him.

"The Sword of the King? You were always worthy of it." Fares couldn't hide his happiness for his friend; Rafiq had always been one of the good men in the king's army.

Melhel was confused. "What is the Sword of the King? What does he do?"

"I am his voice and presence on the battlefield," Rafiq explained. "I command the soldiers and represent the king."

Melhel still could not fully understand. "So... Where is the king? He doesn't fight?"

King Michel found it best to explain himself.

"No, young Melhel, it is not for a king to fight on the field," he said. "I must be around to lead my people at home."

King Michel calmly described the tradition that a king cannot fight, it being too great a risk, so the Sword of the King is his regent in war.

"Rafiq here represents me and my decisions on the battlefield."

But Melhel wasn't having any of it. "What kind of king doesn't lead his own soldiers?"

No one could believe Melhel had the gall to say this to his face.

Fares once again had to break the tension. "Come! Let's head inside. I'm sure we have much to discuss."

As Fares and Melhel followed everyone in, Fares discreetly slapped Melhel in the back of the head, as the younger Barak still wasn't quite accustomed to the required formalities.

As THE TWO families sat feasting at the table, the mood was still tense. Fares had an idea why the king had come, but that more had to be at stake than his becoming the king's blacksmith. What his ulterior motives were, he could not guess.

"It's a lovely feast you've made us, Fares," the queen exclaimed, trying to set the Baraks at ease.

"I am truly humbled, Your Majesty. I can only hope it is up to the standard your family deserves." Fares forced a smile. It was better to at least try to make conversation rather than sit in painfully awkward silence.

Melhel's dead quiet made it harder. Having learned his lesson before, he now did his best to keep his mouth shut. Prince Sirhan constantly eyeballing him helped: the stare of the snarky prince would quiet anyone.

King Michel sensed Melhel's newfound quietness and tried to get to know the boy better. "You've been awfully quiet, Melhel," he said.

Melhel looked at the king sheepishly, knowing he was aware of his embarrassment, and like the good man his uncle wanted him to be, he gave the king his attention. "Just enjoying the food my uncle has prepared, Your Majesty," Melhel said with a fake smile and forced laughter, not knowing what to do in a situation where his blunt honesty had made him look stupid.

Being brutally straightforward was easy with the locals, but the king was different. He had to be careful; he felt a threat in Prince Sirhan's gaze.

"Tell us about yourself. Where are your parents?" Queen Rania said, trying break the ice.

"They died when I was a young boy," Melhel said as though it was nothing. It wasn't, anymore; he'd learned to move on.

"My deepest apologies. What happened? Illness?" King Michel was inquisitive, relishing the chance to connect with a young subject.

Melhel ran his hands through his dark hair, getting it off his face so he could properly address his king and queen.

"No, Your Majesty, bandits killed them in a raid." His voice became softer. "Ever since then, my uncle Fares has raised me."

The king and queen were moved by Melhel's sincerity. It was true the young blacksmith had moved on, but the memory still pained him, and he still wondered what his life would have been like had it not been for that day.

Fares knew it could still be a sore spot for his nephew. "Make no mistake, Melhel is still a fine young man," he chimed in quickly. "I'm immensely proud to have a nephew like him." He realised Melhel had made a horrendous first impression, and it was only right to put in a good word for him to compensate.

King Michel took note of Fares' care for his nephew, and his bright eyes stared into Melhel's. "Interesting. And you are a black-smith like your uncle?"

Melhel nodded. "Yes. He taught me everything I know. Including how to be a soldier."

King Michel was intrigued. "A soldier? I had assumed that was behind you, Fares."

Rafiq, keeping guard at the door, overheard the conversation and smiled. He especially knew the kind of soldier Fares had been, and knew he would never completely let it go.

"Of course, that life is past," Fares said calmly. "But you heard the boy; his parents were killed by bandits. Unfortunately, in a place like this, he has to know how to fend for himself."

Melhel had gone quiet again. He'd never liked it when his uncle talked on his behalf.

The king, meanwhile, was shocked to hear of bandits in Chekkos. "Bandits? In my kingdom? I highly doubt that could be a major concern."

Fares chuckled disappointedly. This kind of self-deluding vanity was one of the reasons he had left the king's service.

"Your Majesty, they're not a problem in Beiros, of course, because that's where you comfortably live." Fares took a quick sip of his wine; *comfortably* may have been a bit too courageous even for him. But the drink was encouraging. "It's easy to miss the bandit problem, living in a palace where everything is catered for you. Perhaps this visit can be an eye-opener."

The king and queen were stunned. The prince was furious. Melhel took a gulp of water and politely excused himself to the bathroom. Now, you couldn't have cut the atmosphere with an axe. No one said anything for a solid minute. The royals were dumbfounded that Fares would suggest they were out of touch.

Fares himself couldn't believe it, and couldn't help but smile slightly. He was somewhat proud of himself for finally standing up to the king when it mattered, even if it could cost him.

Melhel returned to find everything still quiet, and feared for what might come. As he sat down, he lowered his head and prayed to Lah that he would be fine.

King Michel stood up authoritatively. "A word, Fares," he said, staring his former solider right in the eye, looking down on him as a monarch on his subject.

Fares stood, and though shorter the king, returned the stare of this man he was disappointed to follow.

"Certainly, Your Majesty," he said with audible disdain. He knew what was coming, and intended to have his voice heard.

The two men excused themselves from the table and went outside.

Melhel looked sheepishly around the table.

Prince Sirhan was enraged. "The insolence of your uncle," he scolded Melhel, "to dare to speak to my father that way."

Queen Rania tried to calm her son. "Now, Sirhan, Melhel cannot be faulted for his uncle's words."

Her presence warmed the room, which between them Fares and the king had chilled.

"Besides, Fares has always been blunt with your father. It's why he was so respected."

Melhel attempted a joke. "I guess that's where I get it from."

Queen Rania smiled at Melhel's effort, but Prince Sirhan kept a withering gaze on him. The prince would not forget the Baraks' words any time soon.

OUTSIDE, Fares escorted the king to the side of the house away from the city streets, where they would not be seen. Rafiq was slightly startled and was about to enquire what was going on before King Michel waved him away. Rafiq then dropped his guard. Deep down, he knew Fares was a man to trust, but at the same time, he expected Fares' mouth had gotten him into trouble.

Fares led the king to the field that he and Melhel used for combat training. Alone there with Fares, King Michel got his first proper view of the land the blacksmith owned, and was taken aback by how lush the greenery was.

"My word. This is some place you've got yourself, Fares." Though he was surrounded constantly by luxuries, the beauty of the landscape could yet astonish him.

"Thank you, Your Majesty."

But King Michel was quick to return to business. "I take it you've an idea why I'm really here."

Fares had dreaded this conversation, precisely because he knew it would one day come. Now he had merely to accept his fate.

"I knew being your blacksmith was only going to be the small end of the deal," he said.

King Michel took a deep breath and prepared to win his old friend over with charm. It usually worked.

"You're right," King Michel admitted. "There's something more. The Scandosians."

Fares' face immediately shifted towards anger.

"Scandosians?" he cried. "Haven't I killed enough of them for you?"

Fares had worried for decades that the war would come back to him, and here it was.

"If you hear me out, there will be no killing," King Michel assured him. "This I can promise you."

Fares sat on a bench and rubbed tears from his eyes as he thought. Emotion had overcome him as his worst fears looked like coming true.

But he had to give his king a chance to explain. "I'm listening," he said.

King Michel sat down next to Fares, addressing him not as a subject, now, but as an equal.

"As you are well aware, Scandos is our wealthiest province aside from Alexandros," he began. "Once again, they want greater autonomy and power."

"And let me guess, you want to wage another war?" Fares grumbled cynically.

"On the contrary," King Michel replied. "I would love to avoid one. This is where I need you. You're honest, intelligent, and one of only a few people I can trust. If I'm going to solve this mess, I need good men."

In entreating Fares' support, the king explained how, to his dismay, the most recent senate meeting had seen the Scandosians push unrelentingly for greater powers.

"Why not just grant them what they want?" Fares asked. "If they're still at it after one civil war, could it be worth giving it to them." "You know as much as anyone how power-hungry they are," the King warned. "They don't only seek this autonomy for Scandos as a province; they wish to undermine my authority and take over Nataaros.

"Beilos didn't build the country for this. Our system wasn't built so it could be taken advantage of. We have prospered as a kingdom under Alexandrosian rule, but fair and equal powers and rights have been granted to all our provinces. If I let the Scandosians go, fine.

But then what about the Riosans, or the Parosians, or, Lah forbid, the Venosians?

"The whole kingdom would collapse, and maybe even greater, more bloody civil wars would ensue. To save the kingdom and everything we as a people have created, we need to come to an agreement with the Scandosians swiftly."

Fares considered the king's words.

"I'm no politician. I can't trust any of them. Why do you need me?"

King Michel lamented the corruption that had been seeping into his senate. "That's exactly why I need you. I don't trust them either. But I trust you. Aside from my family and Rafiq, you're the only one," King Michel's voice grew more pleading, and Fares knew he was genuine.

"After twenty-five years, can you really still be sure you can trust me?" Fares was being swayed, but still resisted.

"You're the only one who shunned the old life and retired outside of the capital afterwards, rather than trying to expand his power. If that's not the mark of an honest and decent man—a man that I can trust—then I can no longer be a king."

Fares still loved Nataaros, and knew the treachery of the Scandosians. He didn't want to see another war, nor to see the wars of the past be for nothing. And he understood that men like him were needed in a crisis.

"You are correct, Your Majesty: the politicians back in Beiros are a bunch of lying cowards." Fares chuckled, and even the king allowed himself a smile. "If it means I get to save my kingdom, I'll join you, as a blacksmith or as a confidante, but I cannot shed any more blood on your orders."

"Understood. That is perfectly reasonable," King Michel was grateful that Fares had accepted the offer. "How do you think your nephew will react?"

Fares laughed. "He was too blunt with you before—that won't change. But travelling with me is the very least he can do for Nataaros. Perhaps he'll learn something."

CHAPTER 4
THE ROAD TO BEIROS

It took a lot of convincing for Fares to get Melhel to go with him to Beiros. The younger man felt he didn't owe a thing to the royal family. He admitted he was rash and a bit rude to the king in their meeting, but that didn't change anything. In his estimation, he didn't owe the king service as his blacksmith any more now that he'd spoken his mind. Melhel did owe his uncle, though, for raising him, and it was only Fares' insistence that made him agree to the trip.

Melhel had never even been outside of Chekkos, and knew nothing about Beiros or anywhere else in Alexandros. And now he was asked to pack up, leave his old life, and start anew in a new city — in a whole new world. Fares did promise him that opportunities would come of it. Melhel would build a reputation from his work and be able to set himself up with the future by ingratiating himself with the elites in the capital. But Melhel was too like his uncle for these promises to matter: he wanted the quiet life, not the high life. He would only do this as a favour to the man who raised him, taught him, and made him the man he was.

Rather than selling the shop and property in Chekkos, before they left, the Baraks arranged to rent it to some up-and-coming smiths. Fares decided that he could benefit by making some extra gold while he was away, and give experience and opportunity to an eager learner. If you are well established in your craft, little is more rewarding than mentoring someone who looks up to you and can really benefit from it. The young blacksmiths who would take care of the shop were more than capable; Fares would never have entrusted it to anyone he doubted. His standards were incredibly high, and his trust hard-won.

~

RAFIQ AND A GUARD were loading everyone's belongings onto the king's carriage, which was large enough for all of Melhel's and Fares' necessities on top of the royal family's own luggage. King Michel had promised them a brand-new workshop in the heart of the business district of Beiros, with the best equipment and resources only available to a servant of the king. They would even have a villa close to the palace, with a view overlooking the green Alexandrosian countryside surrounding Beiros. King Michel really had made every effort to impress his friend in enticing him back to the capital. And he would need Fares more than ever, if he was to be believed about how serious the situation with the Scandosians was.

As the Baraks were ready to board the carriage, Prince Sirhan couldn't help but sneer at his new travelling companions. Never had ordinary citizens been allowed to ride in the carriage with the king, and no matter how hard his parents pushed him to be on his best behaviour, there was no hiding his disdain for the commoners, even though it was in his best interests to get along with them. Since Sirhan was to become king after his father, and Melhel to take over his uncle's duties in time, Melhel ought to have been the one the prince befriended most of all, so that the bonds of loyalty could pass smoothly down the generations. But this was not a perfect world.

~

THEY HAD BEEN RIDING for several miles, almost half a day, and the trip had already become tiresome and awkward. Prince Sirhan and

45

Melhel couldn't stop staring at each other, each of them filled with contempt. But the queen had enough of this, and redoubled her efforts to stir up some conversation.

"So, Melhel ... are you looking forward to living in Beiros?" she asked.

Her beautiful, wide smile shone through and broke down all his barriers. He didn't necessarily want to answer—he wasn't in the mood for conversation—but there was something about Queen Rania's radiance that got to him.

A sidelong look from his uncle certainly helped to get the ball rolling, too.

"Well, Your Majesty, I'm a little nervous, to be perfectly honest." Melhel answered as thoughtfully as possible, making sure he looked his queen in the eye, so as not to be evasive. "I've only ever known Chekkos. I know nothing of Beiros, royalty, and the like. It will be quite the culture shock." The queen smiled at him. She saw his innocence beneath his rough exterior; that he was honest, wished for a humble life, and without his parents, had few in the world to care for him.

"Not to worry, Melhel: many a great man in Beiros came from a humble origin," she said calmly. "Why, our Sword, Rafiq, was a simple farmhand before he found his calling to fight for his king and kingdom."

"This is true," the king attested. He was just a simple man from a simple family." He beamed proudly, talking of his Sword's accomplishments. "It wasn't till he was drafted for the civil war that he truly made a name for himself. We needed all hands to fight, and his skill in battle elevated him to where he is now."

Melhel was surprised. "Is this true?"

He had naturally assumed that Rafiq Harrira was of noble birth.

"Ask your uncle," said the king, gesturing for Fares to back him up.

"It's true," Fares confirmed. "He was a nobody. But he was a natural soldier. If weren't for him and his strength, perhaps our battles would have gone differently."

King Michel smiled. "There's a reason he is now my Sword. I wouldn't give such an important position to just anyone."

"I thought swords had to have been nobility," Melhel said.

"Not necessarily," the king explained. "As long as they can do their job effectively, it wouldn't matter if their father was Nataaros's most respected senator or a slave from Venos. There is always opportunity."

Melhel turned to his uncle. "Was he that good in battle?"

He was sceptical, but knew his uncle wouldn't lie.

"Yes," said Fares. "You should ask him about it. He has a lot of stories to tell." His expression was steely: a sign of honesty, Melhel knew.

"You see, there's nothing to be afraid of," the queen said reassuringly, taking hold of the conversation again. "Greatness can come from anywhere. It matters not who your parents are. What matters is who *you* are, and how you apply your gifts. Like Rafiq did."

She looked meaningfully at her son. "It is just the same for us. With Sirhan, we can only do so much," she said. "But we know that to be a great king, he must use what is given to him wisely. His rule will be judged by the hard work he puts in for his kingdom."

Prince Sirhan scowled. "You underestimate me," he said. "I will be the greatest king the land has ever known."

"I should hope so." The king grinned. "You're a reflection of myself and your mother. For our sake, you had better believe you'll make a great king."

Fares thought it best to chimed in supportively. "Not to worry, my prince. I'm sure once I've finished mentoring my nephew, he will be of great service to yourself, as I was to your father."

Melhel looked the prince directly in the eyes, sharing a look in which they both knew the others were right and they were better off getting to know each other.

"I'm sure Melhel and I will do great things for Nataaros," Prince Sirhan claimed boldly, with a hearty smile and the confidence of a young man with wild ambition but little experience.

~

A FEW DAYS into their trip, the Baraks and the royals had become close again. Prince Sirhan and Melhel slowly started to get along with each other, and Fares and King Michel rekindled their old friendship. The younger generation shared their life stories—Prince Sirhan's of growing up as the heir to the throne, and Melhel's as the adopted son of a blacksmith and warrior.

Meanwhile, Fares and the king told everyone stories of the times they'd helped save the kingdom from disaster.

Melhel was wary, though, about getting too far into the details of the Scandosian Civil War. He knew it was still a sore spot for his uncle. But Fares seemed to be enjoying himself for the first time in a long time. Despite what the stubborn Alexandrosian said, he had deeply missed King Michel, and was glad they were reunited.

Prince Sirhan often dominated the conversation with his loud, slightly high-pitched voice. "Once, during my sword training, I was finally able to have Rafiq as my instructor," he began his tale. "And I was only ... maybe ... fifteen years old, but I was certainly more than ready. Anyhow, as we got further into the session, during a spar, I managed to sweep his leg and knock him straight onto his back."

The prince boasted with the most animated and exaggerated hand gestures, selling the story as something that genuinely happened.

"Oh, yes, the great Rafiq Harrira, bested by Prince Sirhan," he shrilled. "I held my practice sword to his throat. Had it been a real fight, he'd have had his throat cut!"

Outside in the driver's seat, keeping a watchful eye around the carriage, Rafiq still heard everything the prince said, and rolled his eyes behind his visor.

Melhel was taken aback at the story and sat up. Could Rafiq, the intimidating Sword of the King be defeated in a sparring match by Prince Sirhan? It didn't add up.

Fares also had his doubts, and leaned forward to stare directly at the prince. His eyes flashed unnervingly beneath his rugged brow.

"Are you sure? Rafiq Harrira?" he quizzed. "That one outside, keeping an eye out for us?" He looked ready to call out the lie if need be.

"I swear it," Prince Sirhan insisted.

"Really?" Fares was an inquisitor now. "Because the Rafiq Harrira I know tore through Scandosian soldiers on the battlefield like they were saplings. The Rafiq Harrira I know saved this kingdom from elven domination through sheer bravery and brilliance." Melhel began to chuckle as his uncle hounded the prince. "Yet, you mean to tell me that you defeated him?"

Prince Sirhan started to quiver under the pressure of Fares's gaze, and lowered his eyes a moment.

Looking to his father for support, the prince instead was met by a raised eyebrow prompting him to cut the lies.

Even the queen sighed at her son's fables.

"Fine," Prince Sirhan confessed. "It was not Rafiq I bested, but a squire."

Fares burst out laughing.

"A lowly squire?" he mocked. "And here I thought the great prince had actually defeated the legendary Sword of the King."

It grated Prince Sirhan's nerves. "It would behove you to not laugh at your future king, Fares." But the old soldier could not be intimidated.

"With due respect, prince," Fares said smiling, as he shifted his eyes to the king and queen, "even your parents can't help but find it amusing."

And he was right, King Michel's wide smile was brimming with humour. He had found his son's feeble attempt at showing superiority rather charming.

Queen Rania, on the other hand, laughed with pity at his embarrassment. He was still her little boy, and kind and generous as she was, though as ruthless and cold as he could be, she still loved him unconditionally. In her eyes he could do no wrong.

But Prince Sirhan's embellishment was not merely that of a boy trying to play grown-up. He was aware of the politics he would be embroiled in when his time came. He knew he had to win people over, and had tried to put up a front of strength for Melhel. If the young smith were to spend several years serving him, possibly even as a soldier or commander, Melhel would also have to fear him, even if only slightly. He had no wish to be able to send such people into a state of panic or paranoia—but he did want them to answer his call and his call only, knowing that disobedience or insubordination would be noticed.

Add that Melhel had no experience of the court or indeed anything outside of Chekkos, and the prince believed he could plant a false idea of the glory of royalty—specifically *his* glory—in Melhel's mind.

But if anyone had made an impression recently, it had been Melhel. Though his rudeness to the king at their first meeting had been an insult, Michel marvelled at his honesty. In the three days of their trip, that innocent candour had taken him and the queen aback. They had simply never seen someone like him.

Too often, people had told the royals what they thought they wanted to hear, not what they needed to. Melhel's lack of knowledge on matters concerning the capital was quite the shock, though simply a testament to his roots as a young man from Chekkos, who had grown up away from the politics and frivolity of the court.

But his knowledge of the world and people around him couldn't be understated. Prince Sirhan may have considered him a simple man, maybe a fool, but rather, he had a different way of thinking. And he hadn't yet made his biggest impression on the royal family.

THEY WERE at the halfway point of their journey, where the road between Chekkos and Beiros was lined on either side by luscious, green grass. The Grasslands made up the vast majority of the natural landscape in Alexandros, where wildlife could roam free and farmers reaped rich harvests from the soil.

Granted, the government and the king took relatively little note of agriculture and natural resources. That was a heritage that had carried on for many generations. Rather, when they looked out from their carriage on the plains, the king thought of war.

The open, grassy fields had hosted numerous battles in the civil war, and seen slaughter and bloodshed. Here, formations and strategies went out the window. It was too vast for an infantry to concern itself with fancy tactics.

Only the best cavalry can enjoy an open battlefield, and they have done so in the battles waged across the Alexandrosian countryside. The hoofprints of the strongest horses could still be faintly seen, all those years later, and the local villagers and townspeople still recalled the slaughter of countryman and enemy alike.

Especially in warmer weather, these fertile plains were a beautiful sight. The Cedar Hills to the west of Beiros and south of Chekkos loomed above them, as did the Snowy Mountains. These were just outside of Beiros's jurisdiction, too far away for anyone from the capital to care about. For as long as anyone could remember, the kings of Nataaros had focused on the economic development of the major cities—like Beiros, Beilos, and Sidos—and left the countryside to itself. And King Michel was among those monarchs whose neglect was most complete. This had made room for lawlessness, of which the king was oblivious.

As the royal carriage carried on down the road, Rafiq spotted a group of men about a hundred yards ahead of them, just off the road and making a clamorous noise.

He and the drivers made nothing of it and kept up their speed, but as they got closer, they could hear the cries and wails of the men more clearly.

"Help us!"

"Save us from our misery!"

Their faces were covered in dirt, their clothing in tatters.

They appeared to be hungry and malnourished, poor and desperate for any sort of help. They were beggars, homeless and in need.

Now the group stood in the road, not letting the carriage pass.

"What say you, young men?" Rafiq bellowed from his high position on the driver's seat. "Are you not aware you are disrupting an important envoy?"

"Please, sir, we are hungry and cold," one of them pleaded. "We can see that you're of substantial wealth. Would be so troublesome to spare some gold for our troubles?"

Inside the carriage, the king grew frustrated at the sudden halt.

"What is the meaning of this?" he wondered aloud. "Why have we stopped moving?"

51

They listened outside to hear what was happening, and heard Rafiq's discussion with the beggars.

"I do apologise," Rafiq said with remorse. "But I am merely a driver and protector. I am not in a position to hand over gold to anyone."

The beggars observed the extravagance of the carriage.

"Say, this is quite the marvel," the leader noted. "The owner must be quite rich. I am sure he can spare some gold."

"Begone," Rafiq warned them. "For I will be forced to use my sword."

The ringleader was taken aback by Rafiq's threat. "You wouldn't slay folk like us, would you?" the man wheedled.

King Michel heard all this and expressed his misgivings to Fares. "Surely, we can spare a few gold coins," the king said. "What is that to us? It would be treasure for these men." He was about to step out of the carriage, presenting himself as a glorious saviour of a king, but Melhel quickly realised what was going on and stopped him.

"These men are not poor beggars, Your Majesty," Melhel said, understanding what may come. "They are bandits. Please, do not dare step outside of this carriage."

"Bandits? In my kingdom?"

"There are a lot of poor folk out in these parts," Melhel explained. "Banditry is what they must resort to if they want to survive."

Fares had seen as much as Melhel and agreed. After all, Melhel had learned from Fares how to judge a man.

"He's right," Fares said to King Michel, who went back to his seat.

"Very well," the king conceded. "What should we do, then? We cannot leave Rafiq on his own out there."

The queen remained calm, but the prince became frustrated.

"Let me take care of these vile creatures," he cried. "I will show them not to threaten me or my parents!"

Melhel was quick to stop him. "You won't do that. You're far too important."

Fares got up. "Melhel and I will deal with it," he said. This was nothing new to them, and unlike the royals, they were unshakingly calm.

Back outside, Rafiq was still in a back and forth with the bandits, who kept up their act of being humble beggars.

"I urge you, step aside and allow us to pass," Rafiq demanded.

He stepped towards the ringleader. His sheer size dwarfed the bandit, who hoped his cunning would pull him through.

"We won't leave until we are given what we deserve," the ringleader insisted.

Fares and Melhel emerged from the carriage.

"Have you not heard the man?" Fares called to the bandits. "Step aside. This is not your business." They inched closer to the quarrel.

"Very well, then," the bandit sighed.

The filthy man had stepped back and drawn his sword to kill Rafiq, when Melhel quickly launched a dagger through his throat, killing him on the spot.

The bandits panicked and tried to rush the blacksmiths, but Rafiq quickly came to his senses and drew his sword, stabbing one of them in the back.

Fares rushed forward and engaged two of them, making quick work as he managed to weave underneath one and used him as a human shield against his friend, killing both.

Melhel made eye contact with the last bandit and approached him but, frightened, the man made a run for it. He tried to head for the nearby woods to hide, but Melhel chased and almost caught him. Before the young Alexandrosian could catch the terrified bandit, though an arrow hit the false beggar in the back and he dropped dead.

Melhel looked back at the carriage, where one of the guards had been able to grab his bow, draw an arrow, and finish off the group of bandits.

The king, queen, and prince stepped outside and saw the mess. They had heard it all: the threats, the sounds of the bandits being cut down by superior fighters, and their screams as they were slain.

King Michel was impressed with Melhel's resolve.

"You saved my life, young man," he said with a sigh of relief. "Excellent work, seeing they were not who they seemed."

To Melhel it had been light work.

"I've dealt with bandits before," he said as he headed back into the carriage. "It happens a lot outside the major cities. People are desperate for money. Truly desperate."

At that moment, Melhel was uncharacteristically low-key. But the king had been impressed with what kind of man he was, and learned the state of his kingdom outside Beiros.

Fares smiled at Rafiq.

"Guess I'm not completely finished saving your life," he chuckled at his former friend. "If we weigh it up, I think you still owe me a few more of those."

"As though I've never saved yours before?" Many times, it had been the other way around.

But there wasn't time to waste on quibbling or to look back. They returned to the carriage and continued onward to the capital.

A COUPLE of hours after the bandit attack, by nightfall King Michel was still thinking about what he had seen on the road.

He had been positive that his kingdom was thriving, that there was no crime of that sort, and that no ill men would dare to rob a carriage of his type.

He stared out the window of his carriage at the stunning night sky of Nataaros, and saw the stars in their constellations.

"How can a world so beautiful be so violent?" he asked Fares. "Is this Lah's cruel plan? To create a world with wonders like the stars in the night sky and the trees in our woods, but fill men with violence and hate?"

Fares made sure to keep his voice as low as possible, for everyone else inside the carriage had fallen asleep. The attack had kept the king and his old friend awake.

"It is not Lah's will to twist our heads in this way, my king," he said.

Like any true Alexandrosian family, Fares and Melhel were

54

devout followers of the Faith of Lah, the worship of their creator god, who was said to be a dragon the size of the largest lakes in the land. It was not uncommon for Fares to sometimes go back to the words preached by the Faith, especially in matters like this.

"I can promise you, Lah's will is to see us live a just and full life," Fares preached. "He has only granted us free will so as not to control us and use us as his pawns. Those men back there—it is a shame they didn't exercise the free will that was given to them justly, and they will be judged accordingly."

Fares' words reassured King Michel that their god was not out to punish or test him.

"Well then, why is that men choose to rob and to commit crimes?" the king asked, probing Fares further. "Have I not been a fair king? A good king?"

Fares stopped and thought for a moment. "You have been a good king," Fares finally consoled him. "But this is the reality: you have neglected the countryside for far too long. If it weren't for the local communities banding together to maintain order and a stable society out here, there would be chaos."

"Are you saying I've ignored my people?"

"With all due respect, yes," Fares told him. "You've focused on what can generate wealth and haven't paid attention to the people who need your support to survive. Your presence simply isn't felt outside of the major cities. It is almost as if we do not have a king, or that you are a king in name only, not in practice."

"What would you have me do?"

"It is not the time for politics, Your Majesty." Fares yawned. "When we are in Beiros, you can discuss it with those fools in the senate."

Fares had always been one of the few people who could be so blunt to the king. To refuse to discuss an important issue until they arrived in Beiros was a presumption only a few could take. He had earned it through his service. And King Michel knew that Fares was doing him a favour and would leave abruptly if he felt it appropriate, his rank aside. Fares could not be commanded to act against his conscience or better judgement.

The king had a lot to think about on his own as he once again gazed at the night sky.

If Fares had always had the king's utmost trust and respect, Melhel had made an impression too. For him to have seen the bandits' attack before it happened, and to act swiftly to save Rafiq and the king's life, had been a remarkable thing to do. King Michel certainly had big plans for the young blacksmith upon their arrival in the capital.

CHAPTER 5

THE HEART OF A KINGDOM

I n the outskirts of Beiros, the horses pulling the carriage trotted along. It was just before dawn, and the black sky was slowly being replaced by grey with a slight tint of orange indicating that the bright, Nataarosian sun would soon appear over the horizon. The walls of Beiros came into Rafiq and the drivers' view, and what a sight it was.

The city's walls had been built using the finest concrete in the land, and developed over time by the kings of Nataaros to ensure the city's defences were strong. 'Impenetrable' the word most often used to describe Beiros's walls, as it was said that no assault could ever succeed against the city, and those that had tested the walls had sorely perished.

Those walls were fifty yards high, and no one unwelcome could easily go in or out so long as they remained intact. No catapult, no battering ram, nor even the largest army assembled could penetrate Beiros; the king and his family could rest easy knowing the city remained forever safe.

Surrounding those walls was a moat, approximately thirty fathoms deep, as if impenetrable walls weren't enough. The moat's circumference was roughly that of the city itself, around twenty miles. A rumour persisted that piranhas imported from foreign lands inhabited the moat's waters, since none dared put it to the test: an ingenious way to keep people in line and prevent attacks.

Ahead of the city gates was a drawbridge, stretching across the moat, which the city guard kept constantly manned, with not a second's break. There were the workers who pulled the gears to lower or raise the drawbridge, lookouts to warn of any potential threats, and archers to dispatch them, posted at equal distances the whole length of the city walls.

There were armed infantrymen in case of a confrontation, and a commander for each shift. Every order trickled down from him to the lowliest guard.

On top of the walls, gunners manned cannons that ensured an explosive and forceful defence in event of a siege. The king had put great expense and effort into defending the city, and no one dared to attack. The guards were often bored and dismissed the excessive defences, and the pay was minuscule for the work asked, but their commanders kept them in line, punishing any insubordination with a lap around the walls. To the king, this was as serious a job as any, if not more so, and the punishment was to be handed out accordingly.

THE CARRIAGE now halted at the gates of Beiros, waiting for the drawbridge to be lowered.

Two minutes passed and Rafiq, annoyed, Rafiq was annoyed and wondered what was holding them up.

"Do these young men not know what the royal carriage looks like?" he exclaimed to his fellow drivers.

Atop the walls, the guards were dawdling inattentively, playing a simple word game to prevent themselves from falling asleep.

"Sword," one said.

"Dagger," said another.

"Rats."

Rafiq yelled out to them. "If you carry on not paying attention to whomever arrives at the gates, we will surely lose the city in a matter of hours!" His booming voice quickly grabbed the guards' attention, and panicking, they rushed forward to see whose the voice was.

As they looked over the walls, they saw Rafiq ahead of the dazzling carriage with his arms wide in impatience and frustration.

"Rafiq Harrira! Sir!" one of the guards quickly barked to him.

"Yes, I know who I am," Rafiq answered. "Now, open the gates and lower the bridge. The king doesn't have all morning!"

The guards hurriedly lowered the drawbridge and opened the gates, letting it pass.

It was still barely daybreak, and there were yet few enough people in the streets that the carriage could pass without drawing much attention. With the city empty, Rafiq could marvel at Beiros in the serene glory of its architectural achievement.

Starting near the gate were the various housing quarters, reserved for the finest workers in each craft throughout all the lands. These houses stretched across the city and surrounded the centre, which was focused on industry. Rafiq couldn't help but smile at the ease with which they passed through the streets. Here and there he caught the aroma of freshly baking bread, the bakers being among the few people already awake and working.

Further into the city, Rafiq began to spot the schools—the finest in all Alexandros—where the city's children and youth were taught the essentials of life: mathematics, literacy, and physical education. Only later, when they reached adulthood, would an Alexandrosian choose a profession, be it medicine, law, politics, the military, or a trade such as blacksmithing. For certain careers, such as those involving politics and the law, it was advantageous to study the Scandosian language as well as Nataarosian, and the availability of this option in the schools of Beiros had done wonders for diplomacy and relations in the aftermath of the civil war. As a speaker of Scandosian himself, the king had stressed the importance of the language in education.

Not too far from the city's best schools was the military academy. For those who chose the life of a soldier, this was where they were taught combat, battle tactics and strategy, weaponry, and the history of war, down to the earliest uses of sticks and stones as weapons. Martial education took high priority in Alexandros, and along with the city guard and the common and elite soldiers of the army, even some politicians were educated in war. They, along with the king, bore responsibility for major military decisions.

Rafiq and Fares had found themselves at the academy at a young age, and there their skills had been honed until they were adept if untested soldiers. It seemed a lifetime ago; they had almost been different men.

Melhel awoke early and looked outside his window. Seeing that he was in Beiros, he was awestruck by its beauty. Chekkos paled in comparison.

The carriage moved so slowly it allowed Melhel to climb up outside and hop onto the driver's seat next to Rafiq, who was shocked to see the young man awake and next to him.

"What are you doing?" he asked.

Melhel rubbed his eyes, still not fully awake.

"Thought I'd come check out the capital." He yawned. "Look at this place. How did they build such a city?"

Rafiq was surprised. "Your uncle never told you how our city came to be?"

Melhel shook his head, "Not really, no." He harkened back to his education under Fares. "Just that it was the capital. But look at these buildings!" "How did this all happen?"

Rafiq leaned back, realising it might be time for a story.

"We still have some time before the palace." He cleared his throat. "Why don't I tell you the origins of Beiros and the major buildings we pass?"

Melhel liked the sound of this. "Alright, let's do it."

Further in towards the centre of Beiros, Rafiq soon found his first landmark. "Here, we have the museum," he explained to Melhel. "Any archaeological find, painting, sculpture, or piece of artwork and history can be found here."

"*Any*?" He asked.

"Anything," Rafiq affirmed. "Be sure to visit whenever you have spare time. It seems as though your uncle hasn't taught you nearly enough about our kingdom."

Melhel smiled at this sly knock at Fares. It was becoming increasingly plain to Melhel just how little he knew of the world around him. A sword or a hot iron—sure, he knew his way around those, and he could defend himself and the people around him from a bandit raid. But ask him to discuss causes and effects in Nataarosian history and he wouldn't have a clue where to begin. He knew the glory of war from stories he had read as a child, but to examine the complexities and dynamics behind such events and the people who drove them was beyond his ability.

"Why store such things in a museum?" he asked. "Why not leave them where they were?"

"Because they must be preserved," Rafiq answered. "To let them gather dirt would be a disservice to the people, who deserve to see them. Especially if—like you—they are clueless about history."

Much as he knew the truth of it, Melhel felt slighted.

"I'm not clueless."

"Perhaps that is an unfair way to put it," Rafiq allowed. "But to say you're an aficionado of history, or an expert on all things in our kingdom, would be false. Yes?"

Melhel had to nod, despite his pride.

"And the artworks?" Melhel wondered. "Why are they there?"

Rafiq smiled. The thought of the museum brought him joy, despite his apparent roughness. "When you and your uncle craft a fine shield or sword," he said, "made of the finest materials and with a design to make others envy the bearer, what do you do with it?" he asked.

"Well, we sell it to whoever is most interested."

"Exactly." Rafiq grinned. "Your work doesn't go unnoticed, and you are rewarded for it. So it is for the finest artists: their work is admired and bought at a high price, to be put on display for all to see.

"It may depict anything: famous figures, famous events. You may see a painting of the civil war; you may see a sculpture of Beilos himself. Art is precious and should be admired by all. And if you are talented and gifted, then you should be celebrated."

Melhel took this lesson to heart: your hard work will be rewarded and it is well for the world to see it. If you can create something that represents the pinnacle of your craft, why hide it, when you could show the world its greatness?

Several blocks from the museum, Rafiq and Melhel found the citizens had risen and the streets were increasingly bustling. The activity of the capital was swinging into life for its newest resident to see.

People could be seen making their daily trip to their jobs, and it wasn't hard to separate the nobility from the lower classes. The nobles were dressed head to toe in the finest material from the cloth factories of Paros, in all the colours of the rainbow. The lower classes went about in all they could afford: simple—though often dirty—light-coloured robes and tunics of cheap cotton.

Melhel noted the disparity. "Is this the divide between the rich and the poor?" he asked. "The rich dress like living artworks, while the poor look as though they were given the scraps that were left over?"

Rafiq paused, unsure how best to answer. "It is the way society functions. The rich gained their wealth through hard work—and fate."

Melhel looked to his left and saw a barefoot child whose face and bare limbs were smeared with dirt. "I doubt the poor have chosen to live this way," he observed.

"There is every opportunity to gain wealth in Beiros," Rafiq said. "This life is just what you make of it."

"But poverty like this hardly exists in Chekkos. You don't see people barely clothed. I'm sure the king could do something about it."

The horses ahead of the carriage were trotting merrily through the streets.

"Open up schools for the poor," Melhel suggested. "Make it easier for these innocent people to receive these opportunities you speak of."

Rafiq chose not to debate the matter any further. He was the Sword of the King, and it was neither his place to comment nor to judge. No matter what, he would always defend King Michel. "Whatever you would like to say, I'm sure the king is open to suggestions," Rafiq said.

Melhel couldn't help but feel that from his privileged position, Rafiq did not understand the plight of these poor people.

As their journey continued, they slowed by the huge Beiros Amphitheatre, which could seat thousands. "Here you can see all the performances and plays by the best musicians, and actors in the land," Rafiq explained.

Melhel was keen to finally attend the theatre. "What kinds of plays?" He asked.

"All sorts," Rafiq said enthusiastically. "Comedies, dramas... You could come see a re-enactment of a famous battle in our history. Why, you could see the funniest comedians bring the crowd to raucous laughter!"

The young blacksmith was eager to delve deeper.

"What kinds of comedies are we talking about?" he queried.

"Any kind," Rafiq explained. "Satires on family life, observations on the world we live in—"

"Political comedy, then?" Melhel interjected.

"What do you mean?"

"You know, making fun of the senate, politicians ... even the king?"

Rafiq was shocked. "Making fun of the king?" he said in disbelief. "Would you be so crass?"

Melhel shrugged, unaware of the seriousness of his suggestion. "Shouldn't comedy be taken lightly?" he said. "I mean, it is for laughter, is it not?"

Rafiq shook his head, embarrassed. "Yes, but even comedy has some truth to it," Rafiq said darkly. "Some seriousness. To make fun of the king in public—it's unheard of."

"So?" said Melhel. He didn't share Rafiq's delicate sensibilities. "Would he care? Is it not within a man's rights to criticise another openly?"

"Yes, but not the king."

"Is he so feeble that he cannot defend himself?" Melhel asked. "Or cannot take a joke? He's a reasonable man. I'm sure he wouldn't mind some good-natured ribbing."

"Melhel, young man," Rafiq sighed, "the king is the most exalted in the land. To mock him is to mock the very foundations Nataaros was founded on."

"I thought those foundations were democratic at their core?" But the Sword had had enough.

"It's out of the question, Melhel," he said, ending the debate. "That's final."

Melhel stayed quiet as they continued past the amphitheatre and on to the palace.

~

EVERYONE ELSE WAS STILL fast asleep inside the carriage, though the sun was slowly making its presence felt across the city.

In the royal district, the architectural marvels of Beiros really began. Here, in the richest and most noble of all neighbourhoods in the capital, only the finest buildings and designs were on display, much like the artworks in Rafiq's beloved museum.

Melhel looked to his left and right and saw history unfolding before him. Where there had been mere huts in the times before the kingdom, now stood towering structures as high as its technology could manage. When Beilos conquered and built up Nataaros, this was what he had envisioned: people in sheer wonder over what Alexandros—what Nataaros—was capable of. It was a place where travellers from near and far could revel in what he had spent his life creating.

These buildings were awash with gold and marble that reflected the sun and gave the city an almost otherworldly glow, as if it were the work of forces beyond our comprehension. The designs and forms placed together could have been merely paintings by the finest artists, but they were real.

Alexandros was known for its intellectual heritage, and it was in Beiros, the capital, that the best lawyers, doctors, politicians, architects, and practitioners of any field requiring intellect, could be found. It was vastly different from the small, single-storey world that Melhel had come from back in Chekkos.

"I may grow short of breath navigating a home of this size," he joked to Rafiq, trying to slowly defuse the tension. "I've never seen anything like this."

Rafiq stayed focused on the road. "You'll get used to it," he said. "And who knows? Perhaps it'll make you a better soldier should we ever need you to be one."

"A better soldier?" he retorted. "Did you not see me against those bandits?"

"Bandits are not an army." Rafiq said. "Report back to me when the enemy isn't stupid enough to think they could rob the royal carriage."

Melhel returned to being stunned by the buildings as they passed. Just the fact that they were homes amazed him. The amphitheatre, museum, library, and gallery had all been institutions. The royal district was different. People lived in these magnificent structures: the king's closest relatives and friends, Nataaros's most powerful politicians—all could call the royal district home.

But even among these astonishing buildings, the royal palace still stood out. It was truly a home fit for a king. Standing so tall that the tip of its highest spire could be seen from outside the city's walls, the compound was very roughly cubic, with the outer walls enclosing an inner courtyard. The palace itself was decorated in royal red and white to distinguish it from the rest of Beiros. Whether you were a resident or a visitor, you would know this was a place for a king. The front gates, warding off threats, were jagged and black, and constantly manned by only the finest guards in all the land for twenty-four hours of every single day.

The carriage reached the front of the gates and stopped. Rafiq dropped down from the driver's seat to awake the sleepy passengers inside.

The burly general banged on the doors of the carriage.

"Wake up!" he screamed, with no regard for just who was inside.

Naturally, Prince Sirhan took offence.

"Does that oaf have no shame?" he moaned.

"Apparently not," King Michel mumbled.

Fares was the last to fully awaken, and when he realised that his nephew was no longer inside, he panicked. "Where's Melhel? Has anyone seen him?" Then he rushed outside only to see Melhel standing right there, giving him a confused look.

"Good morning, Uncle," Melhel said.

"What are you doing awake?" Fares demanded. "And how long have you been up? It's barely morning!"

Melhel had paid no attention to the time.

"A little while now," he replied. "Rafiq gave me a little run through and a tour of the city as we passed through. Did you know comedians are not allowed to mock the king?"

Unfortunately, he said this just as the royal family were making their way outside.

"Did someone say my name?" the king wondered.

Rafiq used this chance to embarrass Melhel, as if the young man hadn't been doing enough himself.

"Well, young Melhel over here is suffering quite the culture shock right now." Rafiq explained. "He has yet to fully understand the customs that a denizen of Beiros should follow."

The king brushed this off coolly.

"I'm well aware of that," he chuckled. "In fact, I was aware of his lack of awareness of our customs within thirty seconds of meeting him."

Fares rolled his eyes at Melhel, who couldn't hide his sheepishness.

Queen Rania placed a gentle hand on her husband as if to remind him to only speak kind words of his new guest, especially as Prince Sirhan was giving Melhel his trademark cold stare.

"But, in saying that," the king continued, "he will learn. It's evident to me that where he's from is vastly different to where the rest of us are from. Besides, I appreciate his honesty."

Melhel smiled, thankful for the king's understanding nature.

"And he is a fine young man," the queen said, encouraging him further. "You should be immensely proud of the man he's become, Fares." She beamed. It was her almost ethereal radiance, rather than her words, that most swayed her people, and Fares couldn't resist blushing at the compliment.

Rafiq laughed and rubbed Melhel's head playfully. "I'll make sure he does learn," he told the king. "Or so help me, Lah, he will know about it."

"As will I," Prince Sirhan chimed in, far less jovially.

Melhel wanted to hurry everyone else up.

"Enough about me, please," he insisted. "Let's head inside."

~

THE GROUP HEADED inside the palace through the front doors, as large as could be, made of the finest wood in all Nataaros and polished at the beginning of each week to maintain the gleam of royalty.

As they stepped into the front hall, Melhel looked up and saw portraits and paintings of past kings and battles. At the very top, right in the middle and the largest of the bunch, was the portrait of Beilos, the conqueror and founder of the kingdom. His portrait was strikingly regal even in next to those of his counterparts: he stood tall and strong in garments decorated in a bloody crimson red. He faced the viewer with his body angled slightly to the left, with his dominant right hand in the foreground, clutching a sword that shone as bright as the sun, threatening to blind onlookers even from within a mere painting. His gaze turned directly at the viewer with a stern look of authority: the portrait had been commissioned shortly after his conquest and unification of the kingdom.

King Michel noticed Melhel's awe. "I see you have met the Conqueror. My ancestor," he said. "Had it not been for him, none of us would be here today." Melhel looked at King Michel, to Beilos, and back again as he registered the similarities between the two men. "He looks a lot like you, Your Majesty."

"Of course!" King Michel chuckled. "We are of the same blood, you know."

Elsewhere, Fares had overlooked the portrait of Beilos, which he had seen all too often in his time, and was captivated by a painting commemorating the victory in the Scandosian Civil War, following the Siege of Beiros. Set outside the city walls, it depicted a larger-than-life King Michel, as the governor of Scandos at the time, Hasson Nasallah, surrendered himself at the king's feet.

Surrounding the king were familiar faces: Rafiq Harrira and even Fares himself, who had often been seen as the hero of the day. His actions, decision-making and leadership during the siege were considered by contemporary historians to have won the battle for the Alexandrosians and royalists.

In all the talk of Beiros being impenetrable, and impossible to besiege, the battle was the closest anyone had come to disproving that theory.

Fares sighed at the memories the painting brought back. He knew the truth behind the romantic depictions of Nataaros and its history.

"So, what are your thoughts on our great city?" he asked Melhel warmly, wanting to continue their conversation.

"It's beautiful," he said. "But there is one thing that struck me."

"And what would that be?" he wondered.

"I haven't seen any women on the street at all," Melhel recalled. "Not in the shops. Not in the stables. Nowhere have I seen a woman. Have we stumbled upon a womanless society? Is everything here for men only? Do they even exist in Beiros?"

The king was taken aback by Melhel's abrasiveness. "Well... You see, Melhel..." He stumbled to find an answer. "We do have women here, of course ... we do. But they're at home, being loving and caring mothers and wives to their families."

"That seems fair," he allowed. "They're just kept inside, and the men do all the work?"

"Correct," King Michel replied. "That's how we function as a stable society. It's how we've always functioned, so there's no need for it to change any time soon."

King Michel turned his head and saw Fares still staring longingly at the painting of the siege. "You saved our lives that day, Fares," the king reminded his old friend. "We owe you a lot."

"We should've fallen that day," Fares said. "We have no right to be where we are today."

"Lah willed it," the king asserted. "If it were not His will, we wouldn't have won."

But Fares was still haunted by that day. "I do not think Lah would've willed the things we did," Fares said. "What kind of god would?"

King Michel made no comment but knew exactly what Fares

was referring to. Neither of them wanted to touch on it, especially while Melhel was within earshot.

Fares decided to put a smile on his face, and at the very least attempt a joke. "Still," he said, "the painter could've at least made me more handsome."

CHAPTER 6
A FRESH START

It took longer than predicted for Melhel to adjust to his new life in Beiros. Fares had no such trouble; the habit of living at the kingdom's heart returned to him as though it were muscle memory. But Melhel was like a bird with clipped wings, no longer able to fly and forced to walk or run.

Prince Sirhan did as he said he would and offered his friendship and guidance, albeit in his own unique way. During the first week of Melhel's stay in Beiros, the two spent the evenings together swapping stories of their lives. Having come from vastly different backgrounds, they were encouraged to further get to know each other to understand their motivations and character.

Queen Rania was especially encouraging of this idea, as she knew all too well from experience that understanding her people went a long way towards making great leadership possible.

In one conversation between the two young men, Prince Sirhan listened to one of Melhel's stories of how he and his uncle had fended off bandit raids.

"It happens more often than you would think," Melhel explained. "That's why we weren't as fazed as everyone else during that attack on our carriage." during the trip here."

Prince Sirhan tried to remain unfazed and indifferent to Melhel's world-weariness, and tried to impress his new friend himself. "You know, I've dealt with my fair share of banditry as well," he claimed.

"You haven't!" Melhel said disbelievingly. "Your dad—"

"His Majesty, thank you, very much!" Sirhan interjected.

Melhel paid little heed. "Anyway, *your dad* was completely oblivious to the bandit problem facing our town," he continued. "There is no way you have any experience in dealing with bandits."

Prince Sirhan was annoyed, firstly because Melhel was ignoring protocol and secondly because he was downplaying the prince's experience. Sirhan hated to be underestimated and talked down to, not least by a commoner like Melhel.

"Fine," the prince huffed. "Let me tell you my bandit story." He drew himself up as if to regale Melhel with the greatest story ever told. "About two years ago, when I was on a scouting mission with the army, we were ambushed by a gang of bandits and my companions were swiftly killed and I was kidnapped," he declaimed, as though relating the most epic tale in history.

"They took me away to their stronghold and held me ransom, upon noticing I was a nobleman. Twenty talents of gold they demanded as their ransom. I told them to raise the amount to fifty, for I was the Prince of Nataaros. The fools had no idea who I was and whom it was that they had in their capture."

Melhel found it hard to believe any of this.

"In the meantime, word was sent out to the nearest armies that fifty talents were my worth, and they worked endlessly to raise such an amount. While I was in captivity, I made it known to those animals that I was in charge."

"How?" Melhel questioned.

"I am getting to that," Prince Sirhan said impatiently. "Their brains were no match for mine. I read them poetry, had them wait on me and serve me. When I wanted to sleep at night, I simply told them to be quiet and they did just that. If they laughed at me or made fun of me, I threatened to have them hung from the gallows for the whole of Alexandros to see."

"What happened in the end?" Melhel asked.

"When the gold was eventually raised, I was released from captivity and free once again," the prince claimed.

"And that was that? That's how you dealt with bandits?" Melhel nearly laughed.

"Of course not. Don't be silly," Prince Sirhan said, rebuffing Melhel's mockery. "After I was free, I returned with an army, captured them all, and had them hung from the gallows just like I promised."

Melhel was still sceptical of this entire story.

"Okay, so, to summarise your story," Melhel recapped everything he just heard, "the army of Nataaros was defeated by some bandits, you were captured, they didn't initially know who you were, you told them to raise your ransom, you acted as if you were in charge, you threatened to have them hung, once you were free you did just that. Is that correct?"

He looked at Prince Sirhan right in the eyes, who remained as defiant as always.

"You don't tell it as wonderfully as I do," Prince Sirhan was disappointed in Melhel's summary. "But, yes, that's basically what had happened."

"I still don't believe you," Melhel said.

"What? Why not?" Prince Sirhan was defensive.

"When our carriage was attacked you were nowhere to be seen," Melhel commented. "The army of Nataaros would have in no way, shape, or form been defeated and killed by bandits, no matter the circumstances. There is no chance the bandits didn't already know exactly who you were. And I highly doubt you'd have been so composed and superior during a kidnapping as you claim."

"Have it your way, then," he said, before storming out of Melhel's room, offended.

Melhel couldn't help but laugh. "Dominated bandits as if he were their leader..." he chuckled to himself.

And Melhel was right: the prince's version of events was the complete opposite of the truth. The real story was that he had been captured while on a walk around the city walls, and was beaten and tortured in captivity. The bandits did ransom him for fifty talents, because they knew exactly who he was and set their price accordingly. The king was furious about what happened and promptly sent a small squad of his best soldiers, including Rafiq, to retrieve the prince, who after the bandits' defeat was found in their hideout quivering, malnourished, and bruised. For a month after the ordeal, he was so traumatised that his usual arrogance dissolved, though he slowly returned to normality.

Prince Sirhan remained ashamed of the event and took every chance he found to tell a version of the story that made him seem brave and heroic, to paper over the truth. He had thought Melhel stupid enough to believe him, but despite his ignorance of city life, the youth could easily spot a lie when he saw one, and was not shy to point it out.

Nevertheless, Melhel knew that those who bend the truth for selfish motives can often be the most dangerous kinds of people.

THE MORNING after Prince Sirhan's attempt to impress him, Melhel woke to the sun beaming through his window into his eyes.

Despite the relative luxury of the home he and his uncle were afforded in Beiros, it had no curtains, and the sun served as their wake-up call early in the morning. As he struggled to open his eyes, Melhel resolved to remember to tell his uncle to have that fixed.

He dragged himself out of bed, almost zombie-like, before putting on his clothing and heading downstairs to the kitchen.

The kitchen was something else, compared to what they were used to in Chekkos. The king and queen had given them the finest pots and pans, plates, bowls, and utensils, as though they were royalty themselves.

Every week, a vendor replenished their supplies, following's the king's command. They seemingly never had to pay for anything.

While Melhel brewed himself a cup of coffee—a necessary pick-up given the early hour—Fares came downstairs to join him, looking far more refreshed.

"Morning, Melhel," he said, chuckling as he noticed the bags under Melhel's eyes. "You look well."

"It doesn't help when the prince of all of Nataaros keeps you awake at night with story after story," Melhel moaned. "And since we have no curtains, when the sun is awake, so am I."

Fares laughed at Melhel's supposed struggles. "As you should be," he remarked. "We've got a lot to do today. No use wasting time by sleeping in." He poured himself a cup of coffee and grabbed some bread to go with it. "How was Prince Sirhan?" he wondered.

"About how you would expect," Melhel answered. "Did you know he was once captured by bandits, but forced them to raise their ransom for him and spent the whole time in captivity ordering them around, before having them executed?"

"Is that so?" Fares said sceptically.

Melhel managed to shake his tiredness and crack a smile.

"Well, he *thinks* that's what happened," he joked. "I highly doubt a man like him would be so calm and controlled. You saw him when we were attacked."

"I didn't see him at all," Fares remembered.

"Exactly," Melhel replied. "Nowhere to be seen. He stayed inside the whole time until it was safe. A far cry from the brave prince he believes himself to be."

Fares was a little concerned over Melhel's contempt. "Regardless, Melhel," he said, "you have to learn to make friends with him, for the benefit of everyone."

Melhel sat down to breakfast, and stuffed his face full of bread, eggs, and fruit. "I know," he mumbled with his mouth full, "but it's hard when he keeps lying and making everything about himself. I can't make friends with someone like that, let alone serve them."

"You can't make friends with anyone in general," the older blacksmith scoffed. "This is the time to learn."

Melhel didn't warm to the comment, despite its truth. His bluntness had made it hard for him to make friends, even growing up. He had always spoken his mind more than other children. He didn't know how to pay a compliment or spare someone's feelings, and he didn't know how to smile and nod at someone proud and powerful to hide what he felt.

Fares knew that if Melhel were to survive in Beiros, that would have to change.

~

BY THE BEGINNING of the working day, Melhel and Fares were in their new workshop admiring the equipment at their disposal. The king had spared no expense in affording the blacksmiths the finest tools and materials that could be had.

"It's almost as if he's preparing for war," Fares said.

A voice came as if in answer. "I see you have acquainted yourselves with your new toys." Melhel and Fares looked up to see King Michel greeting them, beaming proudly at his own largesse.

"The best tools for the best blacksmiths. The king of Nataaros should spare no expense," he bragged, shaking the hands of his new workers.

"Your Majesty, it is an honour," Fares said in appreciation. "But this is too much."

"Nonsense!" King Michel downplayed it. "As I've always said, you have to invest. It's no use using cheap materials and labour to get a job done. Not if you want it done effectively."

The king was only half right, and only half consistent with his philosophy. Expenses had historically not been spared, but in matters of war. This extravagance reminded Fares of the civil war, where the kingdom's budget had been put mainly towards financing the military. In times of peace, spending instead went to infrastructure, which in times of war was foregone as the king set his sights on victory.

Melhel was overwhelmed by the workload he expected along with all these materials, fretting over the change in lifestyle that was upon him. "Your Majesty, are we really supposed to work with all of this ourselves?" he asked, gesturing at what was laid up for them.

"Of course not!" King Michel replied. "There are some fine blacksmiths on their way, ready to begin working for you."

Fares was confused. "Working for us?"

"That's what I said," King Michel reiterated. "You two won't be blacksmiths, you'll be *in charge* of blacksmiths. You will be leading production for the army. Come now—did you really think I went to all this trouble so just the two of you could spend all day and night hammering metal against an anvil?"

King Michel expected the Baraks to be honoured, but they were closer to being overwhelmed.

"That's great, Your Majesty…" Fares said, "it's just that we've only ever worked as a pair. We've never been in charge of other smiths before."

"And that's why now is a good opportunity for the both of you!" King Michel maintained his excitement. "You'll get to oversee an enormous project and help usher in a new golden age of black-smithing. Think of the legacy you will leave. When Alexandrosian —no, *Nataarosian*—metal and weaponry are the most renowned in the world, they will be traced back to you two."

The Baraks didn't quite share King Michel's grandiose view of the whole idea. They simply had never worked with others before, only together. As private as they were, it let them focus on their work, excelling by use of their own techniques, which they'd rather not pass on to every blacksmith that walked on through.

But that concern was thrown aside as one of the king's soldiers burst into the room.

"Your Majesty, come quick!" He urged.

The king quickly turned to see the soldier panting; he'd bolted his way to the workshop.

"What is it, soldier?" the king asked.

"You have to see this, my king. Come."

The soldier ushered everyone out. Whatever it was, it was important.

EVERYONE RUSHED to the throne room, which was also where the king's table of advisers met, including the land's most respected and influential politicians and senators, hand-picked by the king himself.

Now that Fares was in the capital, the king had asked him to join this table. Today there was no meeting, just a woman under arrest, dragged to her knees by two guards.

The king was outraged. "What is the meaning of this?" he demanded.

The woman was barely dressed. Melhel looked away, embar-rassed. Fares, too, was shocked.

"Why have you brought her before me like this?" the king asked the guards.

"Your Majesty, we caught her having an affair with a guard in his house, while his wife was gone," one of the men said as he struggled to subdue the woman. "We must have her punished."

The king's face showed his dismay that such a scandal would involve one of his guards. These men were meant to be the finest in the kingdom.

King Michel pondered before making his decision.

"Adultery is a heinous offence," he said. He looked to the woman with disgust. "What do you have to say for yourself?"

Though panicking, she looked the king directly in the eye. You could almost hear her heart pound. "I was not aware the man was married, Your Majesty," she said in her own defence. "He approached me at the bakery where I work and seduced me. Told me that if I were his, all my dreams would come true—that we could be together forever."

The woman was visibly angered by the way she had been tricked, even as she was distressed that it was about to get her into serious trouble.

Melhel noticed the man was nowhere to be seen, just the woman. "Where is this guard you slept with?" he asked, trying to avoid the embarrassment of looking at her.

"We left him in his bed, full of his own shame," the guard said. "His wife will be very disappointed in him."

"No matter," King Michel said. He had come to a decision. "Young woman, whether you were of the knowledge or not, adultery is adultery, and laws must be upheld. The punishment for adultery is death. The guards here will take you to your prison, where you shall remain until your execution."

The woman couldn't believe it, and burst out crying. "No! Please, Your Majesty! I beg you!"

The guards began to drag her away.

Fares was appalled, and lowered his head. Melhel quickly ran after the guards to block them from leaving with the woman. "Wait!" he shouted. "There must be another way."

But the king was adamant. "The law is the law," he said. "I can't make any exceptions."

Melhel was trying to buy the woman time, and trying madly to think of some defence, if no one else would come to her aid. "Hear this, then, before you take her away," he pleaded.

The guards looked at King Michel, who gestured for them to stay.

"The two men said she was caught committing adultery, correct?" Melhel said.

"Correct," the king replied.

"Well, adultery is a couple being intimate without any marriage to signify their union," Melhel continued. "That involved a man, too, who in this case is arguably more culpable. Why is he not being punished?"

Those present exchanged glances without answering Melhel's point.

"Can a woman not choose what to do with her own body, as a man can?" Melhel argued. "She was unaware that he was married, and of the impression that they were in love and would be together. Will she die for an honest mistake while the man behind it keeps his life, and nothing changes for him?"

The king was impressed by Melhel's impassioned plea, but not yet completely swayed. "That man was a guard, though, Melhel," King Michel countered. "I can't kill one of my own guards."

"They both committed the same crime, Your Majesty," Melhel said, "and should be treated the same way. If she dies, so should he. If he lives, so should she."

The woman was brought to tears that her life had come to this. The only man that had ever shown her any respect was the one now pleading for her to not be executed for an honest mistake.

Fares approached the king, knowing he would always take his opinion into consideration. "The boy is right, Your Majesty," he said. "She did nothing wrong. You can't kill the poor woman while the guard can run free."

That seemed to move King Michel. His trust for Fares was nothing new, but to have his old friend concur with Melhel cast a halo on the younger man, who had already won his admiration by taking on the bandits on their way to Beiros. The king knew that Fares would not have backed Melhel out of familial loyalty alone, but only because he shared his judgement.

"Let her go," the king ordered his guards. "No one is going to be executed."

The guards dropped the lady to the ground indifferently. The law was the law; an order was an order. Melhel rushed to the woman to comfort her.

"You deserve a better start to your life," he told her.

She was far too emotional to respond. The king approached them and commanded the woman to rise.

"Young lady, you are in this man's debt," he said. "It's not often I bend the laws, but he makes an excellent point. You did nothing wrong, and only you should decide what can be done with your body."

The king stood up and beamed at Fares. "Be proud of him," he said in praise of Melhel. "Now, to your workshop."

Fares and the king both returned to the workshop to continue their discussion of the blacksmithing to be done, but Melhel and the woman remained as he comforted her after the ordeal. She cried on his shoulders as he held her. He may not have been the most socially adept, but he understood what a moment like this needed.

"Why bother saving me?" she asked.

He looked the woman in the eyes, and it seemed to her as if it were the first time anyone had ever been genuine with her.

"This city has already begun to annoy me," Melhel said. "What with the lack of women doing anything at all, the prince boring me with his fake stories of adventure, and even the work we've been set by the king. Some good needs to be done."

He held her face and with a large and calloused thumb he helped wipe away her tears.

"What is your name, by the way?"

"Marissa Hussan," she replied.

"Marissa. I'm Melhel Barak. It's a pleasure to meet you."

He helped her up as she tried to dust herself off and straighten her dress.

"I wouldn't call it a pleasure," she said. "Not like this."

"It's okay," he reminded her. "No one is perfect. Why, on the way to Beiros myself and my uncle had to save the king and the prince from an attack."

Like everyone else in Beiros, she had little idea of what went on outside the walls. "Really? By whom?" she inquired.

"Bandits," Melhel replied. "The king was asleep, and the prince... I think he was crying."

Marissa couldn't help but laugh a little despite her pain. The thought of Prince Sirhan crying was rather amusing. "I take it you're not a fan of the prince?" she asked.

Melhel wondered if his mouth was going to get him into more trouble than it already had. "It's not that," he began. "I guess I'm just not used to him. Or anyone like him, or his parents. Nothing here is what it seems. It's all so fabricated, and even dangerous for someone like you, despite your innocence. They have these fancy walls and guards constantly posted, but it seems like Beiros needs protecting from itself more than from the outside. Granted, I've only been here a short while..." Melhel trailed off, realising he was doing a poor job of hiding that he wasn't having a good time in Beiros at all. "But I digress," he said, snapping out of his funk. "Are you able to go back home, to work?"

Marissa looked at Melhel as if he had just stripped naked in front of her.

"Are you serious?" she cried. "I can't go back to my old life!"

Melhel was startled by her outburst, and stumbled back a step. "Whoa, whoa... Calm down... I was just asking..."

"Do you really think I will be allowed back at home, back at work, back at my old life, after this? I'm broken." Her voice cracked as she heard herself state the truth that this one mistake had cost her everything.

"That can't be fair," Melhel said. "It's on him not knowing where to put his stuffing where it's appropriate." Marissa rolled her eyes at him. His naivete almost impressed her.

"You saw what just happened. I nearly got killed. Somehow, I survived. But I've got nowhere to go."

Melhel looked at her, an idea forming. "Nowhere?"

"I may as well ready myself for a life on the street. That's what comes to women like me."

She slumped against the nearest wall, regretting every decision she'd ever made. What had her life come to, she wondered, to owe her life to the mercy of this man she knew nothing about, who happened to have the ear of the king.

"It doesn't have to be that way." Melhel offered his hand to her.

"What do you mean?"

"We have plenty of room in our home, plenty of work," Melhel said. "It may not be ideal, and it may take a lot of negotiating with my uncle, but it's a place you could stay."

Marissa looked at him, shocked by his generosity. Never before had any man been so kind to her with so apparent a lack of ulterior motive. It would be an escape from her messy life.

"But you've done so much for me already," she said in refusal. "I can't accept it."

"We have plenty of money and room," he reassured her. "While we're busy working for the king, we'll need help around the house. We'll pay you well and treat you fairly. If you're unwell, you may rest. If you are tired, you may sleep. If you are hungry, you may eat. All we'll ask is that you work hard and do a decent job."

"Then I'll do it," she relented. "But only if your uncle agrees."

Melhel brushed that concern aside. "Come with me now, and I'll talk to him about it. He'll listen to me, I guarantee it."

~

"ABSOLUTELY NOT!" Fares didn't listen at all to his nephew's proposition. The idea of them inviting that woman to live in their new home was preposterous. "How can you bring yourself to ask me such a thing?"

Melhel was disappointed, but he was as stubborn as Fares and not liable to take no for an answer. "Uncle, please. She has nowhere to go. She cannot go back to work; she cannot go back home. What is she meant to do? Are we supposed to leave her on the street?!"

"Not our problem," Fares said dismissively. "She got herself into that mess. She can get herself out." His apparent callousness came from his anxiety about their new life. "She should be grateful that we helped her avoid getting executed. We've done more than enough."

As Fares went back to reading through the list of work they had to co-ordinate in the workshop, Melhel tried to think of how best to bargain with his uncle.

"We can hire her," he suggested, as he had proposed to Marisa. "She can work for us."

Fares looked up at Melhel with a look of confusion.

"She's not a blacksmith. She wouldn't know the first thing about our craft. And we already have enough workers, thanks to the king."

"She doesn't have to be a blacksmith, Uncle. And yes, we have enough workers. But with all that work to do, who's going to look after our home? We won't have the time." This suggestion intrigued Fares, who stood up from his desk to face Melhel.

Outside, Marissa waited. Melhel hadn't wanted to bring her in straight away, for fear of provoking Fares's resistance.

She could hear the men's discussion and grew anxious that they seemed to be arguing over what to do with her. Men had decided her life's direction enough.

"What did you tell her we'd do?" Fares asked.

"That she'd have work to do and a place to stay," Melhel wouldn't back down. He used to get intimidated by his uncle, but not any more—not at his age.

"Are you in love with this girl?" Fares probed Melhel.

"No, Uncle!" Melhel rejoined. "I just want to help. As soon as I walked into Beiros, I saw what kind of a backward society this is. Let's do our bit to improve it—be a force for change."

Fares considered this. It would save the two of them the hassle of housekeeping.

"Where is she now?" Fares asked.

"Outside," Melhel replied. And he headed off to bring Marissa in, while Fares sighed at having been outmanoeuvred.

Fares put on a smile to welcome the woman as she entered with Melhel by her side. Hospitality demanded as much. "Thank you for inviting me in, Mr Barak," Marissa said nervously.

Fares laughed at her formality. "Just 'Fares' is fine," he said. "Now, I understand Melhel has offered you a job."

She nodded. "Yes, Mr—" Fares cut her off with a wave of his hand. "Yes, Fares," she corrected herself, "your nephew has been so kind."

Fares nodded with a slight grin. "Good, good. He is a kind boy." Melhel worried that Fares might be getting her hopes up before rejecting her.

"Just so we're on the same page, please, tell me exactly what he promised," Fares asked.

Marissa began to stumble over her words. "Well... Um... That I could work around the house, live here and... Housekeeping, essentially."

"Very good," Fares nodded. "Exactly what Melhel told me. But I haven't exactly agreed. He has done this without my permission, and it is my understanding that my decision could affect your future."

Marissa lowered her head in shame. Melhel was about to step in and defend her before Fares continued. "Luckily, he gets his generosity from me." Fares extended his hand to her. "I will give you six months. You will work for us, and work well. You will have a bed to sleep in and a room to call your own. But in six months I expect your life to be sorted, and you to be ready to go out on your own. Do I make myself clear?"

Marissa was brought to tears, as she thanked Lah and his wonders for this blessing. She hugged Fares and Melhel as though she was hugging her mother and father. "Thank you both so much!" she said, crying into their shoulders. Though it made them uncomfortable, they willingly accepted her gratitude.

Melhel took her hand to escort her around the new house. "Come, I'll show you your new room," he offered.

Just then she realised she had brought nothing with her. "But, what about my things? My clothes?"

"I'll have it taken care of," Melhel said, brushing it off.

Fares looked at the two of them and chuckled begrudgingly. Though he was inclined to regret agreeing, it was right to help someone in need. Fares had worried that his nephew wouldn't survive in Beiros—that his bluntness and lack of social grace would see this town of politicians and deceit swallow him whole. But those qualities seemed to have helped him find his feet. He had already won favour with the king and queen, convinced the king to bend the rules for Marissa, and saved a life from a harsh law. But he still worried: in such a place, apparent success could abruptly come crashing down.

Still, he wasn't going to be the one to stand in Melhel's way. Not yet, anyway. He had far too much love for his nephew, and far too much work to do to bother getting too involved in Melhel's personal business.

Fares now had to be not only the king's personal blacksmithing operator, but also a politician. On top of being informally one of the king's closest advisers and confidantes, he was likely going to be asked to attend the senate with him.

Playing politics was already dangerous enough as it was, perhaps even more dangerous than it had been during the civil war itself. And while the war would still haunt him, Fares would soon long to fight Scandosians rather than arguing with senators.

CHAPTER 7
NEWS FROM THE FRONTIER

Politics and new friends aside, Fares and Melhel settled into a routine life. They got their blacksmithing operations underway, leading a team of the finest smiths in Beiros. Young, hard-working, and eager to learn, the men reminded Fares of the working classes back in Chekkos.

Before long, they were churning out all the weapons and armour the king could dream of for his army, at a rate almost as if they were at war.

Even outside of smithing, Melhel kept himself busy, managing to always fit in his daily weapons training, practising all the techniques he had learned from his uncle, though on a dummy as opposed to a living man. It would have been nice for him to have sparred with Fares like in the old days, but he was far too busy running the smithy.

Marissa had become well acquainted with their new home, doing her best to make a good impression not only on Melhel and Fares, but anyone else of import that she stumbled across—even, perhaps, the king. She wasn't going to waste her chance at redemption and end up on the brink of death again. She did make quick friends with Melhel, who was more than happy to be her protector if nothing more.

Now settled in, the two smiths were ready for whatever the city could cough up at them. Melhel was even learning to tolerate Prince Sirhan's arrogance, while Fares had learned to calmly shoulder the trust King Michel had placed in him. In those times, trust would become more valuable than ever.

~

FIVE MEN SAT with the king at a table in the throne room, in a meeting of his closest advisers. Fares, naturally, had been chosen by the king to be there.

Then there was Al Jasha, the king's adviser on financial matters. Fares would have described him only as a slimy opportunist, looking to bank on any chance he could have at wealth and glory.

Also seated was Al Aanif, the adviser on war and the military. He saw violence as the only reasonable solution to every dispute—even a game of cards.

The fifth man seated, right next to his father, was Prince Sirhan. King Michel felt it imperative that Sirhan sat in on these meetings to learn how to rule. Experience is the greatest teacher.

Rafiq was also present, by the door with the guards, ready to listen quietly while the politicians bickered.

"Gentlemen," said the king, "we have met here to address the issue of the Scandosians." He rose from his seat. "As we meet in the senate later today, I have no doubt they will continue to argue the issue of their autonomy."

He looked around at his advisers with steely-eyed conviction. "Promise me that each and every one of you will have my back on this," he demanded. "They cannot win."

Al Aanif was the first to chime in, being his usual aggressive self, "You already know the answer to this, my king," he said. "Strike them before they strike us. The Scandosians are nothing but egotistical wimps; we can crush them in battle in a heartbeat."

Fares rolled his eyes. "Have you no memory of the civil war, Al Aanif?" Fares asked of his counterpart. "Or is my recollection correct that you sat here ordering young men to war?"

Al Aanif looked at Fares angrily. "I suppose you have a better solution, blacksmith? I'd love to hear it."

King Michel tried to calm everyone, not willing to mediate a spat just yet.

"Gentlemen, not here and not ever can you behave in such a way," he admonished, before turning to another of his advisers. "Al Jasha, can we afford a war? What are their finances like compared to ours?"

For Al Jasha, this was an opportunity to plant an idea in king Michel's head. "We have more than enough, Your Majesty," he said. "Enough to sustain a campaign for months on end."

"Which wouldn't be beneficial to anyone," Fares warned. "You want to drain our economy? You want to waste lives, time, and resources? Then you wage war. If you don't want to do any of that, you resolve this diplomatically, in the senate."

El Salam defended Fares. "He is right. We will only hurt ourselves. Our relations with the Scandosians are already fragile as it is. Let's not shatter them."

Every man in the room was Alexandrosian, and their people had historically dominated the ruling classes of Nataaros, beginning with Beilos the Conqueror. The Elvish Scandosians had their own identity and way of governing themselves within the kingdom, which they felt the Alexandrosians impinged on. In turn, the Alexandrosians felt the Scandosians threatened the kingdom they had built. That was why the civil war had such wide-reaching implications. It affected everyone in Nataaros, but especially its two most significant ethnic groups, conflict between which spelled disaster if not properly managed.

El Salam pressed his point by suggesting a different focus. "Besides, we have a bigger issue at hand. Those two young men who investigated the disturbance north of Alhayit are due back any day now."

Those scouts, Ahmid and Salal, had already been gone a long time, and their arrival with a report must be imminent. But this was the first time Fares had heard of their mission.

"What do you mean, 'north of Alhayit'?" he asked.

"We sent two soldiers up there," King Michel explained. "We're waiting on their news as we speak."

"You never told me this?" he almost yelled at his king. "Who knows what is there? Potentially the army of the dead, for Lah's sake." Fares knew the stories all too well. If they proved to be real, the dead would be a bigger threat than any army of elves they could dream of.

Al Aanif tried to dismiss Fares's outrage. "I wouldn't pay attention to the concerns of a man who willingly houses and employs a whore."

"It's because I show more decency and resolve than any of you politicians do," Fares said. "My nephew and I have done more in the few weeks we've been here than you lot have in the years since I left. Fools, all of you."

Prince Sirhan grew irritated. He hated attending these meetings and the senate, and saw politics as the business of bitter old men with nothing better to do but squabble at everyone else's expense. And he may have had a point.

King Michel worked valiantly to keep everyone's emotions in check, especially now the army of the dead had been brought up. "Fares, it is my fault I didn't warn you about that, and I'm sorry." He couldn't afford to lose Fares' trust, given what might be ahead.

The king then turned angrily to Al Aanif, his military adviser, "As for you, you idiot, Fares and Melhel took that woman in as a gesture of compassion. Maybe you should try something similar."

Al Aanif looked sheepish having just been yelled at by the king in front of everyone, his enormous ego was poorly equipped for the slight.

"Now, as for the disturbance north of the frontier," said the king, getting things back on track, "those two men will be back very soon with their news. Then we will act accordingly. He looked meaningfully at Fares. "There is no need to panic," he said, and then, turning to Al Aanif, "or to behave like a bunch of animals."

"And if the rumours are true, that there is a dead army beyond Alhayit?" Al Jasha asked.

"Well, then," said the king, "you can use all that money at your disposal to direct it at killing them all."

ELSEWHERE, ONE SUBJECT OF THE POLITICIANS' quarrel had done his best to get away from Alhayit. Salal had done exactly as the hooded figure told him, and ran for whatever was left of his life.

As he made his way inside the wall, he closed the gate that he and Ahmid had entered through and made extra sure it was locked.

"Never again," he said to himself. "Now, to civilisation."

Salal continued his walk slowly, praying that the darkness would be his as cover against whatever else might want to kill him. Even his own shadow frightened him now, never mind an army of the dead, or even the wild animals that roamed these parts.

Only a few hundred yards from the frontier, Salal was near collapsing. His breathing became heavier, and he grew more and more tired, the result not only of exhaustion from his flight, but also from the trauma of what he had seen. Who could stay cool after that? This was something more than war, and far worse than he could have imagined.

As he went deeper into the woods, sleep began to overtake him. His eyes shut for seconds at a time against his will, before he snapped them open again. "Just ... five minutes," he panted to himself, and fell to the ground face first before he could think of the danger this might put him in.

The sky was black as could be, with the moon below the horizon and nothing but stars for light.

He was far enough from Alhayit not to worry about the dead, but also well away from any nearby cities or towns. Who knew what else might lie in wait for him in the forest. But he didn't care: he was so tired he had lost even the will to protect his life.

WHEN MORNING ARRIVED, Salal was still where he had fallen, having slept there without moving for several hours. The ground had proven an adequate bed.

As a horse galloped by, its rider saw the man on the ground and, suspecting murder, dismounted to investigate. When closer, having seen no blood and checked the man's head for blunt trauma, he at last looked for breathing. And there it was, though only fainting.

A check of the ground nearby turned up nothing to show what had happened. So the man tapped Salal's shoulder, and the scout immediately sprang to life, screaming, and ran. "Run! Run!" he shouted deliriously as he tore away in a dead sprint towards the horse. When he reached it, the startled animal kicked him in the ribs, breaking several.

Salal cried in pain and fell to the ground again, clutching his side while the man shook his head. "I'm dying!" Salal screamed. "This beast has killed me!"

The horse was panicking too, neighing and kicking about, before its owner could calm it down. Then he tended to the writhing Salal.

"Slow down, my friend. It's gonna be okay."

Salal stopped rolling around like a menace and realised that he was not dead. "Rejoice! I am alive!" he yelled, and winced at the pain it caused him. "But your horse broke my ribs!"

The man was unusually patient. "You frightened it," he chuckled. "Did you not think it would kick you if you ran past screaming?"

"It makes sense when you put it that way," Salal conceded.

"What happened to you?" the man asked.

"Your horse kicked me, that's what!" Salal replied obtusely.

"I mean before that! Why were you sleeping on the ground?"

"Oh…" Salal felt silly now. "Long story. I haven't got much time. I need to get back to Beiros as soon as possible."

The man was impressed with Salal's resolve. "But how can you expect to go walking if your ribs are really broken?"

Salal tried to get up, but was in too much pain and fell down again on his behind. "Maybe not," he said. "So much for getting to Beiros quickly." He lowered his head in dismay that he would not be able to complete his task.

"I can take you there," the man offered.

"What?"

"I can take you to Beiros."

Salal tried again to rise, and this time managed it laboriously before dusting himself off.

"Why do this for me?" Salal asked.

"Whyever you need to be in Beiros, I'm sure it's very important," the man said. "For a soldier of Nataaros."

"Thank you, good man." Salal appreciated the gesture. But then he pointed to the horse. "As long as *he* doesn't kick me again."

"*She*," the man corrected him. "And on the way, you can tell me exactly how you ended up here. It's a long ride."

Salal was hesitant, but had no choice. Forgetting everything else, he focused steadfastly on delivering the news to King Michel as quickly as he could.

The man helped him up on the horse that had shattered his ribs, and jumped up in front as they began to head off.

"Josif, by the way," the man said, introducing himself, breaking the ice as the horse had Salal's ribs.

"Salal."

And so the two of them began the journey back to Beiros.

THE KING'S confidence that news from north of Alhayit was on its way proved not to have been misplaced. By the time Salal and Josif finally approached Beiros, Fares's first meeting at the table of the king's advisers was still to begin.

The sun was barely coming up and the sky was still orange as they came to the gates. On their long trip back, Salal had told Josif everything he had witnessed: of the woman who reported the incident, the investigation, and what tiny part of the world beyond the frontier that he had seen. Salal told Josif of the strange writing and silhouettes they had seen, and of Ahmid's death.

If Salal was to believed, the ghost stories had come true, Josif realised. The scout had much to report to the king.

The guards straightened up as they approached the gate. "Who goes there?" one of them demanded.

"I have a soldier back from the Wildlands!" Josif called out. "He was sent on an investigation by the king!"

Salal waved to them, still wincing slightly as his ribs hadn't properly healed.

"It's Salal. I'm back!" he called out.

The guard shook his head when he saw the state of him. "Wait, wasn't there two of you?"

Salal's was deflated. "About that... Bring me to the king and I'll tell you everything on the way."

"The king, I think, has the senate today. He'll be busy," the guard said.

"This is more important. Just let me in." The guard chose not to argue and began to lower the drawbridge even at that ungodly hour, letting Salal and Josif pass into the city. The two men met the guard at the front gate.

"I want to know everything," the guard said. "Do not skip any details."

"It's not pretty," Salal warned.

~

BY MID-AFTERNOON, the men inside the throne room were still bickering over what to do about the Scandosian situation and the threat of the dead army.

"We can't afford to go into another war!" Fares tried to remind them.

"Think of the riches that we could gain," Al Jasha retorted. "We could subjugate them and make them pay tribute."

Fares considered this notion barbaric. The idea of entering a war purely for financial gain was sickening. Holding power was one thing. Thirsting for it and for glory was another. To want to fill your pockets at the cost of other people's lives was on an entirely different and horrible level.

King Michel was inclined to agree. "I do not want to subjugate a province of Nataaros, you animal," he bellowed. "Get that thought out of your head immediately!" The greedy little man shrivelled back in his seat.

Al Aanif maintained his stance of advocating for a mobilisation of troops to invade Scandos. "The Scandosians have been arrogant enough to provoke us," he argued. "Let's show them force. With Fares leading the blacksmithing program, we have the weapons to launch a swift invasion."

Fares balked at the last point. "I will support no such thing," he said definitively.

"Why else have you been brought here, then?" said Al Aanif. "To make weapons and armour for the fun of it? Don't be so stupid."

Fares looked at his king in frustration, right in the eyes. "Your Majesty, if you have brought me here purely to support an invasion of Scandos, say so now and I will pack my bags to return to Chekkos."

"Coward," Al Aanif scoffed. Fares was ready to slap him across his smug face, when Rafiq's voice boomed from the door.

"Need I remind you, Al Aanif, of who is painted in the front room of the castle?" Rafiq belittled him. "Not you, but Fares. He stood and fought while you hid in your home and waited for it all to blow over."

"Quiet, Sword," Al Aanif said, scowling. "You leave the politics to us. We'll save the killing for the likes of you."

"Just as well," Fares said. "You couldn't handle what we have. When you've actually fought a battle in your life, against the Scandosians or anyone, as opposed to sitting on your arse and letting young men do the hard work, you'll understand why this is a terrible idea."

Fares was right, Rafiq thought. These politicians didn't know the horror of war, or even much about how to wage it. They only knew how to start a battle that others would fight. It was ironic that Al Aanif, who oversaw the military, had no experience of war beyond the advisers' table. Even battle strategy and tactics were left to generals and the Swords of the King like Rafiq. All Al Aanif and men like him ever did was point at the enemy and effectively say, "Kill them. Don't care how you do it, just see to it that's it's done."

"Unless the dead army ends up being real," Fares said, bringing the discussion back around to that topic. "Then, maybe, I'll reconsider my position."

"And what if they're not real?" Al Jasha chimed in.

"Then I won't go to war."

King Michel stood. "Until that young man comes back with news, there'll be no more talk of dead armies." He stared at Fares as Fares had at him before. "Understood?"

Everyone went quiet.

"Good. We can continue this Scandosian discussion in the senate. I'm glad I got to hear differing opinions. Always good to see discussion and debate. Even if you men may not appreciate it."

With that he ended the meeting. But before the king could dismiss everyone, there was a knock on the door.

Rafiq, startled, opened a small hatch in the door to examine whoever had knocked.

"The king is busy. See to him another time," he said to a guard. Behind him, though Rafiq could not see them, stood a grimacing Salal, supported by Josif.

"Sir, it is urgent," the guard insisted.

"How urgent?"

"Remember the expedition beyond Alhayit? *That* urgent."

"Alright, one moment," Rafiq said, startled.

He shut the hatch and addressed the king as he was dismissing everyone. "Your Majesty, it's important."

"I'm sure it can wait," the king replied.

"It's about Alhayit. Salal is here."

King Michel's eyes widened with surprise. "You're kidding. Bring him in."

There was an air of near panic in the room. The advisers could hardly believe the mission had really been completed. Fares feared what they might hear.

The guard brought Salal and Josif in.

"Who's this man?" said the king, looking at Josif.

"Josif, Your Majesty." He bent his knee to the king. "I escorted Salal from the frontier all the way to Beiros."

"A very honourable thing to have done. You may rise." The king then looked to the guard. "Sir, see to it that Josif is rewarded. You are both dismissed."

The guard nodded his head and escorted Josif outside.

King Michel looked at Salal, "What happened? Where is the other one? Ahmid?"

"Your Majesty, sirs…" he said, acknowledging everyone in the room, "you may all want to take a seat for this."

∽

IN THE SHOPPING district of Beiros, Melhel was walking with Marissa as they bought food for the house. Melhel had taken them to a bank, to withdraw some gold from the account the king had asked to be set up for him.

The bank's grandeur suited an establishment enjoying royal patronage. Clerks stood behind desks that supported a colonnade of arches, atop which rested a vaulted ceiling of varicoloured stained glass. Somewhat overawed by the surroundings, Melhel crossed marble tiles to a counter, with Marissa on his arm, and put on a cavalier manner with the clerk.

"Good day. I would like to withdraw some gold, please," he said.

"Name."

"Melhel Barak."

"How much would you like?" he asked, almost like a machine.

Melhel looked at Marissa, "How much do we need?" he asked Marissa, uncertain. He still had little idea of what things were worth in the capital, or of how much they spent in their new life and work.

Before Marissa could respond, he hit on an amount. "A thousand gold coins."

"A thousand?" Marissa exclaimed. "We don't need that much."

"Whatever is left over I'll put aside," Melhel said, turning his attention to the clerk again. "A thousand, please."

"Certainly," the man obliged. "That will incur a small fee of one percent of the withdrawn amount."

Melhel was puzzled, "One percent? Excuse me?"

"It is standard, sir, that upon withdrawals you are charged a fee of one percent." He seemed to have said this many times before, so that it had become a habit.

"So, you're telling me I have to pay to get my own money out?" Melhel was about to blast the man. "What stupidity is this?"

"Sir, it is common practice."

"Not where I come from," Melhel said. And indeed, the bank in Chekkos did not charge such fees. This only happened in major cities such as Beiros and Beilos, as he was finding out.

The clerk presented the money. "These are the regulations, sir," he said, standing his ground. "If you do not like it, you can tell the king."

"Luckily, I know the king personally," Melhel said, smirking, "so I will tell him."

Melhel grabbed his money and stormed off with Marissa. "How stupid!" he grumbled.

Marissa was embarrassed. "You didn't have to yell at him like that. He was only doing his job."

Melhel sighed, feeling a little apologetic for his outburst.

"It's not him I'm angry at," he said, calming himself. "It's this whole city. This whole royal, aristocratic society. In fact..."

He dashed back inside the bank to speak to the clerk, whose guard was up. "Sir, we've been through this—" he said as Melhel approached.

Melhel cut him off. "I know. And I would like to apologise for my behaviour. I didn't mean to yell at you. You're doing a great job, and I thought you should know that," he apologised. "The world needs more people like you, honest and hard-working. Keep it up."

The clerk was humbled by this. "Much appreciated, sir."

Melhel thanked him for his service again before heading back outside with Marissa.

"What was that?" she asked.

"I wanted to apologise," he said sincerely. "He didn't deserve to be yelled at like that, as you said." But as they walked off to continue shopping, he couldn't help ranting. "Anyway, the whole society annoys me," he said. "I wonder how Uncle Fares is coping in the throne room."

SALAL HAD FINISHED HIS STORY, and no one was more stunned than Fares.

"We have to do something," he pleaded with the king. "I will double my efforts if it means defeating this threat."

The king agreed, "You're right. It will be the first item on our agenda in the senate."

This irritated Al Jasha. "But what of the Scandosians?"

"Damn them and their elven heads," the king said. "This is bigger, and I will make them see that." Salal's report had opened his eyes, and not just his. Everyone looked around to confirm that the others, too, saw that they may be facing a greater threat than anyone had expected.

"What if it's just a madman playing cruel tricks?" Prince Sirhan wondered aloud.

Salal looked at him with fearful eyes. "This is no trick, my prince," he warned. "What we all feared is real."

King Michel stood. "To the senate," he commanded.

As they hurried out the door, the king rushed to Fares and told him quietly, "Grab Melhel on your way in. I want him there."

"Why him?" asked Fares, baffled.

"He could do with the experience."

CHAPTER 8
THE SENATE

After the debacle of the throne-room meeting, the politicians headed to the senate, where a meeting was due among the senators of Nataaros to discuss the day's agenda—namely what to do about Scandos—and, unbeknown to them, the apparently very real threat of an army.

Rafiq had stuck by the king's side as he travelled in a small carriage, not pompous or extravagant like the one in which they had travelled to Chekkos. This one was less conspicuous and more nimble: better for city streets.

Prince Sirhan joined his father and their Sword inside the carriage, scowling at the thought of dealing with more boring politics for the rest of his day, when he would have preferred to be reading and learning. King Michel would always tell his son that experience was the best teacher and *this* was real learning, but the prince was unreceptive.

Fares was now outside the castle, heading to the shopping district to find Melhel and Marissa. Even with two guards by his side as an escort, he breezed hurriedly through the immense crowds in the streets and marketplaces.

Some areas were filled with upper-class people shopping for luxuries: the finest clothing that came only from Paros, or the most sumptuous foods harvested from Rios. Like his nephew, Fares disdained such people. "They would stick their neck up at you while you stuck your neck out for them," he had told his nephew many times, describing their ingratitude to those who had fought in the civil war.

It mattered not. There were bigger issues at hand, and Fares needed to find Melhel so he could get back to them.

"He couldn't be too far from here," Fares told the guards. "I know they're grocery shopping, so they must be around somewhere."

But everywhere they looked, they saw only the hordes of people. Finding Melhel and Marissa looked like a hopeless task — until one of the guards spotted a young man arguing over the price of a pound of apples.

"Is that your nephew?" he asked Fares.

Fares saw the young man and chuckled. "Of course. Only a man from Chekkos would do such a thing."

Melhel and Marissa had been in the middle of their shopping when Melhel decided to debate a vendor on the price of apples. "These are not that good," he argued. "I know good apples; these are not worth what you're asking."

"I'm telling you now, best in all of Alexandros. In all of Nataaros!" the vendor bragged. "This is my price. You take it or leave it."

Melhel had met his match for stubbornness, and relented, "Fine. Here." And he paid the set price. "But if these apples aren't as good as you say, I'll be back demanding an explanation, with swords." He raised a finger as he said this, and when he was finished, he turned around.

"Uncle Fares, what are you doing here?" he said with surprise, noticing the guards with him. "Did something go wrong at the meeting?"

"Sort of," Fares said. "Come with me to the senate. The king wants you there."

"Is everything alright?" Melhel asked.

"Not quite." Fares was weary. "Come, I'll explain on the way."

"But I can't go: I have to help Marissa," Melhel was anxious about leaving her on her own, after everything she has been through.

Fares had an idea. "You two," he said to the guards accompanying him, who looked at him attentively. "Go with the young lady and help her finish the shopping," he ordered. "Then, take her back to the house and do not leave until I get back."

Melhel wasn't keen on this. "Are you sure, Uncle?"

"If anything happens, I know who to blame." Fares grinned menacingly at the guards before handing them two bags of gold coins. "One for the shopping. One for your troubles. Understood?"

"Yes, sir," the guards said.

"Good."

Fares turned to Marissa. "Be safe, my dear," he told her. "Do avoid trouble. If anything seems suspicious, these men will protect you."

Marissa smiled at Fares' concern and leadership. "I'll be safe." She hugged each of the Baraks. "Thank you both."

She went off with the guards, leaving Melhel and Fares on their own.

"What happened?" Melhel asked his uncle, eager to know. "Did it go badly? Why am I wanted at the senate?"

"The king thinks it's appropriate you attend. To learn," he grumbled, his annoyance plain. "His son is there as well. Prince Sirhan hates the idea of it. All of it. That, you have in common. But this is part of the king's plan to train you both to be future leaders. You had better accept it."

Melhel couldn't believe what he was being dragged into, and moped all the way to the senate.

~

MELHEL AND FARES reached the front of the senate building, not too far from the castle and, like the castle, something to marvel at.

The entire building was circular, with a domed roof. Made of marble, it was adorned with statues and figurines of the greatest kings and warriors in Nataarosian history.

At the very top of the dome stood a fierce, domineering dragon

100

—Lah, the god of Nataaros and their religion. Lah stood tall, over-looking the senate and Beiros as their guardian and protector, as he was said to do from atop the Snowy Mountains, in the clouds.

Each statue and figure on the building was crafted with incredible realism and the most lifelike detail, as intricate and precise as the portraits of the kings in the museum and at the castle. The level of craftsmanship and artistic merit was extraordinary.

Various politicians and officials, mainly men, streamed in and out of the building as they went about their busy and tumultuous life. All the peoples of Nataaros were represented among them; alongside the Alexandrosians, there were also Riosans , Parosians, Venosians, and, of course, Scandosians. The Riosans stood out with their darker complexions, as did the Parosians with their shining, pale skin. Venosians gave a robust, coarse impression, while Scandosians wowed onlookers with their ethereal elven beauty. If there was any place in the kingdom where all races were evenly and adequately represented, the senate was it.

Melhel approached the front entrance and read the inscription there, "For the Senate and People of Nataaros," highlighting the core value of the institution and the kingdom: that their system of government was to be fair and just to all, not only Alexandrosians. Not all would have agreed that was the reality.

"Impressive, isn't it?" Fares said to Melhel.

"Not bad. Good size," Melhel observed. "Who would've thought politics could be so pretty?"

"No one," Fares grunted. "This is the only pretty part about it." Fares started to head in, dreading the drama to come. "Once you get inside, the beauty is sapped away."

Melhel was confused. "Is the design inside not as good?"

"No, it's still pretty good," Fares said. "The paintings and architecture are still up to standard. It's just a shame the people inside are ugly."

The younger Barak couldn't help but agree, even before seeing for himself. His impression of Beiros and its people had already been mixed, and that would be putting it politely. He couldn't imagine what the politicians would be like. "I assume it's full of vultures?" he said.

"And rats and snakes too," Fares said. "Whatever animal you would not like to be known as, the senate is filled with them."

Fares mustered the resolve to finally head in.

"Let's go."

⌇

THE BLACKSMITHS ENTERED the senate building and Melhel was wowed yet again, by its sheer size and beauty. It was a painting come to life.

People were spread throughout the halls and corridors, rushing to and fro as they tried to get their work done. They dressed like nobles, in robes and tunics of silk, fine cotton, and brocade, awash with colour.

The walls were lined in paintings and designs, many in gold and silver, which along with polished stone made the interior of the building gleam. Much as in the castle, paintings showed famous figures and events from history: battles, kings and queens, soldiers and senators.

Fares and Melhel headed towards the senate chamber, the door to which was flanked by two heavily armed guards. Fares shot them a look and they nodded to allow him entrance, already familiar with the king's newest adviser.

The older Barak walked through, but a guard stopped Melhel. "You can't go through here," he said.

"He's with me," Fares vouched for him.

But almost as soon as Fares could step in, King Michel, Prince Sirhan, and Rafiq arrived, and the king spoke for Melhel too.

"I wanted him to be here," the king said. "Thank you, soldier."

The guard understood and stepped aside, allowing everyone through.

King Michel smiled to Melhel, "Glad to see you've made it," he said to Melhel, beaming. "You'll learn a lot."

"Where is the queen, Your Majesty?" Melhel asked, on noticing she wasn't with them.

"She is helping the poor," King Michel explained. "As she always does while I'm stuck in here dealing with these idiots."

Melhel found Fares' and the king's contempt for the senate discouraging, but supposed that if he had to be there, it must have been important enough.

"Melhel," Prince Sirhan said in acknowledgement, "nice for you to join us." His voice was rich with sarcasm.

"It would be nice—but you're here," Melhel quipped with a grin, unwilling to let the prince get the better of him.

As they walked into the senate chamber, Melhel saw it was as circular as the building that housed it. The seating in the room was divided into sections representing each province—Alexandros, Scandos, Paros, and Venos—with each having ten senators elected locally every two years.

In the middle of the floor, deliberating and acting as a moderator, was the head of the senate, who was elected every four years from among the senate. When they moved into their new position, another senator replaced them in the allotment for their province. For example, the head now seated was an Alexandrosian, Saad Jaja, and he had been replaced by a new Alexandrosian senator. The head of the senate was effectively the president of the kingdom, ranking just below the royal family.

In their own little box sat the royals and the king's advisers from the throne room. Melhel took a seat next to his uncle, nervous about his first political experience, unsure of what to make of the situation and of what to do.

Senators debated each other on how best to approach whatever issues were presented to the senate, and they set the laws that all Nataarosians had to follow. Should a senator, group of senators, or even an entire province propose a new law, the senate would debate the content of a bill before it was drawn up by the head of the senate. All fifty senators had to agree on it before it could be drawn up, to which it was then presented to the king and queen.

If the king and queen agreed with the draft presented to them by the head, they would sign off on it and it would become a part of the law of the land. If they disagreed, they send it back to the head to redraft it before it was accepted as law.

Behind the laws stood the constitution, based on the principle that Melhel saw engraved above the entrance of the senate building,

"For the senate and the people of Nataaros". And behind even that, the king and queen still had the final say on all matters, and veto power over the senate, if they felt things were getting out of hand.

From the royal box, King Michel, Rafiq, Melhel, Fares, Prince Sirhan and the king's advisers watched the senate commence its business.

Saad Jaja stood up from his position in the middle of the floor. "All rise, to the king of Nataaros," he commanded as per custom. King Michel waved and nodded his head, as all stood to attention, acknowledging the senate's service—theoretically—to his people and kingdom.

"We begin the day with a motion for the law on tax increases to be placed." Saad began. "Those not in favour, please make it known."

No one got up or said a word.

"Very well. I shall move the motion into a draft."

Saad moved to the next agenda item, "Next, we have the Scandosian issue."

Saad looked at the Scandosian delegation, whose prominent senator Ismal Haiya moved up to speak.

"Thank you, honourable Saad." Ismal's elven features stood out among all in the room, with a glow outstripping even his brethren, which made him a charismatic leader of the Scandosian delegation.

"We never had the chance to finish our discussion the other day on our quest for greater representation, after we were rudely interrupted by the Alexandrosians," Ismal jabbed, visibly angry. "May I be assured we can continue without delay?"

Saad nodded. "I can promise this."

"As I hoped, your Alexandrosian ethnicity has not impinged on your judgement," said Ismal.

Alexandros's most notable senator, Yassin Benzi, stood to defend the head. "You dare accuse of the senate of bias?" he blasted.

Ismal looked at Saad, who had promised no interruption.

"Do not speak out of turn, Yassin," Saad warned. Ismal grinned.

"Of course, not, I would never," said Yassin. "And the head has just provided us with evidence of his impartiality."

The Scandosian cleared his throat before reading from a paper handed to him by his fellow elves.

"It is beyond evident that in the years since the civil war," he said, "which saw the near decimation of my people, of my home, that Scandos has done nothing but prosper for Nataaros.

"We have provided education, health, and wealth to all in and out of Scandos. Our language is taught to the higher classes, and our methods and systems are examined in the schools. It's clear to me and all in the kingdom that Nataaros might not survive without us."

Saad took over. "And what is it you propose, Ismal?"

"Greater representation in the senate, for all of Scandos," Ismal stated.

Whispers and murmurs broke out around the room. King Michel himself was nervous and on the edge of his seat.

"Quiet!" Saad commanded forcefully. "How much greater?" he asked.

"On par with the royal family of Alexandros," Ismal demanded. "For too long, you bearded brutes have ruled this kingdom. It is time for what is fair."

Ismal had directed his words directly at King Michel, who gave the elven senator a steely glare reserved only for when he had been wronged.

The senate room erupted, with everyone yelling and talking over the top of each other.

Among the uproar, Melhel made out "What about Rios?" and "Venos has been neglected for too long! It can't all be just Alexandros and Scandos!" Barely anyone could get a clear word in. Ismal remained standing, revelling in the dissension he had created.

Saad had no choice but to slam his gavel down to restore order. "Enough!" he roared. "Ismal, explain yourself. The royal family is the royal family *of Nataaros*, of which Scandos is a part. Theirs is a royal blood that has lasted hundreds of years. To question them is to question everything our kingdom is built on."

"They're Alexandrosians! Theirs is the blood of a cruel tyrant!" Ismal declaimed. "Alexandros is faltering, and you are all too blind to see it. Look how Scandos prospers and progresses. And yet we have to answer and submit to a weak province and an ignorant king?" His words rallied the Scandosians behind him, who all screamed in support.

This enraged King Michel, who stood up from his box to exercise his kingly authority.

"That's enough of you and your poisonous tongue, Ismal!" he bellowed. "I will not have any more of your demagoguery in my senate! Do not dare to undermine me or my kingship."

King Michel had long detested the Scandosian faction's tendency to incite fear and prejudice to gain political support. Ismal's tactic was clear: boast of Scandosian prosperity while denigrating Alexandros and claiming the king was a tyrant in the hope of gathering more support for his cause.

Ismal noticed Fares in the box with King Michel. "I see you have brought a friend, your majesty." The Scandosians jeered the unassuming Fares. "We have a name for Fares Barak back home, 'the Butcher', for all he did to us on your orders." Fares held his breath to avoid saying anything that would provoke further discord.

But the insult drew the ire of Melhel, who leaned over to ask his uncle what Ismal was saying. "Uncle, what do they mean?"

"I'll explain it to you another time." Fares waved his nephew away.

King Michel leapt to Fares' defence. "He did what any good soldier would do. But the senate is not for debating history. It's for debating the present."

Ismal laughed. "And you won't even do that, my king," he said. "You continually undermine Scandos and the elves."

"If you want greater representation in the senate, I am more than willing to discuss it," the king said calmly. "But what you demand is ludicrous. You seek much more than representation." The Alexandrosians applauded in support.

"Ismal," said Saad, resuming control, "I think your back and forth with the king has gone on long enough. What is it you seek?"

"Greater representation, as per the terms I have written up," Ismal reiterated.

"I will draw up a law on these terms and leave it to a vote among the senate, and then the king," Saad explained. "Understood?"

Ismal nodded.

"Good." Saad banged his gavel. "Next on the agenda…"

Ismal interrupted with one final comment. "Your Majesty," he said, "where is the beautiful Queen Rania? Have you left her at home again?"

Ismal's continued pressure on the king infuriated Rafiq. Meanwhile, Al Aanif leaned towards Fares to say quietly, "This is what I mean. We can't trust these people with democracy. Only force will shut them up."

"Only for about twenty-five years," Fares replied. "Before the handsome bastards pipe up again."

King Michel smiled at the suggestion his queen was at home. "You're wrong once again, Ismal," he smirked at the elf. "The queen is visiting an orphanage, teaching the young souls. It's all a part of our philanthropic program. I suppose an arrogant elf like yourself wouldn't know about helping others in need. You only know how to serve your own selfish desires."

The senate—bar the Scandosians—broke out in laughter at King Michel's jibe. Ismal clearly wanted to bite back, but his fellow senators held him back, urging him to let the senate get on with its business.

The cold Prince Sirhan, though still dreading all the politicking he still had to endure, went on chuckling at his father's joke.

Melhel looked around, confused. "It wasn't even that funny," he whispered to Fares.

INSIDE AN ORPHANAGE in the heart of Beiros, hundreds of disadvantaged and orphaned children were gathered in an atrium of sorts, eagerly anticipating the queen's arrival. Such visits were rather frequent, and the children valued her warmth and generosity as they struggled with their lives and uncertain futures.

The children all sat in a circle on the floor, in rings around a space where the queen would come and stand among them, talk with them, and tell them stories, which they loved. Her eloquence could make even the darkest tale, true or false, come off sweetly enough for youthful ears.

When the queen arrived, the director of the orphanage preceded her into the circle. "Alright, kids," she announced. "Her Royal Majesty, Queen Rania."

The queen glided into the circle on her own, with no guards by her side. She wanted the children to see her more as a mother than a queen, in place of the mothers they had lost. Granted, it was hard for her to give a down-to-earth impression when her beauty shone like the summer sun on the surface of a lake.

Although she stood alone, guards had still been posted all around the orphanage. The queen may not have wanted to elevate herself above the children, but you could never be too safe. In those times, you had to keep your guard up.

Rania walked to her spot in the circle with smiles and waves, blowing kisses to the children, who were ecstatic to see their queen.

"Good morning, my children," she said. "How are we today?"

"Good," The children said together, almost singing.

The queen smiled. "I've been told you've all been well behaved since I last visited. Is that right?" The children, wide-eyed, all nodded. "You've all done your homework, and not got yourselves in any trouble?"

"Yeeeeessss," the children answered in harmony, eager to see what she had in store for them.

Queen Rania pulled out a storybook and paced across the circle, turning as she did so that she didn't turn her back on any of the children for too long.

"That's wonderful to hear," she said. "I think you've all earned a story."

"Yaaaayyyyyy!" the kids squealed with excitement.

The queen laughed as she began. "Today, children, we read from *A History of Nataaros.*"

This book was the standard text, covering the entire history of Nataaros, that was read to children as an introduction to the study of history. It spanned the thousand years BB—before Beilos—and the more than six hundred years AB—after Beilos. This was how Nataaros counted the years: from Beilos's conquest and unification of the kingdom, with the years AB being those after his coronation.

The children cheered, eager to learn more from the queen.

" 'King Beilos's Wars of Conquest'," she announced to the children. This chapter covered the wars that Beilos the Conqueror had waged to unite the kingdom.

As she coughed gently before continuing, the children's eyes were fixed on her with anticipation.

"It was ten years before Beilos," she began, "and the Republic of Phoenicos was on the brink of another war. Tension had boiled for over a century as the elves of Scandos received greater representation in the government. These reforms were met with anger and disdain, as for years, the elves had been seen as invaders, intruders in the land. To grant them greater representation infringed on the very foundations of the republic.

"Wars had already been waged, leading to these reforms, but the changes had done nothing but aggravate the situation, bringing more turmoil and chaos." Queen Rania's resonating voice was like music to the children, who sat entranced as she read. Only she could make history so fascinating for them.

"By the birth of Beilos the Conqueror, various battles and skirmishes had been waged among rival factions and provinces, all seeking independence or greater representation. Beilos was born into a warring country, drenched in violence and bloodshed.

"When he was just eighteen years old, using his exceptional charisma and leadership skills, he rallied an army and started a civil war himself, seeking to unite Phoenicos and end the fighting once and for all.

"For eighteen years the war went on, and step by step, Beilos established his power in each province: Alexandros, Rios, Paros, and then Venos. Only Scandos remained, and the elves were not going to give up without a fight. They would not willingly relinquish the independence that had been given to them."

"So, what did Beilos do, Your Majesty?" an eager child asked.

Queen Rania smiled. "Well, our first king wouldn't let the Scandosians stop him, and he continued his conquests deeper and deeper into their country," she said. "Eventually, they fell, and the kingdom of Nataaros was formed, which stands today in the glory among which we live."

She said this with a conclusive tone that signalled the chapter had ended, and the children applauded. Each episode was brief, as the book glossed over the whole story of Nataaros, giving only the basic outline—it was for children, after all. Further details were reserved for the elites and those undertaking higher education, who would learn more minutely what had happened in the great battles and movements of their country's history.

After each of her readings, the queen would give her own interpretation, taking it upon herself to give these children some semblance of an education.

"You see, children," she said, "when people do not want to cooperate—do not want to get along and work together, it can lead to a lot of trouble. When reforms drastically changed the government and people couldn't agree on them, many innocent people were hurt.

"Beilos saw the problems he was born into and took it upon himself to unite the country and form the kingdom. That is why, no matter what, we must hold onto our ideals and preserve unity."

Neither the king nor the queen were above propagandising to children. In fact, they wanted to instil a sense of pride and national belief, in the state, its institutions, and the monarchy. This was vital for the kingdom's survival.

But the reality may have given a contrary impression. The queen wouldn't tell the orphans of the brutal wars Beilos and his successors had waged, and nor would schools. Only those with the money and opportunity to study further could access this sort of information, and then what they discovered would shape their thinking for or against the kingdom.

Melhel, for example, as a humble blacksmith from Chekkos, hadn't taken much of an interest in history. Now, working with the royal family, he had the chance and the reason to learn, but that was only from a position of privilege.

Although the queen was giving an unduly rosy picture of history, and for somewhat self-interested reasons, that didn't take away from her generosity. She firmly believed that education was of the utmost importance, and that the kids loved her teaching. It may have been a biased and simplified version of history that she offered them, but what account is not biased? What story is completely true? At the very least, she was lifting these children out of the most profound depths of ignorance.

"We can all use Beilos's example and work hard and cherish what we care about," she told the children. "When you see a need for the right thing to be done, do it. Do not hesitate to follow what you believe is right."

And that was a fair lesson, which had long made an impression on the youth of Nataaros, and of Alexandros and Beiros in particular.

∾

BACK IN THE SENATE, Saad waited calmly for the disquiet surrounding King Michel's clash with Ismal to die down. "Gentlemen, are we done?" he asked. "Can we keep doing our jobs?" Everyone quietened down.

King Michel resumed his seat and gestured for Saad to continue.

"Thank you," Saad said. "Next on the agenda, we have the expedition beyond Alhayit. It has just been discovered that what we suspected from the initial report is true: the army of the dead is real, and they are back."

At this, there were panicked mutters of disbelief around the room.

"Of the two soldiers that investigated, only one, Salal, returned to report to the king and his advisers," Saad went on. "Salal reports that an army of dead men were gathering, surrounded by suspicious imagery and writing. A hooded figure— presumably their leader—stood with them, and warned Salal to run. Ahmid was killed by one of the dead: his body has not been recovered."

Melhel was startled by this. "Dead army? They're here?" he said quietly to Fares.

"Yes." Fares sounded disappointed. "Salal returned as we were meeting with the king in the throne room."

"And you didn't think to tell me? This is everything we've read about!"

"I didn't exactly have the time," Fares said, gritting his teeth. "We had to be here, where you were bound to hear the news."

"I'd rather have found out from you, Uncle. Not like this."

"Look, I'm sorry," Fares apologised. "A lot happened in our meeting, none of it good. We'll talk about it at home."

"Okay." Forgiving his uncle, Melhel went back to listening to Saad.

"When ready," said the head of the senate, we will send an expeditionary force to quell this army before it can pose a greater threat," Saad glared around the room. "If what we have all read about the dead army is true, this is matter we must take seriously. The king has urged me to impress this upon you."

Ismal shot to his feet. "And how do we know this is true?" he demanded. "How do we know this isn't just you Alexandrosians distracting us from the issues at hand?"

Prince Sirhan took offence to this and stood up. "Senator, are you calling my father—your king—a liar?" His steely eyes pierced into Ismal's. "Be careful."

Ismal stayed cool and tried to reason with him, though mockingly. "Prince Sirhan, do you seriously believe this evil army of the dead, which your people seem to believe in with all their hearts, is more than mere superstition?"

"You weren't in the room when Salal told us what happened," Prince Sirhan said. "You didn't see the state he was in. I'd be quiet if I were you. You seem to speak out of turn a lot, and often on topics you don't know anything about."

Ismal's pride took another hit as muted laughter erupted around the room at this second jab from the royal family.

"Just because your father is the king doesn't mean you can speak to me in that manner," Ismal warned the prince.

"No, of course not," Sirhan agreed. "I speak to you 'in that manner' because I am unfortunate enough to be in the same room as you and these idiots."

Melhel had to stifle his laughter, as he was on the brink of busting out. He never expected someone as cold as Prince Sirhan to go on the attack with such humour.

King Michel chose to take a back seat, letting his son take over.

"The fact is a man has died, and another barely survived to give us vital information," Prince Sirhan continued. "We do have to take this seriously. This is not some conspiracy or whatever you're suggesting. Don't be moody because you didn't get your way before."

Ismal was visibly insulted, and turned to Saad. "I thought royalty was supposed to keep out of senatorial discussions? To maintain neutrality. Or can we bend the laws for them and their brethren?"

Yassin Benzi decided to step in and defend his prince and king. "I think I'm allowed to speak, Saad?"

Saad nodded. Ismal rolled his eyes, knowing Yassin would side with the royals.

"Thank you," Yassin began. "Senators, we must always look to defend Nataaros at all costs and protect the kingdom. This is our duty. Forget factions, forget this tribalism—if what we have heard is true, none of that will matter in the end. The dead army is far worse than laws and politics. The king wouldn't have put this on the agenda for nothing. It is real, and it is coming."

Everyone seemed to agree but the Scandosians.

"I agree," said Rios's senior senator, Mansour Alal, speaking up to rally others to the cause. "Saad, in the next meeting, draw up a vote to have this issue dealt with. We can't let it go any longer."

"Of course, senator," Saad said, nodding. "We will have it decided upon. Each and every one of you will get a say on the issue of the dead army. Do the right thing by your hearts."

He put his notes away and raised his hands. "That's it for today. You are all dismissed!"

Before anyone else could leave, Ismal stormed off, furious that his wishes for greater representation had been waved away and that everyone was more concerned over the dead army, which he saw as superstition and myth. As he walked away in anger, his fellow senators wondered why he was so upset.

"Leave him," Saad said. "He'll realise this is the bigger issue."

Melhel and Fares stood to make their way out of the chamber, but not before Melhel approached Prince Sirhan. "Never took you for the humorous type," he said. "I never realised how annoying elves can be."

"You haven't dealt with them as often as I have," Sirhan said discontentedly. "You'll learn to mock them too."

"Shouldn't be hard. They seem to make it easy for us."

"Indeed," Prince Sirhan concurred. "Anyhow, this Salal—I want to speak to him, get a full idea of what he faced. I want you there with me."

This surprised Melhel. "You want me? For something like this?"

"Father did say we'd better learn to work together. What better way than to do this?"

Melhel pondered a moment before agreeing. "Good idea. Although, can we wait till tomorrow? That was enough politicking for a lifetime, let alone an afternoon."

Prince Sirhan smiled. "I think you may be right."

CHAPTER 9
THE GLADIATORIAL GAMES

A day after the commotion in the senate, neither Melhel nor Prince Sirhan could be bothered to deal with more politics. Though they had asked to speak to Salal, both of them almost regretted the decision. Neither of them wanted to relive what they heard, nor whatever horrors Salal had faced beyond the frontier, and on the journey back home.

Fortunately for them, the king had decided they were due for a trip to Sidos to see the gladiatorial games, the kingdom's national sporting event.

The trip was to take about a week. From Beiros to Sidos, mostly through the Grasslands, was an even longer distance than to Chekkos, with the Cedar Hills making the journey more arduous.

At the same time, Salal was back in Beiros, receiving medical treatment, and blessings from the priests of Lah, following his ordeal. This gave everyone else time to recover and regroup too, before returning to deal with the issues at hand. The king's previously planned trip to Sidos to show Melhel and Fares the games was the perfect excuse for a holiday.

While Melhel and Fares were at home packing their things, they tried to talk Marissa into accepting their invitation to come with them. She felt unworthy of attending such a prestigious event with the royal family. The games weren't just any entertainment—they were the sport that united everyone in the kingdom. People of all ranks could enjoy the spectacle of seeing the greatest and most ruthless fighters beat each other with reckless abandon. It was the Nataarosian national pastime.

As at the senate, the king and queen had their own box, seated high above the arena where the whole crowd could see them, and where they could even influence the outcome of a fight. Royal attendance at the games was an honour for the fighters who quested for glory under the gaze of the king.

Marissa, still embarrassed to have been the girl who had an affair with a guard and ended up at the king's mercy, didn't feel like she belonged.

"Nonsense," Melhel said, dismissing her worries. "Of course, you're welcome to come!"

But after what happened, Marissa didn't want anything to do with the royal family. "I was stripped half-naked on the floor of the throne room, in front of the king," she said. "And you expect me to be sit in the royal box with his family?"

Melhel thought about this for a moment. Fares was still busy trying to pack. "Did he not save your life?" Melhel asked. "Was it not the king who spared you in the end?"

"No, it was you," Marissa said.

"All I did was make a convincing argument. The king still made the decision. He obviously saw some good in you—that your mistake wasn't all you are."

Marissa kept her head down, refusing to make eye contact with Melhel.

"Besides, you're with us now," Melhel said. "You're a part of the family. And we are close to the king. Therefore, so are you."

"The only time I've properly met him was when he was about to approve my execution," Marissa retorted.

"He's a forgiving man. He won't hold that against you." Melhel smiled and put his arm around her reassuringly. "When I met the king, I didn't even bow to him or bend my knee," he laughed. "As it turns out, that's not how you treat a king."

Marissa chuckled. She definitely could picture Melhel doing something like that, lacking the awareness to greet his king properly.

"Do you think he's held that against me?" Melhel said. "We both realised my mistake and now I am close with his family. He'll do the same with you."

Marissa took a deep breath, allowing her friend to sway her.

"I guess you're right," she conceded.

"And the king loves my uncle and values his opinion heaps," Melhel added. "If he's seen my uncle was willing to take you into our home to live and work with us, then he'll have no issue with you being our guest at the games. Like I said, you're family now."

Marissa teared up a little, overwhelmed by Melhel's generosity and kind words. She would soon have gone from the brink of execution to fraternising with the king and queen. It was a lot to take in.

"Then I'll go," she agreed. "But who's looking after the house?"

"The guards will make sure no one does anything funny," Melhel said. "Especially the Scandosians."

"They really hate us, don't they?"

"I wish I knew why," Melhel said, shaking his head. "They seem to hate my uncle, especially, judging by the reception they gave him in the senate."

"Wasn't he the one who defeated them in the civil war?" Marissa asked, remembering a chat they'd had. "I'm pretty sure you both told me that one night over dinner. He turned the tide of the battle?"

Melhel wondered for a moment. "Yeah, but this hostility—it's more than just losing a battle. Something's up." He couldn't hide his weariness. "I suppose it is all politics, in the end. Glad we're getting a break."

And just as he had finished, someone began banging on the front door of the house.

"Answer it, Melhel!" Fares called out from inside his room.

"Got it, Uncle!" he replied, hastily making his way to answer. When he got there and opened the door, he saw the prince standing there with a host of guards.

"Prince Sirhan!" he said with surprise. "What brings you here? We're not leaving for a little while."

The prince held his head high and proud. "Father asked me to check up on you, to see if you're ready," he said. "I take it everything is going as planned?"

"Uncle's just packing the last few things now," Melhel replied.

"You don't want to help him?"

"He won't let me," Melhel laughed. "Thinks I'm horrible at organising myself."

Prince Sirhan smirked. "I'll take his word for it."

He looked around the inside of the house presumptuously. "Mind if I come in?"

Melhel knew he couldn't say no. But before he had said anything, Sirhan had already stepped inside.

Prince Sirhan brushed past Melhel to check out the Barak's home. He inspected every last nook and cranny with the professional thoroughness of a building inspector.

"I see we've looked after you quite well," he commented. "Father was always fond of your family."

"That's why we're here," Melhel said.

Having finished scrutinising the house, the prince finally noticed Marissa, sitting sheepishly on the couch. "And you must be Marissa," he said, flipping on the charm as he always did when in the presence of a beautiful lady. "Prince Sirhan," he said magisterially, introducing himself.

Marissa looked up and was immediately smitten by the handsome young man.

"My pleasure," she said with embarrassment, transported by the prince's good looks.

"The pleasure is all mine," he said, grinning and taking her hand for a gentle kiss.

Marissa blushed all over, and she could feel the skin on her face heating up as it reddened.

Prince Sirhan turned to see Melhel rolling his eyes as he looked on.

"Have you kept this beautiful creature from me this whole time?" Prince Sirhan asked him.

Fares had joined them, and was determined not to let the prince assume he was the alpha male in the house. This was still Fares's domain, and the elder blacksmith was determined to let the Sirhan know it.

"Just from you, young prince," Fares said, walking up to shake his hand in welcome. "We didn't want her falling for your charms."

Fares may have been sarcastic, but he was right. Marissa was already infatuated by the prince, and her face had continued to redden so that now it somewhat resembled a cherry.

"Excuse me," she mumbled, having become so flustered she had to excuse herself to the bathroom, much to everyone's amusement.

Sirhan turned to Melhel and Fares, awestruck. "She's the most beautiful woman I've ever seen. The most beautiful in all of Alexandros—no, in Nataaros! After my mother, that is."

"Yeah, your mother is quite beautiful," Melhel said in a dig at the prince.

Sirhan took exception. "Pardon?"

"Nothing." Melhel grinned, causing Fares to give him a look of warning, so he changed tack. "Yes, Marissa is beautiful, and a great woman," he said. "She'll be coming with us to the games."

Prince Sirhan was plainly excited by this prospect. "Excellent," he said. "More time for me to get to know her."

Fares looked at the prince sternly, not wanting the poor woman to be embarrassed further. "Do keep your voice down, please," he said. "She's just in the other room, you know."

"I know, and I don't care," the prince said. "She ought to know how I feel. I'll be making her my bride soon enough."

Melhel was taken aback by the audacity of the prince, who seemed to think this perfectly normal. "Is that how marriage works?" he asked. "You just point to any woman and say, 'You, we're getting married'?"

"When you're me, yes. Father does stress the importance of having a smart and beautiful wife; this Marissa could be the perfect candidate."

The prince had half a point. Rania was the very model of a queen, and Prince Sirhan may have thought that if he found such a woman himself, he would have to do what he could to marry her, even if it meant asserting himself rather forcefully—including against the wishes of his parents if he must.

Fares placed his hand on the prince's shoulder. "So long as you take good care of her, understand?" He looked deep into the prince's eyes, frightening him a little. "She's like a daughter to me now, and I'm sure you know of what fathers do when silly men wrong their daughters."

The prince gulped, trying to keep his composure, but his wide eyes showed genuine fear. "Of course," he stammered.

In the bathroom, Marissa washed her face to cool her feelings for the prince. She could hear the men bickering over her. Despite her recent shame, she allowed herself to be flattered by Sirhan's interest. Just imagine—a prince wanting to marry her! Now her sense of unworthiness to attend the games with the royal family turned to an eagerness to impress the prince with her beauty and brains.

In the living area, the men stood uncomfortably waiting for Marissa to finish in the bathroom. Fares's warning had made the two younger men awkward.

Sirhan tried to avoid danger by steering the conversation away from Marissa.

"Melhel," he said, looking to his friend, "have you ever seen the gladiators before?"

Melhel shook his head. "No, I haven't."

"Not to worry," the prince said hesitantly. Out of the corner of his eye, he could see Fares still glaring at him. "They're a joy. I'll give you a rundown on the way in."

HALFWAY BETWEEN BEIROS AND SIDOS, Melhel, Prince Sirhan and Marissa had taken the driver's seat of the royal carriage as Rafiq took a well-deserved rest inside with Fares and the king and queen, who were discussing the Scandosians and the army of the dead.

In the driver's seat, the prince was explaining the gladiatorial games to Melhel and Marissa, who had no idea how any of it worked—Melhel for his provincial background, and Marissa for lack of interest.

"So, every fighter is a prisoner from Venos," the prince said. "These men are the worst of the worst. Smugglers, murderers, rapists. You name it, they did it."

Sirhan's dramatic flair was in full force, and his guests were fascinated. "If they're fit and willing enough, they fight in these games," he continued. "If they choose not to, then they're executed."

"The same way your father was going to execute me?" Marissa scolded.

"You're not a murderer or a rapist, my dear." The prince smiled, eager to stay on her good side. "You didn't deserve execution. I'm glad Melhel convinced my father of that." Melhel rolled his eyes, amused that Marissa couldn't see through his insincere flattery.

"Anyway, where was I?" the prince went on. "Ah, yes. So, these men have been chosen to fight each other, with weapons and armour, if they choose to not just get executed."

Melhel was typically sceptical. "So that's it? They just fight?"

"Not 'just fight'," the prince answered. "They have at each other until one of the brutes is either dead or too wounded to fight on. If one is wounded, it's my father's call as to what to do with him. He can signal to have the wounded fighter either spared or killed."

"And what makes a man worthy to spared or killed? What influences your father's decision?" Marissa asked.

The prince sat up and gesticulated energetically to illustrate his next point.

"The crowd," Prince Sirhan explained. "They'll be crying to either spare him or finish him. If the fighter fought well—bravely—he'll likely be spared. But if the fighter was weak, or a coward, then they don't deserve to be spared."

Melhel still had more questions. "Why not just send these men to the army? They're willing to fight each other to the death. Why not put them to good use and fight for the king?"

Prince Sirhan scoffed at this. "These men do not deserve to fight for my father. We only want the most loyal and honourable soldiers.

Besides, this *is* putting them to use. Entertaining the masses is a public service. They're artists."

"Didn't realise there was art in two men brutally trying to kill each other," Marissa commented.

"There is if you have the best of the best fighting for glory and honour."

"What glory? What honour?" Melhel didn't believe that such a thing could bring glory to a man.

"The glory of proving your mettle in the arena. Of having an entire crowd of people worship you, idolise you for showing the peak of what man can do with a sword and shield. To be the best at physical competition and be loved for it—what a privilege!"

"Surely, a great privilege—to be forced into this as a prisoner," Melhel said, clearly sick at the sound of these games.

But Prince Sirhan wasn't going to let Melhel's reservations spoil his fun. The games were his favourite spectacle, and he spoke of them with an energy and enthusiasm that one seldom saw from him.

"You'll understand it when we get there and you watch a fight," he assured his guests. "The pageantry and excitement of it all. You won't ever see anything like it. It's better than a play. It's not scripted like what you would see in an amphitheatre. This is real drama and emotion: the best piece of entertainment in the whole kingdom."

SEVERAL DAYS LATER, the party arrived in Sidos, and Rafiq stepped down from the driver's seat to request entrance at the gates.

These gates were not as large and extravagant as their counterparts in Beiros, as apart from serving its mission of hosting the games, the city was not of great political or economic import. The citizens were mostly middle-class and nearly all served the games in some way, as promoters, armourers, weapon-makers, trainers, or even as cooks for the fighters and the crowds.

Sidosians worked for the prisoners to keep them in peak condition as athletes. They worked for the spectacle and the show. They worked for the games. That was how Sidos functioned as an economy and served the kingdom.

That was true of the men, at least. The women were wives to the men at work, and sometimes humble spectators. The children, too, would sit and watch, in awe of the skill and physicality in front of them.

Rafiq approached the front gate and called for the attention of the guards. "I bring King Michel and Queen Rania of Nataaros!" he announced. "Here to enjoy the games that your city graciously hosts."

One of the guards approached the gates and recognised Rafiq's armour and distinguished face. "No need for the niceties, Rafiq," he said, "I can recognise the Sword of the King and the royal carriage any day of the week."

"Then you can let us in without delay," Rafiq ordered.

The guard nodded and began to open the gate.

Rafiq stood with his arms folded and tapped his feet impatiently as the heavy gate slowly swung open. It felt like it took an eternity, and when Rafiq returned to the seat he told the driver, "Remind me to try and introduce a reform to have the gates open faster."

The carriage began its way into the city, heading straight for the games, which were due to start in only a few hours, hence Rafiq's impatience. When the king and queen were in attendance at the games, they were always expected to arrive at the arena early and inspect the fighters for the day's events—to see them for themselves and make their personal predictions of whom they thought would be victorious. The king's picks were always scrutinised carefully, and if he deemed a fighter worthy of victory, as a favourite that fighter's prestige rose substantially.

Betting was widespread, and the odds were greatly affected by the king's favour. If a fighter was selected by the king to win, then his odds rose, as would his fame if the prediction came to be. He would demand more expensive equipment, and better training, food, and housing. Though they were only prisoners, fighting to escape execution, the gladiators were revered by the public as athletes, and their celebrity throughout Nataaros was guaranteed.

As the carriage passed through Sidos, Melhel could immediately see the arena, which was visible on taking just a single step into the city. The structure was a behemoth, towering over the smaller buildings of the city, testifying to Sidos's dedication to the games.

The royal party rode past the housing complexes for the fighters, the training barracks and hospitals, the armouries and smithies, and the cafeterias. This was tourism in Sidos: you were a fan of the games, or you were nothing.

Even Malia, the woman that Salal and Ahmid had spoken to when they investigated the reports of trouble at Alhayit, was a cleaner for the games, and her late husband had been a labourer. They were a true Sidosian family, which served the games.

Watching the city pass by through a carriage window, Melhel noticed how bland it really was. "This is pretty poor," he observed. "And this is where you choose to host such a prestigious event?"

"Sidos is not about the city, Melhel," Prince Sirhan explained. "It's about the games. Wait until you see the arena."

"It'd better be worth it," Melhel warned, already fed up. Disappointed in Sidos, he wished he were back in Beiros, where he could work on his smithing and quiz Salal on the dead army.

"It is, I promise you," Prince Sirhan reassured him.

"This our national pastime, Melhel," the king chimed in. "The whole kingdom unites to watch these games." The king and his son were both big fans. But while Sirhan revelled enthusiastically in the violence, King Michel saw their potential to unite everyone, distract them from the harshness of reality, and reinforce Nataarosian traditions.

"I'm aware of that, Your Majesty," Melhel said. "But couldn't you have picked a better city?"

"You'll see how it doesn't matter once we reach the arena, just as Sirhan said," King Michel confirmed. "The adrenaline, the thrill, the roar of the crowds—there's nothing quite like it. It beats going to the senate, that's for sure."

Melhel looked at Fares, who nodded as if to tell him to shut up and agree.

The young man decided to take his uncle's lead. "Sure, I understand." He smiled. "A lot of people travelled from Chekkos to attend the games, and they all had good things to say."

This was only half true. People did attend the games, and they did always talk about them, debating the merits of fights and fighters. But Melhel have never given thought to whether that talk was good or bad; he could not have cared less.

"And you've never decided to head off yourself?" the king asked.

Melhel shook his head. "Guess we were too involved in our work; we never found the time to do it," he answered. "Luckily, we have the opportunity now."

Fares took over, trying to keep his nephew out of trouble. "It was really up to me," he said. "I focused him on his work from such a young age, he never really gave thought to doing any sort of travelling."

"It's clear that he never left Chekkos," Prince Sirhan, said, digging at Melhel's struggle to adapt to his new life.

Melhel didn't take too kindly to this. "And I've noticed you've never left mummy and daddy's care," he said with a mischievous grin.

Before Prince Sirhan's ego overwhelmed him and this became an argument, Queen Rania interjected.

"Boys!" she admonished, going from queen to parent, "you are friends now, remember?"

The prince tried to smile and wiggle his way out of being told off like a child, something he hated. "What friends do not joke with each other, mother? I'm sure Fares and Father always kept high spirits with laughter."

"On the contrary," Fares said, "I wasn't the most humorous type when I was younger."

"What's changed?" Melhel joked.

Everyone in the carriage shared a laugh, breaking the tension for the time being.

"This is true," King Michel added. "He was always deadly serious, no matter the task. He could've seen the funniest of plays, and a statue of Beilos would still show more emotion."

"I guess that's part of being a soldier, my king," Fares explained. "You have to suppress your emotions, no matter what you see or do. All in the name of the king and his kingdom."

King Michel, like everyone else, knew Fares was alluding to the civil war. The joking mood dissolved and the tension returned. Fares simply couldn't let the war go, especially when the king made such comments.

Queen Rania knew her husband's and Fares' history better than anyone, and, seeking to calm the situation, turned to Melhel with a new topic.

"So," she said, "what are you most interested about in the games?"

THE TIME HAD COME: the carriage had arrived at the arena, right in the heart of Sidos and so big it could be seen from anywhere in the city, and even many places outside. Sixty metres high, inside it was roughly three hundred yards square, though a lot of it was just the stands for the crowd. The arena was reputed to seat what they said to be over one hundred thousand adoring, screaming, fanatical supporters, whose cheers created the atmosphere of war.

That's what each fight was like to the fighters and the fans—war. The crowd were tribal about which fighters they would support, and some fans of the more popular gladiators had to be separated into different sections of the arena to prevent crowd violence. Years before, there had been a disaster at the arena when rival fans became even more violent than the fighters they supported, causing a deadly human stampede, but memory of the event had been swept under the rug by the powers that be.

As King Michel, Queen Rania, and their guests stepped out of the carriage, the host of the games, Adil Karom, was there to meet them. Adil had a sharply defined goatee, with the moustache curling slightly upwards and wide of the rest of his beard. He had a devilishly cheeky grin, and unmatched enthusiasm not only for hosting the games, but for all things entertaining and theatrical.

126

He greeted the royal family warmly. "Your Majesties! Welcome to Sidos," he said, smiling and bending his knee enthusiastically.

"A pleasure as always, Adil," King Michel replied. "How are we looking for today?"

Adil couldn't shake his excitement, "Even more spectacular than always! The fighters are fit and ready. Can't wait for you to meet them." Adil always made sure every minute detail was perfect for a visit from the king and queen.

Once he stood back up, Adil noticed Fares and Melhel. "New friends of yours?" he asked the king, excited to see fresh faces.

King Michel beamed, proud to introduce them. "This is Fares and Melhel and Barak," he said, "They've taken charge of our blacksmithing program, and are close advisers to myself and my beautiful queen."

Adil's eyes lit up at discovering whose company he was in. "*The* Fares Barak?" he exclaimed. "The hero of the Siege of Beiros?"

Fares nodded humbly. "I wouldn't say 'hero', but yes."

"What an honour!" Adil shook his hand excitedly before turning to Melhel. "And who might this young man be?"

"Melhel is his nephew," said the king.

Adil examined both men carefully. "Ah, I see the resemblance," he observed. "You both have that Alexandrosian vigour about you."

He looked at Melhel's face. "I take it you're not from Beiros."

Melhel shook his head. "Chekkos," he said.

Adil then turned to Marissa, and his face brightened even further as he regarded her beauty. "And who is this lovely lady?" he wondered.

"Marissa Hussan," she replied.

"And what brings you here?" Adil asked, approaching her slowly.

Marissa was nervous, as though she was under the spotlight and stardom was upon her. "I work with Melhel and Fares," she said. "Well... *for* them," she explained.

"Ah, what fortunate men to have you in their company!" Adil proceeded to gently kiss Marissa's hand, leading her to blush.

"This is Melhel and Marissa's first time attending the games, Adil," Queen Rania explained. "He was very excited to see the fighting techniques on display. And Marissa is keen to see the show you will put on."

Adil got between the two newcomers, ramping up his showman persona to sell them on the games. "Good, good. You'll see plenty of that here." He put his arms around Melhel and Marissa chummily. "Come with me, young people, I'll explain everything on the way."

Having tried to encircle Melhel with one arm, Adil now more clearly saw how in shape and strong he was. "Why, you're quite strapping yourself," he said. "Say, can you fight?"

"My uncle taught me," Melhel said.

Adil felt he had missed a big opportunity. "Shame," he sighed, "if you weren't such an upstanding citizen, you'd make a fine gladiator."

Melhel laughed. "Well, I don't have any plans to murder or rape anyone, sorry to say."

Adil's own laugh sounded forced.

As everyone headed inside the arena, Prince Sirhan lagged behind, feeling neglected. Adil had been so intent on the newcomers, he hadn't even acknowledged the prince. "Am I being ignored?" he cried.

The queen tried to comfort him. "Not at all, my love! You know how excited Adil is to see new guests, and how excited your father was to show Melhel and Marissa the games."

"I don't care," the prince said, putting his foot down. "A prince should never be ignored like this. And the way he kissed Marissa's hand…!"

The queen smiled. "Do I sense a bit of jealousy?" she teased.

Prince Sirhan became flustered, and his face reddened. "No…"

"Not to worry. When the crowd notices you, I'm sure they'll cheer as loudly as anything."

The prince raised his head, determined not to led Adil's slight dampen his mood.

"Damned right they will be," he said. "And when I am king, no one will ever ignore me."

As Rafiq walked past the prince and the queen, he said, "Until then, you'll have to settle for being beneath your parents." Prince Sirhan scowled at him.

"We'll see how long that lasts," he muttered under his breath.

OUR PARTY HAD ENTERED the rooms in the arena where the day's fighters were preparing for battle. There was astonishing variety among them: some were big and strong, others small and agile, or nimble but powerful, but all were physically gifted specimens. Often, fights became a battle of brute strength against agility, and the outcome was seldom certain.

They were oiled up and rubbed down to prepare their muscles for the fighting ahead, making sure they were in top condition to give their best performance. Fighters could be seen stretching and miming their techniques, loosening themselves up like the best athletes do. Some were already fitted with their armour, to which Fares and Melhel took a keen eye.

"Not a bad job for criminals," Fares said to Adil. "They're nearly as well equipped as the army!"

"We treat these men not as criminals, Fares, but as athletes," Adil explained. "These men provide us with the greatest show in all the land."

King Michel went off to inspect each gladiator, examining their condition, shape, toughness, and apparent mental fortitude. The gladiators did their best to keep their cool before the king, and not be awestruck.

They had greater trouble when they laid eyes on Queen Rania, whose beauty easily stunned the weaker-willed. Their difficulty in keeping their eyes off her drew dirty looks from the prince.

King Michel noticed a gladiator in the back of the room on his own. This brute of a man was taller and wider than anyone he had ever seen, with muscles on top of muscles, a bald head and clean-shaven face, and a big patch of hair across his chest. He wore no armour, only trousers, the sole piece of metal he had on him being the battleaxe that he was sharpening methodically.

Adil approached the king. "I see you have noticed the Beast of the East," he said by way of introduction. "He is the headlining gladiator for today. You will see him fight at the very end of the day's proceedings."

King Michel looked him up and down, almost frightened of the man. "What poor soul wants to fight him?" he asked.

"A man with nothing to lose," Adil commented. "Good luck to them. This one is Rios's finest criminal export."

Melhel and Fares had also noticed the Beast. "That's the biggest man I've ever seen," Melhel exclaimed.

"Would've been nice to have had him in the siege," Fares chuckled. He shook his head in pure disbelief over the man's size.

Queen Rania came to put a comforting hand on Fares' shoulder. "Ah, but then you wouldn't have had your moment," she said, trying to lift his spirits.

"If that's what you want to call it," Fares replied. "I would've gladly let this giant have it."

Melhel was still transfixed by the Beast. "Who's got the guts to fight him?" he asked.

"Whoever it is, I cannot wait to see the little man get crushed," Prince Sirhan said gleefully.

"You told Marissa and I how much of a spectacle these games are," Melhel said. "What kind of show is a large man crushing a smaller one?"

The prince was ecstatic. "The very best kind!"

"I fail to see what's entertaining about a one-sided fight," Marissa said. "Is it not unfair to match him with a smaller man? Shouldn't he fight someone his own size and strength?"

"There is no such thing as fair in a battle," Prince Sirhan claimed, "only who is strongest, and who is victorious."

Melhel laughed at Prince Sirhan's belief, "What a base mentality to have."

"Base, but winning," Prince Sirhan boasted. "Besides, if I were you, I wouldn't be so self-righteous."

"What do you mean?" Melhel asked.

"Well, you're watching, are you not?" the prince sneered. Melhel's directness was becoming too much for him.

"Only because you're making us watch it," Melhel hit back.

"You've never been in a battle, anyway! What do you know about what happens in one?"

"Whatever the reasons, we are here to enjoy the show," Prince Sirhan exclaimed.

King Michel returned to the front of the room to address the gladiators. All eyes turned to him, as they tended to. The fighters all bent their knees: even these criminals, with nothing to lose, knew how to yield to custom.

"Honoured gladiators of Nataaros," he called out, "I bid you welcome to the games. We are blessed to be able to witness your strength, power, and skill as you fight for glory. You may rise." He gave an upward gesture with his outstretched hand. "Stand strong and proud of who you are, warriors. Thousands of people cheer your names. They are here for you. All of you carry on a legacy, a tradition, of rigour and valour. May you all see it out, and may the best fighters win. I shall see you all in the arena."

As the king walked out of the room, he stopped to whisper in Adil's ear.

"My money is on the giant."

A FEW FIGHTS had already taken place before the king and his party could even take their seats in the royal box. It was tradition for the royals to only make their presence known during the main event, as anything less was seen as beneath them.

The ground was wash with the blood and viscera of the poor men who had already met their fates in these games. The crowd cheering and jeered, electrified by the day's action. Just the sight of two people desperately fighting each other to the death, with nothing held back, is enough to drive one into a frenzy. Competition can bring out the best and the worst out of people—sometimes at the expense of others' lives.

The workers at the arena hastily cleaned up the gore left on the ground in preparation for the royal entrance. In Adil's view, this was not something for the king and queen to see.

Then Adil himself took centre stage, and in a surprisingly

powerful voice, projected through a horn that lifted it to the far corners of the stands, he began to announce the proceedings.

"Ladies and gentlemen, are we having fun today?" he called out.

His question was met with a raucous cheer from the crowd, who were thirsty for the main event.

"It is with great pleasure," he boomed, "that I present to you our esteemed guests. All rise for the rulers of all Nataaros: King Michel and Queen Rania!" Swinging an outstretched arm, he pointed theatrically to the empty royal box, placed right in the middle of the stands but away from the squabbling crowds and high enough to offer a better view of the games than from anywhere else in the arena.

King Michel and Queen Rania ascended the stairs from below to reach the box, and stood at the parapet to acknowledge the adoring subjects and supporters all cheering and chanting their names.

The king had a cheesy smile plastered across his face, while the queen was more reserved as she gently waved to the people.

Behind them came Prince Sirhan, Melhel, Marissa, and Rafiq. Sirhan waved at the crowd with a veiled smile, less expansive than his father's.

Fares, Melhel, and Marissa smiled and stood awkwardly, not sure whether to wave or wait to be seated.

Rafiq, unfazed by the crowd's attention, nonchalantly took his post behind the seats, guarding against potential threats from the rear, as a good Sword should do.

Adil, knowing Fares was with the royals, decided to draw some attention to the humble blacksmith. "Beautiful people in the crowd, it has just come to my attention that the king and queen have some guests with them," he said disingenuously—he had known all along who would be in the box with them. "And none more esteemed than that fine gentlemen with the shy face. I present to you the hero of Beiros, Fares Barak!"

The crowd erupted when they realised that it was indeed Fares in the royal box, and chanted his name in recognition of the deeds he had done in saving Beiros.

Melhel looked to Fares. "I never knew you were this famous," he said.

"I'm not," Fares waved this off as he always did. "I just can't shake that stupid battle."

When the hysteria over Fares' appearance had died down, Adil took a deep breath, ready to reel in the crowd.

"And now, for our main event—the moment all of you have been waiting for!" he pointed to one end of the ground, where a gate was being lifted for the Beast to make his way in. "Introducing Rios's finest export, a man so big even Lah shakes in his home on the mountains. A man with muscles upon muscles, the Beast of the East!"

The Beast strutted in unarmoured, just as in the rooms. His battleaxe was sharpened and gleaming, and he let off an energetic roar to the crowd, getting them onside to cheer for him.

Even from the height of the royal box, his sheer, brutal size was terrifying.

"No man could beat him," Prince Sirhan claimed. "That's the best fighter in all of Nataaros."

Rafiq heard this and quickly leaned over to the prince, "I hope you say that only because I am in a league of my own. After all, this brute wasn't the one saving you from bandits while you cried for your mother."

Prince Sirhan blinked and carried on watching, with Melhel and Marissa flanking him on either side.

"What poor soul have they possibly convinced to fight him?" Fares asked the king. "Look at him."

Adil then pointed to the opposite end of the ground, where another gate was opening.

"Now, his opponent," Adil said, introducing the other fighter. "He's quick. He's nimble. Blink and you will miss him. Our challenger, Daviso the Poison!"

Out stepped a significantly smaller man, even shorter than Melhel, and far less muscled. Daviso had covered himself head to toe in armour, with just a short sword his weapon of choice.

The crowd booed the man, whom they saw as clearly inferior. The Beast egged them on.

Prince Sirhan laughed aloud. "That's who they've got to fight the Beast? What a joke!"

Melhel's eyes expanded, shaken at the contrast between the two fighters. "He's gonna be crushed," he said.

Marissa was shaking, scared for the little man about to be squashed like a bug. "I'm not sure I can watch this," she said, and shuddered.

Prince Sirhan placed his arm around her. "Come now, my dear, let us enjoy a true show of force." The prince relished the prospect of the bruising brawl about to take place. "What a joke of a name, though — 'The Poison'. They couldn't have thought of something better?"

"And you would have?" said Melhel.

"Yes. No one could be more creative than I," Prince Sirhan bragged. "In fact, I shall be having a word with Adil about this."

Melhel rolled his eyes at the prince's arrogance.

On the ground, Daviso the Poison stood unassumingly, waiting for the introductions to finish so the fighting could begin.

Adil took the focus one last time. "Our fighters are locked in and ready. The question is, beautiful audience, are you ready?"

The crowd screamed in excitement.

"Then let our main event begin!"

The drums banged, signalling the start of the fight. As Adil walked past Daviso, he whispered to him while looking at the Beast. "I sure hope you know what you've got yourself into."

Adil made his way to his seat, leaving the two fighters staring at each other.

The Beast tried to intimidate Daviso by slamming his axe on the ground with a furious scream, igniting a cheer from the crowd. "You're a dead man!" he warned. "To think you can challenge me, the Beast of the East!"

Daviso stayed silent. Instead, he grabbed his sword and entered a fighting stance.

The Beast laughed at him. "You really think that little needle is going to save you? I'm going to quarter you with my axe."

He made his move towards Daviso and swung, but the smaller fighter ducked underneath and slashed at the Beast's exposed stomach before quickly creating space.

The Beast was stunned, and the whole crowd gasped. They couldn't believe Daviso had actually drawn blood either.

Melhel nodded in approval, impressed by Daviso's move.

"That's how us shorter men fight," he joked to his uncle.

"That's exactly how *I* fight," Fares noted.

Daviso waited patiently while the Beast licked blood from his wound off his fingers and spat it back out.

"Just a scratch," the Beast said, even though the wound was still open and he could feel the blood leaving his body.

His anger and aggression rose up and he lunged at Daviso, who sidestepped and parried the attack away. The Beast swung repeatedly at Daviso, who dodged or blocked every attack.

"Why won't you die?" the Beast cried out in between swings. Daviso still hadn't said a word, concentrating only on defending himself.

Up in the royal box, everyone had leaned forward in their seats, eager to see the outcome of what was turning out to be a thrilling fight.

"This is not going to be the bloodbath we may all have expected," Queen Rania said. "I guess size really doesn't matter."

"I guess it doesn't, my love," King Michel responded, surprised at this apparently new revelation.

Fares looked at his king. "You would know if you'd actually stepped on a battlefield," he remarked.

"Don't get on your high horse, Fares," the king said. "You wrote the little man off as much as the rest of us."

The Beast took one massive swing at the head of Daviso, who quickly ducked and sliced the back of the Beast's knee, ripping through the tendons.

The bigger fighter winced in agony and dropped to the ground.

Daviso stood over the Beast, who was now unable to stand, and had dropped his weapon to clutch at the back of his leg, which was now pouring blood.

"I hope this teaches you a lesson," Daviso remarked. "Always be on guard."

Daviso then took off his helmet and revealed his face, which bore a soft, gentle expression unexpected one capable of destroying the Beast. He put his sword to the throat of his vanquished foe and looked to the royal box. "My king!" he cried. "Make your call. Do I spare him, or kill him?"

The crowd now favoured Daviso, cheering for him and calling for the Beast to be killed. The king rose to address them amid the commotion. "Young man, you have fought valiantly, and bravely. I commend your skill and your spirit," he began. "I cannot lie; I did not predict this."

Daviso smiled. "I get that a lot," he said. "I think it's my height ... or lack thereof."

"I see now that size doesn't matter," he said, somewhat in awe, "as the queen graciously pointed out to me a moment ago. Your opponent has disappointed me. I expected better of him."

"He has to spare the man," Fares whispered to Melhel. He looked at the Beast, unmoving in a pool of his own blood. "He's in agony. You can't kill a man this way."

Prince Sirhan was growing tired of his father's rambling. "Get it done with and kill the brute!"

"I have made my decision," King Michel said on hearing the crowd call for the Beast's head. He raised his hand and showed Daviso the thumbs down.

Fares looked at the king with disgust, while Prince Sirhan sat up ready to see the death.

Marissa buried her head in her hands.

"I *really* can't watch," she cried.

Melhel looked at the gleeful prince and lowered his head in shame, appalled that violence like this could be a form of entertainment.

Without question, Daviso lifted the Beast up by the hair, placed his sword along his neck, and in one slice chopped head clean off. He held the Beast's head aloft for the crowd to see, and they revelled in the slaughter.

King Michel applauded the spectacular end to this underdog story.

Marissa buried her head in Prince Sirhan's shoulder, unable to look at the Beast's severed head.

The prince cared not; he was too busy cheering and clapping.

Fares was disappointed in his king and in the world that he had fought for. He felt ashamed that after the civil war, and with the threat of another looming large, people still found this senseless violence entertaining.

Melhel and his uncle both arose from their seats, and stormed off out of the royal box, away from the action. No one noticed; their eyes were fixed on the show in front of them.

CHAPTER 10
REMEMBERING THE HORROR

On the way back to Beiros, the carriage was full of awkwardness and tension. Melhel and Fares were none too pleased with what they had seen in the games, and even less with King Michel's and Prince Sirhan's enjoyment of it all.

Melhel and Sirhan had been sitting ahead of the carriage with the driver, and since setting off, Melhel had done little but stare at the prince with a look of contempt between glances at the passing landscape. His respect for Sirhan had dropped dramatically, especially since seeing his glee at the slaughter while he sat alongside a horrified Marissa.

"Are you alright there?" Prince Sirhan barked at Melhel during another long stare.

"Just daydreaming."

"About what?" the prince snapped.

"About the horror show you put us through." Melhel couldn't have been blunter. "Apparently your idea of entertainment is seeing a man's head chopped off."

The prince laughed, failing to see why Melhel hated the experience.

"It's sport, Melhel," he said. "The winner takes it all."

Melhel rubbed his face in frustration and disgust.

"Takes what, though? A life?" he replied. "People die in war, and we want to make a game out of it?"

"The games are a tradition of our kingdom," the prince asserted. "So, yes, we do want to, and we have made a game out of it."

"Well, it's a stupid tradition."

"And what would you suggest, then?" Prince Sirhan asked.

Melhel thought for a moment. "I don't know…" he floundered, "throw a ball around … kick it around? Maybe just limit the violence to wrestling of some sort … anything to not have people's heads chopped off in front of people who have already been through so much."

Prince Sirhan waved these suggestions off as though Melhel were a deranged prophet telling him the apocalypse was coming. "The people won't find that entertaining," he said. "Face it, they all adore the games and the gladiators. You saw them: they were wild!"

"Then the people are idiots." Melhel looked back to the carriage. "And you had better explain this to Marissa."

"What do you mean?"

"Don't give me that," Melhel said. "It's obvious you like her. It's obvious she likes you. It was obvious from the moment you two met. But she was really put off by the games. She hates violence. And she's only here because she was nearly executed herself. If you truly want her to be your loving wife, you'd better make this up to her."

Prince Sirhan couldn't contain his laughter. Everything Melhel had to say was like one big joke to him.

"You think I care?" he scoffed. "When she is my wife—and she will be—she'll most certainly be attending the games with me."

Melhel shook his head in annoyance, and was ready to give up arguing. "You'd better talk to her about it, then," he said, "because she is very stubborn. Very. I don't think you could make her go again unless you can convince her otherwise."

The prince moaned. "Lah, in your infinite wisdom as you reside atop the Snowy Mountains, please tell me why women are such complicated creatures." He stared to the sky, hoping Lah would be at his beck and call. "For the trouble they bring, I struggle to think if they're worth it."

Melhel scowled. "Maybe they are. Maybe they're not. But here's an idea: don't take them to a killing show and expect them to like it!"

Prince Sirhan still didn't get it. Melhel wasn't enabling him by telling him what he wanted to hear. Instead, Melhel was the only man who dared contradict him, and it rankled.

"Between women and politicians, I'm not sure who I'd rather deal with," the prince cried.

"Lucky for you, you get to deal with both," Melhel mocked. "You're the future king, as you always remind me." Melhel could see from the prince's face that he didn't take too kindly to this, and immediately tried to change the topic. "Speaking of politics, are we meeting with Salal when we return?"

Sirhan looked at him sharply. "You're quick to change the subject."

"I'm not trying to convince you of anything; I never do," Melhel explained. "I've said my bit. It's up to you to take it on. Now we have to get back to the real issue at hand: the army of the dead."

The prince nodded. "That I'll agree with. I'll see to it that we meet with the scout as soon as we return."

"What are we going to ask him?"

"Just what happened. What he saw. Maybe even what happened on his way back after he was found by that man … oh, what was his name?"

"Josif," Melhel said.

"Yes! Him."

Melhel was confused. "What does that have to do with anything?"

"We can find out if he saw anything as well. If not, we at least have an adventure story."

Melhel took this on-board and continued to look at the country-side surrounding them. He was forever impressed by the beauty in Alexandros, but a part of him knew it could all disappear if things did not work out like they were meant to.

MELHEL and the prince both agreed to hold the meeting with Salal in Melhel's house. While not far the castle or other busy areas of Beiros, it was low-key enough to not draw attention. No one would think twice of one ordinary man entering the home of another.

Marissa was away in the kitchen, preparing food and drink to be presented to Salal on his arrival. Hospitality was key, and softening Salal to make him lower his defences could let them extract more information. Marissa was only too happy to help.

Fares was at the workshop, overseeing their ever-bustling black-smithing operations. Melhel and Prince Sirhan were to work alone together. As Queen Rania had stressed, this was their chance not only to prove themselves to Fares and the king, but to show they could cooperate well, as Queen Rania had stressed.

Melhel answered a knock at the door. Salal. "Welcome," Melhel said, shaking his hand. "Thank you for taking the time out to do this."

"More than happy to help," Salal responded graciously. Then he saw Prince Sirhan. "My prince," he said, bowing his head and bending his knee.

The prince took pride in this. "You may stand, soldier," he said with a smile.

Salal stood and walked towards the living area while Prince Sirhan smirked at Melhel. "That's how it should be done," he said.

Melhel rolled his eyes. He didn't have time for Sirhan's attitude, and in his head he prayed that the prince would not ruin this opportunity.

The three men each took a seat on one of the couches around a table. Melhel and Prince Sirhan leaned back, relaxing while Salal remained bolt upright.

"You can make yourself at home, Salal," Melhel offered.

"Thank you," Salal replied, loosening up a little.

Marissa walked in with a tray of biscuits, bread, and tea, and placed it on the table, smiling at Salal.

Melhel stood to introduce her. "Salal, this is Marissa. She helps my uncle and me around the house."

Salal politely stood up and gently took Marissa's hand. "Lovely to meet you. It's a wonderful thing that Melhel and his uncle have done."

Marissa was surprised. "So, you know?"

"Everyone knows what happened," Salal said, somewhat embarrassed that he had let his knowledge slip. "Well ... every soldier at least."

Marissa turned to Melhel and Sirhan. "How does word get around so quick?"

"Because people cannot keep their mouths shut!" Melhel exclaimed, looking at the prince.

"I didn't say anything," the prince parried.

Marissa brushed it off. "Regardless, it's nice to meet you as well, Salal" Then she glanced at Melhel. "I'll be around if you need me," she said already walking off to leave the men alone.

Salal was more at ease now, and finally leaned back into his seat, acquainting himself with his surroundings, "It's a nice place you have," he commented.

"Courtesy of the prince here, and the king," Melhel said. He extended his hand to the food. "Have something to eat. Please, don't wait for us."

"If you insist." Salal, apparently ravenous, started by taking bites of biscuits and bread. "These are incredible! Who made them?"

Melhel grinned. "Marissa was a baker, you know."

Salal was delighted. They were the best biscuits he'd ever tried. "Well, give her my compliments," he told Melhel.

Prince Sirhan stepped in. "Alright, don't get too comfortable," he said gruffly. "She is their maid, after all." Already, the prince had grown protective of the woman.

"I just wanted to pay a compliment, my prince," he stumbled.

"Only joking, young man," the prince jested, smiling at him. "You're allowed to compliment."

Salal chuckled uncomfortably and continued stuffing his face to avoid saying more that would give the prince fuel for jokes at his expense.

Melhel tried to break the ice with some questions. "So, Salal, how have things been since your return?"

"It's just the normal soldiering life," Salal said. "Back to my duties for Nataaros."

"That's so good to hear," Melhel nodded. "What made you want to become a soldier?"

Salal had already taken a huge bite, swallowing a bread roll almost whole, and gasped for air as he tried to form his next sentence. "My father was a soldier," he began. "And his father before him. And his father before him, as well. I come from a family of soldiers."

"*Esteemed* soldiers?" Prince Sirhan asked.

"No, my prince. Just normal infantrymen."

"I assumed as much. Otherwise, I would've already known who you were," Prince Sirhan remarked. "Not to worry; I'm sure they all fought bravely for my father, and his father before him. And, as well, his father before him."

Melhel noted Salal's increasing discomfort with the prince as he blatantly belittled his family for their lack of prestige.

"Yes," the soldier agreed, and smiled obsequiously. It was all he could do.

"As you will fight for me when I am king," the prince reminded him.

"Of course, my prince," Salal said. "I would never think of anything else."

In contrast to Sirhan, Melhel was doing everything he could to be welcoming and reasonable. He knew full well the kind of person Salal was: soft and timid, responding best to cordiality and gentleness. Prince Sirhan didn't seem to appreciate this, and seemed committed to treating their meeting as an interrogation.

"You never had a say in your career path?" Melhel asked.

"Not really, no," Salal said. "As soon as I was of age, I was off to the academy."

Melhel beamed. "Where I'm sure they churn out fine soldiers," he reassured Salal, and glanced at the prince as if to tell him that's how it should be done. "And how have you found the weapons and armour we've been supplying?"

Salal looked at Melhel with surprise. "That's you who's making them?"

Prince Sirhan looked perplexed. "You didn't know the Baraks were the new blacksmiths for the army?"

"No, I'm so sorry." Salal jumped up to shake Melhel's hand. "That's some fine work you do."

Melhel shrugged it off. "Thank you," he said warmly. "But it's mostly my uncle, Fares. In fact, we don't even craft, we just run the operation. Everything goes down to the talented smiths working for us."

Salal smiled. "Well, it's your technique," he complimented. The new weapons and armour coming from the Baraks' smithy had been wildly popular with the soldiers. "I can't wait to tell the others I met the man that will save us all."

"Save us all?" Melhel and Prince Sirhan were confused.

"Yeah," Salal said. "When the dead army comes for us, we're gonna need the best equipment gold can buy and metal can make. Isn't that what we're here to discuss? The dead army?"

Melhel and Prince Sirhan looked at each other, realising there had never been any need to break the ice. Salal was eager to tell what he had seen. It was time to get down to business.

"Yes," Prince Sirhan said, a friendly note creeping into his voice. "That night, beyond Alhayit. We want you tell us everything."

Salal sat back down, ready to tell the story with as straight a face as possible. Melhel and the prince hung on every word.

"Well, I and another soldier, Ahmid, we went to investigate a report made by a woman in Sidos," Salal began. "She said she saw a flash of light and heard a screaming so loud it was unbearable. We spoke to her, and she told us what she saw, what she heard, and we ventured beyond the wall.

"When we got there, there was nothing. It was empty. Until we saw something on the ground..."

"What did you see?" Melhel asked, leaning forward, engrossed in the story.

"I don't know. Some strange writing in some foreign language," Salal continued. "It wasn't the common tongue ... it wasn't Scandosian either. It was something that would be new to even the most esteemed scholars." Salal took a long, deep breath, unwilling to relive that moment even though he knew he had no choice. "And when we saw it, before either of us could react, Ahmid's head was sliced off and I was surrounded by these dead men, and they were approaching fast.

"Then, I saw a hooded man, who told me to run. So, that's what I did. I ran. I ran as far as I could until I collapsed, back inside the frontier, in Alexandros."

"Who was the man?" Prince Sirhan probed.

"I don't know." Salal shook his head, "I didn't see his face. All I remember after that was waking up, and Josif finding me."

Melhel sat further forward. "And what happened with Josif?"

SHORTLY AFTER JOSIF had found Salal in a state of panic, and the two of them had begun venturing back to Beiros, they got into a deep conversation about the dead army.

They had both been firm believers in the myth growing up, and now Salal's experience had confirmed their faith in the stories.

"It was everything we read about," Salal told Josif. "A living nightmare. I saw a man die in such a horrible way. Who knows what may have happened to him...?" The best Salal could hope for was that Ahmid's body still lay where it had fallen, beyond Alhayit. But that could not be guaranteed.

Josif turned on his horse to look at Salal. "You and I have read the stories," he said, "I'm sorry to say this, but he's likely one of them, or was a sacrifice to whatever god or perverted demon they believe in and work under."

Salal panicked. "Oh, Lah. What if I have to fight him? And he dies again?" His face grew pale. "What if that hooded man is the demon behind this all?"

Josif remained stoic, trying to keep a cool head so Salal wouldn't panic any further. But inside, he was quaking. Josif was the kind of man who could hide his fears exceptionally well.

"What do you know about the dead army?" he asked. "I heard

they were to come back during times of upheaval. When a vacuum was created in our society, they would come in and destroy us all."

Salal pondered this. "Well, based on hearsay, things aren't looking too good in the senate."

Josif guided his horse towards Sidos. They were away from the woods now and back in more domesticated regions, where they began to see small farmhouses standing in fields and the path widened enough to almost be called a road.

"What are they saying about the senate?" he asked.

"That we could be on the brink of another civil war. That Scandos are having another try at independence."

Josif shook his head. "Those dirty elves," he cursed. "Why do they bother? They have nearly everything they want. We give them autonomy, freedom, and a good society to run for themselves. But of course the ungrateful shits want more."

"It doesn't matter," Salal warned Josif. "Soon, we'll all be dead. All of this fighting, warring, politicking... It'll all be for nothing."

Josif nodded in agreement. "You're right. The dead army doesn't discriminate. Elf or man—they don't care. They don't see race. They don't see species. They see themselves, and the rest. To them, the rest of us are fodder and must be killed... But why?"

Salal's breathing caught; the thought frightened him no end.

"If my memory serves me correctly, they serve a greater purpose than themselves," he recalled. "Something about Beilos the Conqueror, and events happening during his wars."

Josif thought back on the stories he read. It sounded familiar, and he was glad to have met someone on the same page.

"You're right!" he realised. "As the story goes, 'The sons of Beilos will suffer for the Conqueror's thirst for glory. Our day will come, and yours will end.' " He repeated the words of the folktale he'd heard countless times growing up. "The only question is— whose day is coming?"

"I'm not sure," Salal said. "But I believe it has something to do with that hooded man."

"We should investigate."

"Unlikely!" Salal cried. "I'm going home to my bed. I will take

146

no part in fighting dead armies. Or elves, for that matter. At least, not for a while."

Josif's face tightened. "And you call yourself a soldier?" he scoffed.

This put Salal on the defensive. "I didn't choose to become one, you know."

Josif smirked. "Oh, really? I couldn't tell."

"I don't need stupid comments from you."

"And yet, were it not for me, you'd be the newest recruit of the dead army, and still unwilling," Josif reminded Salal. "Instead of a new recruit in the army of Nataaros."

Salal hung his head, contemplating every life decision he'd made up to that point. He knew it was time to man up and be a soldier, not a frightened child. "You're right," he said. "I'm sorry. I'm just a bit shaken up. After everything that's happened..."

"I don't blame you," Josif said warmly. "Had I been in your situation, I'd be way worse. In fact, I may not have made it out alive, even if someone had found me. Maybe they'd have found a corpse. You're a brave man, Salal."

Salal smiled genuinely for the first time in what felt like years. It had been an arduous, interminable day for him, and he was glad he could finally get some rest.

Halfway between Sidos and Beiros, Salal and Josif had set up camp in the Grasslands, off the side of the road.

Their camp wasn't much, certainly not of the extravagance the royal family would have enjoyed, but it was enough to keep two resourceful men comfortable. By some people's measures, it was more than enough, and that is exactly what two rough bandits thought, when they found Salal and Josif sleeping and vulnerable.

One of the bandits started rummaging through their belongings while the other kept an eye on the sleeping men.

"They've got nothing!" the rummager cried. "What a waste of time!"

"Quiet, you fool," the other one whispered harshly. "You do

realise the best way to steal is to not have them know you're doing it."

"I'm just letting you know that your idea to rob these men was a horrible choice."

"Would you shut up!" The watcher was in a temper now too. They didn't seem to know how to rob people properly.

The incessant arguing of the two bandits woke Salal and Josif, who were startled to see themselves getting robbed.

"What is the meaning of this?" Salal screamed out.

The bandit keeping an eye on him quickly grabbed Josif, hoisted him up, and put a sword to his neck.

"One word and I'll cut his throat!" he warned Salal. "Stand up!"

Salal stood while the other bandit kept going through his and Josif's belongings. This gave the hostage-taker the chance to see his armour.

"You're a soldier!" he exclaimed. "You'd have a lot for us somewhere." He turned his head to his friend and cried, "Idiot! Keep searching!"

"Good man," Salal said, "I can give you anything you want, so long as you let my friend go."

"Not a chance," the bandit responded, tightening his grip on Josif, who remained calm. "Any movement from you and he's a dead man, soldier."

The other bandit stumbled upon some gold in Salal's bags. "I think I found something!"

"What is it?!" the one holding Josif demanded, looking to his friend greedily.

As the captor's head was turned, Salal quickly pulled a dagger from his pockets and flung it at his captor's throat. It caught with a spurt of blood, and the bandit clutched at it coughing and gagging, before falling to the ground in his death throes.

The surviving bandit screamed in horror as Salal quickly ran to retrieve his dagger and Josif ran behind him.

Salal pointed his sword at the bandit, warning him, "I will show you leniency. Go, now," he said. "Take your friend's body with you. Let that be a reminder to you and your thieving associates of what happens when you try to rob a soldier of the king."

The bandit whimpered as he hastily picked up his friend's life-less, bloodied body and ran off.

Salal helped up Josif, who was crouched behind him. "Are you okay?" he asked.

"I guess you're not such a bad soldier, after all," Josif said, brushing himself off.

"You know we don't accept anything less than excellent," Salal smiled. "Now we're even."

The two of them set about cleaning and packing their things, ready to continue to Beiros.

"I just hope you fight like that when the elves and the dead army come for us," Josif said.

SALAL FINISHED TELLING his story to Melhel and the prince, who were intrigued by everything he said. The prince had especially loved the end. "So, you killed the bandits robbing you?" he inquired.

"Just one of them," Salal answered modestly.

"Interesting. You know, Melhel and I had a similar situation on the way here from Chekkos, where he's from..."

"You mean *I* had a similar situation," Melhel interjected, cutting him off. "You sat in your carriage waiting for it all to finish. How many times must I remind you?"

Prince Sirhan gave Melhel a dirty look but continued. "And then what happened?"

Salal shrugged. "We made it here."

Melhel stood. "Thank you, Salal. You've been most gracious."

"The pleasure was all mine." Salal shook the hands of his inter-viewers and then Melhel showed him out, but not before Salal ducked back to grab another of Marissa's biscuits for his walk back to the barracks.

As he closed the door, Melhel sighed anxiously. What they had just learned seemed proof that the dead army were really coming. They would need to act fast to stop them.

"You know what this means?" he asked the prince.

149

"What?"

"I have to read those stories on the dead army. Do you know where I could find such things?"

Sirhan stared at him blankly. "The Library of Beiros, I suppose?"

Melhel rushed to grab his things and head for the door. "Fantastic," he exclaimed. "Let's go!"

CHAPTER 11

SCANDOS

While Melhel and Prince Sirhan had been investigating the dead army, Fares kept churning out equipment at an alarming rate, Queen Rania read to children, and King Michel talked fruitlessly with his advisers, the Scandosians had not forgotten how they had been slighted in the senate.

On his journey from Beiros, through the Grasslands, and up across the border to Scandos, all Ismal Haiya had thought about was how he could possibly get his revenge on Alexandros and the king.

It was a long carriage ride home to Stock, the Scandosian capital, so Ismal had plenty of time to mull over what had happened. He couldn't believe the king, the prince, and Fares had all been there to oppose him. He couldn't fathom how no other provinces had been willing to stand up to what he saw as Alexandrosian dominance — no, imperialism.

If you had asked any patriotic elf, with a sense of elvish pride and Scandosian nationalism they would call the country in which they lived not Nataaros, but the Alexandrosian Empire.

To the elves, King Michel and those before him were not just kings ruling a kingdom, they were emperors, overseeing a dominion of multiple nations, which now answered to their every desire. From their point of view, the kings controlled the wealth and military of the empire to suit their ambitions, and the provincial governors were mere puppets.

The kings and queens of Nataaros would not have put it that way. In the famous words King Michel used, when after the civil war he was asked if he would turn Nataaros into an empire and consolidate his power, "The only emperor of our land is Lah, and none are greater than he." It was straight from the Book: wisdom passed down on their native religion.

But to the Scandosians, those words were only pretty lies: many of them believed the race of men, and Alexandrosians specifically, hated elves and everything they stood for, and felt threatened by Scandos's prosperity. The elites of Scandos thought war was inevitable, now or someday, and were determined to be ready for when it was on their doorstep.

As the Scandosians fought and lost the civil war, being routed during the Siege of Beiros, Ismal had witnessed the heroics of Rafiq and Fares, and felt humiliated. Ismal felt he'd let his people down as a soldier and vowed to one day win the elves not only greater power in the senate, but their own state.

The Scandosians had always had their own identity, after all. Being elves, it wasn't just that they were different to men: they had an entirely different culture.

While Alexandros, for example, gave women relatively little status, exemplified by their general exclusion from important roles and the way Marissa had been nearly executed for merely sleeping with a man, Scandos was far more equal. Male and female elves alike had access to opportunity and justice. By contrast, Alexandros seemed backward to them.

Scandos treated wealth differently, too, taxing the rich and spreading it around. Medicine and education were free to all, administered by the provincial government. This was afforded by those higher taxes on the wealthy, who largely had no issue in paying. Granted, of whatever tax Scandos received as a province, a portion went back to Nataaros. Though Scandos had its own identity, it wasn't separate from Nataaros nor exempt from its laws, and the elves felt this held them back.

The provinces that sided more closely with Alexandros and the king saw things differently: while the king took a hands-on approach to governing Alexandros, Rios, Paros, and Venos, to them Scandos looked like it had been left to rule itself. So long as Scandos participated in the senate, paid its taxes, recognised the king as theirs and otherwise kept its mouth shut, Scandos was indeed free to do as it liked.

But this was not enough for Ismal, and if he had his way, everything would change. He had plenty of time, on the journey home, to think about what he would tell the politicians in Scandos, and to imagine their reactions to having their proposals blocked in the senate yet again.

~

WHEN ISMAL ARRIVED IN SCANDOS, he was always shocked by how beautiful it was. The comparison with Alexandros was stark.

Though Alexandros was lush with greenery, the Grasslands and Cedar Hills making its landscape worthy of painting, Scandos was snowy and mountainous all over, as though it were the festive season all year round.

The Snowy Mountains—where Lah was said to have lived, perching atop the highest point of the world he had created and given life to—encroached into Scandos, straddling the Alexandrosian border. Ismal regarded them as his carriage went on past, slowly, to better navigate the perpetual snow of Scandos.

While the Snowy Mountains tapered off further into Scandos, it didn't stop the rest of the province from being mountainous. In fact, Scandos's two major cities, Stock and Copen, stood behind mountain ranges, a strategic decision to better ward off invasion.

During the civil war, Alexandros and the king were never able to launch an invasion of Scandos: it was simply too cold and too risky a manoeuvre. The king won through his defence of Alexandros and Beiros, tiring and weakening the elves to the point of quitting—plus some ingenuity from Fares himself. But still, the Scandosians knew they were never likely to lose their lands or semi-autonomy. No one could ever attack them, and that gave them continual confidence.

As Ismal came along the edge of the Snowy Mountains towards Stock, from his elevated position but still far away, he saw the lights beaming from his home city. He could already picture the streets as people finished work and came home to their families.

The elves could enjoy whatever life they desired. Should they choose a family life, so be it. Should they choose to be in the military, so be it. Should they choose to live a life of service or solitude, then so be it. And they were proud that, unlike those of the other provinces, their people's destiny was not determined by their birth.

Melhel would have noticed none of his gripes in Scandos, chief among them their poor treatment of women. Female elves were freer than most human men, holding positions in government, the military, education, service — anything they would choose for themselves. They stood on equal ground to the males, and lacked none of their rights.

Men and women of all elven races were free to work where they pleased and marry whom they pleased. They could sit in public wherever they wanted. The death penalty had been long abolished, and adultery was not a crime. The wealthiest residents paid a higher provincial tax, funding medicine and education. Wealth was spread relatively evenly across all people. Unlike the other provinces, where there was an upper class and a lower class, in Scandos a large middle class bridged the gap between the downtrodden and the especially fortunate.

It was, in nearly all respects, a perfectly harmonious society, where freedom and equality reigned, and prosperity was shared by all. They knew neither debt nor hatred, only progress. And the Scandosians used this to their advantage in every negotiation and every senate meeting. Ismal and his fellow politicians would be damned if their way of life was going to be threatened or belittled, and they would surely not allow some "brutish Alexandrosians", as he would call them, impinge on their paradise.

Ismal arrived in Stock during the early hours of the morning. The workday had already begun, but the climate was so cold that it felt like a winter morning before dawn in the rest of Nataaros. At this time of year, the elves worked in the dark of the morning, and took for granted the lights brightening their lives. They felt the constant illumination made them function better as a society, letting them stay always alert and adaptable, and to work well in all conditions, especially in matters of war, which lately was always on their minds.

As Ismal stepped out and began to walk to the governor's palace in Stock, where he would meet with the governor of Scandos and other prominent figures, the deep snow slowed his strides slightly. He didn't feel the cold, having stayed in a thin, characteristically Scandosian silk robe and wearing no headdress to warm his scalp or protect his long, pointed ears from the cold. There were no gloves on his hands or anyone else's: this was the preferred climate for the elves—the icy-cold mountains of their home.

Ismal hated the warmer, sunnier temperature of Alexandros. There, he would often feel as though he was melting, and the whole world was against him and conspiring to hinder the elves' progress. If Ismal wasn't battling what he would call the "biased" senate, he vied against a sun that he felt was magic worked by the Alexandrosians to try and burn him and all elves who dared to leave the cold comfort of their homes. "Always up to their dirty tricks, those men," he would say, lambasting Alexandros. And then he would often reassure his fellow Scandosians, "Wait till they see what we have coming for them."

Now Ismal walked through the snow, watching all the passers-by go about their lives. He saw youths with piles of books in hand, laughing and conversing among one another as they make their way to their classes. He turned to look behind him at the markets, not as bustling or aggressively commercial as those of Alexandros, but operating with all the efficiency and affordability that Scandos prided itself on.

He would have stopped longer to admire all that his people had built in Stock, but Ismal knew he had a bigger job at hand. The governor would not be keen to wait when everything was at stake. All the city life that Ismal saw, and all that they had built, was on the line. His meetings here at home and later in the dreaded senate would shape the lives of the elves for generations to come. He and the governor had much to discuss.

~

MALA HABEB, the governor, was in her office at the palace. Of all the women of Scandos, she was by far the most resilient, ruthless, cunning, and determined. It was not uncommon for a Scandosian governor or politician to be female, but whenever one appeared at a major event outside the province, it struck others as strange. No other province seemed to appreciate equality between the sexes as Scandos did.

Mala still reeled from the civil war. She had never fought in it, for Scandosian women were still kept from the army, but that didn't mean she'd had no stake. She was already a senator at the time, and had watched as her people and her soldiers grasped at victory but crumbled and lost everything. It was under her leadership that Scandos had been rebuilt, and the people thanked her for it nearly every day. No politician in Nataaros was more loved by the people.

What set her apart from someone like Ismal was her pacifism. She had never wanted Scandos to enter the civil war, and was never as gung-ho as her fellow politicians. Mala had advocated for diplomacy on the eve of the war, and only changed her position reluctantly when her pushes for negotiation came to naught. Even now, as governor, she was committed to pushing for change peacefully. This was why Ismal and his fellow senators had been presenting bills and reforms, rather than agitating for another war. It was all Mala's doing.

However, as peaceful as she may have been, she also knew that war must be waged sometimes. While she had preached being peaceful and negotiating, she was clear that any deliberate act of aggression by the king or his people would be seen as provocation and an act of war. Mala would not hesitate to have Scandos fight back. That steely core had gotten her to where she was—she had eliminated many political opponents along the way by having them thrown in prison for the rest of their lives, and every time she framed it to herself as a moral necessity. And it was not entirely ruthless: they would not go to that "wretched prison" in Venos, as she would call it, nor to the gladiatorial games, which the elves also loathed, but to a Scandosian prison where the prisoners were treated with dignity and taught to reform themselves, even if they were guilty of crimes against Scandos.

But despite the relative leniency with which her enemies were punished, the unsparing streak in Mala had gotten her to the governor's office. She was the perfect blend of peaceful and strong. Everyone knew this, including Ismal—who was even a little bit afraid of her. Now he was outside the doors of her palace, he took a big gulp, and knocked on the door, dreading what was to come.

Guards appeared to usher him inside, one each to his left and right. It wasn't needed: though he was bold enough to taunt the king in the senate, he dared not show force or even much resistance to his governor. If anything, this showed his contempt for the monarchy and his belief in Scandosian supremacy. Ismal wasn't the only Scandosian like this: most of the senators were both blindingly proud of their nation while abroad, and fearful of Mala while at home. It wasn't that she was violent—on the surface at least, she was as gentle as her reputation for pacifism would suggest. But she could be intimidating when she wanted to, even loud. You didn't want to hear her loud.

Granted, Mala thought the efforts in the senate fruitless. "What weak elves I send on diplomacy," she would bemoan. She knew that for them to achieve their goals, Scandos's representatives had to be stronger, and she intended to remind Ismal of this.

When they reached the door to Mala's office, one of the guards stepped ahead of Ismal to open it, hiding the senator behind his bulk.

The governor looked up from her papers to the doorway. "Is he here?" she asked.

"Yes, governor," the guard said, nodding.

From behind him, Ismal made himself known. "Governor, how

long it's been," he said, stepping out from behind the guard and extending his hand.

"About six weeks since I last sent you to that hole," the governor said standing to shake Ismal's hand.

Ismail shuddered when thinking of Beiros. "Oh, you have no idea of what I saw!" he complained. "King Michel has really let the place go."

"And I bet that old fool is as stubborn as ever," Mela said with a smirk, then gestured to the guards. "You may leave us now."

The guards promptly exited the office.

When they were on their own, Mala offered Ismal a seat, which he gladly took, after his long journey, though the governor remained standing. "Tell me, how is the king?" she asked.

"Good. Annoying, but good."

"And the queen?"

"I rarely saw her," Ismal said. "She kept going out on her philanthropic missions. A load of shit, if you ask my opinion."

"No, she really does care," Mala disagreed. "At least someone in that family does. The world knows Michel has stopped caring, and as for their brat of a son…"

"He's even brattier now," Ismal interjected. "He's developed an attitude. No doubt he's been groomed to be just like his father."

Mala shook her head. "No matter. We won't let them get in the way of our plans." She paced around the office while Ismal sat rather uncomfortably, having to turn continually to make eye contact with her. "The king has again rejected our bill, yes?"

"Yes."

"And he refuses to acknowledge us as autonomous?"

"More or less."

"How many times has this been the case?"

"I think this is my seventh time being sent to Beiros," Ismal said sourly.

"Seven times we have been rejected," Mala mused. "And seven times the so-called king of Nataaros has ignored the wish of one of his provinces. We want independence—he says no. We asked for autonomy—he refuses. So, we compromise and ask for greater representation in the senate—and does he give it to us?"

"No."

"No, indeed," she cried. "What's my reputation in the senate?"

Ismal's face burned. "Do you want the honest answer?"

"Please," she said. "You know I prefer honesty."

"They think that while you are an intelligent and good leader, you're too weak-willed to ever seriously push for reform—that you are too shaken up to ever march and begin another civil war."

Mala considered this and faced away from Ismal, hand to her chin, pondering the accusation.

"They're right, you know," she said. "I hated the war, and that those idiots decided to wage war on the king. Because of them, thousands died on both sides. Not soldiers, but innocent people who had nothing to do with it.

"We elves are meant to be better than humans. While they crave violence and bloodshed, we crave peace and honour. But to say I'm weak-willed..." She paused at the sting of the insult. "Wow. I would never have expected they would think this. Scandos is what it is today because of me. After those animals destroyed our armies, we had no hope. It is because of me that we are in this position."

She turned back and faced Ismal, who shrank away from her in his chair, fearing her aggression.

"Absolutely," he agreed. "Anyone can see what a great leader you are. Anyone can see how strong you are."

"You know what it is?" Mala chuckled half-heartedly as she realised something. "I'm a woman. They feared our old governor during the war. Because he was a man. They're yet to take women seriously in that world. Well, I'm about to make them."

"What do you plan to do?" Ismal asked.

"While you were gone, I had a thought about who I am as a governor," she said. "Peace has been fantastic. It has brought us wealth, but it hasn't led us anywhere else. We're still where we were after the war, albeit richer. Peace can only get you so far. If you want something, you have to grab it."

Ismal quailed. "Are you suggesting another war?"

"I have taken measures to prepare for an invasion," she revealed. "When we are ready, and when the king and those fools in the senate again reject our demands for greater representation, we will march on Alexandros."

"But last time we lost everything," Ismal pleaded. "You saw what they did to us on the battlefield. It ruined us. Don't go to war. You're better than this!"

"Last time, our leaders were naive and didn't know their enemy. Yes, I saw what they did to us, and I'll be well prepared for it."

Ismal stood and stared into Mala's piercing blue eyes. "And if we lose? They're preparing for war, too. They're better soldiers; they live for war and violence. In fact, Fares Barak is running their armoury."

"Good!" Mala exclaimed gleefully. "We can finally have our revenge on him."

"But what if we lose?"

"I have a contingency plan," she reassured him.

"What is it?"

"All I can say is that it will change the world as we know it, and we will finally achieve our dreams. Whether we win this war or not, we will still be victorious in end. It will be a new day for Scandos and the elves." She beamed. "Our ancestors have waited for this moment for a long time. Now, it is coming."

Pleasantly surprised, Ismal took a deep breath. He was rather happy to see Mala willingly take the fight to Alexandros and King Michel. Like-minded Scandosians would similarly love to hear the governor had decided to fight fire with fire, as they had often called on her to, and take revenge on the Alexandrosians for what had happened at the Siege of Beiros. That day had changed the lives of all elves, and nearly ruined their country. The king's comeuppance would be sweet.

ISMAL RAN HOME IMMEDIATELY to begin writing his new bill for the senate, which was due to meet again in the coming weeks.

With permission from the governor herself, Ismal was to be more ruthless in his demands for autonomy. Scandos as a province was to threaten the king that war may come and more blood would be spilled if they didn't get their way.

Mala had asked nothing about the dead army, and Ismal hadn't volunteered the news. Neither of them believed it was a genuine threat, or that it had anything to do with their plans. The Alexandrosians could deal with their own myths. Scandos had bigger and realer concerns, and its leaders had no intention of letting superstition get in the way of their designs.

CHAPTER 12
UNLOCKING THE PAST

T hose who loved Alexandros and its king now faced threats from all directions, though outside of the orbit of the senate, the army, and the court, they may not have known it.

But Melhel and Prince Sirhan knew full well that Scandos wasn't going to back down from its demands, and that the dead army loomed beyond Alhayit. So they and Marissa scoured the Library of Beiros tirelessly for information.

Marissa, perhaps unexpectedly a swift and voracious reader, kept her head buried in book after book at a desk while Melhel and Fares hunted down anything they could find on the dead army throughout the bookshelves.

"Anything, Marissa?" Melhel asked, turning his head to her.

"No," she said, disappointed. "Nothing. That's got to be at least the fifth book I've skimmed through to find any hint of a dead army, but there's nothing in this one either." She tossed it aside, placing her head in her hands in frustration.

Prince Sirhan was busy analysing every book title he saw. "What *did* you find, Marissa?" he called from the shelves.

"I know of Beilos's conquests. I know of what this land used to be called..."

"What was it called?" Melhel interjected.

"Phoenicos," Marissa answered. "It was a republic that stood for hundreds of years. Everyone lived here, the earliest Alexandrosians, Parosians, Riosans, Venosians, and eventually Scandosians. They had a bunch of civil wars before Beilos conquered them and united us into a kingdom."

Prince Sirhan laughed. "Hm, civil wars. Sounds like nothing has changed."

"Does any of it have anything to do with the dead army?" Melhel asked.

"No," Marissa said.

"Then keep looking," Melhel said.

Marissa stood up, a little bit annoyed at Melhel's abrasiveness. "I, for one, think it's rather interesting," she maintained.

Melhel carried on sifting through what he could find, "I'm sure it is," he said. "I'll be sure to educate my kids on it, provided they don't die in a war with the dead army. And the only way we can stop that is if we find the right damned book!"

In anger he slammed his palm against a bookshelf with a loud bang that made everyone in the library turn in his direction with annoyance.

"I'm only trying to help," she said, herself irritated by Melhel's mood. "If you want me to leave, I can leave."

Melhel let out a sigh and turned to face Marissa. "No," he said. "I'm sorry. I'm just frustrated. We can't find anything on this stupid dead army, and meanwhile we have a bunch of pretentious elves on our backs."

Prince Sirhan looked at Melhel, aggrieved. "You're complaining? I'm the poor one who's going to become king and have to deal with it all someday."

"And I'm gonna be the poor blacksmith who's going to make all the equipment to help you," Melhel retorted. "You're not the only one with problems."

The prince lowered his head. "You're right. And as long as Marissa is by my side, there's no problem that can weigh me down."

Marissa blushed and Melhel rolled his eyes. "Come on," he urged. "Let's get back to this."

Hours went by and they still had no luck. It had grown late and the library was all but empty: the patrons had all left, and only they remained, at the order of the prince.

Their search seemed bound to be fruitless, until Marissa, having churned through at least her eighth book, had a realisation.

"Do we have any confirmation that the dead army is real?" she asked. "I mean, before Salal?"

Melhel and Prince Sirhan looked at each other and shrugged.

"Not that I'm aware of," the prince said. "I think it's just all myth and speculation at this point."

Marissa jumped up, eager to present her eureka moment. "That's exactly it."

"What's it?" Melhel wondered.

"We've been looking in the wrong section."

"Wrong section?" the prince was confused.

Marissa tried to grab the boys to hurry up and get moving, "This whole time we've been going through history books," she began. "But the dead army aren't history. They're a myth, a folktale, at this point. We've got to go to the sections where all the myths are."

Melhel and Prince Sirhan stared at each other in confusion, but both figured they had nothing to lose, and nothing to gain from continuing to search where they were.

"Beauty and brains!" Prince Sirhan marvelled as they ran after Marissa, who by now was way ahead of them, both mentally and literally. Surprisingly, she was quite the sprinter.

WHILE THE YOUNGER GENERATION FORMED A NEW golden trio to hunt down solutions, the older generation seemed to rest on its laurels.

In the face of the threats facing him and his kingdom, Fares felt the only thing he could do was work, keeping up the quality and professionalism to fulfil the king's expectations. Beyond that, he would have to rely on what his nephew, who had seemed to take it upon himself to tackle the army of the dead, reported of events outside the armoury.

The king and queen sat seemingly on the sidelines, worrying about the quotidian details of rule and administration, leaving the prospect of war to Rafiq and the dead army to whichever lunatic took up the task—in this case, Melhel.

Still, there was a lot on King Michel's mind. Although he took a hands-off approach to war and even monitoring the senate, he still cared deeply for his kingdom.

He and his queen now sat together in his throne room, alone. There were no senators or advisers, and not even Rafiq protecting them. It was late at night, and while their son and his friends tired themselves in finding every secret of the land, King Michel and Queen Rania reflected on more than two decades of rule.

"My darling," King Michel said, looking at Rania. "Am I a good king? I thought I had already given everything to my kingdom, after the civil war. Hadn't I put an end to all the bloodshed and hatred? And now it seems to be coming my way once again."

Queen Rania looked her husband in the eyes and laid her hands in his, smiling. Hers was the only smile that could really comfort and soften him. "My king," she said, "I am so proud to call myself your queen. Where others would have fallen, it was you who rose up to defend this city, this kingdom, and everything our ancestors built."

She held his hands tight as she praised him. "Everyone that lives and breathes in this kingdom owes it all to you. I never saw such leadership from a king before you, the man I fell in love with."

The queen ran her fingers through his now-unkempt grey hair.

King Michel sighed, "I did terrible things to achieve this. Terrible, terrible things."

"We've all done things that we're not proud of," Queen Rania reassured him. "You. Me. The Scandosians. Everyone. No one is perfect and we've all made mistakes. What matters is how we learn from them and improve."

"I ordered the deaths of so many elves," the king lamented, turning his head from her. "Innocents dead at my hand. It's no wonder Fares and many others wanted nothing to do with me for so long."

Queen Rania gently took his face in her hands to make him look at her again. "And what have you done since?" she asked. "You have helped rebuild Scandos and turn it into the prosperous province that it is. They govern themselves, they have their own language still, their own culture and history. You could have wiped it all away, erased it from the history books and from the world, but you didn't. I doubt many would've been so merciful."

The king stood slowly and paced around the room, reflecting on what his wife had said. For the first time in a long time, King Michel felt the world resting on his shoulders, and found himself desperate and out of his depth.

"Then why do they insist on independence?" he asked. "You say I have given them a lot, that I have helped them prosper, yet still they want more, and they undermine me and the kingdom."

"Some people don't know when to quit," Queen Rania answered. "I have no doubt you will reach a solution peacefully. Governor Mala is a kind and just woman. If you write to her, I'm sure she will be willing to discuss the matter at hand."

King Michel considered it for a moment. "It could work. But I fear she has that snake Ismal Haiya in her hearing. I have never liked him. If I wanted to, I could have him removed from the senate, but I show kindness and fairness—and he does nothing but make trouble."

Queen Rania stood herself and faced the king. "I trust she will not listen to him," she said. "For decades she has helped build up Scandos with your aid. She wouldn't turn her back on you for a bitter man full of hate and contempt."

"I'm not too sure. Haiya has a way of persuading people. He's already got a majority of the Scandosian senators behind his agenda. I fear Mala Habeb may soon yet be under this spell."

"Then beat him to it," Queen Rania urged. "Write to her. Tell her you're willing to discuss terms."

King Michel shook his head. "I can't. If I do, I will be admitting my fault in all this, and I may be giving up Scandos as a province and starting perhaps another civil war entirely."

Queen Rania felt almost ashamed. "That's it? You're going to let your pride prevent any hope of peace?" she lambasted him. "You don't have to do any of what you just said; you're just frightened of being negotiable."

She was right. No one knew the king like she did. "Please, my love," she said, "write to Governor Mala. Write to her and tell her you can discuss an arrangement, on *your* terms. Save Nataaros."

The king's head drooped, as it often did when the queen had proven him wrong. He could not reminisce about all the good he had done for Scandos to make up for the war, and then turn around and give up trying for peace because of pride.

"I'm willing to organise some agreement. After all, I've always been approachable," he said. "But I won't give them what they want."

Queen Rania smiled. "I'm not asking you to," she said. "No one is. Just that you at least talk to Mala and hear her out. She may realise that being a province of Nataaros is still the best thing for Scandos. You can only know if you talk with her."

"Okay," he said. "But if she can't agree to our terms, then any deal is off."

"That's fine. At least you'll have shown you're willing to negotiate."

∿

MELHEL AND PRINCE Sirhan now found themselves sifting through the sections on myths and folktales in the library, as Marissa had suggested.

Again, she had her head buried in the pages at a nearby table while the others threw her any book they could find that might be relevant.

"Anything?" Melhel asked her.

"No," she said. "Not in this one. Just stories on the werewolves that supposedly live in Rios."

"Werewolves," Prince Sirhan scoffed. "What a load of nonsense."

"After everything we've seen and heard," Melhel said. "I

wouldn't rule it out. Who knows, maybe one day we can investigate that too."

Prince Sirhan grinned. "Have fun with that."

Marissa called out to them as she stumbled upon something. "This is interesting," she said. "Werewolves are only created artificially, by magic. No one is born a wolf. This applies to all creatures of myth, it says." She looked up pensively. "I wonder if this applies to the dead army."

Melhel remembered the scout's report. "Salal did say there was a hooded man or figure," he said. "Maybe he had something to do with creating the dead army."

"Maybe," Prince Sirhan agreed. "Would've been nice to have had Salal with us tonight."

"Leave him be," Melhel said. "He's been through a lot. Let him rest."

"Rest?" the prince was angered. "What rest? He's a soldier. He should act like it."

Melhel laughed. "Says the one who won't see a day of combat in his life."

"Enough, both of you," Marissa intervened.

Melhel and Prince Sirhan didn't stop bickering, but they did at least lower their voices. Arguing would not change that they were stuck in the library in the middle of the night. It didn't help anyone to have them argue. And, though they may not have admitted it openly, Marissa had a pacifying effect on both of them, especially the prince.

"Still doesn't excuse his weakness," Sirhan grumbled.

"Well, you can let him know how you feel when you see him next," Melhel said as a parting shot, looking the prince in the eyes. "I'm sure it'll do wonders for his morale."

Just as Fares was the only person who could be upfront with the king, Melhel was taking on the same role with Prince Sirhan. The prince may not have particularly enjoyed Melhel's honesty, but he was learning to respect it.

"Careful, now," Prince Sirhan warned. "Or else I'll have to send you to the battlefield."

"We'll probably have better luck if you do." Melhel said, "So, by all means, send me there."

Marissa shot out of her chair, her face red with frustration. "Will you both shut up!" she yelled. "For the sake of my sanity, stop fighting. If neither of you quit it, I'll kick you both out of the library and do this myself. Lah knows I've already been doing all the work here."

Melhel was slightly frightened by Marissa's outburst. She may have been his subordinate, but that didn't mean her quick temper couldn't scare him.

The prince, on the other hand, was rather impressed by his new love's resolve. "I love it when you're angry, my dear."

"Good," she scowled. "Now, stop being so self-absorbed and start being useful."

Melhel couldn't help but crack a smile. "Does the queen yell at the king like this behind closed doors?" he taunted Prince Sirhan.

Prince Sirhan squared up to Melhel, his taller frame towering over the smith, and stared him down. "Careful, Melhel," he said. "Your mouth is going to get you in trouble one day."

Melhel didn't back down, and stared right back at the prince, letting him know he considered them equals and intimidation wouldn't work.

"The king probably isn't as annoying," Marissa quipped. "The same way your uncle isn't as annoying as you are." Melhel's smirk quickly vanished. Marissa rolled her eyes and gave up, choosing to get back to investigating, "It's like I'm dealing with a bunch of little boys."

Prince Sirhan grinned and offered his hand to Melhel, "Marissa's right," he said. "But we must work together. After all, we'll need you for a long time."

"I don't exactly have a say in the matter," Melhel said begrudgingly as he shook the prince's hand.

The two of them got back to hunting down books, while Marissa gave them the silent treatment, doubly focused on her reading.

By the time they were already halfway to dawn, the three of them were beginning to fall asleep and still thought they had achieved nothing. Melhel sat down at a desk to rest for a few moments and ended up nodding off, falling asleep with his head resting on his arms.

Sirhan and Marissa continued searching at a leaden pace. Marissa could barely keep her eyes open as she tried to keep reading, and could barely understand the words, which were to now almost indecipherable shapes. It was as though she was reading Scandosian and not the common language—as though she had forgotten how to read entirely. She had even caught herself drooling on a page when she closed her eyes for a moment, and was contemplating using the biggest book at her disposal as a makeshift pillow.

The prince wasn't even looking at the titles any longer, but simply grabbing books at random and instinctively either throwing it on the ground or on the table for Marissa to haplessly read. His fingertips had grown numb to the feeling of the bindings, and his arms were heavy from grabbing volumes from the shelves.

All hope of ever finding anything here seemed lost. It must be time to quit and go home. In the morning, after some rest, perhaps they could think of another approach to the problem of the dead army—one found anywhere but in books. And then Sirhan, having thoughtlessly wandered into the children's section, pulled out a book titled, *The Dead Army Beyond Alhayit*. It was a version of a famous children's story, from which many Alexandrosians learned the myth of the dead army while growing up, and formed their superstitious beliefs about its existence.

Rubbing his eyes, Prince Sirhan realised what he had grabbed and perked up. "I think I've found something!" he exclaimed. "That dreaded nursery tale!"

Marissa roused herself to see what he was holding. "Finally!" She beamed. "This wasn't all for nothing."

Melhel was still fast asleep without a care in the world, in dreams relishing the escape from all the problems he had to face.

The prince had other ideas. "Wake up, idiot!" he cried as he shook his friend awake.

Melhel leapt to his feet, frightened but ready to fight. "What is it? The dead army? Are they here?" All those books had primed him to expect a threat.

"No, you moron," Marissa yawned. "Prince Sirhan has found a

book on the dead army. The children's book where this myth came from."

Melhel calmed down but was bemused. "Oh, well, that's good." He stretched as he woke up. "What now?"

"Now, we sleep," Marissa said. "Tomorrow, we can read through it."

"Why not now?"

"I'll kill you before you can force me to read another book tonight."

"Good point," Melhel concurred. "Grab what we've found and let's get out. I'll explain the mess to the librarian tomorrow."

Between them they gathered every book that Marissa had found anything relevant in, and she and Melhel left the library with teetering piles in heavily laden arms.

As they both moved off to begin the journey home, a dumb-founded Prince Sirhan finally found what he thought a fitting comeback to Melhel's impudence. "I don't need your encourage-ment, Melhel!" the prince called out after them, "Just your loyalty."

Then he ran up quickly behind his companions, who were beaming wearily at the thought they had made some progress and could finally get home and get some rest. Melhel then escorted Sirhan to the palace gates, before he and Marissa doubled back to the Baraks' place.

MELHEL AND MARISSA took care not to make any loud noises as they stepped inside their home. Melhel closed the door with unchar-acteristic gentleness, and Marissa made sure they both removed their shoes at the door to quieten their footsteps.

But their efforts were for naught—the lights were on, and Melhel's guard went up. "Someone's here," he said. "Did we leave the door unlocked? Did Uncle leave it unlocked?"

"Maybe it *is* your uncle," Marissa whispered.

"No way. You know him: he's an early sleeper."

Convinced it was an intruder, Melhel readied his sword and

slowly walked further into the house, with Marissa close behind him.

But when he had tiptoed his way into the kitchen, he saw Fares sitting there with a cup of tea.

"Argh!" Melhel screamed in startled frustration.

Fares looked at him with amusement. "What is wrong with you?" he asked. "And why is your sword out?"

"I thought you were an intruder."

"Why would I be an intruder?"

"Well, since when are you up this late?" Melhel asked.

"No—since when were *you* up this late? Where were you?"

"We were at the library," Marissa explained.

"This late?" said Fares.

"It took us literally all day to find what we were after," Melhel replied.

Fares's curiosity moved him to his feet. "And what was it?"

"We were investigating the dead army," Melhel said. "And we thought we'd find something in the library."

"And…?" Fares asked.

"We don't know, yet," Marissa said. "Tomorrow we'll need to read up on what we found."

"Okay," Fares nodded. "Was anyone with you?"

"Yes, the prince," Melhel said.

"Oh," Fares said, lowering his tone. "I see."

"Why?" the younger Barak asked, wondering at Fares's disappointment.

"Nothing," Fares said, sitting back down. "Just thought he'd have other things to do. He probably came as an excuse to see Marissa."

"I don't think it was just for that." Marissa was a little insulted on the prince's behalf. "He's smart, you know."

Fares scoffed. "But do you think he cares about anything other than himself?"

"Whether he does or not, he was still there," Melhel interjected. "And if I'm defending him, it means I think he had honest intentions."

Melhel sat down across from his uncle. "Besides, like Marissa said, at least he was there. Where were you tonight?"

"You ask a lot of questions," Fares rebuffed him. "Maybe you should learn to just shut your mouth."

Melhel and Marissa were appalled. "Are you serious?" Melhel exclaimed. "Me, shut my mouth?" He stood again, leaning towards his uncle with his hands on the table. He raised his voice as he continued. "I've been running around with Marissa and the prince until who knows what hour it is, trying to save the kingdom. You want to know where *we* were, but the moment I ask where *you* were all night, you mean to tell me to stop asking questions?"

Fares sighed. He knew he was in the wrong, and there was little he could say in response.

"What's the matter, Uncle?" Melhel asked.

Marissa stood back slightly, scared she was about to watch them brawl, something she wanted no part of. She'd rather have gone to bed and simply continued with their work the next morning. But that luxury would be denied her if a screaming match was on its way.

Fares chose not to bite back. Instead, from his pocket he pulled out a sheet of paper and slid it across the table. This puzzled the young man, until he picked it up and read it. Unfolded, the small letter said,

Fares Barak. You will pay for your sins in due time. We do not forgive. Nor do we forget. The blood you spilled will be avenged. The lives you ruined will be avenged. On the twenty-fifth anniversary of that day, you will rue your actions. May your false god, Lah, offer your wretched life some peace.

A death threat. Melhel's face froze. And for the first time since he had been a baby, he was moved to the verge of tears in front of his uncle, fearing for the safety of the man who had been a father to him.

Marissa now stood behind Melhel, trying to read the letter over his shoulder. He passed it on, and her reaction was equally of shock.

Fearful, she covered her mouth with her hands as she looked at Fares.

"When did you get this?" Melhel asked.

"Today," Fares answered. "At the workshop."

"Who sent it?"

Fares didn't answer.

"Who sent it?!" Melhel demanded again.

"I don't know," Fares said.

"Don't lie to me. You know!" Melhel cried. Fares looked down. His nephew had called his bluff. And more than that, Melhel could guess the sender for himself. "It was Scandosians, wasn't it?" he asked.

Again, Fares wouldn't answer.

"How dare they," Melhel said, clenching his fists. "How dare they threaten my family?"

"You don't know the full story, Melhel!" Fares yelled.

"What full story? They lost a war, and now they're mad about it."

"It's bigger than that," Fares said quietly, trying to calm Melhel. "Much bigger."

That stopped Melhel for a moment. Marissa put her hands on his shoulders to try and relax him.

Then Melhel remembered the reception Fares had received since they moved to Beiros. "This is about the siege, isn't it?" Melhel asked. "About why they say you're the hero."

"Yes," Fares said softly.

"That elf in the senate didn't seem to think you were the hero," Melhel remembered. "Why?"

Fares took a sip of his tea before getting up, pouring a cup for Melhel and Marissa, and handing it to them. He then went to sit back down and gestured for the other two to do the same. "Take a seat," He said.

Melhel and Marissa looked at each other before deciding to take Fares up on his offer.

"It's time I told you about what happened all those years ago," Fares said.

CHAPTER 13
THE SIEGE OF BEIROS

T wenty-five years before those days of dead armies, petulant princes, and death threats, Alexandros—and Nataaros as a whole—had faced the biggest threat since Beilos went and conquered it all.

The war had raged on for years at this point, and most battles were merely skirmishes along the border between Scandos and Alexandros.

Other provinces had flipped back and forth in their allegiance, depending on who was winning or could promise more to its allies after victory.

Scandos's wealth had let it amass a strong army with archers and missile weapons at its core. Elves were known to be the most accurate long-range fighters in history, they were well trained, and theirs was as large an army as anything the king could muster.

But their camaraderie and sense of purpose lifted the elves above the soldiers of the king's army. They fought not just for their lives, but their vision of the future. If you want to unite people, you need to give them a common enemy or a common interest. Scandos had both: an enemy in Alexandros and King Michel, and a common interest in autonomy and independence.

All it took to galvanise the Scandosians for war was for their elite to point at Alexandros and the king and say, "This is who is keeping us from independence. Let us unite and defeat them, so we may finally achieve our centuries-old dream."

While for years the war was a stalemate, with no one achieving much beyond exhausting their resources, it was Scandos that eventually landed a decisive blow to turn the war in their favour.

Northwest of Beiros, where Scandos met Alexandros, an army of tens of thousands of elves crossed the mountains into Alexandros, where the king's army was camped.

The elves had the advantage of high ground and in their scouting could see not only Beiros and its walls, but the camps around it. That let them flank the Alexandrosians and their allies to catch them off-guard. By the time the king's army realised the Scandosians had crossed the mountains and were heading for them, it was too late, and they had to hastily take up defensive formations to try and hold them off.

Every camp in the vicinity was warned. Archers were ready at the back, working out their aim to try and halt Scandos's progress. Alexandros's infantry lined up across the front of their position, ready to meet Scandos's army head-on and stop them there and then.

Cavalry flanked the infantry on either side, holding back for now, but ready with strong horses to charge the Scandosian line once it looked like breaking. This was the defensive tactic the king's army began with, sure it would work.

Except it didn't.

From their higher positions on the hills and mountains, with glee the Scandosian generals saw that their counterparts had assumed a defensive formation—the Alexandrosians had taken the bait.

Scandos had no intention of engaging Alexandros head-on. They could not beat them in a battle of infantry. No, their strength was their advanced archery. They saw the line of infantry and cavalry at the front, and licked their lips at the easy pickings. Without hesitation, Scandos's elite archers spread themselves out and took aim.

The Alexandrosian generals saw the enemy wasn't moving, and

grew worried that they had stumbled into a trap. Scandos's army was too far away for them to see, so all they could do was wait nervously and see what would happen. They couldn't go up the hills and attack: that would've been suicide. Nor could they retreat, which would have left their rear exposed. They could only sit and wait.

On the hills, Scandos's archers drew and fired. Their bows and arrows were made with a new technology that gave them greater travel without losing any speed or power. Whether it was fifty or five hundred and fifty yards away, the arrows could pierce their targets. Alexandros's sitting duck of an army was the perfect first victim of this advancement.

The arrows rained on Alexandros like a storm, and just like that, a quarter of the army was wiped out and the rest was exposed. The arrow storm had put the troops in disarray, and they routed, running for their lives towards Beiros and an escape from the hell they found themselves in.

Just like that, Scandos had won the battle without even having to move forward and engage the Alexandrosian line. The elves now had a free run to Beiros, where they could execute their ultimate plan to lay siege to the city, hoping to starve the people out and force the king's surrender.

When King Michel got word that his army had been routed and Scandos was on its way, he was in a state of near panic as he began his city for a siege. This was to be the biggest test in his then short reign.

~

ABOUT A WEEK after their resounding victory in the field, Scandos's forces had moved through Alexandros and closed in on Beiros.

They set up camp not far from the city, knowing its defences were weak and the king's army was already on the brink of capitulation. The Scandosian generals on the ground then drew up plans for the siege.

The Scandosians built a wall around the outer edges of Beiros's surrounds, trapping themselves in with the city and its inhabitants.

This was a cunning trick, as the elves had enough supplies to last them months on end, and lines back to their own territory, while Beiros was cut off and poorly provisioned. Scandos could drag out the siege for as long as it needed, while Beiros would be desperate to end it quickly.

With the double wall around Beiros, communication and supplies could not go in or out. No general within the city could call for reinforcements, for letters would simply be intercepted by the Scandosians camped outside. If the king's allies saw the siege, the Scandosians' outer wall would block their path as they tried to render aid, while an extensive defence ensured no one could sandwich Scandos between the wall and their hostile captives.

Anyone on the outside could see pikes and spikes sticking up from the wall all over, rendering any attempts to climb it suicide. The ground around the wall was rigged with traps, including pits, bear traps, and retractable blades. And along with the armies assaulting the city, other units patrolled the edges of the wall, ready to attack anyone trying to relieve Beiros.

For the townspeople, the siege was a living hell. They could no longer leave the gates, for they'd have been massacred if they so dared, in revenge for the killings of elves the king had ordered during the civil war. Beirosians could no longer go to the marketplace to buy food or supplies, as everything was rationed. Their farmlands and crops were ravaged. They had become prisoners in their own city, and their time under siege was spent on the brink of death. Beiros, which had been the hub of an entire kingdom, was reduced to madness.

When soldiers walked the streets, readying the defences, everywhere a foul stench polluted the air. People hadn't bathed in days or weeks. No one ate properly, being reduced to one meal a day. They were all malnourished and impoverished. Businesses and institutions closed down; the masses were out of work and out of money. With the local economy crippled, the city began to look more like a wasteland than a metropolis.

The senate hadn't met in a long time. Politicians living Beiros hid in their homes, and some even took to their beds, lying near-catatonic while they waited for it all to end. King Michel and Queen

Rania spent more and more of each passing day within the castle, refusing to speak to anyone who didn't have good news—which, after the first week of the siege, meant speaking to no one at all. There was nothing to report but death, disease, and dissolution.

It wasn't a violent siege, in that the Scandosians were not taking up arms or attacking Beiros's walls or infrastructure. They simply waited for the people to starve and the king to surrender and give in to their demands.

Only the elves that lived in Beiros were afforded any refuge; if they could get past the guard and escaped the city walls, their fellows outside would offer them safe passage to Scandos, where they were told to wait until victory and freedom came their way.

The Siege of Beiros went on, slowly turning in Scandos's favour. Barring a miracle, it looked like King Michel would have to relent and surrender, giving in to whatever demands Scandos made. If he chose otherwise, Beiros would surely crumble and Nataaros with it. And no king, including Michel, wanted to be known to history as the one that lost his kingdom.

SEVERAL MONTHS INTO THE SIEGE, Beiros was on its last legs, as its food and supplies were nearly spent. You couldn't walk the streets without hearing wailing as people begged for even a measly piece of bread. But no one had a piece to spare.

The stench in the air was no longer of uncleanliness, but was now the smell of death. Bodies began to litter the streets. Funerals could not be arranged, as the city lacked the means to bury people appropriately, according to their laws and customs, within the city walls. They couldn't even commit the sacrilege of cremating the dead, as there wasn't enough wood to build funeral pyres, unless they took to tearing apart carts and buildings. Even then, no one was prepared to make the smell even worse, and further pollute the air, by burning a body. Instead, the dead were stuffed in corners and alleys along the streets, the best option in the worst situation.

Those that were still living became gaunt. Alexandrosians, known for their stocky builds and hearty eating habits, withered away to skeletons, as though the dead had come to life. Even the dead army that Salal would encounter years from now looked more human than many Beirosians did then. People came to fantasise about death. Whispers of mass suicide passed among the population, which King Michel—whose spirits roused as the crisis intensified—became adamant not to allow. He set more troops to patrol the streets to prevent a coup, a mass suicide, or any other kind of madness that sprang up among the people. There was panic in this, as it meant less people to defend the city, and increased the likelihood that the siege would end with Scandos breaching the walls, but at least the king was taking action.

And yet, while his people suffered, King Michel was still quite literally living like a king, holed up in his castle with Queen Rania by his side and as much of the city's remaining supplies as he desired at his disposal. Prince Sirhan was not yet born, as the king and queen were still relatively newly married, and succession was among the king's top priorities. He wanted to keep himself and his queen alive long enough that he could father a son to take over as his heir. He would keep himself and his queen healthy even if those on the streets had no such option.

As cruel as this may have sounded, the king no longer neglected his people, and had mustered faith that he could win the siege. He planned not for defeat, but for victory.

And he did, indeed, now have a plan to turn the siege in their favour. Had it gotten out, though, it would have spelled the Beirosians' doom. So it remained a secret known only to the king and his most important commanders, Fares and Rafiq. To them was entrusted the execution of the plan, and the king now waited patiently for them as they prepared underground where no one would know.

All the king's eggs were in that basket. If the plan worked, they would win the war. If not, everything Beilos the Conqueror had won would be lost.

Mind you, it was not exactly the *king's* plan, but Fares's. This was the zenith of his military genius, and the king, seeing as much, had put the fate of Nataaros in his hands. It all came down to Fares.

IN THE MOST HIDDEN AND secluded part of Beiros, deep underground and under heavy guard, Fares was working with Rafiq and a group of Riosan scientists to save the city.

Their laboratory was so well hidden, no one outside the project knew it existed. The Scandosians would never have attempted the siege had they known of this place. It was the king's best-kept secret, which he thought of as his pet project even though Fares was the architect. Michel and those working in the lab knew the results could change the war. It was just a matter of time before it was ready, and the scientists were working themselves to the brink of exhaustion, knowing Beiros was on its knees.

Though credit mostly went to Fares, Rafiq was also among the brains behind the idea. When Scandos had gained significant ground in the war and the Alexandrosians knew it would drag on a long time, Rafiq had proposed to the king that they work on a brand-new weapon that would change the course of the war and for the elves into submission.

The king had then contacted his Riosan allies to employ a team of the province's best scientists. Though Rios was known best for its agriculture and farming, its rich lands and diverse products had also fostered the craft of brewing potions and other concoctions for use as weaponry, medicine, or tools. They could make healing potions, potions that restored stamina—and those that could be used in war.

After the king made the call, and well before the Scandosians had laid their siege, Rios's best scientists made their way to Beiros, headed by one known only as Al Eelam, to spearhead the development of the weapon.

Now, although the war had raged a long time and Beiros had been under siege for several months, the team kept up a tireless pace. Progress had been swift, but Rafiq and Fares still grew impatient. Their time was running out.

One night, deep into the siege, the temper Rafiq had been known for giving rein to in his youth showed itself.

"How long left?" he berated Al Eelam. "You and these so-called scientists are holding everyone's lives up!"

Al Eelam, in his makeshift office reviewing notes when Rafiq barged in, didn't even make eye contact with the soldier, but carried on working, not dignifying Rafiq's burst of temper with a response.

Rafiq, insulted, threw Al Eelam's notes onto the ground. "Answer me!" he screamed.

Al Eelam got up and calmly collected his notes, placing them back on his desk before facing Rafiq and looking up as he did so. "Rios has the finest scientists in Nataaros," he said. "We have the finest scientists from Rios. That means we have the finest scientists in all of Nataaros working to save Beiros from its doom. These things take time, so forgive me if you're too impatient."

"How much time do you think we have?" Rafiq demanded angrily. "Have you been up there lately? People are no longer human; they're monsters."

"No, I haven't been up there," Al Eelam answered. "I've been stuck down here as the only hope this city has."

"Well, hurry up!"

Al Eelam grabbed his notes and shoved them at Rafiq. "Read these," he said, "And tell me if you can understand any of them."

Rafiq read through some of Al Eelam's work, confused about what to look for. His tone shifted when he realised just how complicated Al Eelam's work was. "No. I don't understand anything."

"And I wouldn't expect you to," Al Eelam said. "Not as a soldier." He snatched his notes back and returned to his desk. "Now, imagine me, as a scientist. Not only do I have to make sense of the research we have undertaken to make this weapon possible, I have to be able to put these notes into practice and test every experiment we make before we can make it a reality. These things take time, so beg our pardon if we want to get it right."

Al Eelam started to focus deeply on his work again, writing and underlining in his papers. He paused for a moment to address Rafiq again, sounding far-off as if his thoughts were elsewhere. "I mean, could you imagine if we tested this out on the field? How embarrassing. If it fails, the king has egg on his face and looks a fool, the Scandosians know of our plans, and the whole effort is for nothing.

They will raze Beiros to the ground and all the beautiful little Alexandrosians will either be dead or enslaved, and their way of life a mere memory."

Rafiq stayed quiet, contemplating the stakes. He still didn't understand all the scientific work; in his younger days he hadn't been nearly as shrewd as he grew to be. "How hard can it be to create a weapon?" he asked. "After all, swords and arrows are made by the thousands."

"Well, what you ... what Fares has asked me to create, is a little more complicated than a sword, Rafiq," Al Eelam explained. "You're asking me to create a deadly weapon that will change the whole course of a war. Please, have patience. Go upstairs and you can see my team is working hard to create the formula behind this weapon. They're not being lazy. We are not taking success for granted."

Fares entered the room and saw Rafiq standing over Al Eelam. "What's going on?" he asked.

"Nothing," Al Eelam said. "I was just explaining to Rafiq the complications of the weapon we're creating to save this city from its doom."

Fares was a little confused. "And he wasn't bullying you?" he said with a stern look at Rafiq, who lowered his gaze to hide his sense of guilt.

"No bullying," Al Eelam affirmed, avoiding the truth. "Just curiosity. I am always willing to educate the uneducated, if they ask nicely."

"Good." Fares approached Al Eelam at his desk. "And any progress?"

"At the risk of repeating myself in front of our tall friend here, we *are* making progress. We just need more time."

"How much longer?"

"I don't know," Al Eelam said.

"You don't have an estimate?"

The scientist rolled his eyes and got back up. Putting his work down was one of the things he hated most. "Come with me," he said to the soldiers.

Al Eelam led Fares and Rafiq up to the laboratory, where the scientists were mixing ingredients to try and create the perfect formula for their potion. All were wearing gloves and had their faces covered, to avoid severe exposure to the dangerous elements used in the weapon. Each had phials and bottles close to hand as they tried different doses and measurements to get it right. The team had worked tirelessly for months to not only be able to create the weapon, but to mass-produce it.

"It's a good thing the main ingredient can be found in Rios," Al Eelam said. "That way, we have easy access to it and can make plenty of these weapons when they're ready."

"I know you can't give us an exact time," Fares began, "but can you at least answer me this: are we closer to the weapon being ready than we were yesterday?"

"Do you really want to know?" Al Eelam asked, adjusting his eyewear and running his hand along his shiny, bald head.

"Look, Al Eelam," Fares said gravely, "I was just with the king. He's nearly gone mad. I'm worried for him and the queen. Any more of this siege—any more of the horror—and who knows. The elves may storm the gates eventually and sack the city, and if they uncover this plot, who can say what the punishment may be?"

Al Eelam scrutinised Fares. "Are *you* willing to face the consequences?"

"Well... yes ... but—"

"No 'buts'," Al Eelam said. "You came to me and my team with a plan to end the war quickly, and that involves something the world has never before seen. Something so deadly and dangerous, it could lead to great troubles. Are you not willing to face the repercussions?"

"I am," Fares said. "Are you?"

"I'm totally fine with it," Al Eelam said lightly, brushing it off. "I'm only here because you're all paying us to do our best job."

Rafiq couldn't believe what he was hearing. "That's it?" he said. "You're just in it for the money?"

Al Eelam chuckled, "Well, that's not entirely true. I do hate Scandosians; this I will admit. Bunch of arrogant, self-important worms. I would love to see them suffer. Maybe not as much as you do, seeing what you're having me make."

Fares quickly butted in to correct him. "Not because I want to see them suffer, but because I don't want to see our people suffer."

"Speak for yourself," Al Eelam said, shrugging. "They're not my people. *I* want to see the Scandosians suffer." He turned his attention to his team, who were still intent on their work. "Do you smart souls want to see Scandosians suffer?"

They all nodded their heads without looking up.

Al Eelam turned back to Fares and Rafiq. "We have a common enemy," he explained. "That's more than enough for me to do this and willingly face the consequences. Besides, if we do get captured, I'll just tell the tall creatures it was all your idea in the first place."

Fares grabbed Al Eelam by his collar. "You do that," he growled, "and I'll make sure you receive no forgiveness from Lah when we all die."

The scientist—diminutive and dark-skinned like most Riosans, and with a double dose of their known propensity for invention—brushed himself off. "I was just joking."

"No jokes," Fares warned. "Now, are we any closer to a result than we were yesterday? And don't waste my time."

Al Eelam sighed before going to one of the workstations and grabbing a sample. It was a small device, much like a bomb, which glowed a fluorescent green and emitted thin tendrils of smoke. It even smelled like it could wipe out anyone unfortunate enough to breathe in a solid lungful. But that was nothing. Al Eelam took Fares and Rafiq away to a sealed room and asked them to wear masks and suits of a strange material something like leather but much smoother, to protect them from the fumes that may have poured out from the weapon.

In this room, where the trials for the weapon were being held, rabbits were caged as subjects for testing. "We obviously can't use humans," Al Eelam had said—so they had to make do with rabbits.

Al Eelam grabbed one of the weapons in his hands and readied it. "Is your gear secured?" he asked Fares and Rafiq, to make sure they were safe. It wouldn't do to go killing Alexandros's greatest heroes.

"I can't breathe in this thing," Rafiq complained.

"Good. It means you won't inhale anything," said Al Eelam. Then he activated the weapon and rolled it towards the rabbits.

It opened up, and from it green smoke poured out all over the room. The mist clouded the men's vision, but several moments later it cleared enough for them to see the effects on the rabbits.

Had Rafiq and Fares not known what they had been when alive, they wouldn't have recognised them as rabbits at all. They looked more like the sort of rotten stew that would be served to prisoners in Venos.

Fares was equal parts fascinated and disgusted. "Was that supposed to happen?" he asked Al Eelam.

Al Eelam stood there in awe. It was the first time he'd tried this particular iteration of the weapon.

Rafiq was now incredibly uncomfortable in his suit. "I'm getting out!" he cried. "I need fresh air."

Fares waved him away, while he tried to get Al Eelam's attention. But the scientist ignored him, and just stood there enraptured. He'd done it. After months of tireless work, he had finally created the weapon he'd been asked to create. The war was won. Once they could manufacture and produce these little bombs in the thousands, Scandos would no longer be able to threaten Alexandros and the rest of the kingdom.

"*Yes!*" Al Eelam cheered. "I've done it! Those elves will be destroyed forever!"

Fares didn't believe him. "You mean, that's it?" he asked. "It's ready?"

Al Eelam gleefully ran out of the room and Fares hurried after him. The scientist threw off his suit and began barking enthusiastically to his team. "Listen, you beautiful creatures: *you have done it!*"

The team looked up in amazement.

"It worked!" Al Eelam yelled at them. "Your latest experiment worked, damn you! It was a resounding success. Those rabbits are nothing but muck. Which reminds me, do see to it that they're cleaned up."

The team hugged and shook hands to congratulate each other,

proud that their hard work had borne fruit. It was their greatest accomplishment as scientists.

"The job is not done yet," Al Eelam reminded them. "We must make these things by the thousands. Once we are ready, we will send them to the defenders, and rid Beiros and Nataaros of this elven infestation."

While the scientists cheered, Rafiq approached Fares. "Your idea worked," he said quietly. "You may have just saved us all."

"Yes..." Fares said uneasily.

FARES AND RAFIQ personally went to deliver the news to the king. The three sat alone in the throne room, discussing their next course of action.

"It's ready?" the king asked, as incredulous as Fares had been.

"Al Eelam believes so, Your Majesty," Fares confirmed. "They're now making thousands of them using the same formula. They should be ready by the end of the week."

"So that's it? We've won?"

"Not yet, my king." Fares was anxious not to get too far ahead. "But we are a step closer to lifting the siege and winning the war."

The king sat up in his throne. "And then what?"

"Well, the hope is that when the elves see the destruction this bomb brings them, they'll be forced to lift the siege and surrender, ending the war," Fares explained. "Then, we can negotiate terms that favour us."

"And if the arrogant bastards refuse?"

Fares took a deep breath. What he was about to say shook him to his core. "Then ... we continue," he said. "We make more and more of these bombs, and we attack every regiment we see. If they refuse, we take the fight to Scandos itself, and rain this creation down on them until they give up or cease to exist."

"Which we don't want it to come to," Rafiq chimed in.

"No, we don't," the king agreed. "Alright, you said by the end of the week, this thing will be ready? That's a few more days of suffering. Lah ... I hope my people can take it."

"You should really speak to them," Fares suggested. "At least see them. Let them know their king has their back."

King Michel refused this notion. "No—what will they think of me? When this siege began, I hid in the castle for fear that I would die before fathering an heir. They know their king eats and drinks like a glutton while they starve and thirst like prisoners in their own city. They don't want to see me. I couldn't bring myself to think that they would even want to hear from me."

"Your Majesty," Fares began. "With all due respect, you *have* handled this siege rather poorly. But this is your chance at redemption. We are close to winning. Remind the people that their king is still fighting for them."

Rafiq stepped forward. "If I might add something, my king?"

"Yes, Rafiq."

"I've found that people, when they're at their most desperate, will take any sign of hope with open arms," Rafiq said. "When they see you emerge from this castle, they won't think less of you. They'll remember that they have a king, and that as long as he is willing to face the reality of the situation, there is still hope that this nightmare may end."

King Michel considered this thought, and nearly brought himself to tears thinking of everything he'd been through in his short time as king of Nataaros.

He stayed quiet so long that Fares felt compelled to check up on him. "Your Majesty?"

"I won't deliver a rousing speech," King Michel said. "I will see the poor and the hungry, and let them see my face. While you and Al Eelam work on saving us all, I will bring hope to the people. I will remind them that I am with them, and they are with me."

"That's all we ask of you, my king," Fares said.

"Now, to victory," said the king.

∼

BY THE END of that week, the king had made his presence felt among the people strewn throughout the city streets. Even in their hunger, pain, and thirst, knowing the king was with them gave them peace. Fares and Rafiq had been right in their prediction that once the people saw their king, they would forget they had been left alone.

And now the weapons were ready. Fares and Rafiq had begun to transport the bombs from Al Eelam's laboratory to the defenders at the walls.

As the three masterminds of the project watched their vision come to fruition, they couldn't help but feel uneasy.

"It's fascinating, isn't it?" Al Eelam said. "You hate a race of creatures so much, yet your conscience tells you to not utterly destroy them."

"You learn to shut your conscience up in war," Fares remarked, "If you let the little bastard get too many words in, you'll fail as a soldier."

"You're not really humans anymore, are you?" Al Eelam observed.

"Not really." Fares lamented, "Humanity has long since left us. From the moment we make our first kill we are no longer humans, or on the side of living creatures. We are machines sent by a powerful man in a fancy chair to do his bidding."

Al Eelam shuddered at Fares's negativity, but wasn't one to get on his high horse. After all, he was helping the cause, and his motivation was hate.

When the work of getting the bombs to the defenders on the walls was well and truly underway, Fares and Rafiq headed to join the garrison and ready for the counterattack.

At the battlements, they found the defenders looking as depleted as ever. The archers, with worn-out arms, could barely draw their bows to fire at the Scandosians.

Looking over the walls, Fares saw the Scandosians camped outside and living freely, without fear of an attack. But seeing the walls they had built around Beiros, he realised they would soon find themselves trapped inside their own prison.

"Lah help those that die from this," he told Rafiq.

"Lah curse them, you mean," Rafiq replied. "Look at what they've done to us. I cannot wait to see it all end."

"Has it ever occurred to you that they were also just doing what was ordered of them?" Fares asked.

"Yes, elves are like us, if that's what you're saying," Rafiq said. "They have as much free will as we do. They chose to imprison us, and we have chosen to fight back."

When the supply of bombs reached the walls and was being readied for distribution, Fares descended a ladder to ground level to explain the plan to the defenders, with Rafiq by his side.

"Soldiers of Nataaros," he began. "We thank you for your loyalty and your dedication in the defence of our great city. When this siege started, we feared, and we were right to do so. All hope seemed lost. Yet, you brave men have stood strong and kept the elves at bay, despite overwhelming odds.

"What we have here is a new weapon, designed by Al Eelam of Rios. It is a type of bomb—a small device that can be carried by hand. We have thousands of them. Each of you will be issued one. Do be careful; it is very deadly. On my signal, we will unleash these weapons on the Scandosians and weaken them to their bones.

"Then, while wearing the protective gear that we will be issuing you, we will assault their encampment, kill any survivors, and lift the siege. Have I made myself clear?"

The soldiers stayed quiet. They'd heard everything Fares had to say.

"Soldiers, are we ready?" Rafiq demanded.

"Yes!" they bellowed back.

"Are we ready to take back our city?"

"Yes!"

"Then let's go!" Rafiq cheered.

One by one, the soldiers collected their gear, bombs, and protective equipment. This was the moment they had waited for until they lost hope it would arrive—their chance to strike. That morning, Beiros would be saved.

When the first squad of Alexandrosian infantry left the front gate, wearing not only their armour but protective gloves and helmets to protect them from the bombs, they formed up and faced the Scandosian camp directly.

The Scandosians emerged from their camps and saw what was

facing them. "What is the meaning of this?" a Scandosian commander on the front lines asked the infantrymen.

They Alexandrosians were silent.

"Answer me," the commander ordered, "or we will attack!"

Still, there was no answer.

"Have it your way," the commander sighed. And then he barked, "Attack!"

The Scandosians formed up and attacked the small squad of Alexandrosians facing them, hoping to wipe them out quickly.

From atop the walls, Fares was watching this all unfold. The trap had been sprung.

"Now!" he roared at the soldiers.

Thrown, launched, and fired, the bombs fell upon the elven camp like a storm, opening when they hit the ground to engulf the elves in green mist like they were rabbits in Al Eelam's laboratory.

"What is this? I can't breathe!" the Scandosian commander wheezed, clutching and clawing at his throat.

Their attack halted, and they could no longer face the Alexandrosians in front of them.

Second by second, the elves were dying. Their faces began to melt. While their eyes rolled out of their sockets, they coughed up blood and left puddles of bodily fluids all over the ground. Their nervous systems ceased to function, and they fell down twitching and convulsing, their excrement, vomit, and blood fouling the camp. Beiros stank badly enough of dead and unwashed bodies, but the Scandosian camp, by comparison, now made the stench of Beiros seem like the perfume of roses.

Fares watched as the destruction wrought by his bombs kept raining down, and the elves melted like ice in the summer. The corpses they left behind said nothing of the beauty they had in life: bones thin as broken kindling and grey as storms, resting in a slosh of blood and shit. It was the most horrific thing anyone had seen.

Rafiq turned to Fares. "Shall we stop?" he asked. "I think that's all of them."

Fares raised his hand straight up, and the hail of the weapons from hell stopped. "Finish them."

The soldiers inside the walls now rushed out through the gates and massacred any elves that had remained. If an elf hadn't been left completely unrecognisable by the gas, they were cut down with the sword. Any elf still breathing, fell to the blades of the Alexandrosians, who after months of starvation to the brink of death, were half out of their minds and thirsty for Scandosian blood. This was no longer a battle: it was personal vengeance.

From high above, Fares saw what was happening and wept. He knew what the result would be when this was over.

"It worked," Rafiq muttered with amazement. "It's actually worked."

"I know," Fares said softly. "That's what I was most afraid of."

Within the hour, all that remained of the besieging force was entrails and gore. An Alexandrosian soldier picked up what was left of the Scandosian commander's body and carried it inside Beiros, meeting Fares at the gates. He tossed the body to the ground, showing Fares and Rafiq the devastating effect of their creation.

The commander's body was almost purely skeleton, as his skin and flesh had melted away. His armour and clothing hung limply off the bones.

Fares nearly threw up when he saw this, and had to look away. There was no taking back what he had done. At least, once word reached Scandos, the war would be over.

Just like that, Fares had saved Beiros, ended the war, and made his name synonymous with death.

⌒

BY THE TIME Fares had finished telling Melhel and Marissa the story, the two were holding their faces in shock.

"That's horrible," Marissa said.

"You don't think I know?" Fares said. "Why do you think I always feel insulted when King Michel calls me a hero? Is that his idea of heroism, turning living creatures into a pile of muck?"

Melhel pushed himself up from the table, exhausted. "What a night this has been," he said. "What happened next?"

"Scandos was forced to negotiate its surrender," Fares

explained, "There was no way they were fighting on after that. No way."

"And you?"

"The king asked me to be his Sword," Fares said.

"And?" Marissa asked.

"I said no," Fares sighed. "And he gave it to Rafiq instead."

This surprised Melhel. "So, Rafiq wasn't his first choice?"

"No. The king always wanted me," Fares said. "But I couldn't serve a king that would willingly do that to his own people."

"They're elves, though," Melhel said.

"As long as they live in Nataaros, they're still his people," Fares affirmed. "Afterwards, I retired back to Chekkos. And now here we are again."

The younger Barak was solemn, finally seeing, after all these years, where the pain that always burned in Fares had come from. "I get it now," he said, "why you hated the king. Why you always criticised him in front of me. You did it for him. And now, you've been brought back to face it all again."

Fares chuckled, "And you want to know what's funny?"

"What?" Melhel asked.

"The king has invited us to a party." Fares handed a piece of paper across the table. "To commemorate the twenty-fifth anniversary of our victory."

"Wow," Melhel laughed grimly. "I guess they have to rub it in."

CHAPTER 14
CELEBRATIONS

"Who the hell celebrates a war crime?" Melhel asked Fares the next morning. They and Marissa were seated at breakfast, struggling to decisively open their eyes after a late night of revelations.

"The king, ironically," Fares said.

"Some king," Melhel grumbled. "I thought I was right not to bend my knee when I met him."

Fares took a gulp of his morning coffee, which Marissa had brewed extra strong to fight their account for his exhaustion. "You know it was my idea," he reminded Melhel.

"And you're one of the sulkiest men I know," Melhel responded. "Plus, you never spoke about it. If it were up to you, it'd have been kept from the history books forever, I suppose. But King Michel wants to throw a party? What's he commemorating? Sure, we won, but at what cost? Scandos is at our throats about reforming the constitution, the dead army I won't even go into—and the king wants to throw a party?"

Melhel's outburst gave Marissa a massive headache. "Mel, it's way too early to be yelling," she complained.

"I don't care," Melhel said. "What sense does the king have, insulting the Scandosians like this?"

"Oh, so you're on their side now?" Fares taunted.

"Of course not. But this isn't exactly helping the king's cause. Imagine if you're on the fence about this issue. The Scandosians have been trying to get their independence for hundreds of years. We practically ate them alive in the civil war, and now when they want to try again—peacefully, I might add—we ignore them and throw a party to celebrate their defeat."

Marissa was still rubbing her eyes. "Fares, when he puts it like that…" she said gently.

"You're right, Melhel," Fares said, nodding, "it would only bring sympathy to the Scandosian cause. Especially if we're there."

Melhel stood to grab some bread from the counter, and started munching before turning back to face. "Then let's not go," he mumbled through a mouthful. "Show that Scandos's greatest enemy —if that's what they think you are—doesn't support this."

"Want to tell the king that?" Fares laughed. "We have to be there. Imagine how bad it would look for the king if we stay away. It would show disunity. Scandos will think the king is weak and losing his grip."

"Stuff him," Melhel said.

"Really? Shall we be mature about this?" Fares stared into Melhel's eyes. "Do you want to defeat Scandos or not?"

Melhel sighed. "Yes. But this isn't how you do it."

"Maybe not," Fares said, "but neither is turning our backs on the king and his kingdom. We have to show unity and togetherness. Even if we disagree, it's all about perception. If the people see that we're united, it'll show we're strong."

Melhel chuckled. "I guess I'm not cut out to be a politician."

"No, you're really not."

~

ELSEWHERE, the king was in the castle hall, where all major functions were held, helping to plan the festivities.

The queen and her organisers were deciding on the room layout for the party. Rounded tables filled one half of the hall, where people would be allocated seats according to their family alliances

195

and prestige. They would fill the tables with the richest and most famous and influential people in Beiros, until they ran out of places.

Ahead of the tables, open space had been reserved for dancing, which was still a big part of Alexandrosian culture. Even in a martial age like this, people would dance at any cause for a celebration. This wasn't a grim commemoration of victory in the civil war, but of the triumph of the Alexandrosian culture over the Scandosian.

Finally, across the dancefloor, elevated and overlooking the entire room, was a long table spanning much of the width of the hall, where the king, his family, and his closest friends and advisers would sit. Melhel, Fares, and Marissa would all be at this high table.

"I want a minimum of five drummers, all playing at once as we dance," the king demanded. "All of them should be dressed in the traditional garb of the Alexandrosian drummer."

The organiser busily noted the king's requirements on a piece of parchment, with a rather more flamboyant quill than many were used to seeing, tipped with gold to match the ornate brocade of the organiser's outfit.

"And the band will be here," the king said, pointing to the edge of the dance floor. "The singer, the musicians—the lot. They will play mellow sounds as we talk and mingle, before kicking things off with a livelier tune as we get into the celebrations."

"Understood, Your Majesty." The organiser smiled and nodded, finding space on the already crowded parchment to scribble another note. "And food?"

"The queen has seen to it," King Michel confirmed. "Only the best Alexandrosian food for this event. No expense is to be spared."

The organiser made a further note. "And seating?"

"The wealthiest and most important guests should be seated closest to the dance floor."

"And on your table?"

"The royal family. The Baraks and their assistant. Saad Jaja and his wife, and my advisers and their wives: Al Aanif, Al Jasha, and El Salam."

The organiser grinned. "You say those names with contempt, my king."

"That's because I hate dealing with them in the senate," King Michel sniped. "Do you think I *want* to deal with them on such a special night?"

"Do not worry, we will make sure it will be fun, and full of celebrations," the organiser reassured the king. "Nothing will go wrong, and you will have the best of times. Why, you won't even notice the politics or idiocy of these men." King Michel wished he could believe the promise.

Queen Rania returned to the two of them after having spoken to the caterers about the food. "You look stressed," she said, noticing the overwhelmed look on her husband's face.

"Just the thought of us having to sit next to my advisers fatigues me."

"You could always get new advisers," the queen suggested.

"Maybe once the matter of Scandos is resolved. It's not a bad idea," the king agreed.

"My queen, how has everything gone with the catering?" the organiser chimed in.

"Very good," she smiled. "Everyone will be well-fed. All five hundred of them."

"Have fun mingling among them all," the organiser joked. "I shall be watching closely to make sure the night goes as smoothly as planned."

King Michel shook the man's hand. "And this is why we trust you with everything. This deserves the best celebration the land will see this year. Which reminds me..." He turned to Queen Rania. "Remind the prince to visit the tailor. And get him to take Melhel with him."

In her office, Mala Habeb sat with a fuming Ismal Haya, who had just stormed in in a rage, bringing news of the upcoming celebrations in Beiros and denouncing the king and everything Alexandros stood for. Just as Melhel and Fares had predicted, Scandos was not responding well.

However, Mala stayed stoic, in stark contrast to her counterpart.

"Some king he is," Ismal ranted. "After all the moral superiority he puts on in the senate, he goes and does this. It's despicable."

Mala listened patiently.

"They're very good at playing the victim, Alexandrosians," Ismal went on. "Do they forget what they did at the siege? The lives they took so heinously? Do they forget everything they took from us and will not give back?" Ismal stood and slammed Mala's desk with the palms of his hands. "It was *you* who built this place back up to its glory! It was *you* that ensured our survival and our legacy for the future. Not them, but you!

"King Michel took our homes, our lives, and our culture—our history and our heritage—like that pig Beilos before him. And neither one of them helped us come back from the devastation their ruthless hands had wrought. We've done everything ourselves, and yet we cannot be given independence. The very thought of it threatens that twisted animal and everything he stands for."

Ismal, already worked up, was now even becoming infuriated by Mala's protracted silence. How could she say nothing while he praised her and denounced her enemies? "Are you just going to sit there?" he asked. "Say something, Governor!"

Mala looked at him with contempt. "Do you ever shut up?" she asked.

"I'm sorry?"

"Maybe the reason we cannot be given independence is because I send you to represent us in the senate," she rebuked him. "*I* can barely cope with your whining; I cannot imagine how the king feels."

"You and I both know the king won't grant us independence because he fears Scandosian autonomy," Ismal defended.

"Perhaps," Mala said softly. "But perhaps it's also because his impression of Scandosians is that we're little children—like you."

Ismal was taken aback.

"Besides," Mala continued, "when have you ever seen him visit or pay any attention to us whatsoever? Twenty-five years as king and he wouldn't even know where to find us on a map. He is a fool and the fact that he is my king insults me to very core, every day of my life. No matter what I do, I have to answer to him. Even if I have proven myself to be the best administrator in this jungle of a kingdom. Even if we have proven ourselves to be the best province in all Nataaros, still... He shows himself for who he truly is."

Mala got up from the desk and stood right in front of Ismal. "After what he and that horrible man Fares Barak did to us, that I have to still answer to an Alexandrosian shakes me to my bones. The king's authority is a living insult to every elf that lives and works in Nataaros, provides for *his* kingdom and gets no thanks for it. And now has the gall to throw a party commemorating a war crime."

Ismal leaned back, frightened by his governor's intensity. "What would you have me do?" he asked.

Mala breathed in and took a step back. "Nothing. You've done all you can. I hear the next meeting of the senate is coming up soon, after this stupid party. I'm coming with you."

"You are?"

"Maybe I can talk to the king myself, present our case as best as possible, and finally be given what we have deserved for centuries."

"And if you still have no luck?" Ismal asked.

"Then we may have to fight once again," Mala warned. "Only this time, I won't make the same mistakes as my predecessors."

AS THE KING and queen continued organising the festivities, Fares lamented his mistakes in life and war, and Mala excoriated King Michel, Melhel and his friends were at the tailor's.

The shop, belonging to Elies Sabe, whose talent had brought him out of poverty and obscurity to be the most renowned couturier in all Beiros, was open exclusively for them, so Elies could work with them individually to create the perfect outfit and fit for each of the three.

Melhel was indifferent to the privilege: he would have avoided the festivities if he could, and the ordeal of being dressed for the occasion was making him rethink whether he should ever have come all the way to Beiros with his uncle. "Stay in Chekkos, I should've told myself," he often said to himself that week as he worried about what had happened and what might.

He waited outside a fitting room with Prince Sirhan while Elies was busy with Marissa, pinning her dress for the party. Melhel sprawled over a couch, his exasperation clear, but the prince sat up straight on an ornate chair, waiting patiently to see how his new love would be dressed for the celebration.

When Melhel looked like dozing off, Prince Sirhan leaned over to hit him on the shoulder.

"Do you mind?" Melhel exclaimed with annoyance.

"Have you no manners," Prince Sirhan said, "to be falling asleep right now?"

Melhel rubbed his eyes and sat back up. "Do you honestly think I care?" he said. "This whole idea is stupid. Dressing up is stupid. Everything is stupid. The only thing stopping me from walking out right now is that you will complain to your father, and that Marissa needs an escort home."

The prince shook his head. "Get excited, Melhel. It's going to be a night to remember." He was beaming, picturing himself with Marissa. "We will drink, sing, and dance the dabke."

"I don't know how to dance the dabke."

Prince Sirhan was stunned. "What do you mean you don't how to dance the dabke?"

The dabke was the folk dance of Alexandros, and involved a large group of as many people as necessary, holding hands in a circle and rhythmically stepping to a beat while moving to the side. The top of the circle was usually led by one or two leaders, who would have their right hands free and would be the ones with the most entertaining and acrobatic moves. These men were typically the fittest, strongest, most skilled—and drunkest—of all the dancers.

"I thought you hated this sort of stuff," Melhel said.

"Correction: I hate the politics, but I love the partying."

Melhel rolled his eyes.

"Besides," the prince said. "This night is going to cost millions in gold. We'd best make the most of it."

"Hmm, millions," Melhel mused. "We could give that to the

poor, the homeless, the needy, the hungry. We could put it towards the war effort or our defences, even." Melhel stood and leaned against the wall. "Instead, we put it towards a party that's insulting people we've defeated and conquered over and over again throughout history."

Prince Sirhan stood up as well. "Don't be so negative," he said. "The Scandosians won't feel insulted."

"Want to bet?"

"It's commemorating the anniversary of the end of the darkest period in Nataaros's history," Prince Sirhan explained. "What's so insulting about commemoration?"

Melhel shook his head. "You really don't know, do you?"

"Know what?" The prince was befuddled.

Melhel realised that Prince Sirhan genuinely had no idea of the devastation caused to the Scandosians in breaking the Siege of Beiros. The history books had either glossed over the story or changed it. The Alexandrosian history books, that is.

"Never mind," Melhel said, trying to change the subject. "You know, you're sounding a lot like your father right now."

Prince Sirhan's face changed, and he rounded on Melhel. "I'm *not* like my father!"

Melhel raised an eyebrow. "Why not? *He's* overly excited about this event. *You're* overly excited about this event. If you can't see the similarities, you're as blind as an old man."

"I promise you I will be a better king than my father," the prince said sternly.

"I'm sure you will be."

Marissa had finished getting fitted as the conversation between Melhel and Prince Sirhan grew heated. "Will you two shut up?" she cried. "I'm coming out, now!"

Elies walked out first, with a smile plastering his face. "My prince," he said, grinning, "your love."

Melhel groaned at this statement. He hadn't figured out what Marissa could see in the prince, but he could definitely see what made Sirhan so keen, as Marissa walked out of the fitting room in a shimmering dress as blue as the sky. It was fitted perfectly to her figure, in a contemporary interpretation of the traditional Alexandrosian costume for women. The fabric was adorned with jewels, imparting a glow that made her shine as never before. For that moment, not the queen but Marissa, a lower-class woman who had nearly been unjustly executed, was the most beautiful woman in all of Alexandros. And on top of that, she had intelligence and force of character.

Melhel was stunned. In all his time with Marissa he hadn't realised just how attractive she could be. He had acknowledged her beauty, but her dress was always simple and her demeanour modest. In this setting, he finally saw what all other men saw. It was unlike him to ogle, but now he made an exception.

Prince Sirhan immediately jumped up in excitement as though he were back at the gladiatorial games. He couldn't believe he would be attending the celebrations with such a beauty.

Marissa stood proudly while the men admired her. No longer was she the woman who had been caught with a soldier, but the prince's date to a royal event.

"So," she said, "what do you think?"

Melhel, for once in his life, was too gobsmacked to think of anything clever to say. "Wow," was all he could muster with a smile; he knew how much this meant to Marissa. For all his annoyance at the festivities, he knew that for Marissa this was a big step, and he wasn't so heartless to not share in her joy.

"This is the one!" Prince Sirhan exclaimed. "Elies, you've done it again." He ran to shake the tailor's hand forcefully.

Elies chuckled. "That's why the king and queen always come to me," he said. "That's why I'm famous!"

"Undoubtedly," the prince agreed before turning to Marissa. "And you—my word, I'm lost."

Marissa grinned. "You approve?"

"Do I ever." Prince Sirhan was still wide-eyed.

Elies stepped in. "Should I put this one aside as a definite 'yes'?" he asked.

The prince beat Marissa to it. "Yes," he said. "Put it aside. This is what she'll be wearing, and she will be the best dressed and most beautiful woman there."

"Excellent." Elies smiled. "Now, who is next?"

Prince Sirhan approached Melhel and tapped him on the shoulder. Melhel was daydreaming now, not paying much attention to anything.

"Melhel and I, please," the prince said. "Time for our outfits."

Melhel let out a groan. He knew how long this would take, and could've thought of a million and one things he would rather have been doing.

He was escorted into the fitting room as Prince Sirhan made a quick request to Elies. "Make him look good," he demanded, "After all, he and his family are friends of mine. But make me look better."

"Understood," Elies said with a nod.

THE NIGHT HAD COME. The twenty-fifth anniversary of the end of the civil war was upon them, surely to be the greatest night in the king's reign.

Once the sun set, a full moon shone upon Beiros, and the streets were festooned with lights. The king wasn't the only one hosting the event: all of Beiros was, as nobles and senators from across the country, with the exception of Scandos, had come to join the celebrations.

Outside the royal palace, flowers adorned the open gates, through which extended a carpet half a mile long. Flanked by guards, it welcomed the entry of the most important people in the kingdom.

Inside, in their chambers, the king and queen were getting ready individually. The queen was with a team of the finest dressmakers and artists, ready to elevate her natural beauty to the realm of the angelic. The king was in his room with the prince, and each had shaved, donned their suits, and parted their hair neatly to the side. Michel was dressed in a red tunic and trousers whose colour symbolised his kingship, while Prince Sirhan's suit from Elies Sabe was in navy blue. Both men looked as sharp as ever, but the prince couldn't help but wonder insecurely whether he truly was the better dressed man, as he had asked to be.

But when they met the queen outside of their rooms, ready to take their positions in the hall, all thought fled of which man was more impressive. Both knew the women would eclipse them. On seeing his wife, King Michel was as captivated as Prince Sirhan had been when he first saw Marissa in her dress. The queen's dress was fitted in a similar style to Marissa's, but in a lavender that perfectly matched her brown hair.

King Michel took her hand and kissed it. "My queen," he said with a smile.

She blushed. "My king."

They lightly held each other's hands and walked off with their son by their side. It was to be their night.

~

LONG BEFORE, the king had already received word that the guests were arriving, but as was his typical practice, the king expected to make a point of arriving late, not only to make a grand entrance once every guest was in their place, but also to secure entry to the palace before the royal family appeared.

The guests were still pouring in through the gates in droves. Hundreds of them made their way inside after extensive checks from the guards, and if not seated at their tables, were mingling with their friends and rivals. Five hundred people were to fill the hall to its absolute capacity.

Melhel, Fares, and Marissa had made their way inside to sit together at the high table. At they did so, they passed the advisers Al Aanif, Al Jasha, and El Salam with their wives, and the Baraks stopped to awkwardly shake their hands while Marissa half-heartedly smiled and waved, knowing that almost all of the senators and courtiers in the room would have had her executed.

Al Aanif tried to strike up a conversation. "So, Fares," he said, "how is the blacksmithing going? Have the king's requests been met?"

"Of course," Fares responded coldly. "I just hope you won't send our young men off to test their weapons too hastily."

Al Aanif took offence. "Now, now, I would never," he claimed. "Only if it is in the best interests of the king and his kingdom."

Fares sipped a goblet of wine that an attendant had poured and handed to him. "You're a persuasive man, Al Aanif," Fares said. "Hopefully you turn him towards peace."

"We're all his advisers," Al Jasha interjected, not wanting to be sidelined. "Let us work together on this."

"Just stick to blowing the budget," Fares jabbed back. There was a strained silence, and the older smith scrambled to recover. "Look, no politics tonight. I am here with my nephew and our guest. We are here for the king and his occasion. He worked hard on this. Let's not spoil it with argument and talk of war." Fares then turned towards Melhel and Marissa, who had begun to move hesitantly towards their own seats at the other end of the table.

When Fares had caught up with Melhel, the younger man leaned in to ask, "Where is the king?"

"You know how he is," Fares said. "He wants to make a grand entrance. He'll be here shortly, once everyone is here and seated." Fares looked down the table at the other advisers, across the empty seats reserved for the royal family. "And it'd be good if he were here, so I don't have to look at those three all night."

"Like you said, no politics," Melhel reminded Fares.

Behind their table, Rafiq stood silently and unnoticed, armoured and upright, guarding the back entrance to the hall, from which the royal family would enter. For him, this was no occasion for partying or small talk.

THE NIGHT no longer felt as young by the time the guests had arrived and taken their seats. Melhel was now bored out of his mind at the high table without Sirhan as a sparring partner, while Fares waited anxiously for the king's arrival. Marissa, though more her beautiful self than ever, was growing impatient to see the prince.

But finally, the master of ceremonies stood in front of the high table, ready to introduce the royal family.

"Ladies and gentlemen," he announced, "I present to you—the royal family of Nataaros!"

Everyone stood and applauded as the royal family walked out to their table with toothy smiles shining at the crowd, waving to their loyal subjects.

"About time," Fares said in Melhel's ear.

The king, queen, and prince took their seats, and King Michel gestured that the guests should cease their applause.

"You may be seated, dear friends," he called to the room.

As Marissa sat, she saw Prince Sirhan blow her a kiss, and blushed at such public flattery. Melhel could only look on with disgust.

The king remained standing as he spoke to commence the evening.

"My closest friends, allies, and confidantes, welcome to the twenty-fifth anniversary celebrations of the Scandosian civil war," he began. "We are here tonight to remember the darkest days in our kingdom's history, when we were torn apart by race, religion, and politics. Never again do I wish this to happen, and I should hope that a quarter-century on, we have learned from our mistakes and will make a concerted effort to never repeat them.

"When the war broke out, I had truly believed that this nation— my kingdom—was going to fall. But thanks to the resolve of you, the people, and my army, we managed to defeat the Scandosian rebellion and restore order to Nataaros, allowing it to return to glory.

"I would like to make a particular mention of two fine men, whom I would not hesitate to say are the greatest heroes of the war: Rafiq Harrira, my Sword..." He gestured behind him to where Rafiq still stood guard. "...and next to me on my left, Fares Barak, my bravest and greatest general in the war."

Everyone cheered for Rafiq and Fares, but Fares lowered his eyes at the table, surprised and embarrassed by his inclusion in the king's speech. Though he should have expected the attention, he had almost believed he might escape it.

"Stand up, Fares," the king asked.

Fares reluctantly obliged, waving his hand and giving an awkward smile before hastily sitting back down.

"Ah, he's as humble as he is brave." The king laughed, and the audience with him.

"Simply stated," the king continued, "were it not for them, for everyone in this room, and your people—our people—we would not be here today." A small tear was forming in his eye. "Let it be known that heroic deeds will not be forgotten, nor bravery go unrecognised. I salute you all as we all strive together to build a better Nataaros."

The king raised a glass of wine for a toast, and his audience promptly stood up and followed him.

"A toast—to Nataaros, to democracy, to justice!" the king called. Then as he took a gulp, a loud bang was heard just outside. "What in Lah's name—" he sputtered.

But before he or anyone could react, ten hooded figures stormed through the front entrance into the hall, all wielding crossbows.

"Scandos will be independent," one shouted.

Fares realised what was about to happen and leapt over the king and queen to cover them. "Get down!" he shouted.

No one else could react in time, as the hooded figures began to fire their bolts and arrows by the dozens. Within seconds, most in attendance had been killed or injured, and the casualty count continued to rise as the hooded figures kept firing rapidly. The guests' suits and dresses offered no resistance to the darts that impaled them.

As the attack began, Melhel had also quickly jumped on top of Marissa to protect her. Now underneath the high table, they looked up and saw Fares lying over the king and queen as arrows flew in the air above them. If they showed their heads above the table, they would've been dead, along with the rest of their poor audience, the survivors of which were now scrambling to escape.

The human stampede they formed did nothing but slow them down and make easy pickings for the attackers to mow them down in a hail of missiles. These figures were expert shots, and knew exactly what they were doing.

Rafiq had moved from his post and now dove under the high table, to ensure the king and queen were safe. When he saw Fares already had them covered, he was relieved. "How the hell did they get in?" he screamed to Fares.

"I don't know! But we have to react quickly," Fares said. "People are dying by the hundreds now."

Fares tried to look up, but an arrow narrowly missed his eye and forced him down again.

"What are we going to do?" Rafiq asked.

"You're the bloody Sword, this is your job to fix!" Fares roared back at him.

As Melhel shielded Marissa, he realised the prince had not been accounted for. "Where is Prince Sirhan?" he asked.

The rest looked up, and soon found him right underneath the table, cowering away from the rain of arrows, crying and panicking with fear for his life.

Melhel shook his head. "Coward."

The barrage continued, felling any unfortunate soul that entered its path, until suddenly it stopped. The bowmen had run out of ammunition.

Realising this, Melhel, Fares, and Rafiq sprang out to attack.

Before they could escape, Melhel drew five hidden daggers from his boots and threw one at each attacker, striking them all down.

Another five men heading towards him froze, and before they could defend themselves, Fares and Rafiq were on them. Rafiq pulled out his longsword and killed one before Fares grabbed a dagger of his own and sliced the necks of two more. That left two men, who quaked as they faced their adversaries. Expecting little resistance, they had made few plans for their exit.

Melhel quickly grabbed one of his daggers and cut one across the shoulder, before Rafiq charged in and stabbed the last one. Between these three men from the king's inner circle, and the guards Rafiq had secretly placed among the crowd, all the attackers were now dead, their bodies slumped alongside those of the murdered guests and attendants.

Of the five hundred guests, not even half would leave the hall alive.

Melhel, Fares, and Rafiq, all heaving with the exertion, turned their heads to survey the bloodshed. The white marble floors were now red and slick with blood, which also smeared the walls and flowed from the piled, arrow-pierced bodies.

With the noise of the attack now ended, the king slowly emerged from underneath the high table. As he stood and saw the scene before him, the horror took several seconds to sink in. His face whitened, and he emitted a shrill and piercing scream, as if he himself had been struck mortally by the bowmen.

The king's night had taken the worst possible turn, from celebration to catastrophe. Someone, he resolved, would answer for this bloodshed.

CHAPTER 15
AFTERMATH

As the king looked at the bodies that lay in front of him, his face went from its usual olive complexion to white as paper. He screamed and fell to the ground almost catatonic, unable to speak or move.

Melhel, Fares, and Rafiq were at the front of the hall after dispatching the attackers, and in the calm, they now had time to process what had happened, and what they were seeing.

Rafiq selected one of the slain attackers and removed their hood, revealing an elvish face.

"Scandosian," he confirmed to Melhel and Fares.

"I knew it," Fares said. "Who else would do such a thing this night, of all nights?"

Rafiq now set about unmasking each one of the attackers, lining them up in the middle of the room, moving the bodies of the victims to the side to make space where necessary.

King Michel finally roused himself and flipped straight into a state of panic. "The queen!"

Still disoriented, he quickly turned, and when he found Rania on the floor beside him, alive, he picked her up and hugged her like he never had before.

Her tears streamed down his shoulder, all over his suit, and his fell on her dress. They weren't crying just for their victims, but for each other. In twenty-five years, this was the closest they had felt to dying.

Melhel looked up and saw Marissa barely standing, trying to hold back the tears forming in her eyes.

"Marissa!" Melhel called out. He ran to comfort her. "Are you okay? Are you hurt?"

"No," she sniffed, "I wasn't hit. Who would do such a thing?"

Melhel turned and pointed to the bodies that Rafiq and Fares were laying out in the middle of the hall. "That's who. I called it. Don't say I didn't know it was going to happen."

"People have just died and all you care about is being right?"

He didn't say a word. She was right to admonish him.

King Michel raised his head from the queen's shoulder and realised Prince Sirhan had yet to be seen. "Where is the prince?" he asked.

He turned again and again, looking around his feet and underneath the high table, but found nothing, "Where is my son?" he pleaded, *"Where is he? Where is my boy?"*

Melhel looked behind them and found Prince Sirhan cowering in a corner, on his backside with his knees tucked into his chest and his head buried, rocking, shaking, and crying. Had he realised the worst was over?

Melhel stormed angrily to Prince Sirhan and grabbed him by the scruff of the neck. "You coward," he berated him, "your woman was within grazing distance of an arrow, your parents — the king and queen, mind you — were nearly killed, half of the room is dead, and here you are crying in the corner. Some king you'll be!"

The prince pushed Melhel's hand away. "Unhand me, blacksmith," he snapped, trying to be gruff through the tears. "I was not crying."

"It sure looked like it," Melhel countered.

Fares stood in the middle of the hall with Rafiq. "Will you both cut it out!" he demanded before turning to the king. "Your Majesty, please, come see this."

Guards accompanied the king as he slowly limped to the middle of the room to see the bodies of the attackers, staining his boots in the blood of the victims, his people.

"Scandos has attacked me on my night," he cried on seeing the elven faces. "On my night, they have committed this act of terror against me and my people."

"My king, listen," Fares said, hastening to calm him. "It may not have been ordered by the Scandosian government. It may have been a few extremists."

"Scandos has done this—"

"My king, listen to me," Fares entreated. Everyone nearby turned their heads at Fares' raised voice. "This is a handful of elves who did a horrible thing. Perhaps they were Scandosian nationalists. Perhaps they wanted to fight for Scandos, or they want you to attack Scandos and ignite another civil war."

King Michel stayed silent, giving himself time to register everything.

"My king, please, this is not the fault of Scandos," Fares reiterated. "You and I both know this is not in Governor Mala's nature. She would never order another attack."

The king looked up and noticed something no one else had. In all the commotion and chaos, some survivors were still curled in a corner of the hall, among the dead bodies of their acquaintances.

"My people," the king said. "My people..." He wiped a tear from his eye. "You may all leave," he told them. "Rafiq, are they safe to go?" he asked, looking to his Sword.

"They should be," said Rafiq. "I'd suggest for them to spread out and leave one at a time."

"You may all go." The king made a motion of dismissal to the survivors, who promptly ignored Rafiq's advice and ran as fast as they could out of the hall and the palace, and to their homes.

King Michel looked at the bodies of the attackers again. "Rafiq, tell me, how did these cruel men get in?" he asked.

"They must've snuck in—bypassed or eliminated security so they would be left unchecked," Rafiq said.

"But how can your security have allowed this?" the king inquired. "Surely they were prepared."

"I do not know. I will have to investigate," Rafiq said, removing his helmet. For the first time in a while, the king saw genuine concern on Rafiq's face.

Melhel walked among the bodies after tending to Marissa, the prince, and the queen. He stepped around each corpse, disgusted by the gore left around them. "That's a lot of blood," he murmured.

"You think so?" Fares shot him a stern look that said such obvious statements were neither necessary nor wanted.

"I'm just saying, Uncle, this is ridiculous. The bloodshed these creatures have poured on us."

"You too argue too much," King Michel blasted at both of them. "If I have to hear any more bickering out of you..."

So Melhel and Fares kept quiet.

"As if this night couldn't get any worse," King Michel sighed. "Rafiq, you are to investigate what in Lah's name happened. Melhel, Fares, you are both are to aid him." He turned back to Marissa, Prince Sirhan, and the queen. "Marissa, your strength and resolve are admirable, but you have earned a rest. You may go home. I trust one of your hosts will see you there. Sirhan, you are to man up. You are the future king of Nataaros. For Lah's sake, act like it!"

"I *am* acting like it, father!"

"You are not!" the king bellowed. "You hid in the corner away from Marissa, your mother, and me. While Rafiq, Fares, and Melhel put themselves at risk to save our lives, you cried like a child and haven't once shown an ounce of gratitude."

The prince, unable to handle being berated in front of everyone, stormed upstairs to his bedroom.

King Michel took a deep breath. "Gather the dead and arrange a funeral," he ordered. "We will mourn them tomorrow at midday. I will deliver a funeral oration before the senate meets. Hopefully, Governor Mala and the snake Ismal are present to see what their words and actions have led to."

He stared at everyone left in the room—his closest allies and the nobles that had lingered despite being told to leave. "Let today be known as a day that peace has failed," the king said. "We will not forget it, for as long as I am king."

A DAY LATER, Mala and Ismal were at home in one of the many inns that provided for nobles, politicians, and diplomats visiting Beiros. They were well acquainted with these hospitalities, having travelled often to the capital, and in fact, their room had been customised to suit their needs and tastes. It was a home away from home, even if they hated everything else around them.

Word of the massacre had only just begun to spread. It had occurred late at night and now it was still only early morning. No formal announcements had been made; the news was still just hearsay.

Mala and Ismal knew little of how impactful and detrimental their stay would be, and how they and their fellow Scandosians would be received in the senate. In the eyes of Alexandrosians and everyone sympathetic to their cause, Scandos would now be an enemy to the kingdom.

Ismal had gone for a routine morning walk, as he did for half an hour after rising no matter where he was. It was not for health of his body, but of his mind. He would often say it was his only chance to think for himself, without hearing or having to deal with the troubles of those around him—including those affected by his decisions.

But as he walked the streets that morning, he was disturbed by people jeering at him and the two guards that accompanied him. While he had never been the most welcome person in Beiros, this was different.

People were yelling, even spitting in his direction, and only restrained their animosity when the guards brandished their weapons at them. Ismal and his guards were tall, with fine features and pointed ears. In Beiros, they stood out like no one else, and whatever was bringing this hostility on, standing out was the last thing they wanted.

It was only when a passer-by screamed "murderer!" that Ismail began to suspect what might be the matter. He decided to do some investigating to get to the bottom of it.

SHORTLY AFTER, Mala was in her room reading over her notes for when she was to appear in the senate. Still blissfully ignorant of what had happened, she dedicated herself to her work as usual.

That changed when Ismal stormed in huffing and puffing, slamming the door open with his guards right behind him.

Mala looked at him discontentedly. "Do you mind, senator?"

"Governor Mala," he panted, "something bad has happened."

"What could be so important for you to barge in like this?"

Ismal noticed she was at her desk. "Governor, I may suggest for you to sit on your bed," he said. "This is a lot to take in."

"Okay…" Mala was confused but did so anyway. Ismal was still hyperventilating, and she began to grow annoyed. "Hurry up!" she ordered.

Ismal shook his head as though trying to throw off his agitation, and calmed down. "Remember how last night there was the twenty-fifth anniversary of the end of the civil war?"

"Unfortunately, yes."

"Well…"

"What happened?"

"A massacre," Ismal said softly. "Some elves broke into the castle hall and killed hundreds. The king and queen were almost among them."

Mala took her glasses off and wiped her eyes. "And what of the killers?"

"Dead, I think," Ismal said. "But not before taking maybe two hundred and fifty with them."

Mala stood and went to look out the window. The streets of Beiros were alive with activity. "And who was it that was killed?" she asked.

"I don't know their names," Ismal replied.

"Not their names, Ismal," she said. "Was it the people who walk these streets that were killed? People who live and work for the king?"

"Oh." Ismal realised what she meant. "From my understanding it was those present for the festivities. Nobles and the like."

Mala turned from the window to face him. "So, the Alexandrosian elite?"

"Yes."

"Hmph," she breathed. "Now they know what it's like."

"Governor Mala, these were innocent people," he pleaded, shocked.

"So were the elves killed on King Michel's orders," she said. "Where was the public outcry for them?"

Ismal stepped closer to her. "We have a memorial for them in Stock."

"Not from us, from them!" she cried. "But of course, when it's their blood that is shed, we must all weep."

"Governor, blood is blood," Ismal said, "no matter whose it is."

Mala sighed. "You're right," she conceded. "If what you have told me is true, it's a terrible tragedy. These men do not represent Scandos."

Ismal was relieved, but she was not done. "However," she began, "this doesn't excuse the party. No, it does not! Innocent people died because King Michel is as arrogant as they come. He will hear about that."

"I— I'm sure he will," Ismal stuttered. "He is giving a funeral oration later today, at midday, before the senate meeting."

"Good." Mala nodded. "Then we'll be sure to be there."

KING MICHEL WAS SITTING in his throne room with Melhel and Fares. Not even his advisers were with him, just the two Baraks. After what had happened, he felt unable to trust anyone else. Considering that Al Aanif and Al Jasha had been aggressively pushing for war, they were the last men he wanted to see, and he felt that El Salam was too weak to turn to in times like these.

The king lay slumped on his throne at the head of the table, reading over his notes for the funeral oration that was coming up and scribbling discontentedly over what he had written.

Fares and Melhel sat awkwardly, at turns twiddling their thumbs and casting their eyes towards the ceiling. The king, usually chatty, was too depressed, and too focused on his speech, to give them much of his attention—part of the reason he had let his advisers stay home. But just by being there, the Baraks, along with Rafiq, made him feel more at ease.

Rafiq stood in his usual spot at the door, extra cautious after the previous night. Framed by his shining helmet was a sad face, no longer stony or stoic. For the first time ever, the toll of being a soldier and the Sword of the King were weighing him down. He accepted full responsibility for the attack, even if it wasn't his fault.

As the king went over his speech, he scribbled more and more violently, becoming ever unhappier with the results. Eventually, he grew sick of the whole thing, grabbed the parchments, and ripped his entire speech in half, tossing it to the floor and placing his face in his hands.

"Your Majesty, your speech!" Fares cried, startled.

"It's not right," the king said. "None of it was right."

The blacksmith stood. "Well, you have to give something," he explained. "Your oration is in an hour. What will you tell the people?"

The king stood up himself, and looked out a window the way Mala had across town. "I will tell them what they deserve and ought to hear, not what they want to hear," he said sternly.

"What do you mean?"

"Whatever I write, it is all going to be a bunch of nonsense," the king said. "It's just to appease the crowd. I can't lie like that any longer."

"So write something honest," Fares said.

"It doesn't come as naturally to me as it does to you and Melhel," the king observed. "I have trained myself to prepare every word I say, and to bend the truth for the benefit of myself and my country."

"So what do you plan to do?" Fares asked, approaching the king at the window.

"No script," the king said. "I will speak from my heart. Whatever comes to mind as I see those people gathered in front of me is what will come out of my mouth."

Fares pondered the proposal a moment. "And what if you fabricate that?"

"I won't. You cannot fake emotion like you can a prepared

speech. When I am up there and I see their faces, I will not dare lie to them. I can promise you both that."

Melhel chimed in from his seat at the table. "And what if we hear you break that promise?" he asked with a grin.

King Michel chuckled softly and smiled too. "Well, then, I give you two and Rafiq permission to kill me on the spot in front of everyone. For if I were to break my promise, I would not deserve to be king, even if I lived."

~

QUEEN RANIA'S stylists were making her up with a muted look to mark the solemn occasion. This was no time for an obviously painted face or a gaudy dress. As was custom on such occasions, she wore a black gown and her hair down. This was no mere facade; she was genuinely upset, and her appearance showed it.

While she readied herself for the speech her husband was to give, Prince Sirhan was in his chambers, sulking on his bed. He, too, was dressed in black.

Hunched forward, he murmured to himself about what had happened the night before. He had been so traumatised by it that he wanted no part of the funeral oration and the expectations now upon him to grieve publicly. He'd rather have swept his problems aside and attended the gladiatorial games to forget all that had happened. In fact, he'd made arrangements to do just that once the oration was over, with or without Marissa next to him.

In his mind, dead armies and dinner guests, not to mention the Scandosians, could wait for him. He wasn't ready to face death as it was in the world. Only once it was transformed into the organised chaos and thrill of the games could he embrace it.

There was a knock at his door. "Come in," he said.

It was the queen, come to take him to the king's speech.

"It's time to go," she said. "We're due there shortly."

"What's the point?" he moaned. "Father will just harp about Alexandrosian culture and heritage and denounce the Scandosians, and then we'll be back where we started. Tensions will still be rife, and we'll have achieved nothing."

The queen sighed and sat beside Sirhan on the bed. "Son, when your father talks about the pride he has in his people, it is real," she said. "He doesn't say it out of nothing. To him, nothing matters more than the people of this kingdom."

"Then why does he insist on resisting the Scandosians' cry for independence?" the prince asked. "If he cares so much, he'd have given them what they wanted by now, and spared the bloodshed."

"Because he knows that the Scandosians will not stop at Scandos if they are given independence," the queen warned. "They'll go further and further, and try to take over Nataaros itself. To grant them autonomy would put the other provinces at risk. While we rule over them democratically, Scandos will rule with tyranny."

Prince Sirhan scoffed. "Is that what they tell you, mother?"

"No," she said. "It's what I know." She grabbed his chin gently and turned his face towards hers. "You were not around during the civil war. You didn't see what we saw."

"And what did you see?"

"What we saw last night," she explained. "A hatred and disdain for our culture and our kingdom. Everything that was built and created, undermined by people with a stain in their hearts, who know only violence, not peace."

Prince Sirhan stood and looked pointedly at the queen. "The Scandosians tried peace," he argued, "and every time they brought an idea to the senate, we shut them down. This was them fighting back. If Father wages war, who knows how many more people will die?"

The queen stood up herself and met her son's eyes. "Governor Mala is here in Beiros," she said. "I'm sure she can answer for what happened last night and affirm Scandos's stance is peaceful. If not, we know where they stand, and your father can take action accordingly."

"But—"

"But nothing," the queen cut him off. "Now, come, we have to go." She grabbed him by the arm, and they made their way to the king's funeral oration.

WITH THE FAITH of Lah being the dominant religion in Nataaros, especially in Alexandros, Beiros was full of its churches and monasteries, chief among them the Harissah Khnisi, a short walk from the royal palace.

It was the standard place for state funerals and similar events, with a balcony at the top of the building from which the king could deliver speeches. Around the building there was space for crowds of thousands to gather and hear, or to pay their respects and worship to Lah. In difficult times such as these, crowds thronged around the building.

Melhel, Fares, and Rafiq were already at the balcony, waiting patiently for the royal family. Rafiq faced the door behind them, making sure no one could get in and assassinate the king from behind.

Guards were posted at every corner surrounding the religious building, on high alert after the events of the night before, to prevent any more innocents from dying.

If the attackers had hoped to crush Alexandros, they were surely mistaken. They had only tempered the people's spirit. The crowd was plentiful and clamorous, more eager than ever to hear from the king.

Mala and Ismal were in attendance, albeit from an extremely safe distance and flanked by guards. The Khnisi was the most unsafe place for an elf at that point. One sight of their height, long hair, and pointed ears, and a riot would have broken out. For the sake of politics alone, Mala and Ismal felt it best to remain distant, especially as the senate was to meet later that day.

Melhel grew impatient as he and his uncle waited for the king, queen, and prince to arrive. "Was he always this late?" he asked Fares, exasperated.

"He's the king," Fares explained. "He wouldn't be doing his job if he wasn't fashionably late."

"He should be doing his job by sparing all of us the anticipation," Melhel said. "This is a funeral, not the gladiatorial games."

Fares grinned. "If he arrives within the next five minutes, I'll consider him as being on time. After the civil war, he once kept the crowd waiting two hours for a speech. Consider yourself lucky we've only been here about half an hour so far."

Melhel rolled his eyes and started tapping his feet rapidly, such was his impatience. He looked at the crowd in front of them—there must have been thousands. The plaza around the Khnisi was cramped with people jostling each other to try and find room for themselves. The young blacksmith was worried a human stampede would break out, as if more people needed to die to underscore the tragedy of the massacre in the palace hall.

But Melhel didn't have to wait much longer. Rafiq approached him and Fares. "The royal family have entered through the back door," he said. "They're coming up now. Look straight ahead, stern, solemn. Keep your composure like I know you can do."

Melhel and Fares held their positions. Rafiq took the initiative to announce the royal arrival. "Ladies and gentlemen: the king and queen of Nataaros," he boomed to the crowd.

From behind him, King Michel, Queen Rania, and Prince Sirhan appeared. The crowd erupted, anticipating the king's words.

King Michel took to the fore while the queen and prince fell behind him, flanked by Melhel and Fares, and Rafiq returned to watching their backs. The queen remained stoic, but the prince lowered his face to hide his emotions. He really did not want to be there.

The king examined the crowd and waited patiently for the cheering and screaming to die down so he could begin. He raised his hands to show he was about to speak, and the people fell silent.

The king breathed deeply and began to speak from the heart. "In our history, we have faced adversity and tough times as we strove for our kingdom and our sovereignty. Before we were a kingdom, we were a series of warring states—before Beilos the Conqueror, my ancestor, united Alexandros, Paros, Rios, Venos, and Scandos, into one unified kingdom.

"If I were to follow tradition, a speech like this follows a battle or a war. This is nothing new to me or to those who were with us during the civil war. However, I choose to break precedent and custom. We are not at war, but I will speak anyway, to honour the hundreds of lives that were lost in a tragedy last night, which will be felt for generations to come.

"I should hope that the reputations of the men and women that perished last night remain intact and honourable, for they were exactly that, honourable people, whose great lives met a tragic end. Whatever I say now, I pray that it adds to their esteem.

"How great is democracy, I often tell myself. Thanks to my predecessors and my ancestors, this is our form of government. The senate meets often to discuss policy and reform, and decisions on behalf of the people of Nataaros are made with the sincerest consideration, with your best interests always at the front of our minds. It is only through voting and deliberation that your lives can be affected by the senate, as it should be in a democracy.

"In the hundreds of years our kingdom has stood, all our provinces have flourished. Under the guidance of Alexandrosian governance, Rios, Paros, Venos, and Scandos all prosper, safety is ensured, and all are free to live a good and just life.

"We provide the means and the resources for prosperity, for education and growth. Men and women are free to engage in enterprise, to learn, and to develop. Agriculture and industry benefit from the foundations our kingdom has laid, which have stood for over six hundred years.

"Last night was a tragedy. A horror. As I lay in the hall by my queen's side, I feared that all this hard work done by our ancestors was to be for naught, and would crumble before us. I implore you all to consider how close we could have been to losing everything we have worked for, all these centuries gone by, if that tragedy were to tear our kingdom apart.

"Scandos as a province is exempt from any blame. I despise those who hate the elves and their culture and way of life. Respect for difference is a core part of democracy, and therefore a core part of our values. The actions of terrorists should not, and will not, be considered a reflection of their government.

"What is worthy of admiration is the swift action of my guards and soldiers last night, who dealt with the sudden attack as quickly as they could have done. Many lives were indeed lost, this I know, and it was as great a horror as any I have ever seen, but many more lives were saved thanks to the brave men who risked theirs to defend those who survived last night, and to save Nataaros as a kingdom. To those brave men—I am forever in your debt.

"Let it be known that the cowardly, shameful attackers tried to kill Nataaros last night by sparking a war that would see all of us suffer, and many of us die. But they did not achieve this. We are all Nataaros, and all of us together will be stronger as one kingdom, as we stand against hate, intolerance, and those who would jeopardise our sovereignty as a kingdom.

"We are all created equal in the eyes of Lah. As I stand here before him, I pray that he grants us mercy and forgives us for all our sins. I pray he understands the folly of man comes from our free will, and that if we abuse it at the expense of others, he will be merciful and kind and will not condemn us eternally.

"As we mourn the dead, we should also celebrate the living, and life itself, for life is a precious gift that should not be wasted. Let us not spend our lives bringing misery and suffering to those who are different to us, but let us spend our lives working together to better ourselves and the kingdom we strive to grow.

"I will leave all of you with this: thousands of men may try to break us as a kingdom, but we will never break, as long as we are united and stand by our values and our beliefs, by everything we have been built upon.

"As you depart to meditate on the words I have said here, and as you mourn and pray for the innocent souls we have lost, I entreat you: live good and just lives that are precious gifts to yourselves, your country, and the ones you love."

CHAPTER 16
THE BRINK

As King Michel finished his speech, he took another deep breath and examined the crowd in front of him.

He raised his hands, palms open and facing his people, in a gesture of gratitude for the people's attention. "Thank you," he said simply, before turning to make his way out the door with his family.

The crowd let out a raucous cheer, screaming and crying over their king's speech. It had left a remarkable impression on everyone. From that speech alone, in the months to follow, would flow a pride not only in Alexandros but in Nataaros as a whole, which would do much to quash the fear and sadness brought by the massacre.

Rafiq escorted the royal family away, leaving Melhel and Fares alone on the balcony, observing the crowd as people tore themselves one by one from their rapture and began to return to their homes and business.

They felt it was time to go, as the senate was due to meet soon, and they didn't want to lag behind the king.

Fares grabbed Melhel's arm. "I'm heading to the senate, now," he said. "Go home first and make sure Marissa is okay. If she's recovered, bring her to the senate. If not, stay with her. Don't leave her alone."

Melhel nodded. "Got it."

"And if you do come late, head straight for the royal box," Fares explained. "Do not go anywhere else in the building or city. Straight for the royal box. Governor Mala Habeb of Scandos will be at the senate, and with her there after everything that has happened, and the speech the king just gave us, I have a feeling this is only just the beginning."

Melhel was shaken by his uncle's ominous words, but for once in his life he felt this was no time to argue, and headed out the back door to get home to Marissa.

Elsewhere, Mala and Ismal were processing everything they'd heard from the king.

Ismal was impressed, while Mala played it cool.

"He's always had a way with the crowds," Ismal said.

"With the masses," Mala said cynically. "Let's see how willing he is to work together later, in the senate. Let's see how great democracy supposedly is."

MELHEL DID EXACTLY as he was told and made his way home, opening the door to find Marissa seated on the couch with a cup of tea in hand, reading some of the history books they'd taken from the library to find clues on the dead army.

Amid all the chaos and the threat of war with Scandos, Melhel had almost forgotten their biggest threat.

"How was the speech?" she asked as Melhel walked in, without lifting her eyes from the book in front of her.

"It was... interesting," he said, "to say the least."

"What did he talk about?"

"Condemned the killings and spoke about how great we are as a kingdom under our democracy."

Now Marissa put the book down. "Do you believe any of it?"

Melhel stepped inside and sat down next to her. "To an extent," he said, "but I have a feeling we won't be seeing the end of this soon." He quickly tried to change the topic. "But how are you? How are you feeling?"

"Better," Marissa said. "These books have kept me occupied."

"That's good," Melhel said. "Do you feel safe? Do you need anything?"

"No," she said, confused. "Why?"

"Just making sure," Melhel explained. "Uncle and I are going to the senate now, and we both wanted to check you were okay. Last night was pretty horrific."

Marissa chuckled. "You met me when I was on death's door at the orders of the king," she bragged. "Last night was horrific, but there's nothing that fazes me anymore."

"Okay," he relented. "But if we come back home and you're dead or missing, don't think that we didn't care about you."

"That'll be the last thing I do," she reassured him.

"Alright. Well, before I go, I'm gonna grab something to eat." Melhel stood and went to the kitchen for some fruit to snack on while walking to the senate.

Marissa returned to her book, but only got through about three lines before a knock came at the door. She looked up and was ready to answer, but before she could, Melhel returned and opened the door to find Prince Sirhan there with two guards on either side of him. The prince was looking agitated, and only the more so having found Melhel with Marissa.

Melhel was in a hurry. "I'm going to the senate now if that's what you're here for," he said.

"It's not," the prince said.

He and his guards moved to come inside, and one of the guards even attempting to brush Melhel out of the way. "Take your hand off me," Melhel ordered the man. "This is my house. You're not forcing your way in."

The prince was in no mood for Melhel's attitude. "May we *please* come in?" He asked sarcastically.

Melhel moved aside. "What are you here for, then?" he asked.

Prince Sirhan walked in and saw Marissa on the couch. "Her," he said, and ran to the couch, where they hugged each other tightly.

Prince Sirhan kissed her on the forehead. "Are you okay, my dear?" he asked.

"I'm fine, I promise you," she said. "What are you doing here? Aren't you supposed to be at the senate?"

"I'm not going."

As soon as Melhel heard this, his face changed. "What do you mean you're not going?" he asked incredulously. "Even I'm going."

"What I mean is that I'm not going," the prince repeated. "After my father's drivel I've had enough of politics for a lifetime."

Melhel approached him. "And where do you think you're going instead, then?"

"To the games," the prince said. "Marissa, my love, come with me. Let's forget our problems. Let's go enjoy the games."

Melhel got closer to Prince Sirhan's face. "You're not taking her anywhere," he said. "She needs to stay here with me and my uncle, where she is safe."

The prince took a step back and eyed Melhel. "You are in no position to give me orders, blacksmith."

"Some prince you are," said Melhel. "In our darkest time you want to run away and not face reality."

The prince ignored him and turned back to Marissa. "What do you say, my sweet?" he asked her. "Will you come with me?"

She looked first at Melhel, who clearly didn't want her to go. But she couldn't turn down the prince. "Of course, my love," she said. "I will go with you. Please just assure Melhel I'll be safe."

"Oh, you will be safe," the prince said. "I would never let anything bad happen to you."

Melhel looked on with disgust. "You both make me sick," he blasted them. "Your whole romance makes me sick. Prince Sirhan, you, as a leader … the idea of it makes me sick. I may not agree with your father a lot of the time, but he's five times the king you'll ever be."

"Excuse me?" Sirhan responded.

"You heard me loud and clear." Melhel stood firm, "You're nothing but a coward, hiding while 'your love' was nearly killed, and now when we need you the most you choose to run away and escape to your fantasy games."

Melhel then turned to the guards. "And you two idiots are

complicit in all of this," he said. "If we do end up in another war, I hope you're not taking up arms on our behalf. You're about as useless as our prince during tough times."

Marissa tried to calm Melhel down. "Melhel..." She laid her hands on his shoulders.

"Don't touch me!" He shook her away. "I rush back here to make sure you're okay, and you want to run away with him against everyone's best judgement. Just go with your prince, then. If it's what you both truly want, you deserve each other."

Melhel looked at Prince Sirhan. "I'll enjoy explaining this all to your father when I go to the senate," he berated. "What a good look this will be for the kingdom after what your father spoke about this morning: the future king of Nataaros running away, while Mala Habeb is here."

Prince Sirhan said nothing, but merely grabbed Marissa and ushered her out of the door with their guards escorting them.

Once they left, Melhel stood shaking his head in shame at Marissa and Prince Sirhan, and at himself for becoming angry with her.

"Coward," he muttered one last time, though there was no one to hear it, before grabbing his things and heading for the door himself.

∾

AT THE SENATE, everyone had begun taking their place. The king and his closest advisers and friends, including Fares, were in their positions in the royal box.

Saad Jaja was in the middle of the senate floor to mediate the potential commotion. And while Yassin Benzi took his place at the forefront of the Alexandrosian faction, so Ismal and Mala did for Scandos. The two rival provinces had been at each other in the last senate meeting, and many were certain they would be again, especially after the massacre at the palace.

Once everyone was seated, Saad rose to announce the day's proceedings. "Ladies and gentlemen of the senate," he announced. "I would like to formally thank Governor Mala Habeb of Scandos for her presence with us on this day. I have no doubt her wisdom and guidance will be very much appreciated as we discuss today's matters."

The senate applauded, and Mala momentarily stood to wave in gratitude before resuming her seat.

"I would also like to commend Our Majesty King Michel for his words this morning," Saad continued, pointing to the king, "I'm sure every one of us here has been touched by his words."

King Michel took his turn to stand and thank the senate. "Thank you, honourable Saad," he said graciously. "I should hope we can now continue the day's agenda in unity, as one kingdom."

"Thank you, my king," Saad said, and commenced business. "I think we can start by addressing last night's attacks, and what the appropriate response is. Ismal, we do not blame you or your province. In fact, we will allow you to speak first on the tragedy." Saad looked to the Scandosians to find Ismal pleasantly surprised he was allowed the first word on the topic.

At the moment Ismal was stepping forward, Melhel had found himself at the entrance to the royal box. Things were quiet as the royal party waited for Ismal to speak. Aiming not to draw attention to himself, he tiptoed discreetly made his way to the empty seat next to his uncle.

Melhel sat, and Fares leaned over to him. "Where's Marissa?" he asked.

"With the prince," Melhel answered. "They're going to Sidos for the games."

Fares was startled. "As in, the prince isn't coming?"

"No," Melhel said. "He doesn't want any part in this. He just wanted to run away straight to the games. He came and took Marissa with him."

"He took her away?"

Melhel shook his head. "She went with him by choice. It disgusts me, their romance, to my core."

"Hmph," Fares scoffed. "What a coward."

Melhel couldn't help a wry smile. "That's what I said too. I'll explain it better later. For now, I just want to see what's going on here." The two of them stopped talking and focused on the senate, where Ismal was ready to speak on the attacks in the palace hall.

"Thank you, Saad," Ismal said. "I am honoured you have given me the chance to share my thoughts—and those of my province—on this tremendous tragedy."

All eyes in the senate were on Ismal and Scandos. What he said stood to cement or demolish relations between the humans and elves forever.

"Last night, we saw hundreds of innocent men and women die, unfortunately at the hands of Scandosians," he said. "While we cannot undo that harm, we understand the frustration and anti-Scandosian sentiment there may be now. After all, we felt the same way after the civil war, so we can empathise with you, in the way we hope you empathise with us."

Yassin Benzi immediately leapt from his seat to protest. "Excuse me," he said. "How *did* you feel after the civil war, if I may ask?"

Ismal cleared his throat, maintaining his air of superiority. "After the atrocities you committed for your own imperialist gains, senator?" Ismal replied.

"Our own imperialist gains?" Yassin questioned. "You are aware that it was a war you started, no?"

"That's enough out of both of you," Saad demanded, seeing things were about to get out of hand. "We will not be having you two squabble again." He turned to Yassin. "Benzi, take a seat," he ordered. "Ismal, you may continue. But be wary of making inflammatory comments."

"Speaker, I would never," he deferred gracefully, with the hint of a mischievous grin. "Now, where was I? Ah, yes. Scandos express our deepest sympathies for those lives that were lost last night, and we trust that the perpetrators will be punished accordingly."

"It is my understanding that the attackers were killed," Saad said before looking to the king. "Am I correct, Your Majesty?"

"You are," King Michel called out from his box.

"Wonderful," Saad responded. "Thank you, Senator Ismal, for your sympathetic words."

As Saad went to change the topic, the king had grown agitated, not only by Ismal's hints that war crimes had been committed during the civil war, but by Prince Sirhan's absence. He leaned over to Melhel. "Where is my son?" he asked.

Melhel leant towards the king's ear. "At the games, Your Majesty," he whispered.

"With who?" The king couldn't believe what he had just heard.

"With Marissa."

"Why?"

"He didn't want to be involved in any of this," Melhel explained. "After your speech he couldn't wait to leave. He's on a carriage to Sidos as we speak."

King Michel rolled his eyes. "Typical of him," he moaned. "Governor Mala is here as well, and he wants to embarrass me?"

Before Ismal sat back down, he noticed Melhel whispering into the king's ear and called out. "You there, the young Barak," he yelled. "What are you whispering to the king?"

Melhel was taken aback by this, and was about to respond before King Michel interjected. "Nothing to your concern, Senator," he said.

"You should never trust the king talking discreetly to a Barak," Ismal said, "nothing good ever comes of it."

King Michel was incensed. "I do suggest you watch your tongue, Senator," he warned, "or I will be forced to silence you."

But Ismal didn't relent. "Typical of your kind," he cried, "scheming behind our backs. As if enough elves haven't perished under your watch."

"What was done in the civil war, stays in the civil war," King Michel said. "Now, if you would please allow the head to direct the senate's business."

Governor Mala stood. "If I may, Your Majesty," she said.

"Governor, you may not," King Michel commanded. "Let us leave everything in the past and focus on the future, please. We have much to discuss."

Mala would have none of it. "You dare shut me down?" she said. "A governor? And all this time we believed you were for Scandos."

The king had had enough, and stood up. "Governor, I am for Scandos," he replied. "I am also for getting on with matters pertaining to the kingdom. As it stands, the civil war is in the past, last night's attack has been resolved, and nothing remains to be said. We must move forward."

"If you were for Scandos," Mala said, "you would have already offered reparations for the war. I wouldn't have had to build everything back up myself. Instead, we suffer, thanks to your actions and those of Fares Barak." She directed her gaze to the blacksmith. "Don't think I've forgotten you, Fares. I will never forget the face of the man who destroyed nearly a whole generation of elves." Her comments drew cheers from the Scandosian senators, and jeers from everyone else in the room.

Fares was shocked to have been brought into the fray. He and Melhel were both about to stand and defend Fares, but King Michel put his arm in front of them as his eyes focused on Mala. "I'll deal with this," he told them.

The king stepped forward to the edge of his box while Mala remained still. Everyone else was seated. This was between King Michel and the governor.

"What are you saying, Governor?" the king asked. "That you were so innocent in the war? That thousands of our men didn't die, or weren't taken prisoner and tortured at the hands of Scandos? Do you choose to ignore the fact that the war started because you chose to ignore the very founding principles of our kingdom?"

"Those foundations were based on bloodshed and conquest," Mala retorted. "And I will never assume innocence, unlike you, Your Majesty. You seem to forget the actions of Fares Barak, and the destruction he brought upon us with his evil weapon. Our soldiers were mutilated by that potion of his design. Do you forget? Or have you not added this to your history books?!"

Fares lowered his head in shame. He knew his actions in the war would come back to haunt him, and now was the time.

King Michel would not back down. "Our kingdom has stood for hundreds of years," he said, "and your 'brave' soldiers starved out our city for months. People were sick and dying, all because of your selfish desires. Fares had to act; it was a tough choice but one he had to take. That is the nature of war, Governor. People suffer, and people die."

"Well, after last night, I can say with confidence you Alexandrosians finally possibly do know what suffering is," Mala jibed.

"I beg your pardon, Governor?"

"When soldiers have had their flesh eaten from inside of them," she continued, "what are a few hundred arrows in some ignorant and arrogant nobles?"

The Alexandrosians started yelling, almost ready to turn to violence over Mala's words. Every other faction watched frozen with disbelief. Never had a king argued like this in the senate, let alone with a governor.

King Michel grew enraged. "Did you put them up to this, governor?" he bellowed.

"No. I am not as cruel-minded as you Alexandrosians," Mala replied. "However, tragic as their actions were, they at least had rightful cause to commit such an attack."

"What are you saying, governor? That you support last night's attack? Between your words and those of Senator Ismal, I'm inclined to think that terrorism has the support of Scandos."

"No, Your Majesty," Mala responded. "I am not saying that I or any Scandosians support terrorism."

"Then denounce them," the king demanded.

Mala said nothing.

"If you truly believe what you have just said, then denounce them."

Still Mala said nothing.

"DENOUNCE THEM!" King Michel yelled.

"I cannot," Mala replied.

King Michel took a deep breath. The whole room was stunned and in silence. For Mala, the governor of Scandos, the most senior and respected elf in all Nataaros, to fail to denounce the attackers was treacherous, and many considered it an act of war.

"Understood," King Michel said. "You have one week, Governor. One week to denounce the attacks of last night, or I will be forced to declare war again, on Scandos."

The whole senate sprang to its feet, everyone screaming, yelling, and talking over the top of each other.

King Michel went back to his seat with the Baraks looking at him with contempt. The king gestured to Saad to bang his gavel and end the senate meeting.

"The senate is dismissed!"

CHAPTER 17

PREPARE FOR WAR

While the senate was in chaos, the prince and Marissa were in a private carriage on their way to Sidos to watch the games.

They stayed seated inside, both still reeling from the attacks and from Melhel's outburst at them earlier.

"You're not saying much," Marissa observed. "You're quieter than usual."

Prince Sirhan didn't bother making eye contact with his love; his eyes were more focused on the grass, countryside, and mountains in the far distance.

Without taking his eyes from their surroundings, the prince replied, "There are some moments when even the most outspoken of us must be quiet," he said. "I saw hundreds of my people slaughtered before me, and then I see my father—the king—try to use it for political gain."

Marissa was confused. "Political gain?" she asked. "What do you mean?"

"You're a smart girl, Marissa. After a massacre, what is most appropriate?"

Marissa's face was blank.

"I'll tell you what is most appropriate," the prince continued.

"Having respect for the fallen and their families, and not using it as an excuse to revive a centuries-old conflict."

"I don't think it is unfair if your father aims to seek revenge against Scandos," Marissa said in the king's defence. "After all, look at what they did to us."

"And look at what we did to them, all those years ago," Prince Sirhan answered.

Marissa was sullen, "So ... you know? About how they won the siege?"

"Of course I know!" he said. "I'm not a fool. I am the prince. It's the public who don't know. That's why, I assume, you and Melhel only just found out."

"Fine," she said, "but that was twenty-five years ago. The war is over and there has been peace for the most part. Why reignite conflict? What will that achieve?"

Prince Sirhan finally got over himself and looked Marissa in the eye. "The very existence of Scandos as a province of Nataaros, under Alexandrosian rule by my father, is an insult to the elven race," he said. "For everything to have been taken away from them —I can understand their pain."

"So you don't blame them for attacking us?"

"No," the prince said. "I blame my father for giving them a reason to."

Marissa sat up in concern. "Do you support Scandos in all of this?"

"I support peace," Prince Sirhan explained. "My father doesn't. He supports Alexandros and Alexandros only. He'll go to war again just to prove a point, especially as long as he has those foolish advisers by his side."

"I'm sure Fares will talk him out of it," Marissa said.

"I'm afraid his voice of reason will be for nothing. After the attack, after everything that has happened, and depending on Governor Mala's reaction, I have a strong feeling my father won't listen to any advice that isn't 'kill every elf in sight'."

Marissa lowered her head in worry, but realised where they were off to. "If you claim you hate violence so much," she said, "why are we going to the games?"

Prince Sirhan grinned. "I hate war," he specified, "but I don't hate violence if it serves as entertainment, and if it's deserved, like it is for these murderers and rapists we put on show."

"What's the difference?"

"War implicates innocent men, women, and children in the disagreements of powerful men, women, and elves," the prince said. "The games only implicate criminals, who knew what they were risking when they did what they did. That's the difference."

~

WHILE PRINCE SIRHAN was expressing his concerns and fears about a long war with Scandos, the king had gone straight to calling another meeting with his advisers.

In the throne room sat the usual suspects: the king, Melhel, Fares, Al Aanif, Al Jasha, and El Salam.

King Michel was furious at Governor Mala's reaction in the senate. He was ready for war, but the room was divided. Al Aanif and Al Jasha were keen to take advantage of this and push him into battle as they had long wanted, while the rest would do everything they could to stop him.

"You can't declare another war," Fares pleaded. "You're only going to drag us into another bloody mess!"

"You saw that cow's reaction, Fares!" Al Aanif said. "They will not show any remorse for what happened. They do not oppose terrorism—they embrace it."

Fares stood from his seat and looked over the table. "I care not for what they do or do not embrace," he said. "I only care for keeping people safe, and another civil war will not do that."

"Weak, as always," Al Aanif laughed. "I wouldn't expect anything less from your kind."

Melhel's eyes sharpened as he looked straight at the politician. "Care to repeat that?" he dared.

"Quiet, young man," the minister said. "You were not there during the war. Know your place."

"And you were not there, either!" Melhel rebuked him. "My

uncle fought on the front lines while you kept yourself locked away. When Scandos was at our gates, you hid like a little child."

"Is that what your uncle tells you?" Al Jasha asked.

Amid all this bickering, the king sat silent, his head buried in his hands.

"Ask anyone, you piece of filth," Melhel's said, his voice growing louder. "You can ask my uncle, the king, Rafiq—any soldier that fought to defend this kingdom as you did not."

Al Aanif stood, attempting to tower over the young blacksmith. "So you know what Scandos did," he said, "and still you don't want war."

Melhel stood himself, keeping his eyes locked on Al Aanif's. "I know. And I know what we did too," he said.

Fares jumped in. "We need to avoid war at any cost," he said. "We can resolve this with diplomacy, not by the sword."

He turned to Michel. "My king, I love this kingdom, but I will not mutilate any more soldiers on your behalf," he said. "Innocents should not be put on the front lines for your sake."

"Then what would you have me do, Fares?" the king asked. "After all I have done in these past several years, this is how they repay me? And you expect me to lie down?"

Fares took a deep breath. "You answered them with war before," he said, "and that cost the lives of thousands. Be a king. Be a leader. Do not put your people's lives at risk. Not for this."

Everyone stood quietly as Fares' words sank in.

Al Jasha looked at El Salam, who had been silent the whole time. "You haven't said much, El Salam," he noted. "Care to contribute anything of substance?"

El Salam stayed seated and shook his head. "History tends to repeat itself, gentlemen," he explained. "Our people have been in conflict with the elves for how long? Nothing has changed. Not since Beilos himself have we seen lasting peace with Scandos."

El Salam looked to the king. "We can go to war with them again, Your Majesty," he said, "but don't be surprised if more people die, if lessons are not learned and people are hurt. War is a stain that society cannot get rid of. If we declare war on Scandos now—even if Governor Mala refused to denounce the terrorist actions of her people—will only add to the mess that years of war and hatred have brought us."

The room was as still as Rafiq guarding a door.

"What say you, my king?" Al Aanif asked. "You have heard us all speak. Are you declaring war on Scandos? Are we to engage in another civil war?"

King Michel took a deep breath and stood, gesturing for the others to sit back down. "Gentlemen, I appreciate all that you have said," he began. "The arguments for and against war are both as strong as they can be, and I have thought about this long and hard, even before this meeting, even before Governor Mala's response, even before my speech, and even before the attacks."

"The decision I have made has not come without months of forethought, planning, and consultation."

King Michel eyed Fares, Melhel, and El Salam, his voices for peace. "You three have gone against calls for war," he said, "and I respect your conviction and advocacy for peace. War brings heartbreak and pain; I know this too well."

The king then looked at Al Aanif and Al Jasha, his voices for war. "And you two have demanded that war—that action—be taken against Scandos," he said. "In my younger days, I would've taken on your considerations in a heartbeat, without any careful planning, as I did twenty-five years ago."

He sighed, "It may shock you all, but I made my decision immediately after the attack," he announced. "What has happened since only shows my decision was correct: we are going to war with Scandos."

The room was in shock. Al Aanif and Al Jasha stayed silent in their victory, but Fares jumped out of his seat in protest. "You cannot do this, my king!" he cried. "Lives will be lost! It'll only be a vicious cycle repeating itself!"

"My decision has been made, Fares," the king said. "What's done is done."

"Call it off! You haven't declared war on Scandos yet," Fares pleaded. "You can change your mind and deal with Governor Mala personally!"

King Michel shook his head. "It is final, Fares," he said. "I have already sent an army of our best forces to attack the elves stationed at their border, in the mountains. This time, they won't surprise us with their archers."

Fares' face grew pale at the realisation that the king had long been willing to send a surprise attack against the unsuspecting Scandosians.

Melhel was stuck to his seat, outwardly stoic but inwardly panicking. He knew full well what the king would expect of him and his uncle. He was about to go to war.

"Fares," the king continued. "Your weapons and armour will be greatly needed, as will your experience and leadership in battle. You've saved us once; you will save us again."

"But..." Fares tried to argue, but the king ignored his pleas and left the throne room, leaving his old friend standing there, not knowing what to do.

~

THE KING HAD INDEED ALREADY MOBILISED an army to go north to the mountainous region at the border between Scandos and Alexandros.

In the civil war, Alexandros had been taken by surprise, but this time the roles would be reversed. King Michel had learned from the past and intended to use the same shock tactics against his enemies.

The king's army had moved north with a stunning speed seen only from the most elite troops. The only thing they lacked was Rafiq Harrira; deemed too vital, he would be reserved for the inevitable major battle closer to home.

The army sent north numbered around ten thousand, a mixture of light infantry, light cavalry, and archers. These were the best soldiers to use for a quick, surprise attack.

By the time the king revealed his intentions to his advisers, the division had already arrived at the border under the cover of darkness. Uncharacteristically, as camouflage against the mountains and snows of Scandos, they wore white surcoats over their armour in place of the usual green, red, and black.

The Snowy Mountains on the border stood between Alexandros

and the habitable areas of Scandos. They had been hard to climb through and navigate: most travellers go around, but the conventional route would have gotten these soldiers killed, so they had first to scale and conquer these mountains before they could surprise the elves.

In a matter of hours, well into a pitch-dark night, they had scaled the mountains and now had a bird's-eye view of all Scandos.

The general in charge of the division saw what was ahead of him—guard posts scattered across the ranges, east and west along the border. The strategy was simple: capture these mountains to control the border, all the way to Alhayit, and pin Scandos deep in their own territory, trapping them and blocking any routes for trade or escape.

In the civil war, Scandos had laid siege to Beiros, holding everyone inside the city for months. This time, the king's grand plan, made in consultation with Rafiq, was to trap Scandos and its armies across the border, controlling the mountains to give the army a full view of Scandos and to allow no semblance of a counterattack from the elves.

Without hesitation, the general ordered the night raids to commence, and one by one the guard posts amid the mountains fell to the rapid onslaught of the king's armies. Every Scandosian soldier there was either slaughtered or taken prisoner, and the massacre lasted well into the night.

By dawn, every Scandosian outpost had been taken, Alexandros had established full control of the mountains and the border, and, leaving garrisons at the captured posts, was moving deeper into Scandosian territory.

The elves would wake to a shock, looking up to the mountains and seeing hell awaiting them. Their army soundly defeated, any control they had over the border, any hope of exerting bargaining power over Alexandros, would be gone. They had been invaded and trapped in their own province. It would take a miracle from Mala Habeb to save them from calamity.

∽

"HOW COULD YOU DO SUCH A THING?" Fares howled at the king.

King Michel, Melhel, Fares, and Rafiq were in the throne room on their own. After the dust had settled on the king's revelation of his plans for war, the Baraks had cornered the king in the throne room later that night, to confront him about his decision.

"Do you know how many lives we will lose?" Fares continued. He was past indulging any niceties or formalities, and had dropped his guard to let the king know exactly how he felt.

The king sat on his throne quietly, waiting for the right time to speak, while his old friend and his nephew paced the room in a rage over what was to become of their kingdom.

"My king," Melhel said, "we have bigger concerns than the Scandosians, anyway. The dead army still looms large. We need to focus our efforts on them, not on the elves."

"I'm well aware of the dead army, Melhel," King Michel said. "But we cannot fight a war on two fronts. To expect us to be able to fight the Scandosians and the dead army is unrealistic. We will defeat the elves first, swiftly, and then focus on the dead army."

Melhel sighed but stood his ground. "Your Majesty, who is the biggest threat," he asked, "the elves who were more than happy to continue negotiating, or the dead army, who will kill indiscriminately until we all cease to exist?"

King Michel stood with his hands on the table and stared the three other men down. "I know *your* answer, but you're wrong," he said. "Scandos are no longer happy to negotiate. They want blood. We will give them blood."

Fares stepped in. "Are you saying the Scandosian government orchestrated the attack?"

"Governor Mala refused to denounce it," the king explained. "Either she is with them, or she supports them directly."

"How do you know she supports what happened to us?" Fares asked.

"If she doesn't, she would have said so," King Michel said. "Instead, she refused. She is as complicit as the terrorists themselves."

Melhel put his hands over his head. "You cannot be serious, Your Majesty!" he cried. "Look at what we did in the war! We gassed and mutilated thousands of them, and we never apologised. We are not the only victims."

The king left his seat to come up close and roar right in Melhel's face. "We did it because they held siege to us for months! My people were starving. They were dying! They turned Beiros into a living hell, so I acted! What would you have done if they nearly took everything away from you?"

For the first time since he had known him, Melhel had seen the king snap. The young man's lack of a filter had finally drawn his ire.

The king drew breath. "Melhel, I know your main concern is the dead army," he said, "but we need to focus on this first. The Scandosians may not be mindless killing machines like the soldiers of the dead army are supposed to be, but they *will* kill anyone who stands in the way of their goals, as we have seen. Besides, they don't believe in the dead army. We know this already. If they somehow win and take power, and spare your life, do you think they will let you focus on defeating the dead? No—they will strip you of any chance you have to stop them, allowing them to grow stronger and invade us through the wall."

Melhel lowered his head, conceding the king might have a point. It was true, that the Scandosians dismissed the dead army as a mere myth—a folktale. If they took power, there was no way they'd allow Melhel or anyone to continue the quest to defeat this supernatural enemy.

King Michel then stepped away from Melhel and went to his uncle. "Fares, you were with us when Scandos attacked our festivities," he said. "But more importantly, you were with us when they laid siege and nearly destroyed us all. If it weren't for your decisiveness, who knows what the world would look like now. You well know their imperial ambitions. I'm not asking you to fight because I want to see Scandos eliminated; I'm asking you to fight to defend this kingdom, its people, and everything that has been built over all these centuries."

"And if I refuse?" Fares asked.

"Then I lose one of my top soldiers—one of my top generals," the king said. "And Rafiq will have a lot more to do as my Sword."

Fares took a deep breath, shaking his head as he realised the king had convinced him to take up arms against Scandos. "Alright. I'll do it. I'll fight," he said. "But we are only defending what we have; we are not conquering Scandos."

"You have my word," King Michel said, smiling.

Rafiq came forward to announce the current plans for invasion. "Right now, the troops sent should be in position, ready to capture the mountains along the border," he said. "Once we receive confirmation of this goal, we will send reinforcements their way to bolster our position up north. While we do that, we will have armies at the ready here in Alexandros for any counterattack."

"And what of our allies?" King Michel asked.

"Rios and Paros will have troops at the ready if needed, and if we are overrun here," Rafiq said.

Fares turned his head. "They're in on this too?"

"I had organised this with their government already, before we sent the troops," King Michel said.

"So, you dealt with them in secret?"

"It had to be done," King Michel explained. "Rafiq and I agreed that the element of surprise, and secrecy and swift movement, was the key to winning this war."

Fares and Melhel stayed quiet, accepting that now they would have to fight and provide the equipment needed with their blacksmithing. They both looked at Rafiq, who understood their concerns but remained stern, knowing this was no time to argue.

There was no turning back for the Baraks. The time for war had come.

CHAPTER 18

THE INVASION

Dawn kicked in and Scandos woke to see the force that beset them. One by one, as they arose, they saw the mountain outposts in the distance flying the Alexandrosian flag. War had come.

Shocked, they murmured and cried among themselves about what curse had fallen on their land, to allow this constant conflict with the Alexandrosians.

Governor Mala herself had begun the day faintly hearing the panic on the streets beneath her. She had put on her robe, walked outside to the balcony, and seen the source of the commotion. Once she had seen the Alexandrosian flags peppered across the mountains, her face changed from an elf's customary pale white, turning pink—almost red—with rage. Without hesitation, she ran back inside and dressed, ready to head to her office. There would be much to discuss regarding this crisis.

～

MALA NOW HAD Ismal seated across from her at her desk. He was even more anxious than usual, and ready for retribution.

"First, they embarrass you and put you on the spot in the

senate," he said. "Then, they refuse to negotiate. And then, they invade. This is war, Governor. We must act!"

Mala remained quiet, her hands palm-together in thought, with her sharp chin resting on her fingertips. After her rage on first seeing the flags in the mountains, the elf's expression was cold again. She had known this day would come. "Remember when I said I would plan an invasion if our proposals kept getting rejected?" she asked.

"Yes," Ismal replied. "Quite well, actually. But how can we invade now? They have the border."

"Not for long. Need I remind you again of how I elevated myself to this position?"

Ismal shook his head. "No, Governor," he said. "But what do you plan to do?"

Mala stood. "I set up a plan for if they rejected your proposals, yes?"

"Yes."

"And true to form, Alexandros has invaded before we even had a chance to ready ourselves, correct?"

"Correct." Ismal nodded, "What does that have to do with anything?"

"You little fool," she berated him, "do you not think I didn't have a plan for if they invaded us?"

From her desk, she pulled out a map of Nataaros, and pointed at the border between Scandos and Alexandros. The map showed cities, terrain, and military outposts, the last of which were now of greatest interest to them after their capture. "It was the most obvious plan King Michel could have drawn up," she said. "Even from Rafiq Harrira—I expected better of him. Granted, this is pretty humane by their barbaric standards."

"Well, what have you done to counter this, if you saw it coming?" Ismal asked.

Mala grinned, "Come with me," she said. "I'll show you why Alexandros won't win with this idiotic plan of theirs."

～

A WEEK LATER, when he returned from his venture to the games, Sirhan was furious when he found out what had happened while he was gone.

In his room, the king, Melhel, and Fares, had all tried to explain the situation to him. But being opposed to politics, never mind wars over political matters, he refused to accept it. For him, going to war was the worst decision the king could have made.

"What choice was I left with, Sirhan?" King Michel tried to argue. "It's time Scandos paid for their sins."

"Their sins?" Prince Sirhan complained. "You mean ours! *We're* the aggressors, not them."

Melhel chuckled. "No, you can't possibly suggest we're the aggressors," he said, "when, as I recall, during the massacre you were hiding in a corner waiting for it all to end."

"Watch it, blacksmith!" the prince warned.

The king continued to plead his case to his son. "Hundreds of people have died for the Scandosians' cause," King Michel said. "What sort of king would I be if I allowed the attackers' actions to go unpunished?"

"A good one," Prince Sirhan replied. "Seriously, I go away for a week, and you give in to those idiots in your council."

Melhel chimed in again. "Well, maybe if you had been doing your job as prince, and were here instead of at the games," he sneered, "you could have offered your input. But instead, you ran away. What does Marissa see in you?"

"Shut up, Melhel," Fares ordered, nudging his nephew.

"I won't. Not when our next in line is more concerned with putting prisoners in barbaric games than with doing his job."

"Careful, Melhel," Prince Sirhan warned again, scowling, "or I'll send you there myself."

"Go for it," Melhel scoffed. "It's a gain for the games and a loss for your army. Without me defending you and watching your back, you'll soon be a dead man, from what we've learned so far."

It grated on Sirhan to be reminded of the numerous times Melhel had saved his life, no matter how much he knew his young friend was right.

Fares tried to mediate. "Look, my prince," he said, "we have seen this before from the Scandosians. They will only rest when their goals are achieved—when they leave Nataaros and achieve their independence. And they are willing to kill to achieve this dream."

"So give it to them," Prince Sirhan said.

"If we do, there'll be no end to their ambition," Fares said. "They become independent—they won't stop. They will go after the throne. Your father will be dead. Your mother will be dead. *You'll* be dead." He hoped this would appeal to the prince's sense of pride and family loyalty. It didn't.

The prince stood up and looked at the men confronting him. "You fools can carry out your warmongering plans," he berated them. "But don't come crying to me when we're under siege again and our people are dying."

The prince stormed out of his room before anyone could say another word. The others stood there blankly, not knowing what to make of all of this.

"Maybe being under siege will be good for him," Melhel suggested. "It's one way to keep him from running away again."

Even Melhel shivered at the ferocity of the look Fares then gave him. A siege was no joking matter.

～

MELHEL DIDN'T HAVE time to reflect on his spat with Prince Sirhan; he had work to do in his workshop office, going over designs for new armaments and equipment for the impending battle with Scandos.

As he examined them carefully, he noticed that the current armour in use was far too heavy for infantry, on the battlefield it would slow them down. If the Alexandrosians were to have any hope against the elves, they would need to move faster and not be encumbered by their own armour. Melhel left a note of this to be looked at later on—quickly though, as a battle was looming.

Amid the sound of metal clanking around him, he heard a knock on his door.

"Come in," he said, without looking up from the designs.

The door opened and in stepped Prince Sirhan, with a sheepish smile on his face, coming in quietly so as to not disturb his friend's work.

Melhel took one glance away from his work and, seeing the prince, rolled his eyes and looked down again.

"How is it all coming along?" the prince asked.

"Fine," Melhel said.

"Good." The prince smiled.

"But the armour is really heavy," Melhel said without looking up. "It'll be nearly impossible for us to keep up with Scandos's speed. We'll have to adjust that."

"I see." Prince Sirhan nodded. "But wouldn't heavier armour make things easier? They'll have a harder time penetrating us, and we can overpower them."

"My prince," Melhel said, "are you suggesting you know more about blacksmithing and battles than I do?"

The prince knew he had no winning response to that.

Melhel would have liked to concentrate, but Prince Sirhan had more to talk about.

The young blacksmith noticed the prince hanging around and finally gave him his attention. "What do you want?" he scolded.

"I just want to talk to you about before," Prince Sirhan said.

"There's nothing to discuss," Melhel responded. "We need to prepare for war, and you being here is hindering our preparations."

Prince Sirhan sighed. "Can we just put this tension to bed?" He pulled a chair across the room, near to Melhel, and gestured to it. "May I?" he asked.

"Do I have any say?" Melhel said.

The prince took this as a yes and sat. "I understand I was a little bit out of order earlier," he said abashedly.

"A little?" Melhel said, "Try 'very much out of order'."

"Okay," the prince conceded. "I was very much out of order. But you have to see it from my side."

"What *is* your side, Prince?" Melhel exclaimed, "A coward's side? A weak man's side of things? What could you say that would make me think otherwise right now?"

Prince Sirhan took a deep breath. "You've been here a shorter time than I have," he said. "I've lived here in Beiros my whole life."

"What's your point?"

"My point is that you don't know these politicians like I do," the prince explained. "You think you do, but you don't."

Melhel looked at him with contempt, but the prince continued.

"You're a smart man. You are," Prince Sirhan said. "Surely you can see that war is not the answer. These politicians my father surrounds himself with only know violence and hatred and destruction. They don't see the humanity behind it all. They're warmongers, Melhel. They only want to see Alexandrosian supremacy across all of Nataaros."

Melhel considered this a moment. "I see what you are saying," he said, "and perhaps I'd take you more seriously if I hadn't seen you cower in a corner while we were under attack, and if you hadn't run away to the games when we were in the middle of negotiating with Scandos."

"I ran to get away from the politics!" Prince Sirhan cried in his defence. "Do you think I wanted to be stuck in a room with those men and hear them babble about how we must wage war?" He sat up straighter. "Besides, these negotiations were always going to be fruitless. I know my father. And he knew Governor Mala was never going to relent. So he was always going to be readying an invasion from the moment those attackers came in. No, I take that back," he said. "He's been at it far longer than that."

He looked at Melhel with worry, hoping his friend would see his side of things. Melhel was willing to entertain his perspective. "What would you do then, if you were king?" he asked.

"I would negotiate," Prince Sirhan claimed. "Properly. None of this half-hearted business my father gets up to."

"What's the difference between the two of you?"

"I'm a better negotiator than him," the prince said. "I'm more reasonable and not as stubborn. When he doesn't get his way, he throws a tantrum. If I don't get my way, I'm willing to adjust and compromise."

Melhel found that hard to believe. "Well, since you're so good at negotiating," he said, "why not talk to your father now?"

"His stubbornness is equal to my ability to compromise," Prince Sirhan said. "We'd reach an impasse."

The young blacksmith finally put his work to the side and looked Prince Sirhan right in the eye. "You do realise he's like this for a reason?" he said. "The attacks from the other week confirmed his fears that Scandos wants control of the kingdom."

Prince Sirhan rolled his eyes. "They don't want control: they want their independence," he said. "Those idiots in the throne room would have you believe that they're seeking to destroy us."

"One of those 'idiots' happens to be my uncle," Melhel said.

"Your uncle is not a politician," the prince explained. "I'm not talking about him. Besides, your uncle's side of things I can understand. Scandosians have tried to kill him multiple times, but this is different. He's been away from everything for twenty-five years, Scandos is as far from wanting war as anyone, and those terrorists aside, they're not out to take the kingdom over."

Prince Sirhan took a deep breath. "Think about it, Melhel," he said. "They are their own race. They have their own language, culture, and system of government. Their province only exists to be administered from here because of Beilos; they had no say in any of this. Surely, you can see where they're coming from—where Governor Mala is coming from."

Melhel folded his arms. "Then explain the terrorist attacks." He looked at the prince, not expecting him to have an answer.

"You cannot expect an entire state to answer for the actions of a few extremists," the prince said. "Every state has people like that. Ours just happens to have them in the senate."

"That's fine, but Governor Mala refused to denounce them," Melhel said. "If they don't represent Scandos as a whole, surely it wouldn't have been hard for her to do so."

And now the prince, usually brash and confident, had no answer.

Melhel smirked at his victory over the prince, and pressed his case. "Besides, if you dislike violence so much, why do you always enjoy going to the games?" he asked.

Prince Sirhan sighed. "The games and war are entirely different," he explained. "Only criminals are subjected to the games. War is different: good men die on the battlefield, as do innocents who get caught up in it all. The games are to punish the wicked for our entertainment; war sends innocents to an early grave over the quarrels of egotistical men in power."

Melhel nodded as if in agreement. "Killing is killing, though."

"I'd rather have murderers and rapists killed than women and children," the prince replied, with a stern eye on Melhel, who promptly raised his eyebrows in surprise at the prince's forthrightness.

And now Melhel had no answer. He began to gather the papers on his desk to continue his work, but the prince still sat before him. "Are you still here?" Melhel asked, freshly annoyed at the interruption to his work.

"On the topic of killing," the prince began. "What's it like to kill someone? What is it like to play Lah for a moment and take someone's life away?"

Melhel shook his head. "What an awful thing to ask."

"Oh, don't be like that." The prince smiled. "I've seen you at work. The way you handled those terrorists, for instance. And I saw you on our way here from Chekkos, destroying those bandits. You have a knack for it. I want to know what it's like."

Melhel sighed. "You'll never have to know what it's like," he said, trying to avoid answering.

"Exactly. So, tell me—what's it like to kill a man?"

"Honestly?" Melhel asked the insistent prince. But he knew Sirhan would not leave him alone without an answer. "At the time you don't notice it. You're usually defending yourself or the people around you. It's afterwards that it really hits you, when the heat of the moment dies down and you have time to think about your actions. That's when you truly realise what you've done."

"How do you cope with it?"

"I tell myself I'm doing the right thing," Melhel said, "that I have killed only those who deserve it."

Prince Sirhan leaned forward. "And do you believe this?"

Melhel just stared blankly.

But he would not allow his mind to wander further, and shook his head and turned again to his papers. "Who knows," he said. "I need to get back to work."

The prince nodded. As he walked out, he smirked at the realisation that he was shrewd enough to manipulate and soften up even someone like Melhel.

～

THOUGH THERE MAY HAVE BEEN indecision among the Alexandrosian leadership over what course of action to take in this new war, there was none in Scandos. As quickly as their border had been overtaken, they immediately prepared a response.

Mala and Ismal stood before the gates at Stock, gazing at the Snowy Mountains, their faces giving no sign that they expected to lose against the Alexandrosian forces.

With the two Scandosians was the architect of their masterplan— the very same Al Eelam who had orchestrated the potions behind the ruin of the Scandosian army all those years ago, who had decided to switch allegiances to Scandos. His loyalties lay neither with Nataaros, nor his native Rios, but with whomever paid him well and supplied him handsomely to conduct his research. Scandos knew this, and despite what he had done to them, they knew his ingenuity would be key. It had been in the first civil war, and it could be so again in this one.

Al Eelam had aged significantly since the Siege of Beiros, but his brains were as formidable, and again he had concocted something of extraordinary power—which it was time to unleash.

"How are things looking?" Mala asked her new ally.

"Very good, Governor." Al Eelam beamed. "I think this might be my strongest weapon yet."

"Have you tested its potency?" Ismal asked.

Al Eelam looked at him with contempt. "I am the greatest mind in all of this kingdom. If I develop any magic or potion, then you should have no doubt that it will work. You will erect a statue of me once you see its effectiveness."

"A statue?" Mala laughed. "After what you did to us? I'd find it hard to commission that."

"That was all the doing of Fares Barak and Rafiq Harrira," Al Eelam said. "This is *my* doing, and it will be twice as devastating. This will win you your independence, you can be sure of that."

Ismal looked nervous. "So, what does this involve?" he asked.

Al Eelam smiled, "It's simple." He stepped forward and raised one hand, about to click his fingers.

On top of being a scientist, he could also perform magic, and his magic had the properties of a weapon. Without hesitating, he clicked.

A loud bang rang across the mountains, and when those in the city looked up, they saw explosions detonating across the range. Every occupied outpost was simultaneously being destroyed.

Months before, the mountain ranges had been laced with a magic powder that detonated upon Al Eelam's click.

And if the blast had not yet destroyed an outpost, the soldiers there had another thing coming. The explosions were so violent that the mountains themselves seemed to crumble. The avalanches that fell along the mountains engulfed every single unfortunate soul that happened to be up there in snow and rock.

As the explosions went off, Mala had looked on sternly, knowing her long-time plan had finally come to fruition. Ismal was dumbfounded with disbelief that Al Eelam could create such a spectacle. And Al Eelam himself was gleeful, celebrating the effectiveness of his new discovery. He was unconcerned with Scandos' ambitions; in his mind was only the fame and riches he had been promised, which dwarfed those given to him by Alexandros in the last civil war.

At the snap of a finger, Al Eelam had demolished the Alexandrosian occupation, freed Scandos, and opened the border once again. Scandos was now free to send in their army and defeat the Alexandrosians once and for all, to declare their independence.

Now, Scandos could fight back.

CHAPTER 19
BATTLE PLANS

With eerily similarity to the way Governor Mala had looked out from her balcony on disaster a week before, King Michel now rushed to the balcony of his room in the palace, summoned by a distant rumble, to see snow and mountains seemingly collapsing on the horizon where his troops were supposed to be occupying the Scandosian guard posts.

He turned his head from left to right as, one by one, the clouds of snow and debris around the mountains cleared. Where once there had been sharp peaks, now, in the distance, the ranges rose to a high plateau. Where Mala watched with glee, King Michel watched on with horror, for he knew that the tables had turned. Having cleared a path to bring their troops more easily through the mountains, Scandos would now be poised to invade.

The king had to act quickly. Any delay in his response could spell doom for his kingdom. He sent word to Rafiq of what had just happened, anxious to meet his Sword to discuss their next course of action.

~

HALF AN HOUR LATER, Rafiq stood next to the king on the balcony, watching with shock that even the Sword's usually cold demeanour couldn't hide. For the first time in forever, his eyes showed signs of fear and panic.

The snow was still falling, and the avalanches were still raging across the mountains along the border. They had even bled onto the Alexandrosian side, and while they had not hit any towns, anyone unlucky to be travelling in those mountains had been swallowed whole by the snow. This was not only an attack on the king's army, but on Alexandros and its people. The king wanted blood.

"How long has it been since I sent for you?" the king asked Rafiq.

"About half an hour, Your Majesty," Rafiq said.

The king turned to look at his Sword. "Half an hour, give or take, these avalanches have been going on," he said, "and they're not stopping. What on earth has that woman done?"

"The governor seems to have rigged the mountains with an explosive potion, or some kind of magic," Rafiq said, observing the disaster in front of them. "She must have known that if we were ever to invade, our first move would be to capture the mountains and corner them in Scandos, between the mountains and Alhayit. She's beaten us at our game." Rafiq sighed with stress, and rubbed his hands through his hair. "That's ten thousand of my best, trapped under tonnes of snow in the mountains," he lamented, "dead because we fell into a trap."

King Michel detected the disheartened tone in Rafiq's voice, and tried to lift his spirits. "We still have the Baraks," he said. "Fares saved us once. He can do it again, as can his nephew."

"He's not going to like this one bit," Rafiq said.

"No one will," the king said, "but you two know each other very well. The siege was far worse than anything we had ever faced, and we overcame it. We just have to meet the elves in battle, where we can surely beat them."

Rafiq nodded. "Correct," he agreed, "but we have to act fast."

"That's why I called you here straight away," King Michel explained. "For all we know, they're already crossing the border. We haven't got time to waste."

The Sword kept staring at the destruction of the mountains. "Al Eelam," he said. "Al Eelam did this."

"Who?"

"Don't you remember, my king? The Riosan man who developed the potion during the siege? He worked under Fares and me. Now it seems he's switched sides."

"That man?" the king asked. "What is he doing serving Scandos?"

"Must be a scientific mercenary," Rafiq suggested. "After all, who else could develop magic like that?"

The king was confused. "Is it magic, or science?" he asked.

"This man blurs the line between what is given to us naturally by Lah, and what his warped mind can create," Rafiq said.

"Are you sure it is him?"

"I'm absolutely certain," Rafiq said. "This will give Fares extra reason to fight. He never did quite trust Al Eelam."

King Michel smirked. "He never trusts anyone."

"In this case, he was right," Rafiq said.

"Let's go, then," the king said as he made to leave the balcony. "You said it yourself: we can't waste any time."

~

AFTER A WHOLE DAY of destruction across the border, the avalanches let up and then finally stopped.

Snow now covered not only the mountains but even the grasslands on the Alexandrosian side, not just in patches but tonnes and tonnes of it, which would kill the ecosystem in the affected areas.

The outposts that once stood in the mountains had vanished, swallowed by snow with the Alexandrosians and Scandosians they had killed sealed inside for good. If they were not already dead, they would soon be frozen inside and preserved like mummies. Sending search parties to dig for survivors, or for dead to bury, was now a luxury neither side could afford, with a battle soon to take place.

Mala now stood in Stock with Ismal, at the head of an army. This was the largest force Scandos had ever assembled, featuring their most elite heavy and light infantry, cavalry, catapults, and the same famed archers that had devastated the Alexandrosian forces in the civil war.

And aside from the size, something else was different about this army. Learning from their mistakes and suffering during the Siege of Beiros, each soldier now sported different armour to what had been worn years ago.

The infantry units not only had armour and protection covering their entire bodies, but also masks and visors protecting their faces to guard against the use of poison gas. Every other unit had been equipped in the same fashion. Mala was not taking any chances.

The Scandosian cavalry sat atop the most stunning, pearly white horses imaginable. In the field, they would so dazzle the eye that it would seem as though a god favoured them in battle.

At the front of each soldier's breastplate was the Scandosian coat of arms: a snow-capped mountain. Banners sprang above each individual unit, each of which had lined up in a strict, rigid formation, ready to march on Alexandros in their counter-invasion.

Mala was confident, for the destruction she had wrought on the mountains was not the only trick up her sleeve. She had something else in store for Alexandros, which could decide the battle in a single stroke.

She took her place at the head of the army, facing the troops. She would not march on Alexandros with them—as governor she was bound not to fight herself—but could plan their strategy and offer words of encouragement.

She eyed up the soldiers in the front ranks one by one, and began her speech. "In this way, we begin the work our fathers started twenty-five years ago," she began. "For too long, the tyranny of King Michel has held us back, but no more. No longer shall we subjected to this tyrant's whim. We shall take back what is ours. Scandos, to arms!"

The soldiers raised their weapons and cheered so loudly that the echoes were heard across the mountains. This was their moment: everything they had trained for. Mala's speech needed to be no longer; she was known for having only one concern—Scandosian independence—and her soldiers shared the cause. All she had to do was appear before them and hold out the prospect of freedom, and they were spurred to action.

The soldiers began their march.

~

IN THE THRONE ROOM, the king was again with Rafiq, Fares, and Melhel, the men he trusted most to help him plan a battle. The ministers had been sent away to deal with senatorial matters, rather insultingly, they thought, when they'd heard Melhel was permitted in the war council. For someone of his youth to be included was unprecedented. But neither the king nor Rafiq cared if the politicians of Alexandros took the apparent slight personally—they knew Melhel's potential and his contribution to their efforts in times of peace.

A shock addition to this band was Prince Sirhan, whose tone seemed to have shifted following his chat with Melhel about war, cowardice, and what it was like to kill a man. Now, he wanted to hear everything that was being said and be an active part of the war effort, to prove his mettle as a future king.

They all stood around a table with a map of Nataaros laid across it, where little figurines represented the armies of Alexandros and Scandos.

Scandos's figurines were placed just ahead of Stock, where Alexandrosian reconnaissance told them the army had commenced its march, while Alexandros's army was marked as being in and around Beiros, where indeed they were being mobilised for the impending invasion from Scandos.

Rafiq pointed along the map. "From what we know, they have already moved forward from Stock," he explained, "and are now moving forward to cross the undefended mountains."

"How do we know they're coming from this side?" Fares asked.

"Our scouts have informed us," Rafiq said. "This is the safest side for them to cross. If they come in from the west, the mountains are too cold, high, and dangerous even for an elf. It's a safe bet that they're coming from the east."

King Michel rubbed his chin and looks closely at the map, "Where does that leave us, then?" He wondered.

"By our estimations, they'll be halfway between here and the border within a week," Rafiq said. "If we want to stop them reaching Beiros, we'll need to cut them off around here."

Rafiq pointed to an area north-west of Beiros.

Melhel noticed this and grew anxious. "That's just outside of Chekkos," he said, "where we're from. Are we going to be fighting near there?"

The Sword noted the grave looks on Melhel and Fares' faces. "There is a strong possibility that we will be," he said, "if our armies happen to meet there. We'll do what we can to spare the villagers and their livelihoods. If it comes to it, we'll evacuate them until it is safe to come back."

Melhel wasn't happy about this. "Rafiq, sir, with all due respect, we are going to be putting innocent lives at risk," he said. "We know these people. There must be another way to do this."

"I promise you we will do what we can to protect them," Rafiq reassured Melhel. "We are not in the business of killing innocents; we are in the business of defeating Scandos."

"Okay," Melhel relented, "but if I see one civilian killed, by our hand or Scandos's, you can say goodbye to my uncle and me. You can win the battle without us."

Prince Sirhan laughed and looked at Fares. "I didn't realise your nephew spoke for you now," he sneered.

"I didn't realise you'd finally grown enough of a spine to join us here, my prince," Fares retorted.

Sirhan was not happy with this comment, but Fares continued to back his nephew. "Melhel is right," he said, "not just because Chekkos is our home, but because those people don't deserve to be caught up in this mess, whether they're from Chekkos or anywhere."

Now King Michel stepped in. "Fares, you and Melhel have Rafiq's word that they will be safe. Besides, what sort of king would I be if I let innocent people get caught up in a war?"

"The same kind as the rest of them," Melhel said with a grin.

"Anyone with anything significant to say?" King Michel asked, putting Melhel back in his place. "No? Good. Next on the agenda, Rafiq?"

Rafiq stepped forward and opened another map, which resembled a battlefield over the location in the Grasslands, across North Alexandros, where the armies were expected to meet. On this map, he laid out further figurines representing each type of unit on the battlefield: infantry, cavalry, and ranged siege weapons.

Alexandros's units were coloured blue, while the Scandosian ones were red. Rafiq started to lay out each of Alexandros's units in their planned formation, to play out the tactics he proposed to use when they joined battle.

He placed the infantry in the middle of the formation. "Our infantry, both light and heavy, will form up down the middle, shields up," he said. "These units will be led by Fares and Melhel — one each."

Rafiq then grabbed two cavalry figurines and placed them on the infantry's left flank. "Our cavalry will form up here," he said, "to protect the left."

"And what of the right?" Fares asked, noticing no protection there, where he and Melhel were positioned.

"I'm getting to that," Rafiq explained. He then placed a further two units of cavalry further back on the left, "This hidden set of cavalry units will swing to the right. I'm leaving the right exposed to bait them into attacking that side, so we can swing the cavalry over and charge them, breaking their lines when they overcommit."

On the left flank, just ahead of this hidden cavalry, were two units of archers, "These archers will protect us from what we suspect is the Scandosians' numerical advantage in cavalry," he said. "If they try to take advantage and mount a cavalry charge, they will be met with a hail of arrows."

Rafiq then placed one last unit of cavalry to hang back on a hill. "This is me," he announced. "I will be overlooking the battle from an elevated position."

Fares looked at the battle map and tried to pick apart the scenario. He noticed that he and his infantry were still on their own. "And where does this all leave us?" he asked.

Now the Sword explained. "Our biggest mistake the last time

we met Scandos in open battle was being too exposed to their archers, and too slow," he said. "The infantry units will start out apart, with Melhel's units and yours further off to the right. You will then come close and pack in tight with the rest of the infantry, before advancing forward with your shields up to deflect any potential arrows."

Rafiq grabbed all the infantry units and moved them forward.

He then grabbed the cavalry on the left and moved them forward too. "These cavalry units will flank and protect your advance," he explained, "and engage their cavalry if they charge."

Rafiq then took the hidden cavalry from behind and swung them to the right. "Our hidden cavalry will swing to the right and engage their units who come to hit you from that side. This will free your advance. We want to engage in melee combat as quickly as we can with their infantry. They won't beat us this way."

He pointed at the archers. "These men will be protecting us the whole way through, mowing down any cavalry that charge us," he said, before turning to the right side of the battle. "Once this cavalry is engaged and you press forward, the plan is that a gap should open up. Once it does, I will lead a charge through the middle and through this gap to their exposed centre, causing a rout.

"For this to work, we need you to engage with their infantry as quickly as possible, and to win," he said. "Then we need precise timing with the cavalry charges and movement, so we can break their lines. Is this all clear?"

Everyone nodded.

"Any questions?" the king asked, happy with the plan.

"Just one," Melhel said, raising his hand.

Prince Sirhan rolled his eyes. "Of course you do."

"Shut it."

"You shut it."

"Both of you, shut it," the king ordered. He looked at Melhel and waited patiently for both young men to be quiet before asking Melhel what his question was. "Yes, Melhel?"

"When this is over," Melhel began, "when the Scandosians are defeated, are we going back to the dead army? We seem to have ignored that since this whole affair came up."

King Michel smiled. "Of course, we've had to worry about the Scandosians," he said. "That's been our biggest priority. You saw what they've done."

"I understand," Melhel said, "but the dead army is our biggest threat, not the elves. Once this is taken care of, can you promise you'll let me to continue the investigation?"

"I promise," the king said. "Once this is all over, and the kingdom returns to normality, we will focus on the dead army and stop that threat as well."

Melhel smiled and nodded, grateful to the king.

"But," King Michel said, "we need to defeat this dead army as a united kingdom, so let us deal with these Scandosians first."

"When will we move?" Fares now asked, impatient to get on with business. His question was for Rafiq.

"Tonight," the Sword answered. "If we are to have any hope of cutting them off before they get deep into Alexandros, we need to move now. I want a decisive battle. If we can defeat a majority of their army here, we can win the war."

Rafiq looked for approval to the king, who nodded his head. "Go, and be ready for this," he said in dismissing the meeting. "The fate of the kingdom depends on all of you."

CHAPTER 20

REUNION

By that evening, the Alexandrosian army stood in formation before the gates of Beiros, ready to be led on its march.

Melhel and Fares stood at the heads of their respective infantry units, helmets off and stone-faced, nervous about what lay ahead. Each of their infantrymen wore the light but sturdy armour that Fares' and Melhel's workers had toiled over. The soldiers felt lighter and more mobile than ever before, and were just as protected.

Each soldier wore a helmet that covered his entire head and face, leaving only the eyes and mouth exposed. Their breastplates and cuirasses stretched across their entire torso, while their shoulders and upper arms were armoured, and their arms had vambraces and gauntlets to protect their wrists, forearms, and hands. Each soldier's legs were covered with greaves along their shins and cuisses above them to protect their thighs.

To aid in flexibility and manoeuvrability, their major joints—the knees and elbows—were covered in chainmail so the soldiers' movement wasn't restricted. This chainmail was also fitted on their necks to let them turn their heads. Speed was essential to their strategy, and they could not afford the burden of heavy armour weighing them down, especially if the Scandosians were to fight at range again.

The cavalry stood at the infantry's flanks, with Rafiq leading his unit at the right. The horsemen were fitted similarly to the infantry, in lighter armour than usual, though their weapons differed.

Where the infantrymen held short swords and round shields—Melhel's choice, though Fares was more a proponent of the longsword—the cavalry were given spears and lances to drive straight through the enemy lines. Their horses, too, were armoured, for if they were lost, so was the plan.

The archers were armoured more lightly still, being draped in chainmail almost head to toe. Longbows were their weapon, to match Scandos in long-range combat. The arrows they used were tipped with the finest steel that Melhel and Fares could smith, ensuring they had every advantage going into battle.

King Michel stood at the head of them all, with the queen and prince on either side as he looked soldiers in the eye one by one and delivered his final words to them before they marched to battle.

"Soldiers, we stand here tonight to determine the future of our kingdom," he said. "The coming battle will define the lives and stories of your families for generations to come. Know what we are fighting for. Know that the Scandosians up north want to take everything from us—everything we have been building as a kingdom for centuries.

"Remember those that perished in the attacks during our festivities, at the hands of evil elves, and understand that their leader, Governor Mala, does not disapprove of their actions. If she is not against them then she is surely with them. Understand that you are not fighting for glory; you are fighting to defend the existence of this kingdom and everything it stands for.

"There are those that strive to steal away what belongs to others, but that is not us. We only hope to defend our kingdom, and our nation, from those that seek to rip it apart.

"Soldiers, I love you. I cherish you." The king looked at Rafiq. "You are in good and capable hands—the best hands. My Sword, Rafiq Harrira, will lead you into battle, and he will succeed, as Lah has blessed him. I couldn't pray for a better Sword. We are all counting on you."

His speech finished, the soldiers erupted in cheers of joy and anticipation.

Rafiq smiled softly, honoured by the compliment paid him despite his nerves. This was the first major battle he would have to lead, and his bold tactical plan would make or break the kingdom.

Melhel grinned though he was scared too. This was all still new to him. He was no longer merely fighting bandits on the road.

And Fares just wanted it all to be over with. He grumbled to himself with regret over his decision to leave Chekkos and join the king in this war. He had guessed that his job as a blacksmith would lead to this, and he had gone to Beiros anyway. Now he and Melhel would be returning only to fight. But he could only put on a brave face, for now he was a general in the king's army and it was not fitting to mope—it would be bad for morale. As far as he could tell, he was second in command after Rafiq. If anything happened to the Sword, he would take charge, and for that he could not let it be known that he hated to take up the mantle.

"We march!" Rafiq called to the troops.

As they passed the king, he smiled with pride to see his men go forward to save his kingdom.

After several minutes, the soldiers were in the distance. King Michel looked upon them and sighed as he leaned towards his queen. "By Lah, they'd better win," he said.

"They will," Queen Rania said, smiling and kissing his cheek. "Lah is on their side and Rafiq is leading them."

"Come," King Michel said, holding her by the arm. "Let's go."

Prince Sirhan followed behind them, rolling his eyes but otherwise hiding his frustration at the king's decision to go to war.

FOR HIS OWN SAFETY, Al Eelam had firmly established his laboratory in Stock to keep himself in the hands of the elves.

The Riosan was now a wanted man by the king's army, and he had known this fate would fall upon him, so he had made sure that the Scandosians would give him all the facilities he needed—and all the luxuries he could want.

The scientist was whittling away at his work when a knock was heard on his door. To his surprise, upon answering he saw the figures of Ismal and Mala towering over him.

"May we enter, Al Eelam?" Mala asked, as if he had a choice.

"Of course, Governor," he said nervously in welcomer.

As they walked towards Al Eelam's workspace, the scientist was eager to hear about the invasion. "I trust everything has gone well?"

"As expected, Al Eelam," Ismal said with a smile. "Our troops have now marched on Alexandros. Your plan—our plan—seems to have worked a treat."

"I told you to trust me," Al Eelam said.

"Forgive us for not believing you in the first place," Mala said. "However, as I recall, your first foray into weaponry involved what looked like my troops choking on their own insides."

Al Eelam lowered his head in embarrassment. "If it helps, you've already shown twice the gratitude the king did in twenty-five years."

"It doesn't help, but it doesn't surprise me."

Mala walked over to look at Al Eelam's work. "What do we have here?" she asked.

"Just some future designs," he said, rushing to cover it. Al Eelam was always protective of his work's secrecy until it was finished.

"Can your benefactor not see it?" she laughed.

"Not my benefactor. Not the king ... no one," he said.

"She won't be your benefactor much longer if your weapon doesn't work," Ismal warned.

"You saw the mountains," Al Eelam said.

"That's not what he's referring to," Mala said. "The one we took with us had better work."

Al Eelam smirked. "The Alexandrosians will be in for a nice surprise," he said, relaxing a little. "Just like the Scandosians were at the gates of Beiros."

Ismal frowned at this, and Mala put a hand on his shoulder to calm him.

"When they write the histories and say who changed the world the most, will they mention Al Eelam? Of course not," Al Eelam muttered to himself while reorganising his work. "They'll only name the kings and queens and politicians, while little Al Eelam is left in the dust even though he won the damned wars himself."

Mala and Ismal could only look at him with pity.

～

AT THE TOP of the royal palace, Marissa was with the prince, looking from his balcony onto the night-shrouded streets of Beiros.

Lights were shining in the windows and oil lamps along the streets. Murmurs of conversation and boisterous cheers reached them from below. A big show appeared to be afoot in the amphitheatre, drawing in crowds.

Of course, the royal family had larger concerns, hence their absence from the evening's entertainment. But the prince would have been happier there, and couldn't help but be drawn to watching from afar.

"I've had a funny relationship with Beiros," Marissa told him. "But it is beautiful when you get a chance to see it. Away from the politicians and the drama, when you can strip Beiros down to its natural state, it is stunning."

The prince beamed and put his arm around her shoulder, pulling her closer to him. He gestured outwards. "This will all be ours someday," he proclaimed, "sooner rather than later."

"And what if we lose the war?" Marissa wondered.

"Have you no faith in Melhel and Fares?"

"Faith can only get you so far," Marissa said. "I'm worried for them. I'm worried I'll never see them again." She took a deep breath. "I'm worried they'll be killed, we lose the war, Scandos marches on Beiros yet again, wins ... and we'll all be killed." She looked at her prince. "I can't bear the thought of that."

Prince Sirhan kissed her on the side of her head. "And you won't have to," he assured her somewhat patronisingly, as though any such fears were foolish. "Win or lose, we will be safe. I can promise that."

Marissa smiled and rested her head on Prince Sirhan's shoulder. "I just hope they'll be okay," she said. "They've done so much for me ... for us ... it wouldn't be fair if they died this way."

The prince ushered her back into his room. "Come, we'll rest," he said. "We'll rest and hope that it'll all be over soon."

Marching up the Alexandrosian countryside was tiring. Rafiq had set a relentless pace, ordering his men to stop only to eat and sleep —and even then, they were hardly given time for that. If the king's army had any hope of winning the coming battle, they had to arrive before the Scandosians to establish their position.

Melhel marched at the front of his unit, head and eyes directly forward. His only mission was to get to the battlefield near his home.

The young leader looked behind him and urged his troops forward. "Keep moving, men!" he ordered. "Don't slack off!"

The soldiers were disciplined and had taken well to Melhel's leadership. They'd heard of his defence of the royal family and the faith the king and Rafiq had in him. Some knew first-hand how brave and talented a fighter he was, having been bested by him in training, as he bested everyone. Knowing they bore weapons and armour of his design only added to his aura of authority.

It was Melhel's first time being a sort of leader, but Rafiq felt his blunt personality and willingness to take risks suited the position. He saw so much of Fares in the younger man, so it was only natural to assume that Melhel could lead like his uncle once had.

Melhel's reputation among the soldiers, spread by men like the one currently sprinting up the formation to get abreast of him, only added to his leadership credentials.

"Melhel!" The soldier sounded excited to be there.

Melhel turned around and saw a beaming smile visible beneath the man's helmet. He was perplexed as to who could be so cheerful on the road to battle.

"Yes?" Melhel asked.

When the soldier removed his helmet, he saw it was Salal.

"I never thought I could ask for a better leader of my unit," Salal said. "I'm so glad it is you."

Melhel smiled in return. "Salal," he said, placing his arm around the man's shoulders, "fantastic to see you with me." He laughed. "Did you only just realise I was your leader?"

"No, of course not," Salal said. "But I only had the chance to talk to you now."

"Well, I'm glad I have brave soldiers such as yourself with me," Melhel said in praise. "We will need it."

Salal grinned. "How are you feeling?" he asked, "I hear we're poised to battle near Chekkos, where you're from."

"Rafiq knows where I stand on this," Melhel explained. "He knows that the safety of the village is of utmost importance. The battle is to be fought away from the village, not in it."

"Do you still have anything there?" Salal wondered.

"Just a lifetime of memories, and people I've known since I was a baby," Melhel said. "Oh, and my family home and business."

Salal laughed nervously. "I'm sure your uncle would be worried to lose that."

"Not as much as me," Melhel said. "He's an old man. He only needs it for a few more years," he joked.

Salal couldn't keep himself from laughing. The other soldiers looked at him in disgust until Melhel gestured to them that it was okay.

"I'm the young man in the family," Melhel continued. "How else can I support myself?"

"You could always work for the king."

"I already do," Melhel said. "But that doesn't mean I want to do it forever. Beiros is nice, but it's also a tough place to make a life. I love Chekkos no matter what. It's my home. This is just an opportunity that Uncle and I took, and the king desperately needed our help."

Salal was confused. "You would turn down all that money to live in Chekkos?"

"Money isn't an issue," Melhel explained, keeping his head

forward. "We have enough. And all the money in the kingdom isn't worth putting up with the senate."

"Is it really that bad?" Salal asked.

"Come with me one day," Melhel laughed, "if you don't believe me."

∾

IN THE THRONE ROOM, the king slumped in his seat, slowly and methodically tapping his hand against the table while the queen sat next to him.

The room was quiet, and the tension was palpable, as the king ran through every possible scenario in his head. The queen, as ever, exercised her famous patience.

"You know our lives depend on this one battle," King Michel said.

"You don't have to tell me, Michel," the queen replied. Only she called him by his first name—in private, of course.

"Everything we have built, everything that we have worked for in the last twenty-five years, is all up in the air," the king said. "If Rafiq and the Baraks fail—we fail as a kingdom. Those elvish savages will enslave us all, and everything Beilos did will be for nothing."

The queen held his hand. "We have Lah on our side," she said in comfort. "But more importantly, we have the greatest army and generals in the kingdom. No province has dared to challenge us for precisely this reason."

"No province except for Scandos," the king scoffed. "Arrogant bastards. After all I've done. I could have burnt the place to the ground and killed every elf I saw once we won the war. I had them coughing out their lungs, and I had the decency to stop when the war was won."

"And the decent man always wins," Queen Rania said. "The evil always get what is coming to them. They will pay for their crimes, do not worry. The world doesn't let the massacre of innocents go unpunished."

"Well," the king sighed, "I sure hope the world lends its power to Rafiq."

Queen Rania kissed the king's hand. "You chose him to be your Sword for a reason," she said. "As a general, he is a reflection of your leadership and judgement. If you can build a kingdom after a civil war, you can appoint an appropriate Sword and general."

Michel let this sink in, thinking of the decisions he had made in his time as king. He wondered if he truly had been out of line in ordering the gas attack on the Scandosians. Maybe the elves truly did deserve their own state. After all, they were their own species — not human, but elves, with their own language and culture.

But then he considered the other side: Scandos had initiated the war. They had been a part of the kingdom for centuries and already had relative autonomy anyway, far more than the other provinces. At this point, it was greed and a desire for power that ruled their thinking, not the "Scandosian cause". If they won this war, as he had often said, the Scandosians wouldn't stop at independence, but seek to conquer Nataaros for themselves and bring the kingdom under their control.

"I pray you are right, my love," the king said. "I pray that whatever I have done, it has been for the good of Nataaros, and not to its detriment."

He kissed her hand too. "And I pray our son can take on my ability to rule."

"Do you not think he is fit?" the queen asked.

"Not yet," the king explained. "He is far too rash, far too selfish. Sirhan is a brilliant boy, but he's not a leader. When we needed him, he ran away with Marissa to the games. His obsession is unhealthy, and his lack of willingness to negotiate and talk to others will be the death of him as king if he doesn't learn to overcome it."

The queen was taken slightly aback. She seldom noticed her son's shortcomings, only his gifts. In her eyes, he was made to be king and practically without fault. Whatever may be wrong with him — whatever the king might be referring to — could in her eyes surely be eased out of him as he grew older and learned to rule.

"He can still learn to rule," Queen Rania said in her son's defence.

"He won't if he refuses to," the king explained. "Sirhan loathes attending the senate with me and avoids it at any cost. He shirks responsibility and runs away when he doesn't get what he wants. I worry for him and the kingdom. I want to die knowing he is ready to be king."

King Michel turned and faced his queen, holding both her hands. He leaned forward and looking directly into her eyes. "Together, my love, we need to raise him to be the man he was meant to be," he said. "Nataaros depends on him being as strong a leader as I've tried to be. He can't refuse to listen or be present when he is needed. If he continues down this path, I worry I will leave the kingdom in hands that are simply not capable."

Queen Rania contemplated this silently. For once she had to face her son's shortcomings; she could see the truth in what the king told her.

"Melhel—now he's a leader," the king said. His eyes lit up talking about his new favourite soldier. "He springs into action when it is not even asked of him. No one ordered him to risk his life at the anniversary of the civil war, but he did it anyway."

King Michel took a deep breath. "I want those two to spend as much time together as possible," he said. "More than they already do. If Sirhan is to be a leader—a king—he needs to follow an example aside from us, and Melhel is that example. I will discuss this with the two of them after the war is over."

It was very late, and it seemed as though the king and queen were the only ones still awake.

Prince Sirhan, however, was awake, and, having come to talk with his father about the war, had paused at the door when he heard voices within. With no one else passing through the hall to disturb him, he had managed to stay there and hear everything. He wasn't happy.

∼

SEVERAL DAYS LATER, the king's army had finally marched its way to Chekkos and set up its camp nearby to ensure the battle took place as far as possible from the town. Their aim was to push the battle further north from Chekkos, closer to the Scandosian border, as Fares and Melhel reasonably wished.

Rafiq, Fares, and Melhel were in the middle of the village overseeing the soldiers and civilians alike. Scores and scores of men, women, and children were being spoken to about the impending battle, with soldiers across the entire village, detailing them on exactly what they should do should the worst happen and Scandos win the impending battle, leaving Chekkos undefended.

The people were reassured that the battle itself would take place at a distance, but the army still needed to take precautions to ensure their safety was secured. It would have been a horrible look for the king to let a battle take place so near a village and let the people come to harm—Governor Mala would be the first to pounce on it to paint the king as a heartless ruler who cared nothing for his own subjects.

Fares was impressed to see that despite the presence of the army, when they were done with hearing the plans for an emergency, his former neighbours went on about their usual business as though nothing was out of the ordinary. The bakeries and butchers were readily selling produce, and even the famous smithies were still clanging. Children were still running around and playing in the streets without a care, not knowing their futures would be decided in the coming days.

Fares sighed, homesick and wondering if different decisions could have changed this moment. Once more, he regretted his actions in the civil war, whose consequences had returned to him as he had feared.

As his thoughts returned to the present, he noticed Melhel and Rafiq talking nearby. "You know my agenda," Melhel was saying, "as long as these people are safe, I will happily lead my men in battle."

"Look around you," Rafiq said, gesturing at the soldiers on the village streets. "You can see our men are going through everything we instructed them to do. The people will be safe. I'm well aware you grew up with many of them—that you know them—but above that they are innocent people. I have no intention of letting them die in this battle."

A group of young men walking past in the distance recognised Melhel, whose face was clearly visible with his helmet off. The young men recognised his distinct and rugged features, and waved at him with a smile.

Melhel returned the gesture. Once those men had been boys he played with on the street, and after that youths he had sparred and debated with. Now, it was his job to protect them.

"I'd like to see the elves lay siege to this place," one of them called out to Melhel. "They wouldn't last a week!"

"Planning to take them all out yourself, Hamoud?" Melhel called back.

"With his bare hands!" another answered for him. The men guffawed and waved as they went on. "Kill a few thousand elves for us, Melhel!" Hamoud called behind him.

Fares couldn't help but chuckle. The Baraks weren't the only implacable men to come out of Chekkos. The whole population was firm as a rock, and too stubborn to let a war get in the way of their lives.

This pride and force of personality was admirable, and mixed with an uncommon dose of intelligence and political savvy, it had caused first Fares, and now his nephew, to rise within the kingdom.

"And what of those scouts?" Melhel was now asking Rafiq, referring to a small party that had been sent north to assess the Scandosians' position and see if plans needed to be changed.

"They should return by tonight," Rafiq answered.

"Provided they haven't been captured," Fares opined pessimistically, inserting himself into the conversation after his long, pensive silence.

Rafiq shot Fares an unappreciative look. "I'll assume you're not suggesting our scouts are incapable of avoiding capture," he said. "You know as well as I do, they are better than that."

Fares grinned. "Always expect the worst," he said. "Failing to do that is how we got stuck inside Beiros for the better part of a year." The siege of long ago had come about in part because of the overconfidence of those in charge.

Rafiq rolled his eyes, but he knew Fares was right. In war, no one played by the rules. The worst was far from a remote possibility.

Melhel chuckled at the older men's sparring and began to walk off. "I'll be back," he told them.

He went in the direction of his old home, and looked at the village around him as he passed, taking in every detail as though with fresh eyes. It felt at once new and so familiar, as though he'd never left, and this could be the last time he ever saw it.

His home was only a short walk away—as was everything in the village—and he looked up to see it and the smithy in the same exact condition as when he and Fares had left. Melhel beamed with pride, knowing the friends they had left in charge had honoured their trust, done the business justice, and carried on the legacy of Chekkos's most notable residents.

Melhel stood in front of the building and marvelled at the care that had been put into its design. Having lived nearby nearly all his life, and having worked in it only a little less than that, he had never truly noticed how much it stood out from the other buildings in Chekkos. But now, as an outsider, he could see just how grand it was for a village smithy—one of the largest buildings in town, built of stone and with their family name displayed prominently on a plate of shining brass by the entrance.

Melhel stepped inside, and as he heard the ring of steel on steel from within, he grinned from ear to ear.

When one opened the door to the shop, a bell rang to signal that someone had walked in. The shopkeeper approached the counter, expecting a customer.

"Hello, can I help—" he asked, before his voice was cut off by an excitement that set his face aglow. "Melhel!" the man yelled, before running around to give his old friend a hug.

Melhel smiled as he embraced the man tightly, as though it had been an eternity since they'd last seen each other, "Jamil, my friend!" This was the man tasked with his keeping his family's business running. "How are you?"

"Very well," Jamil said with a smile. "Business has been fantastic!"

"Good to hear."

Jamil Sassin was an old friend of the Baraks, and Melhel had known him since childhood. When they left, he was the only man Melhel and Fares believed they could truly trust to look after the business while they were in Beiros. Like many people, he was a few inches taller than Melhel, with scruffy hair and a long but surprisingly neat beard. His smile was wide and devilish, and his brow was covered in sweat from the intense work of a blacksmith.

The two young men released each other and sighed with relief to finally be seeing each other safe—for now—after the Baraks had spent several months away.

Jamil was overwhelmed at the spectacle of Melhel in his armour. It was good work, and his friend made a formidable figure, so armed. "I hear you're off to fight the elves," he said.

"Yes," Melhel replied. "And unfortunately, we've chosen a battlefield not too far from here."

Jamil walked past Melhel to look outside in the village. Outlined by the light from outside, he cut a tall, strong silhouette in the doorway. "Is that why the army is here?" he asked.

"We're here to prepare everyone in case we lose," Melhel explained. "That way they can evacuate and save themselves from a massacre."

Jamal turned back to Melhel and came closer to examine his armour. "This is some fine work," he observed. "Did you and your uncle come up with it?" He couldn't help but prod at it, inspecting every detail.

Melhel grinned. "Well, mostly me," he bragged, "but Uncle did have a slight hand in it."

"With armour like this, I don't see how we can lose," Jamil said. "So, what's the plan, anyway?"

"Win," Melhel said.

"Really? I'd have assumed the plan was to lose the war, let the Scandosians take over, and then have all our kids become stupidly tall, grow pointed ears, and speak a stupid language," he joked. "I mean, what is the plan of attack?"

Melhel chuckled. "We need to get up close," he explained. "Their archers have a major advantage against us. But once we get in their faces, we can defeat them."

"Of course!" Jamil exclaimed. "No one can defeat the Alexandrosians in a fight, especially not a bunch of elves."

"It's not that simple," Melhel warned. "The Scandosians are smart—too smart. Never underestimate your enemy, especially when they use tactics that breach the rules of war."

Jamil sized Melhel up. "Like when they attacked that party?"

Melhel nodded.

"I heard about that," Jamil said. "In fact, I heard you killed every attacker."

"Not 'every'," Melhel said, shaking his head, "The king's Sword had a hand too, as did my uncle."

"Ah, so the king is a fighter!" The prospect excited Jamil.

Melhel laughed and shook his head. "Not at all!" He sat Jamil down to explain. "So, the king has a 'Sword', who is his bodyguard and his general on the battlefield. The king doesn't do any leading or fighting himself, that's up to the Sword—Rafiq Harrira, the big man you may have seen—and of course myself and my uncle."

Jamil scoffed, shocked that the king didn't actively participate in battles. "King Michel doesn't fight at all?"

Melhel shook his head.

"What sort of king doesn't fight for his own people?!"

"That was exactly my reaction," Melhel said.

"Where is he now?" Jamil asked.

"In Beiros."

"While you're all here?" Jamil asked.

Melhel nodded and grinned.

"And the prince?"

"Also in Beiros," Melhel confirmed.

Jamil had the most confused look on his face. He sat and pondered, struggling to comprehend.

Melhel smiled. He'd been there as well. "Don't worry, it took me a while to figure out too," he laughed. "Eventually, you get used to it all."

"I don't want to get used to it all," Jamil said, squirming. "I'm rather happy here in Chekkos."

Melhel stood up. "I envy you," he said.

Then, from outside came the sound of a horn.

"What was that?" Jamil said, leaping up and scrambling for a weapon.

Melhel raised his hand to calm Jamil. "Don't worry. It's for me," he assured him. "Well, for everyone. Looks like we have to gather and get ready to march on." He turned to Jamil. "It's been a pleasure."

Jamil gripped him tightly as they said goodbye, worried that his old friend may not make it back. When he let go, he looked at Melhel with foggy eyes.

Melhel firmly held him by the neck, as close friends do. "I'll see you when I get back," he said, patting Jamil on the back of the head and then ruffling his hair. He made his way out of the shop, ready to re-form the troops.

~

MELHEL RAN BACK to Rafiq and Fares in the village's centre to gather up the formation. The three men stood with their under-officers around them.

Fares turned to his nephew. "Where were you?" he asked.

"Checking up on Jamil," Melhel said. "I wanted to see how he was doing."

"And...?"

"He's doing well," Melhel said. "We've left the shop in good hands."

Rafiq was gathering the soldiers, and one by one, they began to form up around him, Fares, and Melhel.

When they were assembled, the Sword's booming voice relayed the orders. "Men, I have just received word from our scouts," he said. "The Scandosians are only a day away from where we have chosen our camp. We must make haste and leave now to be there by tonight, so we can set up and be ready for battle.

"Camp will not be far," he said, "but we need to be there shortly. Am I clear?"

"Yes, Sir!" the men chanted.

"In the event of a victory, we will gather the dead and their standards," Rafiq said. "We will send word to the king and prepare for

279

the next course of action—which is hopefully an end to the war. But should we lose, those that survive must sprint back to Chekkos and the other nearby villages, to evacuate them. The safety of the people is far more important than trying to regroup for another battle. Once they are evacuated, we march back to Beiros and report to the king."

"Scandos will never win!" one of the soldiers yelled from the crowd. This drew a large cheer, including from the villagers who had been standing by in awe to watch the soldiers form up, as though they were watching the greatest performance of their lives.

Rafiq smiled—a rare sight in the circumstances. "Very well," he said, "we march!"

The soldiers cheered and followed Rafiq and the Baraks as they began the march to camp. It was already the middle of the day, and they needed to get to camp quickly, as Rafiq had stressed. The next day's battle would decide the fate of the kingdom.

CHAPTER 21
THE BATTLE OF CHEKKOS

By night, the Scandosian army had camped several kilometres away from Chekkos and begun preparations for the battle.

Their camp was sprawling, with soldiers from across the province spread throughout: infantry, cavalry, and missile. While the Alexandrosians were adorned in strong, heavy armour, the elves had opted for lighter plate that covered their tall frames. Speed was their game, and their plan was to try and keep the Alexandrosians at a distance.

The infantry fought mainly with pikes and spears, knowing that if they got into close combat with the humans, they would surely lose. Despite their superior height, they were not fighters like the Alexandrosians. They knew this and held it against them. The elves fought with their minds rather than their muscles.

The Scandosians' missile units were their strongest, having dealt devastating blows during the civil war. Ranged weapons let them inflict massive casualties from a distance, and their cavalry was fast and adept at chasing down troops that had routed. Scandosian cavalrymen were also expert scouters and could travel to receive and deliver information in a matter of hours—as they had done that day.

The leader of the Scandosian army, General Ahmad, had waited at the head of the camp for his cavalry to arrive with reports of the location of Alexandros's army. He sat silently praying to his gods in Scandosian, for a resounding victory that would grant him ever-lasting glory and fame in the elven world.

In the distance, Ahmad could hear the rumbling of horses' hooves as his scouts approached with their report.

He stood, his long, silver hair flowing, and his height giving the impression that a tree had just gained sentience and arisen from its roots. Ahmad walked forward to meet his scouts and discuss the plan.

"Soldiers!" he called in greeting.

The scouts rode in and dismounted, and the chief among them approached his general.

"Are the reports in our favour?" Ahmad asked him.

"Very much so," the scout replied with a grin. "Our plan is coming to fruition."

"How so?", Ahmad queried.

The scout laughed. "They will fall into our trap," he said. "They're going to look to approach us immediately. This is a battle we will not lose, General!"

Ahmad nodded. "Let's head into camp. We can discuss the plan from there."

FROM THE ALEXANDROSIAN CAMP, the units had been split up and deployed across the battlefield in accordance with Rafiq's tactics.

In position with his unit, Melhel sat in his tent with Salal, enjoying a hearty meal of roast chicken with seasoned vegetables. Though unspoken, the special effort that had gone into the meal had a clear implication—it may be everyone's last.

Traditionally, no one was permitted in their officer's tent save for other officers, but Melhel considered the tradition folly and had allowed Salal an exception.

As they ate, they shared their thoughts on the developments in Nataaros.

"Thank Lah that the cooks prepared this for us," Melhel said.

"Your favourite?"

"Everyone's favourite, from what I've gathered," Melhel said. "We may as well enjoy it. Chances are that many of these brave men will not survive tomorrow."

Salal stopped eating and looked fearfully at his young commander. "Do you really think we'll all die?"

"It's war, Salal," Melhel said. "People will die. I may die. You should know this—you're a soldier!"

Salal gulped his water. "This is different, sir—"

"Do not call me sir," Melhel interjected.

Salal was flustered. "Melhel ... this is different. We're not fighting bandits, as you have done so well. We're not fighting terrorists. We're fighting fellow countrymen."

"You cannot call them 'countrymen' when they are actively fighting to be rid of us," Melhel said, "when they endorse attacks on our king and his family. Who does that to their own country?"

"Desperation can lead you to do crazy things," Salal said. "They've never felt they belonged in this kingdom. Think about it —they're not humans. Their whole culture is different. Do you blame them for wanting independence?"

Melhel leaned forward in his chair and looked his solider dead in the eyes. "Don't go soft on me, Salal," he warned. "If one of us is in danger tomorrow, you'd better be ready to fight."

"I am ready," Salal answered. "Just like they are."

The fresh-faced commander was at a loss for words, a rare occurrence for him.

"They're fighting for what they believe in, just like us," Salal continued. "Don't think that I won't give my life for our cause, but understand that they're doing the same."

"It's the night before battle and I'm being lectured on sympathy for the enemy," Melhel complained.

Salal chuckled. "Don't act like you're not participating in this only so you can get permission from the king to fight the dead army."

Melhel looked sharply at Salal. "Who told you?"

"I have my sources."

The young blacksmith sighed. "You're right," he relented. "That is my main concern, not the king's politics." He stood and paced around his tent. "But don't think I'm not in this fight to win."

"I believe you," Salal said, "but understand that this war is complicated. It's not as simple as 'Scandos bad, Alexandros good'."

"Sure," Melhel agreed, "but despite that complication, war is war, and we have to fight to protect our kingdom, if we don't want to see its foundations destroyed by some power-hungry elves."

Salal willingly nodded.

"And one more thing," Melhel said.

"What is it?"

"When we eventually get to fight the dead army, you'll be coming with me." He smirked.

"Great," the fearful soldier groaned. "That'll be splendid."

Melhel approached him and put his hand on his shoulder. "It's only because I know you care as much as I do about the dead army," he said. "But until then, we have elves to deal with. Get some rest. You need sleep."

Just as Salal was standing up to leave, the tent opened.

One of Melhel's soldiers popped his head through the gap. "Sir," he said.

Melhel rolled his eyes. "Yes?"

"General Harrira wants to see you and the other commanders in his tent."

"What does a blacksmith have to do to get some sleep?" he called out. "I'll be there."

Melhel placed his arm around Salal's shoulder, and they walked out together.

Before they parted, Melhel gripped his arm and pulled him closer. "Be strong—and above all, be brave!" he asked of his soldier.

Salal nodded, and they shook hands and went their separate ways for the night.

～

THE DAY of battle had arrived. It was dawn, and Rafiq was outside his tent, just beyond the borders of the main camp, and looking ahead at what was likely to be the battlefield.

From his position he could overlook the flat grasslands; it was the perfect vantage point for him and his cavalry to form up and examine the battlefield. In front of him and down the hill were miles and miles of grass, not quite long enough to slow soldiers or horses.

Luckily, Alexandros's army seemed to have taken the higher ground where they had camped, as Rafiq's view was not obstructed by hills. Instead, he could faintly see Scandosian flags and standards in the far distance, marking where they were and how they were camped. The rise he had occupied would allow him a near bird's-eye view of the battle while he massed a cavalry charge. The Sword of the King felt invincible.

Looking down upon the grasslands, he realised Melhel and Fares' men would be exposed to archers and cavalry, affirming his belief that they must advance tightly packed, to protect their weak points.

Rafiq spent a good half an hour staring at the field on his own, while the sun was barely up, making sure he was confident in his plan. He was.

Then he slowly walked back to camp, expecting all to have awoken and begun preparations for the battle that would soon commence.

As he made his way back, he could hear the faint sounds of Scandosian horns. The elves were ready for battle; the humans had better be too.

～

BACK AT CAMP, Melhel was overseeing the readiness of his soldiers, making sure all had donned their armour fully and properly and that nothing was insecure.

As each soldier lined up, Melhel inspected their equipment— after all, it was of his design, and as a perfectionist he wanted to make sure it had been crafted exactly to his specifications.

As he reviewed the troops, Melhel spotted Salal, and the two friends shared a smile.

"It's fine work, sir," one of the soldiers said, trying to defuse the tension.

Though he was still displeased by being called sir, now Melhel brushed this aside and grinned. "I know," he said. "I wouldn't be sending you all out there unless I was happy with my work. Let's just hope the rest of the army shares your love for it."

Melhel spotted a young soldier, evidently barely of age to have joined, and with little of the Alexandrosian's characteristic beard on his fresh face. This lad was rather scrawny, and looked as though he may have fooled his trainers to end up at what was likely to be the greatest battle in history.

The blacksmith approached the young man as he stood in the middle of the unit. "How old are you, soldier?"

"Eighteen, sir," the youth said with vigour.

"And what brings you here?" Melhel asked.

"To fight for my king, and to kill those who threaten our kingdom!" He beamed proudly.

Melhel nodded, impressed, while the rest of the unit cheered for the first time since they'd left Beiros.

"He has more bravery than anyone in the senate!" Melhel observed to raucous laughter from his men. "Young man, don't be too zealous. The elves on the other side of this plain are just as tough as you."

"They don't scare me," the soldier replied. "Only Lah scares me."

"I can get behind that," Melhel said with a smile, and patted the shortest member of his unit on the shoulder.

Once he finished his inspections, Melhel stood before his unit and addressed them. "Men, we are here for a reason," he said. "We are here to fight the Scandosians and protect our kingdom. They would see all our heads on pikes and the king's family rotting in Venos for eternity, all because of their unfounded cause. Are you willing to allow this?"

"No, sir!" the soldiers shouted.

"I didn't think so. On the ready!"

NOT TOO FAR FROM MELHEL, Fares was organising his own troops and inspecting their readiness.

Unlike Melhel, he was not eager for battle. He'd been here before; he knew what was at stake and that a number of these men would never return to their families. That was the difference between a commander in his twenties and one in his fifties.

"Sir, you're awfully quiet," one soldier had the nerve to comment.

Fares gave him a withering look. "We're about to go to battle, soldier," he said, "not the amphitheatre."

His was a serious tone, portending the difficulty that lay ahead. He was also wary; though he trusted the plan, when he had surveyed the battlefield himself from Rafiq's vantage point, he had the uneasy feeling that they were walking into a trap. He wanted to lead his men into battle, not into death.

The openness of the field drew his suspicions. Had they been goaded to fight here for the Scandosians' advantage? But he refrained from sharing his uneasiness with Rafiq, who he knew would shut him down. Instead, he prepared himself to do like all good commanders and soldiers, going head first into battle without looking back.

"You're all brave men," he told his troops. "Brave, brave men. I couldn't have asked for a better group of soldiers to lead against the enemy. Know this, and we will surely go on to victory."

The men cheered loudly, encouraged by their leaders' words despite his solemn tone.

Fares forced his mouth into a soft smile, but beneath the facade was the sorrow of knowing that these men's excitement would turn to grief once the day was over.

～

NOT AN HOUR LATER, they were on the battlefield.

As planned, the infantry were placed in the middle and the right flank, spread across six individual units, with the two leading units commanded by the Baraks.

On the left of the infantry, on the grassland, were two cavalry units. The horses panted, the poor creatures eager for a run without knowing what they were running for.

Just behind the cavalry were archers, ready to fire at the elves once they were in range, to thin the attackers' ranks while they were still at a distance.

Behind the main army, atop the hill on the left, the cavalry reserves were ready to be called on when times were desperate and relief was needed.

On the right of the hill stood Rafiq and his cavalry units, enjoying the eagle-eyed perspective he craved. Rafiq looked forward and saw the amassed army of Scandos shining in the bright sun of the early morning. In silvery armour with a tint of olive green, they glinted like beetles in the grass, in contrast to the grey that adorned the Alexandrosians.

The Scandosians had lined up with six units of infantry in the front and middle, tightly packed and wielding spears and pikes.

To their left and right, on either flank, were their cavalry, greater in number than those of the king's army and posing a serious threat to the soldiers that stood in their way.

Behind them, curiously, were not archers as expected but catapults. Men surrounded the structures, standing ready to send a hail of missiles at the Alexandrosians.

One of Rafiq's fellow riders noticed this. "No archers, sir," he said. "Catapults."

"Indeed," Rafiq observed. "No matter. We will engage them quicker, and break their lines quicker. Catapults will be worthless once we get close."

"And what of our cavalry?" the rider asked. "They'll surely be exposed to missile fire."

"Catapults are slower than archers," Rafiq reassured him. "So long as all our units move fast, they will not be exposed. Once we engage them, the elves won't be stupid enough to send missiles into their own men."

Rafiq looked forward to closely examine the catapults. "Besides, they'll merely be hurling rocks and boulders at us," he said. "They're nothing to be feared."

On the Scandosian side, General Ahmad also looked ahead, from his position next to the catapults, which he commanded. He could see the Alexandrosian infantry right in the centre, where he wanted them. His hair flowing in the wind, he smiled.

Without hesitation, he sounded a horn that could be heard across the kingdom.

The Scandosians formed up, donned their helmets, and stood at the ready.

The infantry pulled back and lowered their spears and pikes, tightly packed, so none could get through.

The horses neighed and panted, ready to charge, while the catapults were loaded with their ammunition.

Melhel looked ahead from his position, wearing a gruff expression that masked the dread he felt privately. This was different to fighting bandits or even a squad of terrorists. This was war, and it was like nothing he had faced before.

He looked back at his men, who stood firm, their helmets hiding fearful faces. Melhel nodded to them, in an effort to reassure them that everything would be alright.

Rafiq knew the battle was to begin at any moment, so he came forward from his position in the front lines and addressed the troops as he rode along the front of his army.

"Men of Beiros," he said, "we are here today for one reason, and one reason only—to fight!"

The soldiers raised their arms and cheered.

"Those elves across from us also look to do one thing—to take everything away from us!" he shouted, "To take all that we have worked for, all that we have given, for their own greed and hatred. History remembers those who fight for what is right, who never give in and defend their honour to the last. So, my brave, brave men, how will history remember you?"

Every single soldier roared as Rafiq rode along the lines to rally them, doffing their helmets and raising a fist.

"Will history remember us as the men who defended Nataaros?" he asked. "Or will history remember us as the men who allowed this great kingdom to fall? I know how I want to be remembered. There are millions of people behind us, counting on me—and on each and every one of you—to defend their kingdom. Are you with me?"

"Yes, sir!" they bellowed.

"Are you with me?"

"Yes, sir!" they cried.

"One more time! Are you with me?"

Across the ranks of the Alexandrosian army, men bashed their swords and shields, ready to fight.

Rafiq beamed as he rode back to his position and put his helmet on. "Forward!" he yelled, pointing ahead, and the Battle of Chekkos began.

First the infantry marched forward. Fares' and Melhel's units marched among them, urged on by the words of the Sword of the King.

As the infantry advanced, the units joined up closely, with only a small margin between them, before crouching down and raising their shields for cover as they advanced.

General Ahmad saw this as an opening, looked to his subordinates, and nodded. The Scandosian cavalry on the right wing immediately began to move forward, threatening the Alexandrosian left flank.

The left cavalry of Alexandros moved forward, ready to meet the numerically superior elven horsemen, who glistened in the daylight, almost blinding those that caught sight of them.

Rafiq watched it all like a hawk, then turned to his bowmen. "Archers, take aim," he ordered.

They readied their bows, waiting for the enemy cavalry to get in range.

And then, "Fire!", Rafiq commanded them. A hailstorm of arrows met the Scandosian cavalry, and the sound of their impact reverberated across the field as they met their mark in numerous horsemen.

General Ahmad saw his troops fall and grew frustrated, but shook it off as he readied the catapults for their barrage, and ordered the cavalry on his left wing to charge forward and envelop the seemingly unprotected Alexandrosian right flank—on which Melhel's infantry unit was placed.

The Sword saw this and ordered his cavalry reserves, hidden from the elves' view, to surge forward and meet the Scandosian charge head-on.

As both sides' cavalry units galloped ahead, hooves crashed on the grass like thunder, striking terror into the hearts of those who heard it.

But it was too late for either side to balk. With an explosive crash, the cavalries collided and a fierce melee began between the Scandosians, superior in numbers, and the fiercely determined Alexandrosians, for whom retreat was not an option.

The Scandosian right was still advancing, despite the storm of arrows, and the cavalry on the Alexandrosian left surged forward to meet them, hoping to occupy them long enough to let Melhel's and Fares' forces through.

Melhel and Fares urged their men forward. They marched as one, their resolve holding firm against the chaos around them.

The cavalry battle to Melhel's right had become a bloodbath. The sounds of men and horses dying rang in the air, and the ground became carpeted with the bodies of the fallen, and drenched in their blood.

Still, the Alexandrosian infantry advanced. Seeing this, the Scandosians deliberately began to pull back, sucking their enemy forward.

"Double time!" Fares ordered, and his men picked up the pace.

Ahmad saw this with glee, and looked to the men on his catapults. "On my signal," he commanded.

The Alexandrosian infantry drew ever closer as their counterparts continued to pull back.

"On my signal," Ahmad repeated, making his men wait for the perfect moment.

Melhel's and Fares' forces were in range.

"Fire!" Ahmad screamed, far more furiously than Rafiq had to his archers.

As the elven general's order reverberated, each catapult snapped forward and launched rocks the size of cattle straight into the heart of the Alexandrosian infantry.

But to Rafiq's shock, in mid-air those rocks burst into flame. With the sound of an earthquake, they exploded as they struck the Alexandrosians, sending a shockwave across the whole field.

Al Eelam's new weapon—explosive ammunition—had been unleashed, with devastating effect.

The Alexandrosians were knocked back, with many being torn to pieces by the explosion. Fares and Melhel were lucky to escape alive. They and the other survivors had been blasted away from the impact as the whole infantry line broke apart.

Rafiq looked on in horror and in disbelief that he had fallen into this trap. "Al Eelam, that damned coward!" he screamed.

Melhel was slowly coming to. He could hear nothing but the ringing of his ears. The infantry was in disarray, having lost thousands in the explosion. Their young commander rose unsteadily and set about trying to reform his line.

Fares was a step ahead of him. "Keep moving forward!" the older man screamed.

"The closer we get, the quicker they stop! Keep moving!" Melhel ordered, joining his voice to Fares's as he retook his position.

The soldiers regained their feet to march forward, but the once-formidable line was in tatters. Bodies lay all around them, amid craters formed by the new superweapon created by Nataaros's greatest and most ruthless scientist.

They kept marching as the Scandosians hurled more and more explosive ammunition in their direction. They were good soldiers now, who could not think but only do, pressing on through the hellfire that surrounded and destroyed them.

But hearing and witnessing the devastation, the Alexandrosian cavalry had grown demoralised and were giving ground. Where they had once bravely defended the flanks, now they were slowly being overwhelmed as the elven horsemen cut them to shreds.

Ahmad repeatedly ordered the firebombing of his enemy, and one after another the explosions continued to rock the battlefield. The Alexandrosians were now nothing but feed to the flames.

Al Eelam had paid his debt to Scandos for the destruction he had wrought on its men in the Siege of Beiros.

The Alexandrosians finally closed in on the Scandosian infantry, forcing the barrage of the catapults to stop. As Rafiq had predicted, they would not subject their fellow soldiers to friendly fire.

The opposing lines stared each other down, the Alexandrosians battered and bruised, streaked by the smoke and black earth that had engulfed them in the storm of fire. They could hear the clamour of horses and of swords on steel behind them as the cavalry continued to fight their losing battle.

The Scandosian infantry held strong, pikes and spears in hand, before slowly creeping forward to destroy their weakened enemy. But soon a rogue Alexandrosian unit charged and a melee began as others followed. If they weren't impaled through their guts on a spear, these battle-crazed men judged, they would crash through and kill every elf they could get their hands on.

Melhel shrugged as chaos erupted in the field. The infantry clashed, swords and spears colliding with shields and flesh, the body count swiftly rising by the hundreds as both sides turned what had been a tactical game into a street brawl.

The elves quickly began to spread their line to overwhelm the Alexandrosians, looking to envelop and encircle them, leaving them nowhere to go.

Somehow, within the fray, Melhel realised this. "Fall back!" he called, but amid the sounds of death all around, the men could not hear his orders.

"Fall back!" Fares echoed, again to no avail.

While the Baraks were trying to call their men back and save them from a slaughter, those same men, unhearing, fell by the score to Scandosian blades.

"Damn it!" Melhel cursed. Giving up on retreat, he bolted forward, slicing through any elf he could find as he ducked and weaved between the spears and pikes. A hundred times he was within inches of death, and a hundred times Lah favoured him with life.

Rafiq saw the calamity ahead of him and turned to his archers.

One of his men realised what the Sword was about to order. "Sir, our men!" he warned.

"What choice do we have?" Rafiq called in exasperation.

"Do you want to kill them on the enemy's behalf?" the soldier cried.

Rafiq ignored him and ordered his archers to fire. Begrudgingly, they sent another storm of arrows into the fray, and both elves and men fell.

As suicidal as this tactic was, it seemed to work. The Scandosians bore the brunt of the barrage and began to thin out, opening themselves to a renewed assault.

"They're weakening!" Fares called as he saw this. "Forward!"

At his urging, the Alexandrosians charged, forcing the elves back. Now it was an even fight again: one on one, where men held the advantage of strength over the elves. It was what Fares and Melhel had hoped for in closing the gap with the catapults.

Melhel, arguably the ablest fighter there, as Fares had been in his youth, began to tear through the enemy like they were bandits. He relished the fight, now his pent-up rage was unleashed. It wasn't just the elves he was fighting, but everyone that had ever harmed him and his loved ones. In his mind, he was cutting down Scandosians, the dead army, bandits, terrorists—righting all the wrongs he had seen in his life.

Fares, too, was having his way in battle as the tide turned. The elves' inferior armour was proving fatal as the Alexandrosians skewered them one after the other.

Melhel found himself staring down an elf as they entered a scrap with the battle raging around them. The young commander dashed forward with his shield protecting him from repeated stabs of the elf's spear. He knocked the spear away before bashing the soldier in the head with his shield, knocking his helmet clean off. Melhel slashed the elf's exposed throat, and the soldier went down, clutching at his neck as the blood trickled down. But the wound was shallow, and the man still lived.

The moment changed Melhel's outlook forever. His heart was torn in two: on one hand, he wanted to do what his heart suddenly desired and spare the elf's life, but on the other he knew he had to do his duty to his king and finish his opponent off. Yet there lay an innocent man, a fellow soldier.

Melhel stood over him, ready to kill.

The soldier looked at Melhel with tears of pain in his eyes. Tears formed in Melhel's eyes also—cutting through soldiers rapidly was nothing compared to staring one in the eyes and seeing that beneath their armour they were just like you, fighting for what they thought was right, or simply following orders.

As the battle raged around him, Melhel knew he must quickly decide to spare the man and potentially face the wrath of his king, or to kill him and rob a family of a son, perhaps a father and a husband.

But life has a way of making these decisions for you. As Melhel mulled his decision, a stray arrow struck his knee, piercing right through the kneecap. It shattered every ligament and tendon, and destroyed the cartilage. On either side of his knee part of the arrow stuck out, and he clutched at it in pain, now writhing on the ground.

Melhel roared in agony, unable to get back up.

Salal, who had miraculously remained alive through all of this, saw his leader was wounded and ran to help. He tried to drag Melhel to safety, a bold move in this whirlwind of death.

"Let me at them!" Melhel screamed, refusing to leave the battle.

"Sir, you are wounded," Salal counselled him. "I am not leaving you here to die."

"I am your commander," Melhel said sternly. "I order you to let me fight."

Salal ignored his friend's wishes and dragged him out of the melee. The fight was now mere chaos, each side having suffered too many losses to judge who held the advantage.

Fares looked to his right, unable to spot his nephew. "Where is Melhel?" he asked. "Where is he?"

A soldier ran to him. "He's been wounded, sir," he said. "An arrow struck his knee."

"Damn it," Fares cursed. "Rafiq—how dare he do this?"

Meanwhile, as the fighting continued, Rafiq had spotted a gap opening up on the right, between the melees of cavalry and infantry.

He pointed to it and commanded his men. "We charge through

there, the battle is over," he said. "On me." His cavalry unit formed around him, with Rafiq himself at the front, waiting for precisely the right time to strike.

"Let me fight, damn you!" Melhel was still screaming as Salal dragged him away. Adrenaline coursed through his veins, and he could no longer feel the arrow in his knee.

"Sir, you are unable to continue," Salal told him. "You have fought bravely; I couldn't have chosen a better commander to fight for."

Melhel sulked, as he knew he was in no position to fight with his knee ripped to shreds. He was feeling the pain of it again.

Rafiq kept looking down at the battle from his hilltop. And then the gap he was looking for appeared. The cavalry on the right were holding on just enough to keep it open, but not for long. The time was now: one sharp blow and the battle would be over.

They all charged straight down from the hilltop in a wedge, to feed through the gap and cut down any who stood in their way. The glory of the men brandishing their weapons from horseback was lost on Ahmad, who watched in horror as the Sword of the King bore down on him, as though it were happening in slow motion.

It was as if Lah himself had sent the attack. Light glinted from their armour and their blades as they drove straight for Ahmad and his catapults. The Scandosian general panicked and ordered a barrage of firebombs hurled directly at Rafiq. Fired in haste, no projectile struck a target. Rafiq and his men rode through as though they were unstoppable.

Rafiq closed in on Ahmad. He and his horsemen sliced straight through the Scandosians, mowing down the catapult operators and slashing at the machines themselves that they may never burn men again.

The Sword barrelled on past the catapults towards Ahmad, who now stood ahead of him, still almost frozen but to Rafiq seeming to rush forward, such was the speed of the Alexandrosian's charge. In less than a blink, Rafiq was beyond the elven general, having sliced his head clean off as he passed, and his men had slowed to butcher the elves around him. Then they turned their attention to the mess at the centre of the battle. Their horses turned precipitously, and once again charged straight ahead.

The unit now split into three. One portion veered to the right to deal with one flank and relieve the cavalry unit there, and another did the same on the other side. The third portion, Rafiq's, kept dead on course, smashing into the back of the Scandosian line so that the elves routed, fleeing headlong in every direction from the doom that thundered behind them, if they had not already fallen.

Seeing his enemies in flight from the fury of Rafiq and his men, Fares ordered the infantry to stop. On the flanks, too, the cavalry had so hammered the Scandosians that now they could slow to a stop while the remnants of the elven cavalry galloped away with their lives.

"One more for good measure!" Rafiq shouted to his archers, who unleashed one last hailstorm of arrows at those retreating, aiming to kill any more elves they could.

Melhel, whose knee was being treated by medics on the field, looked up and smiled as he saw arrows fall into the fleeing enemy. Fares sighed and fell to the ground in exhaustion. Rafiq rounded up all his troops—what was left of them—in the middle of the field, and was met with cheers and celebrations.

"The battle is over," he declared. "We have won!"

CHAPTER 22
CONSPIRACY

T he day of the battle, King Michel sat alone in his throne room. Neither his wife, his son, nor his advisers were with him. He was abandoned to his thoughts. Though he normally donned the royal mantle, today he was only in doublet and breeches, forgoing the formalities. He had deliberately sequestered himself alone in his palace, without a care for what was afoot in the world around him.

A loud knock banged on the door. The king ignored it. The knocking came again, and still it was ignored. Then the knocking sped up, and the king thought he would go mad.

"Can't you see I'm here alone?" he screamed at whomever was behind the door.

"Your Majesty, I have news from the battle!" the man announced.

"Already?" This perplexed the king. He stood and let the man in, "This had better be good," he warned.

The man stumbled in, nervous to be alone with the king. "It's from Rafiq," he announced, "it's his official battle report."

"Thank Lah he made it out alive," the king sighed. He took the report from the man, who promptly left, not at all willing to further embarrass the king, as he perceived it.

King Michel opened the report, which read:

On this day, the armies of Alexandros and Scandos met in the fields outside of the small village of Chekkos. Both armies were well equipped, with the Scandosians in particular bringing a new weapon with them, a form of explosive ammunition launched from their catapults. This ammunition devastated our line, but we held firm. Our cavalry were the heroes of the day, holding the flanks long enough that our infantry could advance forward. Fares and Melhel led bravely from the front, tearing the Scandosian spearmen to pieces. I spotted a gap in the lines, and broke forward, charging through the enemy and eliminating those catapults that were nearly our ruin, freeing up the remainder of our army. The battle was won. Though the losses were many on either side, we are now in a position to negotiate terms. Their army is destroyed. No longer can the Scandosians threaten to invade again.

On reading the report, the king began to cry. He had won, and he wanted the world to know it. Without hesitation, he bolted back up to his chambers to ready himself, for this was the greatest day in his reign—in his kingdom's history.

IN THE AFTERMATH of the battle, thousands of lifeless corpses lay draped across the grasslands, already beginning to stink. The survivors of the Alexandrosian army worked to gather their dead and bring them home for the heroes' burial they deserved.

Those that remained of the Scandosian army had fled and were nowhere in sight, likely licking their wounds at their camp. The elven dead were Scandos's problem, as far as Rafiq was concerned; aside from their own losses, they also had the wounded to look out for. Among them was Melhel, now back at the Alexandrosian camp being tended by the field medics, accompanied by Salal.

The arrow was still lodged in his knee, and he writhed in pain as the doctor examined it and marvelled with some dismay at how destructively it had penetrated the joint. Blood continued to pour from the wound as the doctor delivered his conclusion. "This is by far the worst knee injury I've seen," he said. "The bone and tissue are completely macerated."

"What does that mean?" Melhel squeezed out through gritted teeth, still holding back screams.

"It means you may never walk again," the doctor explained, "at least, not for a very long time.

"You've got to be kidding me," Melhel said. "There's nothing you can do?"

The doctor leaned closer to Melhel's knee, which had been elevated in a sling, as though closer observation might change his verdict. "Nothing I can do for the time being," he lamented after a pause.

"What kind of doctor are you?" Melhel screamed, "Fix it—it's your job!"

The doctor was visibly offended, and Salal tried to defuse the situation. "Please excuse my commander," he bumbled. "He doesn't mean what he says; he's just in pain."

"Speak for yourself. I mean everything I say!" Melhel cried. "And I'm serious about this damned doctor fixing my broken knee."

"Sir, your tendons and ligaments are ruptured. Your knee bone is shattered. Consider it Lah's mercy that we don't have to amputate your leg. It's a miracle that there's even a *chance* you might walk again."

Melhel sighed as he began to accept his fate. "So, what next?"

"When we return to Beiros, we will be able to treat you at the hospital," the doctor said. "Until then, this is the best I can do."

The doctor bent down towards Melhel's knee again. "Brace yourself: this will hurt." He snapped off the back end of the arrow with the fletching, and then grabbed the arrowhead to slowly pull the shaft out through the front of Melhel's knee with a squishing, fleshy sound.

Melhel groaned in agony as tears welled in his eyes. He'd never felt such pain, and he clutched for anything he could get his hands on. Salal quickly threw him a nearby pillow with which to stifle his cries of pain.

And then the arrow was out, and the doctor began bandaging the wound tightly to prevent further blood loss. "That will do until we return," he said. "Please, sir, rest up. I can understand this is not easy for you. I will be back soon, once I check on the rest of the wounded." He made his way out of the tent, leaving Melhel with Salal.

But before Melhel could relax, his uncle stormed in, and then froze almost immediately as he saw his nephew on the ground, swathed in bloody bandages with tears all over his face.

"My goodness," Fares exclaimed, "this is my fault." Fares was stricken with guilt, which broke down his reserve so that he rushed to hug his wounded nephew for the first time in years.

Melhel was overcome with emotion. "It's not your fault, Uncle" he said through tears.

"It is," Fares insisted. "I swore at your father's grave I would protect you, and instead I've dragged you with me into all of this."

"I chose to come with you!" Melhel said in exasperation. "Even if I'd never wanted to go to Beiros, I still made the choice to follow you. I could have stayed. And even then, I could be cowering in Beiros right now like Sirhan and the king—but what kind of man would that make me? This is no one's responsibility but mine, and I would go out there again to defend our people, even knowing this would be the cost. Compared to the dead, I got off lightly."

Fares calmed down and his tears abated, Melhel's words seemed to have comforted him in his rare outburst of emotion.

Salal looked on awkwardly.

"Salal, was it?" Fares said, noticing the man at last.

"Yes, sir."

"Sorry about all that," Fares apologised.

"Don't be sorry," Salal said. "This is war, sir. Emotion is a part of it."

But there was no time to philosophise, as Rafiq now barged into the tent, distraught at the news that one of his commanders had been seriously injured. He was greeted by the sight of a tearful Fares and Melhel, as well as a sheepish Salal.

"Out," he ordered Salal.

Without hesitation, Salal began to walk out, but Melhel grabbed his arm.

"He can stay," Melhel said sternly, looking right into the general's eyes.

"So be it," Rafiq relented. "What happened?"

That was too much for Fares. "What happened?" He jumped up and grabbed the Sword of the King by the throat, throwing the much larger man to the ground and pinning him down. "You ordered a barrage on our men! My nephew can no longer walk because of you, you selfish son of a bitch. You just had to win glory for yourself, for the king—at what cost?"

Rafiq struggled to shake the enraged Fares off of him.

"Half our damned army is dead because you led us into whatever demonic creation Al Eelam came up with, and then you decided your archers should fire on the enemy even though we were in the way," Fares roared. "How dare you. What kind of general are you?"

Fares was ready to strangle Rafiq, who had been unable to escape his grip. The blacksmith's eyes were dark with anger—his love for his nephew knew no bounds, and it had made Rafiq the enemy.

The older man had indeed continued to tighten his grip on Rafiq's throat, who now could not breathe and shook his limbs in vain as he tried to free himself from the inhuman strength that rage had lent his comrade. If there had been no one to intervene, Rafiq would have died there.

"Stop it, Uncle!" Melhel cried. "Don't kill him!"

But Fares was deaf to the entreaty, and in that moment cared nothing for the consequences.

Finally, it was Salal's turn to be a hero, as he mustered the courage to run in, drag the enraged Fares off Rafiq, and toss him to the side.

Rafiq turned over, coughing as his lungs fought for air. He scrambled away from Fares, who was beginning to come to his senses and realise what he had done.

Everyone was still, though breathing heavily. Melhel was the first to speak. "Can we not try to kill each other where the elves failed?"

Fares and Rafiq looked at each other in disgust.

"You've got some explaining to do," Fares warned Rafiq.

"Once I catch my breath, after *you* tried to strangle me," he coughed out. "You're lucky I'll not have you sent to Venos for this."

"And why not?"

"Because you're right," Rafiq relented. "It was a stupid decision to order fire. I should never have done it."

The others froze in surprise. This may have been the first time in his military career where Rafiq had admitted a mistake.

"I miscalculated everything," Rafiq said. "I was desperate. We were about to be enveloped, so I turned to the archers to wipe out the elves, ignoring the risks."

"And now my nephew has no knee to speak of," Fares said.

"You don't think I feel guilty, Fares?" Rafiq asked. "From the moment I found out what happened, I rushed here to see if he was okay."

Fares leapt to his feet with indignation. "When you walked in, you asked, 'What happened?'," he called out. "What the hell did you expect to find?"

Rafiq stood himself, apologetically. "I was shocked, I didn't realise what I had done was so destructive." He walked towards Melhel. "You know my respect for you," he said. "I would not have asked you to be a commander if I didn't believe in you. Now, I have to live with this for the rest of my life."

"And now I may have to live with not being able to walk for the rest of my life," Melhel said. "Who do you think has it easier?"

The Sword said nothing; he knew how wrong he had been. He turned to Fares, now calmer after his explosion of rage. "Our little episode just before—it stays here," he warned all in the tent, including Salal. "Is that understood?"

Salal and Melhel nodded.

"I'd hate to go to Venos," Fares said. "Although, it'd be a great billing for the games. Imagine the turnout of people all clamouring to see 'Fares Barak: The Man who Strangled Rafiq Harrira'."

Rafiq gave Fares the blackest of looks. He had been forgiven by the Baraks, but not by his own heart. Like all generals before him and since, he would carry his actions with him there for the rest of his days.

∾

SIRHAN and the king were in the prince's room. The king had just woken him from sleep, ecstatic with the news that they had miraculously won the battle.

Marissa had been in bed with the prince and had left to get dressed in embarrassment that the king had found her there. But the king was too consumed with joy at his victory to pay her any mind.

"Don't you understand, son? We have won!" the king exclaimed, beaming. "Now, we can have our kingdom as it should be, with all the peoples of Nataaros united."

Prince Sirhan was still rubbing his eyes, not fully aware of his surroundings. "That's wonderful news, Father," he mumbled. "How did Melhel fare?"

"From what I can tell, he turned out okay," King Michel said. "His uncle too. Both seem to have done well in the battle. I assume so, anyway. Rafiq would've mentioned their deaths in his report if they were killed."

"So Rafiq is alive too?" the prince asked.

"Yes. In fact, it was he who saved the day. Had it not been for his actions, the Scandosians would be marching against us as we speak."

Prince Sirhan rose from his bed and paced a little as he woke up fully. "It's a good thing we won, then," he said with a smile. "I couldn't bear to have this kingdom ruled by them. It's my throne to inherit, not some filthy elf's."

"Now, now," King Michel said, "diplomacy is important. We're not here to wipe out the elves; we're here to integrate them back into the kingdom."

The prince sighed. "You're right. No killing, only diplomacy."

"Good," King Michel said with a nod. "Now, we will be having a triumph for our brave generals when they return. You will be wearing your finest clothing. This is the greatest day in our history, and you will dress your best."

"Of course, Father."

"And you will fetch down to our vineyard and grab the best bottle of wine," King Michel ordered, referring to the royal vineyard just outside Beiros, "so we can celebrate ourselves, with those fine men."

Again, the prince agreed.

The triumph was a special event reserved for famous and great military victories. Rafiq, Fares, and Melhel were to be paraded into Beiros and welcomed as heroes. The whole city typically turned out for these rare events. In times of war, generals replaced performers and even gladiators as celebrities, and King Michel would be damned if he wasn't to make this triumph a show of his kingdom's superiority over the Scandosians, and use it to unite the people behind his cause.

But first, Prince Sirhan was to fetch the wine.

~

BACK AT CAMP, preparations were being made for the march back to Beiros. Rafiq oversaw all the logistics, making sure everyone was ready and organised.

The soldiers still wore their armour, to look the more chivalrous when they returned for the triumph they expected would welcome them. But they had their helmets off, so that the people would know the faces of the brave soldiers who had fought victoriously for Nataaros.

Fares joined Rafiq at his carriage. There was no use marching in formation anymore: half the army was dead and there was no imminent threat. So the Baraks could sit with Rafiq for the journey home, if they liked, and for the triumph when they entered the capital.

"How's everything looking?" Fares asked Rafiq.

"Better," Rafiq said. "We'll be ready to depart soon. If we're quick, we can be there in three days."

"That's shorter than usual," Fares remarked.

"Hence, 'if we're quick'," Rafiq said with a wink. "The king will be waiting for us."

"Of course," Fares puffed. "Nothing will please him more than dancing on the backs of dead soldiers. Lah knows he loves grandiosity."

Rafiq rolled his eyes. "Would you stop being so spiteful for five minutes?" he bemoaned. "This is the biggest event in our history. Forgive the king for wanting to make an occasion of it."

"It's fine, he can celebrate," Fares said. "Just forgive me if I'm not in the mood to blow kisses at the adoring crowds."

"I get it," Rafiq said, placing his hand on Fares' shoulder. "You're upset. We can worry about all that later. For now, let's just get to Beiros, receive the triumph, and then let the situation cool down."

Fares nodded reluctantly and shook the hand Rafiq had extended.

Behind them they heard a creak and turned to see Salal pushing Melhel in an indifferently crafted wooden wheelchair.

"Oh, Melhel..." Fares sighed on seeing the state of his once-fit nephew.

"I'll get used to it, Uncle," he said. "And who knows, maybe this isn't the end for me."

"Has the doctor said anything else?" Rafiq asked.

"Yes," Melhel said. "He said to make sure that you don't send any more storms of arrows at your men." He smirked as Rafiq took it on the chin.

"Very funny," Rafiq said, deadpan, "but what did he actually say?"

"Although my knee is completely destroyed, they have been working on a healing potion that can restore everything that has been shattered," Melhel said. "The side effects could potentially make things far worse, but it's worth a try."

"Are you sure you want to risk doing even further damage?" Fares asked.

"As opposed to remaining like this?" Melhel scoffed. "Maybe when I'm as old as you two I can accept living like this for the rest of my days, but I'm a young man with my whole life ahead of me. I'm not giving up."

Fares and Rafiq grimaced at the insult.

"And if it doesn't work," Melhel continued, "and I truly am left this way, then I will live with it. But I won't let it overwhelm me, and I won't let it stop me from living."

"That's very admirable of you," Rafiq said. "Again, I am truly sorry for what has happened."

Melhel smiled softly, accepting his general's sincere apology.

It was time to go. As the soldiers began the march to Beiros, Rafiq and Fares made their way inside the carriage. Salal helped the wounded Melhel up, too, before parting to join the rest of the troops.

After all that had happened, the battle was over. For the first time in months, they could walk carefree, not having to think about anything at all.

AT THE ROYAL VINEYARD, deep in the wine cellars, Al-Rifqa, a very enthusiastic winemaker whose great passion was to serve the royal table, was taking Prince Sirhan on a tour.

The prince examined the bottles as Al-Rifqa talked him through them.

"Here, we have wines that have been stored for three centuries," he said. "Some of the best that we distribute your way."

Prince Sirhan waved these away. "Not old enough," he said. "You know my father—this is a big occasion for him. He'd want the oldest."

"The oldest? My prince, is this not for a small meeting?" Al-Rifqa asked.

"Yes, but it's a big deal to Father," Sirhan pressed. "We want the oldest. Can you do that for me?"

"Of course," the winemaker obliged.

"Thank you, my good man," the prince said, smiling. "We can save the more recent wine for the triumph, but this old wine shall only be had by myself, my father, and our victorious generals."

Al-Rifqa knew just where to go. The pair walked the length of the cellar a couple hundred metres further, past all the racks of bottles, to a locked door. The winemaker unlocked it to reveal a single podium inside with a bottle of wine atop it. In this room was also a statue.

"This wine was commissioned by King Beilos himself," Al-Rifqa said, gesturing at the statue. "He told the first winemakers of this vineyard that the bottle shall only be opened at an important juncture in Nataaros's history. Well, I can think of no greater occasion than this, my prince."

Prince Sirhan beamed with joy as he approached the bottle, dusted it off, and inspected it.

"I'll take this one," he said, and walked out of the room holding the bottle by its neck.

"Excellent choice, Prince Sirhan," Al-Rifqa smiled, hurrying after him. "The king will love it! Do give him and Rafiq my congratulations, please."

"Of course," Prince Sirhan said. "I guess King Michel and Prince Sirhan Aounis will have to commission a new, stellar bottle of wine to be opened centuries into the future for another great moment in our history."

Al-Rifqa began to escort the prince back up out of the cellars. "And I'll be ready for such an honour," he said.

JUST THREE DAYS HAD PASSED, as Rafiq had hoped, before the army approached Beiros for the imminent triumph.

All along the streets of Beiros, the people thronged to get a glimpse of their heroes. Notably absent were the Scandosian population, who had wisely kept themselves in their homes.

The royal family waited at the front gates of the palace, where the triumph would conclude after the army marched throughout the streets and city for the adoring crowds.

Now one of the city guards on the walls looked forward and saw the army approaching, spearheaded by Rafiq's carriage. The day was perfect for a triumph, with sunny skies marred by neither cloud

nor raindrop, as though Lah himself had ordained this a day of celebration.

Seated outside the carriage, aside from the driver, were Rafiq,
Fares, and a heavily bandaged Melhel, whose leg still had to be
elevated following the injury.

"Lower the gates!" a guard ordered, and they opened for the
army's arrival.

Rafiq turned to Fares as they passed through. "This is the part
where we stand up and wave," he said.

"My favourite," Fares said sarcastically.

But even so, he stood with Rafiq and the two entered the city
with their broadest smiles on, letting the crowd see their proud
leaders in their glory, having saved the kingdom from disaster. Only
Melhel remained seated, out of necessity, but he did his best to
wave and smile nevertheless, pretending for the sake of the people
that his wounds were just a scratch.

"I need to go to hospital straight after this," he said to Rafiq
while they were still outside of the gates.

"I know," Rafiq answered. "As soon as this is over, you'll go
straight there for your knee. I promise."

Melhel nodded as he and the others braced themselves for the
parade. They had finally reached the gates after a few moments and
began to roll in six abreast with the rest of the army, to the crowd's
applause and raucous cheers.

The people threw confetti in the path of the army, as they
screamed wildly for their heroes. Never had men received such
adulation, not even kings.

Rafiq waved proudly with a broad smile, turning his head to
address everyone he could. Fares was humbler, waving sheepishly
at the adoring crowd, reluctant to look any of his admirers in
the eye.

Melhel, though seated, waved proudly to the crowd, hiding the
agonising pain in his knee.

The rest of the army followed, but were not permitted to wave
or acknowledge the crowd. They must stay firm and walk strong,
keeping formation and leaving the public relations to their generals.

Eventually the triumph made its way to the business district, where the crowd was even greater. The noise was deafening. Roses were among the flowers tossed at the Baraks and at Rafiq, who accepted them with some aplomb as he continued to smile and wave.

Finally, the carriage reached the palace, where the royal family greeted them. Rafiq and Fares stepped down from the carriage and received embraces of gratitude from the king and queen.

"I cannot thank you men enough," King Michel said, on the verge of tears. "This day will live forever."

The carriage driver helped Melhel down from the seat and onto his wheelchair. The queen took notice of the wounded commander and ran to him, "Melhel! What happened?" she cried in shock.

"I took an arrow to the knee, Your Majesty," he said, "straight through. Everything is destroyed."

King Michel, too, rushed to Melhel at his wife's side. "By Lah, Melhel, can you walk?" he asked.

"No, Your Majesty, I cannot. I may never walk again."

"Good grief." The king was perturbed. "What bravery in victory."

"Sure, we'll call it that," Melhel said with a wink at Rafiq, who made no response.

Prince Sirhan approached his friend and put a hand on his shoulder. "You are as strong as you say," he remarked, "I must hand it to you, you've done well."

"Thank you, Prince Sirhan," Melhel replied with a grin. For the first time in their relationship, the prince faced Melhel with genuine admiration—and all it had taken was Melhel's nearly losing a leg.

Now a woman rushed at Melhel and hugged him tightly.

"Ow! Ow! Ow!" Melhel yelped, squirming in what he felt like a death grip. Marissa was ever so happy to see him, but also sad at his condition.

"Are you okay?" Her voice was thick with sorrow for her greatest friend.

"I'll be fine," Melhel said. "We are all here and alive. Nothing can take that from us."

She wiped away her tears before turning to hug Fares. "And you, Fares—I'm so blessed to see you're okay!"

"And I am blessed to see what a fine young woman you are," Fares said, beaming. "I hope you were well looked after while we were gone."

"I was." Marissa smiled and stepped back to Prince Sirhan's side. "We have some important news, actually."

"We?" Melhel asked, raising an eyebrow at the prince.

King Michel stepped forward. "My son and Marissa have been engaged to marry," he announced. "The wedding will be in a week's time, once the mood settles. What a wonderful time in our kingdom."

Fares and Melhel were shaken by a mixture of surprise, worry, and fear. "Marry?" Melhel boomed. "Congratulations!" He wanted to say so much more, but strangely lacked the words.

"Fantastic to hear," Fares said. "A beautiful couple you two will make."

"That's not all," Marissa said, approaching Fares. "I want you to give me away at the wedding."

"Oh…" Fares was taken aback, and felt a lump in his throat. "I don't know what to…"

"You and your nephew have cared for me like family," Marissa explained. "You're like a father to me. I couldn't think of anyone more fitting."

"Thank you, Marissa," Fares agreed. "It would be my pleasure."

A joyous King Michel began ushering everyone inside. "Come, let us celebrate with some wine," he exhorted. "Sirhan grabbed us the oldest bottle in the land."

Fares and Melhel shook their heads. "You know we're not ones for wine, Your Majesty," Fares said.

"For a special occasion, I think you can be," the king insisted.

"I'll join you later," Fares said. "I promise. But I have to get Melhel to the hospital for his knee."

King Michel didn't take kindly to being refused.

"He's right, my king," Melhel said. "The doctor explicitly said that if we were to have any chance of saving my knee, I must seek treatment as soon as we arrived. The triumph, while spectacular, was pushing my limits." He said the last with a wince, finally letting those around him see the pain he was in.

"I understand," the king conceded. "I wouldn't want a strong young commander crippled. Fares, Melhel—we shall see you both later."

"We're grateful for your concern, Your Majesty," Fares said in appreciation, and he and Melhel began making their way to the hospital.

The rest headed back inside the palace, somewhat disappointed. Prince Sirhan, particularly, had really wanted the Baraks there with them.

~

SEVERAL HOURS LATER, Melhel lay abed in the most luxurious hospital ward in the city, still dazed, with his knee elevated and bandaged and his uncle by his side.

The room resembled a hospital less than a hotel suite. Larger than his own bedroom at home, it had a beyond comfortable bed for him to sleep on and nurses at his disposal.

But he only wanted to get better. His uncle was by his side reading reports, keeping quiet as Melhel was not his usual, talkative self.

A knock came at the door.

"Who is it?" Fares asked.

"She says she is family," the nurse said from behind the door.

Fares was confused. They had no family in Beiros. "You may enter," he allowed with curiosity.

The door opened slowly, and a smiling, nervous Marissa tiptoed in. She had flowers with her, which she placed by Melhel's bed before approaching her friend and gently running her hands along his hair.

"How are you feeling?" she asked.

"Better," Melhel said, his spirits lifted by her presence. "I think I may be able to walk after all."

"What have the doctors said?"

Melhel sat so he wasn't looking straight up at Marissa from below. "Well, they've cleaned out my knee, and this potion they told me about might work," he said.

"What potion?"

"It's essentially a healing potion," Melhel explained. "When I take it, it should slowly allow the missing components of my knee to grow back so that I have full use of my knee again."

"And how long will that take?" Marissa wondered.

"Probably months," Melhel said. "But it's worth a shot."

She sat down next to him, on the opposite side of the bed from Fares. "I'm proud of you, Mel," she said. "Not many people sacrifice themselves the way you and your uncle do."

"And we're proud of you, Marissa," Fares said. "How come you're not with the prince?"

"To be quite honest, I wasn't in the mood to sit with everyone, indulge in wine and boast of the victory," she sighed. "I only wanted to make sure you were okay. I have my whole life to engage in politics. This is more important."

Melhel chuckled. "And the prince is okay with this?"

"Not really," she said shyly, "but he was in no place to argue. King Michel allowed me to visit you with his blessing. He sends his regards, as does Sirhan."

"I see you and he are on a first-name basis now," Melhel noticed.

"Well, we are betrothed..." She laughed. "He was disappointed that neither of you were there."

Fares stood to pour a cup of water for the three of them. "We'll celebrate with them soon enough," he said. "But for now, Melhel's recovery is what matters most." He handed the cups to Melhel and Marissa.

Marissa took a small sip. "What happens now?" she asked. "I mean, after he gets better."

"We'll probably still work for the king, I suppose," Melhel suggested.

"I doubt it," Fares said. "The war is over. There's no need for us anymore."

"What about the dead army?" Marissa inquired.

"I'll deal with them when I'm better," Melhel blustered.

"Yes," Fares agreed. "But you can do that from home."

Melhel was confused. "What are you saying?"

Fares placed his hand on his nephew's shoulder with concern. "I'm saying, after you recover, go home. You're not needed here anymore. You've done enough, and it's cost you a lot. You deserve to be back in Chekkos after all of this."

"That's very kind of you, Uncle," Melhel said, "but I am needed here. The king will not take my fight against the dead army seriously unless I am near him, working with him. He won't support me if I'm all the way out in Chekkos."

Fares shook his head with annoyance.

"Besides, I can't leave either of you here alone with all the idiots that roam these streets," Melhel continued with a laugh before turning to Marissa. "And I especially cannot leave you alone with the prince."

"I'll be fine," she scoffed. "You of all people know I can take care of myself."

"But he's different," Melhel warned. "He isn't like his father or his mother. He doesn't have his leadership or her compassion. Truth be told, I don't think he'd make a good king just yet."

Marissa disagreed. "You don't know him like I do," she said. "He's a good man. He is young. He will learn to become a king."

"Hopefully I'll be dead by the time that happens," Fares quipped.

～

THAT SAME NIGHT in the throne room, King Michel, Prince Sirhan, and Rafiq all sat laughing at the table, joking among themselves and proud at their victory.

"I will begin negotiations with Governor Mala tomorrow," the king said. "Now she will have to bend to my will!" He hadn't been this happy in years. He turned to Prince Sirhan and put his arm around his son's shoulder. "Sirhan, my boy, I promise I will leave you a great kingdom, a prosperous and peaceful kingdom, one that will never see the wars that have been seen in my reign."

"Will you be remembered as a wartime king, Father?" the prince asked.

"It seems so," King Michel conceded. "I do hope history will judge me on my actions during war. That would be lovely."

Prince Sirhan stood. "I'm sure history will remember you fondly," he said as he made towards a nearby cabinet.

King Michel was taken aback. "Well, I still have years to reign before history can remember me," he said. "The scholars can judge me when I'm dead."

"Indeed, Father. I'm sure the first thing history will remember you for is how you kept the kingdom united."

"Ah, yes, my proudest achievement," the king bragged. "In no small part thanks to generals such as Rafiq and Fares—and Melhel, of course."

Rafiq nodded with pride. "Lah bless us for that."

The prince returned with the bottle he picked up from the vineyard. "Here she is," he said, beaming. "The most renowned wine in all the land. I cannot think of a better time to drink it." He opened the bottle and poured a glass each for the king, Rafiq, and himself.

The king took a whiff of it. "Oh, this does smell old," he said squeamishly.

"Al-Rifqa was ecstatic I chose this one, Father," Prince Sirhan said. "I'm sure that's a good thing."

Rafiq smelled it himself and, not being a connoisseur, something seemed off about it.

"I should hope so," the king said. "Now, what shall we toast to? Any ideas, Rafiq?"

The Sword shook his head. "Nothing in particular, Your Majesty," he said. "This was *your* victory. You can do the honours."

"Nonsense, my dear boy!" the king bellowed. "You won this battle. The honour should be yours."

"Let us toast to Nataaros and its people," the prince suggested.

"Splendid," the king said. "A toast then, to Nataaros and its people!" The three of them raised their glasses and took large gulps of wine.

The king winced at the taste. "Beilos! You truly did commission this wine!"

"It really does taste six hundred years old," Rafiq commented.

"I agree," the king spluttered, then coughed viciously.

"Are you okay, my king?" Rafiq asked.

"Yes... I think it just went down my windpipe." The king coughed again several times, each more violent than the one before.

Rafiq, too, began to cough hoarsely. Both he and the king sprayed wine—or was it blood?—ahead of them. The prince appeared to be fine.

"Sirhan, what is in this wine?" King Michel rasped as he stumbled to the ground, foaming at the mouth.

"Vengeance, Father," the prince said, smiling without sympathy as he stood above the dying king.

King Michel tried to muster words, but his throat was clogged with foam, blood, and bile.

"You think I don't know how you feel about me?" Prince Sirhan said. "That you don't think I would make a good king?"

The king reached towards his son, but Sirhan slapped his hand away. Rafiq tried crawling towards them, but his muscles were weakening each second.

"Do you want to know how your reign will be remembered, Father?" Prince Sirhan taunted. "As one of violence and bloodshed. The kingdom will consider me a hero. I am saving Nataaros from you, King Michel Aounis."

The king grabbed his throat and began to hyperventilate as the poison overwhelmed his body.

"This is what is right for the kingdom," Prince Sirhan said. "Your death will save millions. You cannot end the war with Scandos. Only I can. You are just too ignorant to see it."

The king tried to speak, but he could only cough more blood and bile onto the floor.

Rafiq had finally dragged himself to them, breathing heavily, a trail of blood behind him, and fell onto his face.

"Goodbye, King Michel and General Harrira," the prince said, looming over them. "You have served Nataaros well. Now, your times have come."

King Michel gasped for air, his dying breaths becoming still faster and more laboured as he tried to cling to life. He reached out to his son one more time before life left his body and his hand dropped to the side.

Just like that, the king and his Sword were dead, their bodies lying on the floor of the throne room. But there was still work for Prince Sirhan to do.

"Help! Help!" he cried. "The king and the Sword have been poisoned!"

CHAPTER 23
A NEW AGE

L ate at night, Melhel lay alone in bed, awake. Fares had left the hospital to go home, as had Marissa, both of them begrudgingly.

It was the first time he could remember that he had been truly alone with his thoughts, with no one close by—neither his fellow soldiers nor his uncle, the only family he knew.

This solitude was a dangerous proposition. After all that had happened, there was now nothing to interrupt Melhel's thoughts of the dead army on the march to kill everyone in Nataaros, and next of how the kingdom would recover and reshape itself after the bloody Battle of Chekkos.

He tossed and turned, and then the memory of the arrow piercing his knee came to him, along with echoes of that sharp pain. Melhel winced, and bit his fist waiting for the pain to subside. But his emotions hurt him more. Going from being a commander in superb physical condition to being unable to walk because of the actions of his own general had shaken him severely.

As if that wasn't yet enough, Marissa and Prince Sirhan then crossed his mind. The poor girl didn't know the prince like he did, he thought to himself. However he acted with her, whatever he showed her, was all a facade. Melhel knew his real character, and that made it painful to see Marissa would end up with him, even if it meant someday she would be a queen.

The wounded blacksmith worried for Nataaros. Prince Sirhan was not fit to be a king, at least not yet. Melhel was convinced he was not equipped to handle the Scandosian situation, the abject poverty all over the kingdom, or, most importantly, the dead army.

But Melhel was in too much pain to afford himself the indulgence of dwelling on such things. He'd drive himself crazy mulling over everything in his head, he knew. Whatever happened, it would work itself out, he told himself. Then he rubbed his knee, slammed his head against the pillow, and went to sleep.

PRINCE SIRHAN STOOD in the throne room with the bodies of King Michel and Rafiq Harrira at his feet. Tears welled in his eyes and his face was red with grief—all part of that facade Melhel had been worrying about on Marissa's behalf.

"The king is dead!" Prince Sirhan called out. "He is dead! He and his Sword! Will someone come to see this madness?"

The door burst open and three guards stormed in to confront the horror of an emotional prince, a dead king and Sword, and bile and blood all over the floor.

"In the name of Lah..." one of the guards exclaimed.

"He's been poisoned!" Sirhan cried. "The wine—it was laced with poison!"

The guard looked on in disgust before turning to the prince. "And why aren't you... What a mercy that you survived, Your Highness."

"Did you not drink the same wine, my prince?"

"They were on the ground, coughing and choking, before I could drink. Lah, how lucky I am—but how unfortunate are they!"

In truth, Prince Sirhan had taken an antidote earlier that night to repel the effects of this particular poison, so that he could drink with the king and Rafiq, but then in the aftermath pretend he never had a chance to taste the wine. Now he must not only keep up the charade, but convince the guards of a further lie: that there had been a conspiracy, entirely apart from himself, to assassinate not only the king, but also his Sword and his heir.

"Where did you get this wine?" the guard asked as he stepped slowly around the scene, looking at the bodies in shock.

"Our royal vineyard," the prince answered.

"And who's the winemaker?"

"Al-Rifqa." Prince Sirhan sprang up, "This must have been his doing!"

The guard looked up at him. "I'm sorry, my prince?"

"He was so eager when I chose this wine at the vineyard," Prince Sirhan said. "I wanted to buy a bottle to celebrate our victory with a drink among close friends. And he was thrilled with my choice. He must have guessed I would take this wine and had already laced it with poison. He's a Scandosian sympathiser! He wanted this!"

"But, Prince Sirhan..." The guard hesitated, hoping to be a voice of reason.

"Arrest that man!" Prince Sirhan demanded.

"My prince..."

"Arrest him now!" the prince ordered. "The king and Sword of Nataaros lie dead at this man's hand. He must answer for the crimes he has committed against our kingdom."

The guards looked at each other.

"Right away, Prince Sirhan," the one who had been talking with Sirhan said begrudgingly.

And without further debate, they gathered a party to arrest Al-Rifqa at the royal vineyard. The prince's plan was underway.

AT THE CRACK of dawn the next morning, guards also appeared at Fares's door, banging loudly. He woke with difficulty, cursing whatever was bothering him at that hour, when all he wanted was some sleep after the battle and the journey home.

"Curse the king!" he grumbled. "What does he want now?" He quickly put on a robe and stomped to the door, furious that his rest had been interrupted.

"This better be important," he warned the guards standing before him in the grey light of dawn, when he had opened the door.

"It is," one of the men said, stepping forward. "We need to come in, sir."

Seeing their seriousness, Fares softened and ushered them into his living room, where he directed them to sit.

"May I offer you men coffee?" Fares asked.

"That won't be necessary, sir," one of the men said in decline.

Fares shrugged it off. "For you, maybe. Since you woke me up at this stupid time, I'm making one for myself." As he clattered sleepily with the coffee pot in the kitchen, the guards were left waiting in the silence of the morning, becoming increasingly agitated with the delay.

The more senior of the two guards was huffing and tapping his feet discontentedly, unsure what to do with himself as he waited to unburden himself of his news.

Fares soon trudged in with his cup of coffee and took a sip.

"Are you absolutely sure you don't want some?"

"No, sir," the guard again declined. "We really haven't much time.

"What is it, then?" Fares asked.

The guard gestured to a chair. "May we ask you to sit down?"

"In my own home?" he remarked with bemusement. "What a world." He hesitated before slowly taking a seat, still sipping meditatively in a continued effort to wake himself up properly.

"Okay," he said when he felt ready. "What is so important that you need to wake me at daybreak and sit me down?"

The guard took a deep, heavy breath. "The king and the Sword have been assassinated."

Fares' face went pale and his eyes widened. His hand weakened and he dropped his cup of coffee to the floor, where it shattered and spilled. But he didn't need coffee anymore.

"I'm ... I'm sorry?" Though his shock and sudden alertness testified that he believed it, consciously he needed more convincing.

"Last night, the king, the Sword and the prince were sharing a bottle of wine to celebrate the victory," the guard said. "Suddenly, the king and the Sword began to choke and cough before falling to the ground and dying. The wine was poisoned."

"And the prince?" Fares asked solemnly.

"He never drank it," the guard explained. "He got the bottle from the royal vineyard, but before he could have a sip himself the other two were in trouble."

Fares got up slowly and paced the room in silence, processing everything. "Just as well," he said, "Melhel and I were supposed to celebrate with them."

"Why weren't you with them?"

"Melhel kind of had an arrow rip through his knee."

The guard speaking stood, following Melhel, and gestured to the others to keep watch at the door. "The news isn't public just yet," the guard said. "The prince and queen will announce it later today."

"Do they know who did it?" Fares asked.

"We've already arrested the assassin," the guard announced.

"Who?"

"Al-Rifqa, the winemaker," the guard said. "Prince Sirhan said that he was ecstatic at his choice of this particular wine. He had planned this all along. He's a Scandosian sympathiser, in fact."

Fares wasn't convinced. "Are we absolutely sure it was him?"

"He will be tried, of course," the guard said. "But the evidence is overwhelming."

Fares returned to the kitchen to pour himself another coffee, and this time one for the guard, too, whether he wanted it or not. "Now what happens?" he said on his return, extending a cup to the guard.

"No, thank you, sir," the guard still declined.

"It's very rude to keep refusing my hospitality, soldier," Fares warned, placing the cup in his hand.

"My apologies, sir," the guard said, accepting the cup and taking a sip. "The prince will be crowned later this week, as King Sirhan Aounis of Nataaros."

"And who will be the Sword in Rafiq's place?" Fares asked.

"That will be for the new king to decide."

Fares shook his head in disbelief. "Alright, I understand," he sighed. "I guess I have a busy day ahead of me, as usual."

"What are you going to do now?"

"First, I'm going to enjoy this coffee and have breakfast," Fares said. "Then, I shall visit my nephew and tell him everything. The king loved him; he ought to know as soon as possible."

The guard nodded his head. "Understood, sir. Thank you for your time." Then he made his way out and Fares closed the door behind him.

Fares breathed out, shaking his head.

"Shit."

~

QUEEN RANIA, still beautiful in middle age, sat silently in her room, clad all in black. The past night had been the first in memory that she had slept alone. Now she had only her son to comfort her, in what seemed the darkest hour of her life.

"What could possess Al-Rifqa to have done this to us?" she wondered aloud, tears streaming down her face.

"I wish I knew, Mother," Prince Sirhan said, and hugged her closely. "He will pay for this. I will make sure of it."

Queen Rania wiped away her tears. "We can't even trust our winemaker," she said. "Who can we trust?"

The prince sighed. "I'm not sure," he said. "But I have a feeling there is a lot of corruption in our kingdom. Al-Rifqa didn't act alone. This was a plot against our family and those we hold dear. I am sure of it."

"So what will you do?"

"Peace must be achieved between us and the elves," Prince Sirhan explained. "That he could never do so is the biggest blemish on Father's reign. I will end all our wars with them, so no one else has to die. Already, in my young life, I've seen suffering on both sides for the Scandosian cause."

The queen smiled through her pain and kissed her son on the cheek. "A noble goal," she said with a sad smile. "I hope Lah blesses you with the wisdom to achieve it."

At that moment, Marissa burst into their room, crying. She ran to hug both the queen and the prince, and the three of them shared a tight embrace.

"I am so sorry," Marissa said tearily. "I wish it had never come to this."

"Do not be sorry, my love," Prince Sirhan said to comfort her. "Those responsible will pay, and no more will people die for this cause."

Marissa buried her head in his arms. "He was a good king, Sirhan." she cried. "He didn't deserve this."

"No one deserves to die this way," Prince Sirhan said. "I promise you, the people that did this will not go unpunished. We will not descend into civil war again. I will move the heavens and the earth to bring peace upon us."

The queen forced herself to speak through her emotions. "We must organise a state funeral," she said. "No later than tomorrow. Let us bury the king and honour the man that he was."

"I'll deliver the oration," the prince volunteered. "We will begin my rule with a clean slate, so that I may lead this kingdom away from bloodshed and into peace."

Queen Rania managed to stand. "Come, my loves. We must have everything arranged. It's what he would have wanted."

The three of them left the room to organise the funeral, to commemorate the tragedy of the assassination and to lay King Michel and Rafiq to rest with honour. Then a new era would dawn on Nataaros, sooner than anyone but Prince Sirhan had expected.

MELHEL WAS fast asleep on his hospital bed. Having tossed and turned the night before, exhaustion had now finally granted him the kind of deep sleep that no one would want disturbed.

Unfortunately for him, Fares had quietly entered the room, and now he softly shook Melhel's shoulder. The young man's eyes fluttered open, and he rubbed them as he woke and slowly realised where he was.

"What's going on?" Melhel asked, still half-asleep. Once his eyes were fully open, he saw Fares standing above him. "Oh, hey, Uncle," he said, less than thrilled to have been woken.

"I have some news for you," Fares said.

"It had better be that the dead army have all died again, and we can go home," Melhel said.

Fares, sitting on the side of the bed, wasn't in the mood to laugh. "No jokes, Mel, this is important," he said.

Melhel sat up to listen properly. "What happened?"

"The king and Rafiq are dead," Fares sighed.

The younger Barak's eyes went wide in disbelief. "Excuse me?" he said.

"They were poisoned last night in the throne room," Fares explained. "The three of them were sharing a bottle of wine, but before the prince could drink, the other two beat him to it and started coughing up their insides."

Melhel covered his head with his hands in dismay. "And Marissa? The queen?"

"Alive, thank Lah."

Melhel breathed out heavily. "Do ... do they know who did it?" he asked.

"They have already arrested Al-Rifqa, the royal winemaker. The prince said he was eager to give them the bottle that was poisoned. Supposedly, he was a Scandosian sympathiser."

"So, let me get this straight," Melhel said. "The prince went to grab the bottle from the royal vineyard. Then, he went to celebrate with the king and Sword. *Then*, before he could have a sip, the other two dropped dead. Finally, they arrested the royal winemaker, who happens to be a Scandosian supporter?"

"Correct."

"And do you believe any of it?"

"Absolutely not," Fares said. "It all seems suspicious to me. I think there has been foul play, and not from the winemaker. He was set up."

"But by whom?" Melhel asked.

Fares shrugged. "Anyone," he said, "the Scandosians, the army, the senate ... anyone could be a suspect. We will see, come the trial."

"Oh, man..." Melhel already felt exhausted by the revelations. "Now what?"

"The state funeral for King Michel and Rafiq will be tomorrow,"

Fares said. "Then, Prince Sirhan's—I guess now *King* Sirhan's—coronation will be later this week."

"Hmph," Melhel scoffed. "What a horrible week this will be. I just said I'm unsure if he's fit to rule, and now he is the ruler. It's almost as if I spoke it into existence."

Fares's face grew more worried with each passing second. "Uncertain times are ahead of us, Mel," Fares warned, "for the prince, the queen, the senate, for Nataaros. It will be dark times for all."

Melhel had no answer. He was looking off to the side, out his window where the rising sun was shining through. It seemed about the only ray of light that remained in his life.

Fares inched closer and waved to get his nephew's attention. "Melhel, look at me," he said.

Melhel obliged.

"Leave," Fares ordered. "Leave Beiros."

"What?" Melhel was perplexed.

"When your knee recovers and you can travel, get out of here," Fares said. "There will be too much instability with the king dead. I've already dragged you in far enough, and now you can't walk. Go back to Chekkos. Recover at home."

"I'm not leaving you, Uncle," Melhel said. "I came to help, not to abandon you. And I need to be with the king to fight the dead army. He needs me to lead."

Fares grew frustrated. "You don't understand. You shouldn't stay here," he urged. "I can handle the politics. You can't. You need to rest and to recover. I will look after the blacksmithing here, and I will guide the new king as I guided his father. You need to get better. Please, Melhel, now is not the time for you be here."

Melhel sighed, knowing his uncle was right. He would have to be wheelchaired to the funeral and the coronation, and was in no shape to remain in Beiros longer than necessary.

"Alright," he relented. "I'll leave when I get cleared from the hospital."

"Thank you, Mel," Fares said with relief. "I promise I will look after myself, if you promise to do the same."

326

Melhel smiled with his lips pressed tightly together. He didn't want to do this, but he appreciated his uncle's love and concern.

∿

AT THE STATE funeral the following day, from the balcony of the Harissah Khnisi, Prince Sirhan delivered an oration for the ages.

Outside of the Khnisi were thousands of mourners, wailing and with tears flowing as they mourned the death of their beloved king and his Sword. It was like nothing that had ever seen before—the largest funeral in history.

As Prince Sirhan stood ready to speak, Marissa and the queen stood to either side of him. All three of them were dressed in black to honour the dead.

King Michel and Rafiq's bodies lay inside the Khnisi in their respective caskets, ready to be buried.

In the upper levels, in a covered area just behind the speaker's podium on the balcony, Fares sat with Melhel, who was still wheel-chair-bound, both preferring to listen to the prince from inside.

Prince Sirhan stepped forward and eyed the crowd with a sad but determined look. Before he had a chance to speak, the noise of the throng grew. The crying could be heard all over the city.

"Citizens of Nataaros," the prince began, "senators and public servants, we are here today to honour King Michel Aounis and his Sword, Rafiq Harrira. Thank you all for being here. An old saying goes, 'It is better to have died young following a life of extraordinary achievement, than to have died old following a life of passivity.' Well, I believe these two men have exemplified this.

"When I was but a little boy, Father used to take me to the countryside to see the glorious Snowy Mountains, to teach me the majesty of Lah. When I became older, he taught me the first steps to becoming a leader. As I became a man, he entrusted me with carrying on his legacy.

"My whole life, I heard stories of Rafiq Harrira's exploits in the civil war—of how he and Fares Barak saved our city from siege. Growing up with him watching over me, I always felt safe and secure. When terrorists attacked a party my father held, the quick action of Rafiq and his soldiers saved our lives and many more. He cared only to serve my father and the kingdom, and to stop those who intend to harm our values.

"My father fought tooth and nail to keep this kingdom united. His whole reign can be defined by one thing: love of Nataaros. He loved all his people, he loved the kingdom, and he was determined never to see anyone break us up. He and Rafiq had just won a victory to secure our kingdom and try for peace—and they paid the price for it.

"Now, those responsible for their deaths will be punished, not just for their murders, but for disturbing the political unity we share as a kingdom. Father, I can only hope to achieve half of what you achieved. As I step into my new role as king, I will think of you in times of trouble and want, when I will need your guiding presence.

"On behalf of all Nataaros, I thank you, King Michel Aounis and Rafiq Harrira, for your lives of service to us all. May Lah bless you in your eternal life."

Prince Sirhan stepped back, tears forming in his eyes, and Marissa and the queen embraced him.

The crowd erupted in a roar of emotion, some overcome with grief for their lost king, others thirsty for the blood of his assassins. The prince chose simply to retreat into the Khnisi and let it all blow over.

LATER THAT DAY, Melhel was back in bed, this time reading the Book of Lah, as he did when he needed guidance.

But as in the morning, when his sleep had been interrupted by his uncle, his time in prayer was cut short by a knock on the door.

"Come in," Melhel said.

The prince walked in with an awkward smile across his face. Melhel put the book down, feigning happiness but in reality rather annoyed at Prince Sirhan's intrusion.

"How's the knee?" the prince asked.

"Better," Melhel answered. "It's less painful, though I am still far from being able to walk."

The prince sat on the nearby chair, facing Melhel.

"How are you doing, anyway?" Melhel asked. "How's the queen?"

"We're coping. Death isn't easy to deal with."

"I know. I lost my father at a young age too," Melhel said. "If you need anything, let me know. I'll be there to support you."

The prince chuckled. "Funnily enough, that's why I'm here." He looked Melhel right in the eyes. "I do need something from you."

"What is it?" Melhel became a little defensive.

"Obviously not now, seeing as you're in recovery," Prince Sirhan began, "but afterwards, when you are healed, I want you to be my Sword."

Melhel froze, at a loss for words. "Your ... your Sword?"

"Yes. Father loved you dearly. He had a lot of respect for you. He always envisioned you and me leading Nataaros to a bright future. He'd have wanted this."

"I'm ... I'm honoured, my prince." Melhel stumbled over his words. "But I cannot accept this. Not in the shape I'm in."

The prince smiled. "That is why it won't come into effect until you are fully recovered."

In his mind, Melhel was scrambling for excuses to avoid the role. "But ... I'm needed in Chekkos for our business," he said.

"Nonsense," the prince said with a laugh. "I will take care of that. You can be my Sword and your uncle can still be our blacksmith."

Melhel was dumbfounded.

Prince Sirhan had one more proposition. "And, I know how important it was to you, so when this whole Scandosian situation is resolved, you may lead the fight against the dead army."

Melhel remained lost for words. He had no way out of this.

The prince took his silence as acceptance. "I appreciate this immensely," he said. "And I look forward to the years to come. For now, get some rest." He stood. "You're going to need it."

As Prince Sirhan left the room, Melhel struggled to process what had just happened. As if it weren't bad enough that Sirhan will be king, he thought, now I'm going to be his Sword.

~

"HIS SWORD?!" Fares cried out on the morning of the coronation. "You cannot walk!"

"He meant after I am healed," Melhel said. "I can't say no, Uncle. I have to oblige him. You can't say no to a king."

"He's not king yet," Fares reminded him.

"He will be in about two hours."

In Melhel's room at the hospital, Fares was dressed in his finest attire and was helping Melhel into his. Fares saw the wheelchair and shook his head viciously .

"Look at you—and he wants you to be Sword!" he scoffed again.

"If this potion is as good as it's supposed to be, I'll be my old self," Melhel said. "And you and I both know what an incredible Sword I'll be." His eyes glinted with humour at this boast.

Once Melhel was fully dressed Fares looked him over. "But you're supposed to leave; you're not supposed to stay here," he said, desperate with worry for his nephew. "This is too much for you to handle. Now, you have one of the biggest responsibilities in the kingdom."

"I cannot refuse him, Uncle," Melhel insisted.

"Oh, Lah," Fares sighed. "So, then what?"

Melhel was looking in a mirror, trying to brush his hair to the side with a stylish parting. "Well," he said, "I guess after the elves are sorted, I can move onto the dead."

"Oh, good. Did he bribe you with that?"

"Very funny."

Fares came closer to straighten Melhel's hair and neaten his clothing. He knew he wouldn't get anywhere by arguing. It was too late: Melhel was to be the Sword of the King.

Both men looked at each other and gave a knowing and resigned nod. They knew what they were getting into. Now they must get the ordeal of the coronation over so they could focus on more important work.

~

IN HER OFFICE, Mala sat distractedly before an array of papers, still reeling over her loss in the battle at Chekkos. She had been so sure of victory. But now she must make other plans.

Just then, Ismal burst through the door without knocking.

"Governor! Governor!" he cried with elation. "The king ... he is dead!"

Mala smiled. "Poisoned?" she asked.

"Yes," Ismal said cheerily. "Rafiq as well. Their victory was fruitless!"

"And what of the Baraks?" she wondered.

"Still alive," he said. "The youngest was wounded in the battle, so he and his uncle were not present to drink the wine. It doesn't matter, though. Prince Sirhan has done what we asked of him. He will be crowned later today."

She beamed. "Good," she said. "Then we can see which province truly deserves its say in this kingdom. I'm sure *King* Sirhan will make an excellent monarch."

THAT DAY, the Harissah Khnisi was draped and decorated with the royal colours of red and gold, and looked more like a festival hall than a house of worship. But the king was and had always been chosen by Lah before anyone else, and coronations were held in the Khnisi to show this.

In front of the altar was a large table filled with documents, and behind it the throne, moved there for the coronation.

Seated in view of all this were thousands of adoring subjects come to witness this historical moment. The bright and vibrant colours marked a turnaround in mood from just a few days before. Grief had given way to excitement.

Now the people awaited the arrival of the new king.

Next to the throne, special seats on either side were reserved for Queen Rania, now the queen regent, and Marissa, who would be queen when she wed Prince Sirhan.

The seats at the front of the audience were kept for the most powerful people in the kingdom, such as politicians like Saad Jaja.

Fares was among them, and off to the side of the pews, allowing enough room for his wheelchair, was Melhel too.

High Priest Maron stood up from his seat at the head of the audience.

"All rise!" he ordered.

Everyone stood tall and turned their attention towards the front door. In came Sirhan, dressed in a white robe covered with gold and jewels. He slowly marched to the altar, smirking at everyone in the Khnisi who had come to see his coronation.

When finally he took his seat on the throne, he sat upright and proud in the knowledge he was now the most powerful man in the kingdom. No—in the entire world.

"Dear people, we are here today to crown our new king," High Priest Maron announced. "Our young king, who by the grace of Lah our father, shall rule with truth, honesty, and compassion."

Melhel scoffed inwardly.

"Prince Sirhan, may you stand," said the priest.

Sirhan stood and placed his hand on the Book of Lah that the high priest presented him. With the palm of his other hand upright and facing out, he prepared to take his oath of kingship.

"Do you swear to serve all the people of Nataaros?" Maron asked.

"I do."

"Do you swear to rule justly and fairly?"

"I do."

"Do you swear that Lah our father will guide you in your kingship?"

"I do."

"In good times and in bad?"

"I do."

"Do you swear to uphold the constitution and the laws of the land?"

"I do."

"Then," the high priest said, "you may kneel."

Sirhan knelt and leaned his head forward. Maron reached to a red cushion on which the crown of Nataaros lay, and placed it on Sirhan's head.

"By the grace and power of Lah, I proclaim you King Sirhan Aounis of Nataaros!"

The people cheered raucously. Even Fares and Melhel couldn't help grinning as they looked around the room. But though they too cheered, it was partly for appearances. Unlike so many, they were not swept up in the moment. Instead, the tribulations their duty to the new king may bring them were foremost in their minds.

King Sirhan now stood and waved to his adoring subjects, smiling from ear to ear.

Queen Rania cried tears of joy, while Marissa stood to applaud her beloved with a toothy grin.

The new king raised both hands to quieten the applause.

"If I may say a few words?" Sirhan looked at the high priest, who stepped aside to let him speak, "Thank you, High Priest Maron, for your blessing. People of Nataaros, I am truly and deeply honoured to be your king. As I said at my funeral oration, justice will be served to those responsible for the horrific murders of my father and Rafiq Harrira.

"I have learned from my father's mistakes. He loved the kingdom, indeed, but he loved it too much. So much, in fact, that he would rather have seen the end of it than to lose any of it. That led to thousands—perhaps millions—of deaths. In my reign, peace will be restored, and men and elves will live in harmony once again.

"As my first decree as king, Scandos will no longer be a province of Nataaros, but a separate kingdom. Scandos will form its own state. Everything else will remain the same."

Murmurs of relief mixed with shock spread throughout the crowd as the people took in how, though the war had been won, the kingdom was still about to change.

Melhel's eyes were so wide they looked ready to pop out of his head, and next to him, Fares gripped his nephew's good knee in horror.

"What is he doing?" Melhel asked.

"He's just sold the kingdom," Fares said.

King Sirhan continued. "There will be no more civil war as long as I am king," he said. "The Scandosians are self-sufficient, with their own culture and way of life. They only ask for independence from this kingdom, which they never wanted to be a part of, but Beilos the Conqueror took their lands from them.

"We will begin the secession process in due time. But for now, let us celebrate this new era. Long live Nataaros!"

"Long live Nataaros! Long live King Sirhan!" the crowd cheered.

Just like that, with Sirhan becoming king and making his declaration, after hundreds of years Scandos was to be independent. Mala had achieved her longstanding goal for her people. What neither politicking nor war could do in decades, a disgruntled prince had done in seconds.

Melhel looked at his uncle with worry.

If the Alexandrosians feared living with the elves as free neighbours rather than subjects of the king, they would soon experience the reality.

The crowd continued is cheers and murmurs, rippled now by both excitement and fear. A new age had arrived in Nataaros, and they knew not what it may bring.

THE END

REVIEW THIS BOOK

Feel free to leave a review. Your feedback and support means the world!

ACKNOWLEDGMENTS

To my aunties and uncles, I owe you everything. Thank you for the first books you put in my hands, and the first movies before my eyes, allowing me to fall in love with reading and writing and the medium of storytelling.

To my grandparents, both here and overseas, thank you for being my connection to my ancestry. This relationship made my world possible, sparked my imagination on this work. I can only hope to honour you with it.

To Lebanon, the birthplace of my parents, stay strong. I love you. Thank you for the culture and history I am so deeply in love with and could absorb all day. This work is my love letter to you.

And, lastly, to my parents. I am who I am because of you. Everything I do is to hope to make you proud, and to repay all of the sacrifices you have made for me.

ABOUT THE AUTHOR

Alexander Farah is a first-time author from Melbourne, Australia. Growing up on any fantasy, sci-fi, and pop culture story he could find, coupled with his love of writing, empowered him to write his own tale of fantasy and drama. When he is not plugging away at his idealised worlds, you can find him staying active, cheering on his favourite sporting teams, and indulging in his favourite cuisines. He is always willing to speak his mind and meet new people—see his socials below.

 facebook.com/alexanderfarahwrites

 twitter.com/Alexanderfarah

 instagram.com/Alexanderfarahwrites